W9-CEG-574

THE RICHEST SEASON

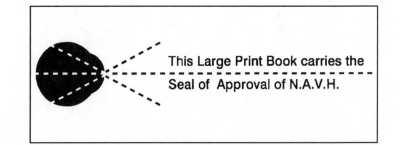

This Large Print Book carries the
Seal of Approval of N.A.V.H.

THE RICHEST SEASON

MARYANN McFADDEN

WHEELER PUBLISHING
A part of Gale, Cengage Learning

GALE
CENGAGE Learning·

Detroit • New York • San Francisco • New Haven, Conn • Waterville, Maine • London

GALE
CENGAGE Learning™

LIBRARY OF CONGRESS CATALOGING-IN-PUBLICATION DATA

McFadden, Maryann.
 The richest season / by Maryann McFadden.
  p. cm.
 ISBN-13: 978-1-59722-822-0 (alk. paper)
 ISBN-10: 1-59722-822-2 (alk. paper)
 1. Wives—Fiction. 2. Middle age—Fiction. 3. Marital
conflict—Fiction. 4. Self-actualization (Psychology)—Fiction. 5.
Pawleys Island (S.C.)—Fiction. 6. Large type books. I. Title.
PS3613.C4375R53 2008
813'.6—dc22   2008022156

Published in 2008 by arrangement with Hyperion, an imprint of Buena Vista Books, Inc.

Printed in the United States of America
1 2 3 4 5 6 7 12 11 10 09 08

*To my family, more precious to me
than anything in this world.*

*For my parents, Jack and Angie
Abromitis, who gave me
the confidence to believe that anything I
reach for is possible.*

*For my children, Patrick and Marisa, who
inspire me
and make me long, always, to be the best
person I can be.*

*For my children-in-law, Karen and
Michael.
You are now like my own.*

*For Alice and Lily, my beautiful baby
granddaughters.
You have brought me love and joy that is
beyond words.*

For Betty, the best mother-in-law in the world.
And Aunt Margie, who we'll always miss. Pawleys Island won't be the same without her.

And for my husband, Pat. Here's to new beginnings.

What Nature did
was remind her that ripeness
is all, that autumn is the richest
season, that preparing for snow means
building a shelter, that warmth within
withstands whatever winter howls
without.
— From the poem "Ripening"
by Joanne McCarthy

■ ■ ■ ■

I
RUNNING AWAY

■ ■ ■ ■

1

The sky was still dark, as it was every morning when Joanna Harrison began walking the two-mile route that serpentined through the development where she lived. The icy air hit her face, the only part of her uncovered, numbing her skin to a dull ache as she walked past massive houses majestically situated on two-acre lots. But unlike other mornings, she wasn't thinking about her day at work, errands afterward, or her children thousands of miles away. She was seeing the weeks unfolding before her in her mind, and she shuddered, not from the cold, but because she knew everything was about to change. And she simply couldn't do it again.

She'd never been a fighter. Years ago, Joanna had learned it was better to keep her feelings under control. And resentments? Well, growing up in her mother's house, she'd discovered how to keep them buried deep inside. The only problem she found was the occasional bout of breathlessness as something vague or long forgotten seemed to bubble to the surface, like a voice struggling to be heard. As it did on that bitter morning in March. Just before dawn, as her sneakers hit the ground again and again with a soft crunching of frozen, dead leaves, following a routine she'd clung to like a lifeline, that voice rose to the edge of Joanna Harrison's consciousness like the quiet crackling of lake ice about to thaw.

Leave.

Pumping her arms, she picked up the pace, her sleep-stiff muscles finally warming up. She stopped briefly, bending her left leg a few times until the knee clicked into place. A little arthritis, the harbinger of middle age. She thought of Sharon and how they would have laughed over this. Sharon was the only real friend she'd made when they moved to New Jersey three years ago. They had jokingly referred to each other as their "surrogate spouses," going to soccer games and movies together while their husbands, more married to their careers, traveled the country. Months ago Sharon had relocated to Texas. She missed her terribly.

The sun was just peeking over the barren hills to the east as she left the sidewalk and headed into the wooded trail that looped behind the houses. Within moments, pale winter sunlight flickered, illuminating the bare trees and the snow-splotched fields in the distance. A glimmer of something ignited inside of Joanna. It had been days since she'd seen the sun, and she could not recall a winter as bitter or endless as this one.

The first snow had come before Halloween, a brief flash of white that was gone within hours as the warm earth soaked it up. By Christmas, life as she knew it had come to a virtual standstill under the weight of nearly thirty inches of powder. She'd stood at the picture window, the cordless phone in her hand, waiting to hear from her children, stranded at different airports. The holiday she'd waited for was cut to a frantic forty-eight-hour visit, as Sarah and Tim rushed back to their own busy lives. And the following day her husband, Paul, was gone on another business trip. Life as she knew it had fallen back into its old routine. Now as she walked through the woods and the world came quietly back to life, longing for her children filled her with an ache.

Just leave.

She was a corporate wife, though. She was used to being alone. Corporate wives were like another breed of single parent. Joanna was always busy, and once the kids were gone, she'd managed to fill the solitary hours with books and videos, or an occasional adult-ed class. In fact, it was the last course she took, in computers, just after moving to Sparta, that led to the job she now had at a local candy company. It was mindless work, punching data into a computer all day, surrounded by buckets of chocolates and the sickening aroma of cocoa beans roasting. Her career, really, had been her family. She didn't mind. As a motherless child, she wanted nothing more than to raise her children herself and give them the love and security she'd never had. They'd followed Paul on his transfers and promotions all over the country, moves that took him higher in the company, like a real-life game of Chutes and Ladders. In twenty-six years of marriage, they'd moved more than a dozen times. As Paul kept scaling that corporate ladder, Joanna's job was to keep the rest of the family from sliding down the chutes.

And now she and Paul would be moving again.

She thought about Paul's big surprise last night. He had told her it was just a business dinner. She'd stood in the atrium of V.I.C.'s northeast headquarters, just forty minutes from their home, in front of the large crowd of coworkers and even some of Paul's clients. Ted, Paul's boss and friend, saluted him for his hard work and sacrifice. And then with great fanfare, Ted announced that Paul was the new vice president of national sales. Cheers erupted and her husband headed for the podium.

Tiny white lights twinkled in the trees, a fountain roared, and then her husband's voice began to fill the atrium with thanks and praise for his company. It was as if his words, echoing off the rising tile walls, had lifted her up, high above the room. She'd watched it all, like a spectator floating above the crowd, and saw the other Joanna far below, smiling, clapping, operating on automatic pilot. After the applause, as Paul walked toward her, she'd plummeted back to earth, breathless. *I can't do this again,* she'd thought. Because she knew what would come next: another house, another town; Paul would be away even more. And she would know no one.

And then she'd begun to hyperventilate. The breath left her lungs as quickly as if it had been sucked out by a vacuum. And she couldn't seem to pull another breath in. She was going to cause a scene. Turning to escape to the ladies' room, she was suddenly stopped by a hand gripping her arm. She turned back and there was Paul, beaming. He must have seen the panic in her eyes because suddenly he pulled her to him and kissed her hard. As the crowd cheered, he whispered in her ear, "I need you here right now, Joanna."

And then they were off, working the room, her husband accepting handshakes and backslaps of congratulations, as she was pulled along beside him.

Now she looked up as a low-flying plane droned through the quiet morning. Through the leafless treetops she saw a jet heading west across the brightening sky and wondered if it was her husband's plane. She remembered Paul telling her he could see their neighborhood on this flight path. She imagined him up there, sitting in business class, his laptop opened, his mind already geared for the meeting he'd be having in California, in spite of their late night. He would be gone for a week or more, again. Did he even glance down or wonder about her, thousands of feet below? Was she anything to him or those he worked with, other than Paul's wife?

As she left the woods, crossing the cul-de-sac behind her house, the newly risen sun flashed off the windows of the houses facing east. Cars sat warming in a few driveways, their exhausts billowing great puffs of steam on this frigid morning. In an hour and fifteen minutes she would be at work, sitting in her cubicle, a poster of Monet's water lilies staring at her from one carpeted wall, pictures of her children at various ages smiling on her from another. After eight hours, she would come home to an empty house, hit the answering machine, and pour a glass of wine as she listened to the endless beeps from endless telemarketers or Gabrielle, their errant cleaning lady, with another excuse. She would turn on the television for company as she ate dinner alone. And tomorrow it would all begin again.

Or would it?

As Joanna walked up her driveway, her own voice suddenly broke the quiet morning. "I'll leave," she said out loud, as she opened the front door.

She drove like an automaton, her mind frozen to thought. Before she knew it, a hundred, then two hundred miles went by. By noon she was on Route 95 South, somewhere in Virginia, and the wall of brown woods that lined the roadside began to soften with new leaf buds. Soon it stretched solid and green. Then there was the first purple splash of wisteria, just before the North Carolina border. At the Welcome Center, where she stopped briefly to pick up a map, yellow daffodils smiled up at her. As she walked back to the car, a silky wind brushed her face, softer and sweeter than she'd felt in a long time.

A short while later, her mood began to sink with the sun. As she followed a detour on a flat, winding back road, dusk settled and lights clicked on in the little houses she passed like beacons in the gray gauze of early night, as families came together for dinner. She felt so utterly alone. A lump of grief swelled in her throat, cutting off her breath, and she veered into a diner parking lot. Frantically, she dumped the remains of her lunch from a McDonald's bag and pulled it to her lips, breathing into it slowly, again and again.

Twelve hours after driving away from her home in New Jersey, Joanna pulled into a motel off Route 95, just before the South Carolina border. Her entire body trembled with exhaustion. Never in her life had she driven alone so long or so far. Hunching her shoulders, she stretched her aching arms high overhead, loosening the muscles in her stiff back. Then she squatted a few times, bending her legs until her knee clicked into place.

She'd never stayed in a motel alone before, and was a little nervous. She took a room near the lobby with an inside corridor. It was stale and airless, and she immediately turned on the vent until cool air gushed in. Dropping her bag on the floor, she collapsed on the bed and closed her eyes. The room began to spin and she felt slightly nauseous. Oh God, what had she done? This was insane. She had no real plan. She was simply driving to Pawleys Island. She'd told herself that morning, as she got in the car and a moment of panic seized her, that she'd figure the rest out when she got there.

She got up and tore the wrapper off a plastic bathroom cup and poured herself a brandy from the small bottle she'd stuffed into her suitcase. Pulling that first sip to her mouth, hands shaking so that the golden liquid trembled in the cup, she thought of her mother for an instant and stopped, picturing the coffee cup that had never left her side. Her mother had fooled no one. Joanna swallowed a big sip, nearly choking as the brandy scorched a fiery trail in her chest that burned even after it was gone. Within moments, the trembling began to ease.

Then she took a hot bath, settling into the shallow tub with a moan of pleasure. After the bath, she poured another brandy, and lay on the bed and turned on the TV looking for the Weather Channel. She had just a few hours driving left in the morning. The weather map for the west lit up the screen instead, forecasting snow up and down the Rockies. She imagined Sarah, up early to clean off her car, wearing some stylish, impractical shoes and no hat, and then driving to her job at the art gallery in Denver. Timmy would probably cram in a few hours of snowboarding between classes, one of the perks of going to college in Montana. She took another swallow of brandy. God, how she missed them. What would they think when they found out she'd left? She wondered if Paul knew yet.

When she was closing the door for the last time that morning, she'd stopped, realizing she'd left no note. And then the absurdity of it hit her. Paul wouldn't be home for days. The note would sit on the counter untouched. So she went in and picked up the phone and left him a voice mail at work, as she'd done earlier with her boss when she quit her job. *I'm leaving,* she'd told her husband. *I've been lonely and unhappy for a long time.* Shame crawled up her skin like a

20

slow heat as she imagined him hearing those words, sounding so banal and ridiculous now.

Joanna got up from the bed and made her way unsteadily to the door and slid the chain across. Then she turned on the bathroom light, leaving the door cracked, and turned off the rest of the lights as she made her way back to the bed. The motel room flickered with the blue light of the mute TV and she reached for a pillow, burying her face, catching the clean scent of bleach just before she muffled the first sob. She was leaving everything she'd ever wanted.

2

From the moment she left the mainland, driving over the small causeway that separated Pawleys Island from the rest of the world, hope washed over Joanna. She saw splashes of snowy white in the wide carpet of green marsh, where egrets nudged in the mudflats for food. A heron lifted suddenly and her eyes followed it up to blue sky, vast bright stretches of it into the flat distance, across the island and to the sea. On the bridge, crabbers dropped their cages over the sides, and she felt as if she were entering another world. A slower place where life is simpler and days revolve around the tides and weather. A three-mile spit of sand, just a half mile at its widest, Pawleys Island was home to nothing but dunes, houses, and beach. Old-timers had wisely kept the hands of developers off the island so it was not marred by hotels or high-rises. Midway up the island sat a cluster of historic homes with low cedar roofs, dense shrubs, and old plantation-style porches that overlooked the sea.

Joanna parked her Jeep beside one of the historic markers and got out of the car. Surrounded by green marsh glittering in the sunshine, she took a deep breath of salty air and relief flooded through her. This was how it looked and this was how she'd felt years ago when she'd first seen it. She was right to come here.

It had been ten years ago, maybe more, when Paul had taken her and the kids to Myrtle Beach for the Easter break. The kids, teenagers then, were bored, and each day was a struggle to find some common ground. Finally on the last day, Paul announced he was going golfing. The kids wanted to go to the Pavilion for the rides and games, alone. Joanna took the car and went exploring, heading for Brookgreen Gardens, but passing it somehow and then seeing the sign for Pawleys Island. She'd turned off Route 17, and minutes later, the world opened up before her — marsh, sea, and sky. The same feeling of peace. And the same wistful longing. Here was a simple place to live.

Getting back in the car now, she followed the single road on the island south to its end and pulled into a sandy parking area. It was late morning, just two hours since she'd left the motel in North Carolina. She got out of the car, followed a boardwalk around a dune, and suddenly the ocean was rolling and shimmering in front of her. A channel that separated Pawleys from the next tiny island washed beside and behind her in a gush of green water as it carried the tide into the marsh. She was nearly surrounded with water. For the first time in a long, long time, real joy bubbled up inside Joanna. Perhaps, she thought, it would all be okay.

Joanna checked into the small Holiday Inn Express out on Route 17, and early the next morning, and each thereafter, she was back on the beach, walking and planning her day. And before she knew it, a week had gone by and she'd established a new routine, although she was no closer to a new life. After her walk, she'd go back to the motel, heat something in the microwave, shower, and dress. Then she would go to the library.

It was nearly impossible for Joanna to enter a library and not think about her childhood. The library had been a sanctuary for her, surrounded by stillness and calm in the after-school hours when her mother had already spent too many hours battling the bottle. Away from her mother's sharp tongue, she would lose herself in books that would take her away to other places, other lives, and for a while she lived vicariously, imagining she was Nancy Drew, pretty and popular, with a dead mother, a fabulous father, and a housekeeper who doted on her. The summer between fifth and sixth grades she'd read the entire series, a book a day, practically living at the library. Or occasionally taking her book to the Sand Bar, the local beach on a stretch of river that meandered through their small Pennsylvania town, reading under a tree far from the laughing families.

Once again she basked in the quiet, the smell of old books and lemon polish. She read the papers, looking for jobs, places to live. The librarian was kind and issued her a temporary card, although she had no local address yet. She even jotted down some places that might have rentals available, but Joanna was determined to get a job before looking for a real place to stay. She'd taken five thousand dollars in cash the morning she left home, but had been using her credit card to pay for almost everything, hoping to stretch the cash. Each morning she left the library with a new stack of things to read in the quiet of the motel at night. And then she spent the afternoons looking for work.

She'd been to most of the restaurants, even many of the stores, including the Harris Teeter grocery she thought would be a sure thing. But it was the slow season, the quiet time between winter and spring, and the answer was the same everywhere: Come back in a month or two when things pick up. Then before dusk settled she'd walk the beach again, eating up the empty hours before dark. It began to seem that walking had become her job.

And soon her joy at first coming here was gone.

Paul Harrison walked into his new office at V.I.C. feeling like a warrior returned from battle. He'd landed that morning after nine grueling days away on business, starting in California. He'd driven straight to V.I.C., assuming he'd be going back to his old office until he could get maintenance to move his things. But his secretary, Diane, was waiting for him and she escorted him with a smile to the corner office on the fourth floor. On the door a new bronze plaque shone: *Paul Harrison, Vice President of National Sales.* He felt his heart expand with pride.

"Congratulations, boss. You deserve it."

"Thanks, Diane."

He closed the door behind him, walked around the massive cherry desk, and sat down. He did deserve this. He'd worked his ass off for years and now, finally, he could relax a little. He swiveled in his chair, looking out the wall of glass. The rolling hills of north Jersey surrounded him. It wasn't officially spring yet, but despite a winter chill still lingering in the air, the world was beginning to thaw.

And soon his wife would thaw, if she hadn't already. When he'd first gotten her message, her trembling voice saying that she was leaving him, he'd been standing in the airport in California, having just arrived. Furious and frustrated, thirty minutes late for his first meeting due to the flight delay, he'd listened to the message three times. On the limo ride from the airport, he'd convinced himself not to worry. He didn't have time to worry. And Joanna would get over it. She always did.

His intercom buzzed. "Ted's on line one," Diane said.

He picked up. "Ted, how's it going?"

"Paulie, my boy, welcome back. What do you think of the new digs?"

"Are you kidding? What's not to like? It was a nice surprise to come in this morning and not have to move."

"Only the best for you, Paulie." Then Ted's voice turned serious. "I need to talk to you later. We just got the figures for the Landmark account and you should look at them. You free for lunch?"

"Sure, as long as it's quick. I've got a doctor's appointment at two. I had to beg to get them to squeeze me in."

"You okay?"

"Sure, it's all this flying, I think. It's killing my sinuses."

"Okay, meet you at noon."

Paul hung up. Then he carefully pulled a small cotton ball from his ear. The flight attendant on last night's redeye had given him a baggie full of them, after the first two had soaked through. This one was clean, not even a spot of pink. And the searing pain had dulled to a tolerable ache. Good. He didn't have time for problems.

He dialed his house then. After four rings, Joanna's voice came on the answering machine. He hung up. She was probably at the store or out walking. There was a quick knock on his door, and before he could reply, it opened. Diane led in a deliveryman with a huge vase of exotic-looking flowers and the biggest basket of fruit he'd ever seen.

"Now that you're back, I'm sure this is just the first of many congratulations." Diane beamed, handing him the cards as the deliveryman carefully set the gifts on the cherry credenza.

When they left, he opened the cards. The first was from the legal department downstairs: *Only the best for the best! Your Personal Legal Eagles.* The second card was from his predecessor, who now headed the international sales division: *Here's to a record-breaking year! Dwight Hobson.*

Of course the previous year had been good. But now, with the shift in management, everyone was predicting big things for V.I.C. He picked up the phone and on a whim dialed his wife's number at work. Her extension bounced him to the switchboard. He hung up. If she had a damn cell phone, like everyone else, he wouldn't have to wonder where she was. But she'd refused to get one, insisting that she was always home or at work anyway. Obviously she was wrong.

Another quick knock and the door opened. Again Diane led in a deliveryman, with more flowers and a bottle of champagne. Paul smiled as she handed him the cards.

"By the way, Diane, I've got a suitcase full

of dry cleaning, and a meeting —"

"Of course, don't even think about it," she said, with a wave of her hand. "I'll have your clothes back by the end of the day."

"Good. Can you get me the Landmark file right away? Oh, and call my doctor and cancel the appointment at two."

"Sure, anything else?"

"No . . . not just yet."

"Listen, Paul, why don't you relax. You must be exhausted after flying all night. Whatever comes up, I'll handle it."

"Thanks, I don't know what I'd do without you."

"Just enjoy this moment," she said, closing the door.

He intended to. Not even his wife's little hysterics could ruin this for him.

3

Ten days after arriving on Pawleys Island, Joanna stood at the same spot on the south end of the island as that very first day, when she'd felt such hope. It was late morning, the sun high and bright, the tide rushing out as water sluiced by her in channels that had worked their way into the sand. She began walking up the beach, trying to relax. There was an old woman on the island looking for live-in help in exchange for a small apartment. Joanna had seen the flier at the library. It seemed too good to be true, and she wondered what the catch would be. But she was desperate.

She began walking up the deserted beach, past the line of oceanfront houses. Although it wasn't April yet, it felt as warm as early summer back home. She continued walking, three, four, five jetties up, until she saw the ocean side of the weathered cape she'd driven by yesterday, after she'd called for the appointment. Stopping suddenly, she turned toward the water, pulling in deep breaths of tangy ocean air, following the rhythm of the relaxation tapes she'd bought.

The house was built on pilings. Walking up the long flight of steps, she stood before a wall of sliding glass doors as her stomach did a little flip. She turned to see the beach spread out below, the light green sea swells shifting and sparkling in the sunlight. And she imagined waking up early in the morning in this house, pulling on sweats and walking the beach as the dune grasses rippled in the ocean breeze.

"You must be Joanna Harrison."

Joanna turned to find a small, gray-haired woman standing at the open slider.

"I'm sorry," she said, embarrassed. She hadn't even knocked. "I was just admiring the view."

"It's lovely, isn't it?" the old woman asked, and then smiled, sunlight flashing off the frames of her wire glasses. There was nothing stooped or frail about her, Joanna thought, despite the fact that she barely reached her shoulder.

"I'm Grace Finelli," she said then, holding out her hand. "Please come inside."

Joanna stepped through the open glass doors into a great room that was surrounded by windows on all sides. Everywhere she looked there was sea and sand. To the far right was a kitchen, a wall of light oak cabinets and a countertop with stools. The dining table sat in front of one set of glass doors. The living area filled the entire left side of the room, with a sofa, chairs, and rocker strategically arranged in front of the other set of sliders. Behind the sofa, more windows offered views of the nearby marsh.

"What a wonderful home," Joanna said, forgetting her nervousness for the moment. "You sit so close to the water."

"That's what I wanted. Most of the houses to the north sit much farther back, with long walkways over the dunes," the old woman said. "That was too far for me. As you can see, the ocean is here, whenever I want to see it. I don't even have to leave the house."

"How long have you lived here?" she asked, following her into the kitchen.

"A month or so," Grace said. "I've always dreamed of living near the ocean, ever since I was a girl. After my husband died last year, I began to think about it again. Anyway," she said, pausing near the stove, "here I am. Would you like some tea?"

"Yes, Mrs. Finelli, I would."

"Call me Grace," she said over her shoulder, filling the kettle at the sink.

Grace set the kettle on the gas stove and motioned for Joanna to sit at the table. Joanna guessed she was in her seventies and must have been very pretty once. Her gray curls were cropped short and the skin on her face was fairly smooth. Her eyes were a vivid blue behind the wire-framed glasses that sat deeply on her nose. Joanna watched those eyes now, assessing her with quick glances. Even in a casual flowered housedress, she could see the erect back and squared shoulders, and thought: this is a woman with a strong will.

"As I mentioned on the phone, I need someone to run errands, shop, drive me occasionally, clean once a week, and perhaps help with some odds and ends around the house," Grace began, as she spooned loose tea into a ceramic pot. "In exchange, I have a little efficiency apartment upstairs free of charge. It isn't much, really, but the view can't be beat."

"I've had twenty-five years' experience taking care of a home," Joanna assured her. "And I do have a reliable car."

The old woman sat quietly. "You're not from around here," she said. "You have no accent."

"No, I'm from New Jersey. Sparta, in the northwest."

"Pretty country," Grace said, and then rose again, placing mugs and a sugar bowl on the table. "I'm from New Jersey myself, actually. Glen Rock, just a stone's throw from Manhattan, and a world from here." She paused as she sat. "What brings you all the way to Pawleys Island, Joanna?"

"I was here on vacation once and thought it would be a wonderful place to settle. And like you, I've always had a longing to live near the sea."

"I'll be honest with you, I've been interviewing nothing but college girls for a week now and I don't think I can deal with blasting stereos and boyfriend problems," Grace said. "But you're a bit of a surprise, I must admit."

She didn't know what to say to that.

"Is there a Mr. Harrison?" Grace asked then, looking plainly at Joanna's wedding ring.

She couldn't help it. Joanna's eyes drifted down to the circle of diamonds on her left hand, a twentieth anniversary gift from Paul that replaced the simple gold band. She looked up. "My husband and I have separated, Grace. I need a job and a place to live."

There was no reply, and then the shrill whistle of the kettle broke the silence.

"Why don't you take a look upstairs, see what you think of the place," Grace said as she got up. "Just through that door. I'll fix the tea."

Joanna stepped through a door in the back of the living room and found herself in a common foyer. As she climbed the stairs, she was certain Grace had doubts about her. She was an oddity, a forty-six-year-old woman who suddenly moved nearly a thousand miles with no job, no place to live. At the top of the steps she walked into a room that was all windows and sunshine, the ocean sparkling below.

A small kitchen and bathroom took up the back of the room. The remainder, facing one oversized sliding glass door to her own deck high over the beach, was a living room with a sofa, rocker, and small desk in one corner, and a futon and dresser in the other. Grace was right; it was small. But it was enough. She imagined waking up in this room each morning to the calling of the gulls, the rhythmic lapping of the tide in the early quiet, and then rising and watching the pink finger of the sun peek over the horizon. At night she could leave the doors open and fall asleep high above the ocean,

like a child rocked by the waves. Longing
hit her in the knees and she sank to a
kitchen chair. This could be home. Here she
could learn to survive without the security
of her husband. And perhaps discover what
she would do with the rest of her life.

If Grace wanted her.

Joanna thought about the old woman, up
and down, her hands constantly busy, her
eyes darting, then staring with shrewd intel-
ligence. She couldn't sit still. She seemed to
have enough energy for both of them; it was
hard to imagine doing anything for her. But
perhaps this was a good day.

Moments later, Joanna sat before her
again, smiling brightly. The old woman said
nothing as she filled the ceramic pot with
steaming water from the kettle.

"You're right about the view," Joanna said.
"The water's so close it's like looking out
the window of a ship."

Grace set the kettle down. "I need someone reliable."

"I am reliable," she answered. "If you'd
like references . . ."

She waved a hand in the air, as if that was
ridiculous. "At my age I don't need references. I can judge a person's character
before they've said a hundred words."

Grace's words hung in the air like a challenge. Before Joanna could reply, Grace picked up the teapot and began pouring hot tea into the cups. And then she was looking straight into Joanna's eyes. "I need a commitment of six months," she said. "Until fall. And I want you to be honest with me if you're not able to make that kind of commitment."

Joanna opened her mouth to speak. And then stopped, her eyes drifting to the waves beyond the glass doors. Could she do this? She wasn't certain she even liked Grace.

"I'll stay for six months," she said. "If you want me."

4

After a weeklong stretch of gray wet days, Grace sat on her deck in the April sunshine, closing her eyes and sighing as the warmth baked her joints and muscles. She could hear the crash of the waves as they hit the surf not more than thirty feet from her deck at high tide, and the soft wash as they spilled across the sand. And then the pause, that moment of silence before it all began again. At such moments in the warm, yellow light of the late morning sun, Grace could almost forget about her illness.

Her house at the beach was the remnant of a girlhood dream — to live near the sea. A longing she'd let drift and then float away on the fast current of her life, like the Evening in Paris perfume she once wore in a simple lifetime that existed before marriage and motherhood. Opening her eyes now, she took in the beach, the clean stretch of almost white sand, and the sea swells, rising and settling as if breathing in and out. It was hard to believe, sometimes, that she was really here. The decision to come had not been easy.

Last year she had watched as her husband, Frank, disappeared before her own eyes. One morning he'd woken with a lump on his neck that she'd been certain was nothing more than an inflamed gland. A few weeks later, the small bulge had grown, like a fertile mound of dough rising with a life of its own. She knew the prognosis before the word was even uttered. Cancer.

Her middle-aged children, Frankie, Sean, and Marie, who lived in Japan, had abandoned their own hectic lives, and suddenly come back under her roof again, like the family they once were. But for Grace, watching them suffer as Frank slowly died was almost as unbearable as losing her husband.

When it was over, when he was gone, her children returned to the busy lives they'd abandoned, furiously trying to catch up on jobs, housework, responsibilities that stopped for nothing, not even death. Grace, numb to the bone with exhaustion, could do nothing but sleep, floating for months in a world of grief as life continued around her. Finally at Christmas, surrounded again with family, she felt herself coming back. Tears filled her eyes now as she unbuttoned her sweater, the morning breeze gone, and she remembered that holiday, already three months past. It was just a week after Christmas, when, unable to shake the exhaustion, she'd finally gone to the doctor. But it was already too late.

"I'm sorry, Grace," her doctor had told her, his voice heavy with emotion, as she sat across from him alone. "It's pancreatic cancer."

His words had hit her like a fist to the stomach. "How long?"

"Six months. Nine at best."

"That quick," she'd whispered, unable to believe it.

"But kinder, Grace, than what Frank endured," he'd said, trying to give her something to hold on to.

As she stared at the ocean now, an old photograph clutched in her hand, loneliness threatened to swallow her. She watched wave after wave crest, curl, then crash onto the sand before her, washing it clean of shells and debris left with the tide. Each day her body weakened a little more, the energy seeping out of her like gray dishwater trickling quietly down a sink. Shopping for food was an ordeal that often drained her

41

for the rest of the day. And simply getting dressed was something she did now to force a semblance of normalcy into her life.

She thought about the woman she'd hired, Joanna Harrison, whose main redeeming feature was her maturity. Joanna rarely talked about herself or her family, and Grace sensed she was trying to escape something. Getting up now, the blood flowing back into her legs after sitting so long, Grace hoped she hadn't made a mistake there. She stepped inside then and found Joanna cleaning up the clutter around her chair.

"No, leave it," she called out.

"But Grace, it's dusty under here," Joanna said, on her knees at the coffee table.

"Really, Joanna, I'm not compulsive. I don't mind a little dust," she said, walking over and seeing her things organized now in piles. Grace liked her little messes. Surrounded by her books, puzzles, letters, and magazines, she saw them as proof of a purpose to her days.

She picked up the pile of Easter cards she'd started that morning and sat in the rocker as Joanna moved to the kitchen, where she began loading the dishwasher. Grace searched the table beside her for stamps.

"Joanna, where did you put the stamps?"

"I didn't see any stamps, Grace."

"But I asked you to get me stamps yesterday, remember? The new ones with the Easter lilies for these cards."

Joanna stood at the counter shaking her head. "No, Grace, you didn't ask me to get stamps."

"I distinctly remember. You were taking those bills to the post office."

Joanna looked at her with a puzzled frown. "Yes, I took the bills, but you never —"

"Oh, never mind, then. Just add them to the list there."

"Whatever you say, Grace," Joanna said, and Grace could hear her annoyance. "I'll just go now."

Joanna took the grocery list from the counter and left without a word.

Grace sat there staring out the sliders at the sparkling ocean, the cards to her children and grandchildren forgotten in her lap. Was it possible she'd never asked for the stamps out loud? So much of her life, her conversations, now took place in her mind. No, not possible, she decided. Joanna was probably just daydreaming and didn't hear her. That was certainly more likely, since Joanna often had a faraway look when she was doing chores.

Just then the dishwasher clicked on, the noisy whirring drowning out all sound of the waves. Grace shook her head. Then she stood, walked slowly to the kitchen, and turned it off.

How many times had she told Joanna she did not like the dishwasher run during the day?

Paul couldn't believe he'd been sitting in the waiting room for more than an hour and still hadn't been seen by the doctor. He should have gone to the damned emergency room. He'd just assumed this would be quicker.

Five days ago, he'd flown to Cleveland to salvage the Landmark account. He shouldn't have flown again. The pain in his ear was worse than on the flight back from California. To top it all, he still couldn't get them to extend their contract. What did he expect, though? He wasn't exactly in top form. Then he was forced to take a train back from Cleveland, too drained to consider driving. When he got home, Joanna still hadn't returned.

He checked the date on his watch and counted back to the morning after his promotion. How was it possible? It was exactly three weeks since Joanna ran away.

But he knew. His already hectic life had kicked into overdrive with the promotion. Christ, he barely had time to sleep since he'd returned from California. And now it seemed there were problems everywhere he turned. At first he hadn't worried about his wife. He'd have bet the house she'd be home before he even returned from California. When she hadn't, he took a chance and called her friend, Sharon, in Texas, who seemed stunned when he asked if she'd spoken to Joanna lately. Forcing a chuckle, he tried to make light of their busy schedules, how they were like ships passing in the night. He hung up mortified.

He drove by her old job three or four times, at random hours, looking for her car. But it was never there. A few times he picked up the phone to call her old boss, but couldn't seem to come up with a plausible excuse as to why he had no idea where his wife was. He thought of the kids and then dismissed that idea, knowing she'd never burden them with her problems. He couldn't imagine where she could be or how she was surviving. The Joanna he knew approached each of their moves in a state of barely veiled dread.

But Joanna was also stubborn. Maybe she didn't like to fight, but she was a master at

45

putting up a wall and keeping it there for days and weeks. Sometimes even months. Punishing him for her unhappiness. Somehow they'd always made peace, though. This time instead of a wall, she'd put distance between them. And the only way to make peace, he realized on the long ride back from Cleveland, was to find her.

He had nothing to go on but a phone number on the caller ID, which could've been just a telemarketer. But the call had come after eleven o'clock a few nights ago while he was away. Telemarketers didn't call that late.

"Mr. Harrison?"

He looked up as a nurse stood in the waiting room with a chart in her hand.

"The doctor will see you shortly, Mr. Harrison. Mrs. Kamaris, you can come with me now."

He looked at his watch again. He'd been waiting now almost an hour and a half. And he'd been forced to turn off his phone when he arrived. He wondered if Bethany, his relocation counselor in Human Resources, had returned his call yet. She'd been expecting him to have the house on the market by tomorrow. Obviously, that wasn't going to happen with his wife still gone. Not that anyone knew about that.

When he canceled a business dinner with Dwight Hobson and his wife last week, he'd simply said Joanna was down with the flu. He hadn't even told Ted yet, and if anyone would sympathize he would. Not that Ted's ex-wife had pulled anything like this. On top of his humiliation was a nagging worry that Joanna might be someplace unsafe. Or worse, in some kind of trouble. And there was nothing he could do.

No, he had to stop thinking like that. Things would work out, they always did. He just needed to buy more time. He would find Joanna somehow and bring her home. Then, in a few weeks, he would tell her about the move to Indiana.

But above all, he needed to focus again. Between the pain in his ear and his missing wife, it was no wonder his business was suffering.

Pulling out of the driveway too quickly, Joanna sent a little spray of gravel behind her. She had nowhere to go. And no one to talk to.

She followed the island road, glittering green marsh to her left, the row of beach houses to her right. Blue sky stretched to the horizon, dotted with white clouds. It was a perfect day. She turned and a moment later crossed the small causeway, empty of crabbers in the late morning heat. The peace that usually came upon her during this drive was nowhere to be found.

What was she doing here?

Driving up Route 17, she took a few deep breaths, telling herself to relax. It was just three weeks, after all, and hadn't she made progress? She had a job with Grace; an unbelievable place to live right on the beach, where each morning she simply had to open her eyes and there was another glorious sunrise, like a rosy beacon of hope. She had to calm down. And give it a little more time.

But she was starting to think that perhaps moving in with Grace had been a mistake, despite the wonderful house. Grace had never asked for stamps, Joanna was certain of that, despite the old woman's accusatory glare. And last week, when she'd stripped her bed, washed the sheets, and then was remaking it, Grace had come into the room just as she was arranging the comforter on top. Grace had lifted a corner of the comforter, tugged, and the top sheet came undone. Grace had looked at her, shaking her head.

"These aren't hospital corners," she'd reprimanded her. "Here," she said then, demonstrating, "this is how you make a proper corner so the sheets don't come apart at night."

Joanna said nothing, although she was simmering inside. She'd been making beds for more than twenty-five years. Few people kept a house as clean and tidy as hers.

Then Grace, who was obviously a fanatic about her bed, showed her exactly how she liked her comforter turned under and her pillows arranged just so. This from a woman who'd just ordered her to leave the dust under her chair!

Maybe the mistake wasn't really with Grace, though. Maybe it was leaving her home in the first place.

In the parking lot of Harris Teeter's, she grabbed a shopping cart. As she pushed it toward the store, she passed a pay phone and stopped. She could call Sharon in Texas. She could tell Sharon everything now, unburden herself, and hopefully feel that boulder of guilt slide off her back.

How many times had they fantasized on their morning walks about running away or reinventing themselves? Sharon, who laughed that her mind was mush after four kids, swore that one day she was going to backpack across Europe, a chance she'd missed by marrying right out of college.

She'd visit the Louvre and the Sistine Chapel and the Acropolis in Greece. She'd finally make some use of that art history degree. Joanna's fantasies were more vague. A little house, a simple life, a beach. And here she was. She'd done it. But reality was far different from fantasy. You didn't just walk away from a lifetime of responsibility and obligation without carrying a fair share of guilt in that backpack full of dreams.

Unzipping her purse, she pulled her calling card out of her wallet. Then she searched the rest of her purse for her little phone book that held Sharon's new number in Texas. She found it, opened it to the page, then stared at the number. Sharon had moved away months ago. They'd only spoken a few times since then. And when she left, Sharon had gushed about her new five-thousand-square-foot house with the media room. Would she really understand?

She put the phone book back in her purse and pushed the cart into the store. Don't overreact, she told herself. This was just a little moment of panic, like the one she'd had the second night after she moved into Grace's house. Walking to the produce aisle, she remembered that night, lying in the dark, unable to sleep. She had seen day after lonely day unfolding before her in this strange place where she still knew no one. Maybe years. An emptiness engulfed her, worse than anything she'd felt before. And a noose of fear began to tighten around her throat, cutting off her air. She'd picked up the phone and called home. After the fourth ring, she heard her own voice and quickly hung up.

She'd flung open the slider and sat on the tiny deck in the dark with a blanket wrapped around her, high over the ocean, longing for home. And finally, she'd calmed down. She'd gotten past the panic that night. She could do it again. She just needed to stay busy.

She pulled out Grace's list, her comments underlined as if Joanna were a child. Tomatoes, *make sure they're ripe. French* vanilla ice cream, French underlined three times, as if she didn't know the difference. She spent the next half hour carefully choosing the items Grace wanted. Then she stopped at the post office and picked up Grace's stamps, with the Easter lilies. Driving back, she got into the left lane to turn off onto the south causeway. But at the last moment, she turned her blinker off and kept going. She just wasn't ready to go back to Grace yet.

She continued down Route 17 and saw

the sign for Georgetown, nine miles. She hadn't been there yet. Maybe she'd just drive around the city for a while, have a quick lunch. The store was out of Grace's French vanilla ice cream, so there was nothing frozen in the bags. And there was little for her to do back at the house, now that it was cleaned.

She passed signs for a new plantation of Southern-style luxury homes, a golf course, and a Mexican restaurant. After a few miles, the signs began to disappear, replaced by a solid wall of green pines on either side of the road. Then a burst of color caught her eye on the other side of the highway. At the next break in the median, she turned and drove back toward it. *Southern Plants & Horticulture.* She pulled in under a canopy of towering live oaks dripping with Spanish moss. Mulched paths led in all directions, lined with gorgeous flowers and climbing plants. It was a gardener's paradise. Joanna got out of her car and smiled for the first time that day. She chose a path and began walking slowly, feeling like a child on Christmas morning.

All around her, shoppers loaded wagons with flowers she could only dream of planting up north. If she were home, she'd be out weeding her beds already, pruning her roses and butterfly bush, even if it was still cold. Her windowsills would be filled with egg cartons where her seedlings would be sprouting by now. She'd be perusing Donaldson's for the clematis she'd hoped to plant this year.

In the greenhouse, she stroked the silky white petal of an angel trumpet, a plant she'd never seen before. Then she knelt, inhaling the sweet fragrance of a potted confederate jasmine. She picked it up and smelled it again. It was heaven.

"Do you need a cart?"

She turned and one of the workers wheeled a cart beside her.

"We do have bigger ones if you're getting a lot of plants."

She smiled. "No, this will be fine."

Loading the jasmine, angel flower, some primrose and Black-eyed Susans and even some fall flowering bulbs onto the cart, she pictured Grace's barren flower beds. Except for a sparse patch of grass that fronted the road, little attention had been given to softening the look of the house. This would transform it. Even Grace should be pleased.

As she loaded the plants into her trunk, from the corner of her eye she noticed a man approaching her. He was tall, light haired, and wearing a suit. Her heart nearly stopped. She leaned further into the open trunk as he came closer. Then he walked behind her and continued toward the greenhouse.

She straightened and quickly glanced over. He was younger than Paul; his hair was lighter. In fact, he was nothing like her husband.

Pulling back onto Route 17, she assured herself there was no way Paul could possibly know where she was. How could he?

5

When he realized a few days ago that he was going to have to make a road trip down the east coast, Paul had bristled at the thought. He'd left that kind of travel behind years ago — budget motels, rest stops, fast-food joints, whatever kept you close to the highway. But his burst eardrum, in addition to half a dozen meetings with his regional sales managers, left him no choice. The doctor had forbidden him to fly again until the tiny hole healed. And then he realized it might all work to his benefit, anyway. Joanna was somewhere in South Carolina. Of that he was almost certain.

Paul put his bags in the trunk of his BMW and hoped he hadn't forgotten anything. Joanna always packed for him. Years ago she'd insisted, and often he'd find a little note tucked into a shirt pocket or a shoe. *Miss you already* or *I'll be waiting!* He would pull the note to his nose and inhale her soft floral perfume. It had been years since she'd done anything like that. Now packing for him was just another chore.

Each night as sleep eluded him and his mind swam with problems at work and thoughts of what his wife might be doing, where she was sleeping, he'd thought of calling that number in South Carolina. But much as he wanted to vent his frustrations and demand she come home, he knew now that wouldn't work. Too much time had gone by. And he knew he'd have to approach her with finesse. He hadn't gotten as far as he had in sales on luck alone. He knew how to read people, gauge a situation, and do what was necessary to close a deal.

Walking around the car, he spotted the small cooler on the floor in the corner of the garage and went to get it. Joanna used to send him off with a cooler full of healthy food — fruit and yogurt and low-fat cheese — warning him about too much fast food on the road. Well, he'd stop at a deli and pick up bottled water and some sandwiches; that was about all he'd have time for. As he reached for the cooler, his foot hit the old metal shelving next to it. The shelf swayed and came at him, Joanna's gardening tools sliding off and crashing at his feet before he caught and righted it.

"God damn it!"

He limped over to the car, his left foot throbbing. Then he heard his cell phone ringing and opened the car door.

"Paulie, I've got good news and bad news," he heard Ted say.

He sighed. "Give me the bad news first."

"That rumor I told you about, when you first got back from Cleveland? Seems there's some meat to it."

"You're kidding."

"Let's not press the panic button yet. There might be nothing for either of us to worry about. I'll keep you posted while you're on the road, I promise."

"All right, give me some good news."

"I got that info you needed on that phone number."

Paul hesitated, still embarrassed at having to tell Ted. "Listen. I owe you one big time."

"Just go get her and make things right. Don't be stupid like I was. Now, got a pen?"

Paul sat in the car, wrote down the address in South Carolina, then hung up. With everything else going wrong in his life, he wasn't putting up with this little tantrum of his wife's any longer. He needed her to fly to Indiana in a few weeks and find them a new house. She had to call Dwight Hobson's wife to reschedule that business dinner he'd already canceled twice. And she was going to have to get this house ready to put on the market.

Limping into the house for the bottle of Advil, he told himself he'd make her see how selfish this escapade of hers was. And that it had gone on long enough.

Besides, she had to be more than ready to come home. She was just too stubborn to admit it.

6

As she stared at the crossword puzzle, the page seemed to blur. Grace blamed it on the brightness of the room now that it was sunny again. It had rained for days, beginning with thunderstorms last week, the afternoon Joanna had left without a word. She'd returned with not just groceries, but a trunk full of flowers, which Grace preferred not to dwell on. After she'd unloaded all the plants, the sky had opened up, and her disappointment was obvious. Since then, Joanna had been cleaning or pacing in her room upstairs as she waited for the rain to stop, and her impatience had taken on a life of its own.

Grace, on the other hand, knew that she was already letting herself go. The house, her appearance, the pleasure of food. Even her mind, as her thoughts bounced across decades, landing on distant memories, vague faces, like the game of Giant Step her mother had taught her a lifetime ago.

The screen door slammed and Grace looked up. Joanna was gone, probably prowling around the front of the house now that the rain had stopped last night and the ground was drying. To Grace, Joanna seemed lost, as if the precious minutes of the life Joanna took for granted, as everyone who isn't dying does, must be filled to overflowing with busyness. Joanna had washed every window, buffed the floors, scrubbed down the porch. Observing her for weeks now since she'd moved upstairs, it appeared to Grace that Joanna was more relaxed when she was busy. Or perhaps less lonely. Or maybe it was just a convenient way to avoid talking because she knew Grace was still annoyed about the flowers.

Grace had been sitting in a chair out front, watching the tide drain from the marsh, when Joanna arrived home last week from grocery shopping. Grace could see that the back of the Jeep was loaded with plants. She got up and walked over as Joanna opened the trunk.

"What's all this for?" she asked.

"They're flowers for the front of the house," Joanna answered and picked up a small box. "And these are bulbs that will flower in the fall."

Bulbs . . . that will flower in the fall.

Joanna set the box back in the trunk. "Don't you like flowers, Grace?"

"Of course I like flowers," Grace said. But it was awfully presumptuous of her to buy flowers to plant in front of Grace's house without even asking.

"But do you want me to return them?" There was an edge to her voice that Grace had never heard before.

An awkward silence grew.

"It's fine. Plant them where you like," she'd finally said, deciding at that moment it would be good to give Joanna something else to do. She was underfoot too much in the house anyway.

Getting up now and looking out a window, Grace saw that indeed Joanna was kneeling on the tiny lawn that fronted the road, gardening tools at her side. Although it was just midmorning, the air was thick and steamy and Grace's face was damp with perspiration. Was she becoming a cranky old woman? She had to try harder. She needed Joanna. She would need her even more in the months to come. She went to the refrigerator and got a bottle of cold water. Then she went out the screen door herself. She pulled up a beach chair in the shade and Joanna looked up.

"I thought you could use this," Grace said, handing her the bottle.

"Thanks," Joanna said, twisting off the cap and taking a long swallow. She smiled briefly, then went back to scooping out hole after hole in the empty flower bed that lined the front of the house.

"What are you planting?" Grace asked, attempting to strike up a conversation.

"I'm planting the jasmine here to climb the railing," Joanna said, sitting back on her heels and tucking a stray hair behind her ear. "I thought I'd line the driveway with Black-eyed Susans. They tolerate the heat well and don't need watering often." She turned from Grace, ending the conversation, and went back to her task.

As Joanna worked, Grace's mind drifted again. She wasn't unreasonable and she liked flowers, who didn't? But flowers had never occurred to her. It would have been one more thing she wasn't certain she had energy for. Like cleaning her own house and shopping for her own things. It was ironic that as her body deteriorated, year by year, cell by cell, her mind grew wiser. How unfair.

After seventy-five years on earth, she knew now that there were stages in life and each one was difficult, laden with decisions. She pictured herself at the precipice of each new phase, shoes glued with the sticky fear of change as she was about to leap into the unknown, the future. Joanna was there, somewhere in that midlife stage. And Grace knew that she herself was at the last stage — cloudy vision, sagging breasts, hair gray and wiry, pains that pulsed a little deeper each day.

Yet here she sat in the glory of another spring warming into summer, knowing each day was a gift. She looked back now, as Joanna gently separated the roots of the jasmine, on the miseries of her youth and saw them as so many wasted moments. She's just about figured it all out, and soon it would be taken away.

She remembered turning thirteen as if it were yesterday, when life stretched out before her like a blank canvas of endless possibilities. By fifteen, she'd convinced herself she was a budding artist and would go to Paris one day. She smiled now, her eyes still on Joanna, her mind years away, remembering how she'd given up her dreams when her heart was captured by a boy in the next phase of her life.

Then motherhood. Nothing prepared her for that ultimate drain on her self. Yet nothing could pull her away from it. She thought of the first moment her son was placed in her arms, tiny furred head turning toward her breast, rooting for its lifeline. Her reason for existing. Even now her heart swelled with tenderness. For three decades she'd devoted all of herself to her three children, who were more precious to her than her own life. And then one day, they were all gone.

A trickle of sweat ran down her chest, bringing her back to the present. Joanna still knelt in the hot sun, wiping at her forehead, her hair curling wildly. Across the road the marsh shimmered in the intense heat, rising with the incoming tide.

One by one, Grace's children had married and left home. Nothing had prepared her for the emptiness in her life. That sudden shift into middle age where everything seemed to come into question. That seemed to be where Joanna was now, on that slippery edge of existence, after motherhood, before old age. It was a dangerous point, she knew, that change of life. She'd seen people sometimes turn their backs on all they'd worked for, even those they loved, in a midlife quest to find themselves. Or some sort of happiness to get them through the second half of their lives. Others puttered on slowly, glued to the same track until they died quietly. *I guess I'm one of them,* Grace thought.

"I'll get us some cold lemonade," she heard then and looked back at Joanna, who must have been talking to her.

And then they both turned as a silver car, foreign and expensive-looking, pulled into the driveway. Joanna stood up and Grace noticed the New Jersey plates. A man got out of the car, tall and nice-looking, squinting in the afternoon sun. Then he turned to them with a puzzled look. Grace glanced at Joanna and saw panic on her face. In that moment, the mystery of Joanna became obvious. She hadn't separated from her husband. She'd run away from him.

And he was here to take her home.

7

Paul wasn't sure at first he was at the right place. Pulling into the driveway, he looked up at the gray beach house, weathered by scouring salt spray and storms. He saw an old woman sitting on a beach chair and near her, a girl kneeling in the grass. She turned at the crunch of his tires, and it took a moment for Paul to look past the deep tan, the mass of dark hair flashing in the sunlight, and recognize the girl as his wife.

Gone for a brief moment was the slight frown, which had long ago stamped twin commas between her brows. Her lips, usually pressed closed in a thin, no-nonsense line, were slightly open as if ready to speak or break into smile. Opening the car door, he was seized by a second of doubt as he realized that after just a month, his wife was already far removed from him and the life they shared. She'd established new routines and habits, an everyday world he knew nothing about.

During the long drive south, he'd decided exactly how to approach her. He would discuss her concerns, ask for a second chance, then take her to Charleston for a night in a romantic bed-and-breakfast before they both returned home. He loved her, and would tell her so. He would also admit to her that in the complicated scenario of their life's goals, she was sometimes neglected.

He closed the car door and stood for a moment in the oppressive heat. Through the wood pilings that held up the house, the blinding sea seemed to rush toward him. He squinted and closed his eyes for a second. He was disoriented, he realized, from too many miles behind the wheel and too many antihistamines. As he'd driven further into spring with each mile south, his allergies had exploded despite his new medication.

"Paul?" he heard her ask.

Even her voice sounded different, softer. She stared at him as if he'd suddenly landed there from another planet. It was at that moment his certainty slipped.

He knew his wife. She was responsible, hardworking. She lived with the ingrained guilt of a wife and mother who'd spent her life trying to make up for the failings of her own alcoholic mother. Home and family were everything to her. But a different woman faced him. A dark, wild-haired Joanna. A stranger who looked as if she were about to ask if he was lost or needed directions.

"Paul?" she asked again. "Are you all right?"

There it was, he heard it. A tremble of uneasiness in her voice, a vestige of the old Joanna. And in that brief moment, he changed his tactic.

"Joanna," he said, smiling and walking toward them. "You're looking all tan and rested."

When he'd first gotten out of the car, she thought she would faint, her heart was pounding so hard. This man who'd become almost a stranger to her over the years seemed, at that moment, like a lifeline to all the familiar things she'd left behind. And he looked so handsome in his gray suit. He stared at her with a pained look, his eyes shining. Suddenly, she had an urge to run into his arms.

"Joanna?" Grace asked.

"Oh, yes, I'm sorry," she said, turning to Grace, who was getting up from her chair.

"Paul, this is Grace Finelli. Grace, um, this is Paul Harrison. My husband."

They shook hands awkwardly and Joanna quickly took Paul's arm. "Why don't we take a walk on the beach?" she asked, leading him away before Grace could say anything further.

It was even hotter on the beach, the white sand nearly blinding in the intense sun. It felt more like August than a day in early April. She walked quickly toward the water and he followed a few steps behind her. When she reached the water's edge, she turned to him and saw that he was perspiring, beads of sweat trickling down his neck.

"How did you find me?" she asked.

"Apparently you called one night and didn't leave a message. Matching your number here with an address is one of the less complicated things I can manage. I'm in telecommunications, remember?" He smiled. "Anyway, it doesn't matter. I've come to take you home."

She began walking north, toward the pier, and he followed. "This isn't a vacation, Paul. I tried to tell you that in my message."

"You mean when you conveniently left it on voice mail so you wouldn't have to talk to me?"

She didn't answer, suddenly feeling

ashamed.

"I thought we could go down to Charleston," he went on, "stay at a bed-and-breakfast on the harbor before going home. Your daffodils are all in bloom, you know."

She thought of her beautiful house. Her lovely gardens ready to burst into bloom. Her children's rooms ready and waiting for a visit from them. How she missed everything familiar.

"I can't." It came out barely a whisper.

"What do you mean, you can't?" Paul asked, taking her arm and forcing her to stop and look at him. "We have a life there, Joanna. We have kids who expect you to be there when they come home."

She shook her head as tears filled her eyes. "What life? You traveling all the time? Me living alone, waiting for you to come home? Another move?" She took a deep breath. "This isn't a marriage, Paul. You've just been too busy to notice."

He dropped her arm and pulled off his suit jacket, wiping his flushed face on his shirtsleeve. "Look, things are crazy at work right now, I admit it. We've got some major problems that came up, things I can't turn my back on. Once this all settles down —"

"There'll be something else, and you know it."

"What would you like me to do, Joanna, walk out on my job? It's taken me more than twenty-five years to get where I am —"

"Oh yes, vice president."

"Most wives would have been thrilled. Or at the least a little supportive."

Most wives would have been told about it, she thought. She turned from him and stared across the ocean at the far horizon, trying not to cry. She was a weakling. For too long she had swallowed each move without complaint, like a bitter pill she had to choke down.

"Haven't I been a good husband? A good provider?" he pleaded, pulling her around to look at him again. "Don't we have two great kids?"

Wrenching herself from his grasp, Joanna turned and began to run, forcing her breath in and out, in and out.

"Am I so horrible?" she heard him shout from behind her. "Or have you suddenly lost your mind!"

A bolt of anger shot through her and she turned suddenly, not realizing he was running after her. He slammed right into her. As she began falling into the water, he reached out to catch her and she hung there in his arms as the wave rushed higher onto the sand, washing over her sandals and his expensive Italian loafers. She could smell the spicy scent of his cologne and feel the sweat coming through his shirt. For a moment their eyes locked. Then she broke free of his grasp and stepped away.

He took a long, slow breath. "You're my wife," he said with sudden calmness. "I love you. I want you to come home."

"What will change?" she asked. "Tell me, Paul. What's going to be different?"

He looked at her for a long moment, and she could see a nerve pulsing in his cheek. "You know, Joanna, I was brought up to believe it's a man's job to take care of his family. I've done that from the beginning," he said. "When you got pregnant, I gave up any dream of law school and married you. And when you wanted to stay home and raise the kids, I worked harder so you could. And now I'm putting our second kid through college. I don't have time . . ."

He stopped suddenly, and she saw that he realized he'd said the wrong thing.

"Right, I'm just another demand on your time right now, and you don't really have enough of it to go around. As usual."

"Come on, Joanna, life isn't that simple and you know it."

"Why can't it be?" she asked in barely a

whisper. "We don't need a huge house, do we? We could live with so much less. Our life was so simple years ago. And we were happy. Don't you remember how hard it was in the beginning? And then even when you went on strike?"

"What are you talking about?"

"We were terrified. We didn't know how we'd come up with the rent, and Timmy was on that expensive soy formula because he was always throwing up." She could hear the trembling in her voice, but she went on. "For weeks we lived on peanut butter sandwiches and spaghetti. We should have been miserable, but we weren't. We had time together, remember? We'd take the kids to the park in the afternoon, then play cards at night because we had no —"

"Life is hard, Joanna," he interrupted, shaking his head as if she were a child. "And things just aren't that simple anymore."

"Why can't they be? Those were our best years, Paul, and we had nothing." She stopped talking, feeling herself begin to hyperventilate, and took a long, deep breath. "I felt so close to you then. We were scared, but we were in it together. Do you remember the little barber's kit we got at a yard sale for five dollars and I cut your hair and you —"

"Jo, stop!" He ran a hand through his hair. "You're just romanticizing, do you really want to go back —"

And then his beeper went off.

"God damn it," he muttered, pulling the pager from his jacket pocket and checking the number. "Let's walk back to the car. I need to make a call."

She watched him walk away. Caught in her throat were all the disappointments unvoiced: taking Sarah to college by herself because he couldn't, or wouldn't, cancel another business trip; countless soccer games he'd missed as Timmy played his way to a state championship, his eyes always drifting to the sidelines in the hopes his father would somehow make it; all the nights and weekends she'd spent by herself, wondering why marriage was such a lonely thing.

Walking back, she realized it didn't matter if she told him or not. He would never hear her.

Minutes later, she found him sitting in his car with the doors and windows closed and the air conditioner blasting as he talked on his cell phone. She sat in Grace's beach chair and watched him pull at his silk tie. Even from there, she could hear the angry edge in his voice, which surprised her, because she heard enough to know that he was talking with Ted.

Then he got out of the car and left it running. He walked over to her and kissed her suddenly.

"I want you to come home now. We're a family."

It would have been so easy to go with him. Things might even settle back down to a peaceful rhythm, they always seemed to. She'd let go of her anger. She would have the comfort of her old life back. And, most of all, her family would stay together.

She shook her head.

"I can't believe this." He stood there a moment. "What you're doing to me is unfair, Joanna. Things are falling . . ."

"Unfair!" she interrupted. "When have you ever been fair to me? Not once did you ever ask me how I felt before agreeing to a transfer and starting over . . ."

"You act like I had a choice."

"You did; you could have at least consulted me."

"So that's it? You're not coming with me?"

"No."

"What am I supposed to tell people? How is this going to look?"

She said nothing.

He walked to the car and opened the

door. "You have no idea what I go through."
And then she watched him drive away.

8

Joanna did her best to avoid Grace after Paul left, knowing that Grace must have heard the heated end to their conversation. At five o'clock she went nervously downstairs to prepare dinner. Grace said nothing of the encounter and offered her a glass of wine, which she drained too quickly.

"I hear it's supposed to be another hot day tomorrow," Grace said from her rocker, where she sat reading as Joanna worked at the counter.

"Yes, seems like a little heat wave," she replied.

"Perhaps we can get some fresh fish from one of the locals near the bridge and have a cookout while it's still warm."

"Great idea," she said, relieved Grace wasn't going to make a scene.

Grace kept up the small talk until they sat down to eat.

"What's this?" she asked, looking at the

salad bowl.

"You said you wanted a salad tonight, Grace."

Grace wrinkled her nose and shook her head. "That's not salad. I specifically asked for fresh iceberg lettuce. This is stems and . . . and leaves. It looks like something you'd pull off a tree."

"It's just baby greens and radicchio," she said, nearly laughing at the ridiculousness of this.

"Well you can eat it," Grace said, pushing the bowl away. "And I'd appreciate it if you'd get me iceberg lettuce next time."

She was tempted to dump the bowl of salad in the garbage. Instead she said, "Fine, Grace."

They ate in silence.

When they finished, Grace put her fork down and looked straight at Joanna. "Your husband seems unhappy that you're here."

She stood and began clearing the dishes. "Well, yes, I guess so," she managed.

"What are you going to do about it?" Grace asked.

"It's his problem," she said, reaching for Grace's plate.

Grace held the plate and forced Joanna to look at her. "Is it going to be my problem, too?"

"I'm sorry, I had no idea he was coming here."

"You lied."

She said nothing, the meal churning in her stomach.

"I need to know if you're going to honor your commitment to me," Grace said coldly. "If not, please tell me now."

"Yes. I gave you my word, didn't I?" she said. "I will stay with you for six months." Then she picked up the plates and took them to the sink.

Grace retreated to her rocker and book, and as soon as the dishes were done, Joanna escaped to the beach for a walk. The light was nearly gone and the ocean and sky were muted shades of gray. She headed for the southern end of the island, walking briskly, anger and frustration at both Grace and Paul simmering inside her.

It was well after dark when she stopped walking. She sat on the cool sand in front of Grace's house, bone tired, and stared at the waves. Their white edges, just visible in the darkness, slid back and forth across the sand in front of her. She wondered if Paul would make it home tonight.

It amazed her that a man she'd spent so many years married to, borne two children with, could feel like someone she hardly knew. But she was beginning to see how it came about. It happened gradually, as it probably did with countless other marriages, over the course of years. Little changes in day-to-day life that were barely noticeable at first. The first school play he missed, the first time he didn't call to say good night. The first supper after Sarah had gone away to college. And then Timmy. Paul's first business trip after they were both gone, when she'd spent a week alone in the house, the first time in nearly two decades. Then again and again. Less and less time together, fewer phone calls, as they moved into lives of their own, separate, yet joined by the common bond of bills, responsibilities, house, and children. She thought about not telling Paul that she'd committed to Grace for six months. Why didn't she? Gutless again.

Leaning back on her hands, Joanna looked up and watched the night sky unfold, a gray velvet canvas deepening to black. She saw Venus flickering brightly, and as her eyes adjusted she saw others, pulsing pinpricks of light burning through the darkness. The rhythmic wash of the waves was hypnotic, and after a while, her arms grew weary.

She lay back on the sand, staring up into the darkness, and spotted a satellite, like a baby star racing across the sky. Her eyes followed it until it disappeared in the fuzzy edge of the horizon, sailing into another part of the world. And it occurred to her she'd done the same thing. She'd run to this world, this different place that sometimes seemed like another dimension entirely. Could she really survive here? Could she become something other than Paul's wife? She let herself drift, her eyes still closed, and just listened to the ocean, the rolling and pulling of the waves, a soothing rhythm, like a long, slow breath inhaled. And then exhaled.

A sliver of moon hung just above the ocean when she opened her eyes. Her head was fuzzy with sleep. She sat up and felt sand falling from her hair. Slowly, Joanna stood, bent over, and shook her head, pulling her fingers through her hair to free all the sand. As she walked back toward the house, she noticed a light on through Grace's glass doors and then spotted her sitting in her rocker, staring out at the ocean. She wondered what Grace was doing up so late.

It was after midnight when Paul turned into his neighborhood. He drove down the quiet streets, past the magnificent colonial homes that sat like fortresses in the moonlight. Then he pulled into his own driveway, touched the remote on his sun visor, and the garage door yawned slowly open.

He got out of the car, bone tired, and breathed in the stale air of the garage, heavy with the smells of gasoline and fertilizer. He walked past the gardening tools where they'd fallen on the floor a week ago. In the dark laundry room that led into the house, he pulled off his damp shirt, shoes, and socks and left them in a heap on the floor, walking across the cool tile through the enormous kitchen, flipping switches that lit a dozen recessed lights.

Since his promotion he'd been home so little that he'd come in and go upstairs to bed and then leave early the next morning, grabbing coffee and a bagel at a drive-through. He barely looked at the place. Now he followed the tile through the two-story foyer, where the week's mail lay scattered beside the double front doors. On top were bills, the mortgage and car payments. He kicked the pile into a corner and turned, heading into the formal living room. He lay on the couch, and the floral Laura Ashley chintz felt smooth and cool on his back as he stretched out, resting his bare feet on the arm. The room, like the rest of the house, was perfect, a tasteful blend of pastels, laces, a Tiffany lamp between two mauve wing chairs, a limited edition print above the gas fireplace. He looked at the hearth and couldn't remember if they'd ever actually used it, although the realtor insisted it was necessary for resale. So much of what was in his house seemed mere ornamentation, planned for the needs or wants of the next owners.

He remembered the realtor walking him and Joanna through the house. Exclusive neighborhood, she'd purred. Homes built with every amenity an executive family could want. This was the kind of house you could flip in a year or two and make a nice profit, she'd gone on, knowing that the odds of Paul's family being in this same house any longer were slim. In the world of corporate families, roots stayed shallow and easy to pull up, something Joanna had never quite adjusted to.

He thought of the first time he saw his wife, twenty-seven years ago, across a bar in a pair of white bell-bottoms and a tight black turtleneck. A heart-stopper, his buddy had called her. He wanted to slide his fingers through the long straight hair that fell around her face like a sheet of dark silk. It wasn't until months later he'd learned that she pressed it every day with a hot iron to flatten the tight curls she'd been born with. Later, after they married, she'd had it professionally straightened each year and then had it cut in a prim pageboy. Her hair today in the afternoon light was like a wild and glorious sun-catcher, and it amazed him how different she looked as she faced him, refusing to go home. And that in twenty-seven years he'd never seen her natural hair.

In the darkened room, he picked up a crystal egg sitting on a brass stand on the coffee table, one of a dozen knickknacks lying around, and tossed it between his hands. His first mistake had been surprising her with his promotion — he'd promised no more moves when they came to Sparta. His second was waiting too long to bring her home.

When he arrived at Grace's house, Paul had half expected Joanna to come flying into his arms, as she used to years ago when he returned from one of these trips. But she didn't. His wife stood at arm's length in front of the gray beach house, a quiet stranger.

He should get up now and listen to his voice mails. Perhaps Ted had left something more about the rumored AT&T takeover. AT&T was vehemently denying the allegations to the press, but Ted believed the threat was real. Acquiring V.I.C. would rocket AT&T back into the number one telecommunications slot in the world. Then the security of jobs at V.I.C. would be anyone's guess. High-priced executives could be axed, bought out, or downsized. Paul's job, which looked solid as a rock after his promotion, was now crumbling under him in small, hard pieces, just like his life.

But Paul didn't have the energy to pick up the phone. He tossed the glass egg in the air and caught it, held it up to the light from the hall chandelier. He closed one eye, peering through the egg like a crystal kaleidoscope, and his house splintered into a dozen shards of light. As he turned the egg, each tiny scene unfolded, a colorful fracture of its whole. Exhausted, he imagined his own existence viewed through such a lens, picturing himself driving, flying, on the phone, in a meeting, sleeping. He was little more than a rat, he realized, working its way through an expensive, beautifully decorated maze.

9

Two weeks later, Joanna went looking for a part-time job, wondering again why Grace felt she needed her. Once a week she cleaned, and that took only four hours or so. Three or four nights a week, depending on Grace's appetite, she cooked supper. Every few days she went to the grocery or drugstore, ran errands, exchanged books at the library. On Sundays, she would drive Grace to the small Catholic church on the other side of Route 17. The routine left too many idle hours for Joanna, hours when she still battled guilt and regret. As she fixed herself tea early one morning, she realized she needed to begin filling her days with something. And since her money was slowly dwindling away, the perfect solution seemed to be looking for a job again.

Later that morning, Joanna drove up and down Route 17, as she had the first days after she'd arrived. This time it was different. Spring was nearly here and with Easter just around the corner, signs for hiring had begun to pop up like flowers. By the end of the day, she had a job at The Chowder House, a local seafood restaurant and bar that was basic, but always crowded when she'd gone by. They offered her two lunches and two dinners a week, a light schedule since they'd done most of their hiring already. But to her it was ideal, not enough to interfere with her obligation to Grace. And waitressing seemed like the perfect job. There was little commitment, the money was nearly all cash, and she thought it might help her mood to be in the midst of people.

She was right. A week later, Joanna found herself looking forward to the days she worked. She enjoyed the noise, the people, the constant good-natured banter and occasional off-color jokes. She was flirted with, teased, and once even asked out by a regular, a cop who came in alone once each week and left exorbitant tips. Goody, the owner, who also tended bar most nights, smiled and told her he wasn't a bad sort if you didn't mind a rifle hanging over the bed. The other waitresses were friendly for the most part, and often stayed for a drink or went out to a club after work. She always politely declined and assumed they thought she was going home to her husband. She still wore her wedding ring.

On her fourth night at The Chowder House, Goody called her over as she passed the bar on her way to the kitchen. She thought her drink order was ready.

"That man's your neighbor," he said, pouring a beer and nodding to a man across the bar. "Come on over, I'll introduce you."

She was mortified — was Goody trying to set her up? But it would have been rude to decline, so she walked around the bar.

"Joanna, this is Hank Bishop. He lives on the island, too," Goody said, as he slid a mug of beer across the bar to the man.

"So nice to meet you," Hank said with a deep, slow drawl and then stretched a hand out.

From across the bar, she'd thought he was old, but he was probably no more than fifty. He had the salt-and-pepper hair and beard of a sea captain. His face was deeply tanned, wind-scoured. Then he smiled and his blue eyes nearly disappeared. Kind eyes.

"Hello," she said and shook his hand.

"Goody tells me you're new here."

Goody was across the bar again, waiting on others.

"Yes, I am."

"From up north, I gather."

"Yes, New Jersey." She smiled, realizing the accent, or lack of it, gave her away.

She could have listened to his drawl for hours, the soft "r" sounds and the slow rhythm of words like music. While Goody began pouring her drink order, finally, Hank told her that Pawleys Island was one of the last strongholds for the nesting loggerhead turtles on the east coast. They were an endangered species now, and those that came to lay their eggs each summer were the last hope for future generations. On each of the two causeways that crossed the marsh and separated the island from the mainland, signs were posted warning all beach dwellers to turn out lights after ten p.m. The turtles, pulled in by the light of the moon and the stars, were often confused by the lights of man. She didn't tell him that she hadn't noticed the signs.

"I really have to get back to my tables," she said, excusing herself.

A few minutes later, as she was carrying the tray of drinks from the bar, Hank put a hand on her arm, stopping her.

"Island dwellers are fanatical about protecting the turtles," he said, "and we can always use a little more help. Would you be interested in joining us?"

"Oh, I've got my hands pretty full right

now," she said. "But thanks."

"Well, how about just thinkin' about it?" Hank asked nicely with a nudging smile.

"Sure," she said, feeling cornered. What else could she say?

Grace didn't seem to mind her having another job. In fact, she seemed relieved that Joanna wasn't always underfoot anymore, and soon they settled into a comfortable routine. But for Joanna, the rhythm of this new life was broken each time she talked to one of her children. She'd been vague with both of them. In the beginning she made the weak excuse that she was just taking a sabbatical for a while, not that she was leaving their father. Timmy didn't even take that well. Always the peacemaker, he wanted things back to normal. Knowing he had finals coming up, she didn't want to say anything to upset him further. Sarah, though, was on to her and thought she was totally justified, that her father was totally selfish and self-centered.

The following Sunday, during their evening call, Sarah was also complaining about money. Her job at the art gallery was soul-satisfying, but left little after paying the bills. Sarah had always been a good kid, a good student. Everything in life came easy to her, except adolescence. And then, just as she was entering her freshman year of high school, Paul had come home and announced another promotion, which meant another move. Sarah seemed to undergo a personality change overnight, venting her frustrations in life at her father. He had dismissed it as the usual teenage angst. But Joanna had seen on a daily basis just how difficult it was for Sarah to start her high school years where she didn't know a soul, trying to fit in and make friends.

"I've got my credit card charged to the limit, just finishing up this apartment," Sarah went on now. "I don't know how people do it. And I'm thinking about canceling cable. I'm never here to watch TV anyway. Or maybe I should just get a roommate."

"But you're happy with your place, finally?" Joanna asked.

"I was never unhappy, Mom. It's just a struggle," she said with a sigh.

She started to ask if she could send a little money to help. That's what the old Joanna would do. And then she stopped. She could hear Paul's voice ringing out from the past. *You do too much for them. You're overcompensating for your own mother.* She would usually throw back *And you don't do nearly enough.* But this was part of growing up, she realized. She had to let them go, even if they struggled. And she had to think about supporting herself first. Sarah would manage.

Her call to Timmy was brief. He was off to an anthropology meeting, so they talked for just a few minutes.

"I miss you, honey," she told him, longing to see him, to touch his face.

"Me, too, Mom," he said quickly. "So what's with you and Dad? Are you going home soon?"

"Dad was here, actually," she told him. "We had a nice visit, but he'll be traveling for a while." Partially true, she thought to herself.

"He works too hard. Why doesn't he take some vacation time and stay there with you?"

"There's an idea," she said, as if really considering it.

She always felt lonely after hanging up with them. As if some part of her, some piece of her life, was missing. Or maybe it was just Sunday night. As a child she'd always hated Sunday nights. When she'd saved all her homework from the weekend, too busy reading or escaping to a friend's house. Alone in her room, she would imagine other families playing games after supper, or watching TV and eating popcorn. It was never like that in her house.

She thought about going down to The Chowder House now, having a drink at the bar and talking to Goody. She'd never gone to a bar alone in her life, and even though she knew everyone, she still felt funny about it. It wasn't like she was working. A woman going alone to a bar meant only one thing, or so she'd been brought up to believe.

In the end, she made some popcorn in the tiny microwave and turned on the TV, not really watching or listening, but thinking about filling up her day tomorrow. The Chowder House would be closed, as it was every Monday.

Wednesday night Grace sat in her rocker writing letters while Joanna was at work. When the phone rang, she was surprised to hear Paul Harrison's voice on the line. Their conversation did nothing to change the opinion she had formed of him that morning he showed up in the driveway. He was a man used to being in charge of his world, used to getting his own way.

"I'm sorry to disturb you, Mrs. Finelli. I was hoping to speak with my wife, and this is the only number I have."

"Well, we share this number," Grace explained. "Joanna has an extension upstairs, but she's not here right now."

"Well, where is she?" He sounded annoyed.

Grace just wanted to end the conversation. "She's at The Chowder House, actually, working. I'll tell her you called."

"What on earth would she be doing at The Chowder House?"

Grace didn't like this, getting in the middle of Joanna's marital problems.

"I think I should just have her call you when she gets in," she said.

"Well, I think I should tell you that things have changed and Joanna is needed here at home."

"Joanna has made a commitment to me, Mr. Harrison," Grace told him.

"She has commitments here."

And before Grace could respond, he continued, his tone less hostile.

"Look, Mrs. Finelli, I don't mean to put you in the middle of this," he said. "But I think Joanna is punishing me. Apparently, she's been unhappy. But whatever it is she's looking for, it isn't down there."

Annoyed at his arrogant prodding, Grace spoke without thinking. "Oh, I don't know, Mr. Harrison. The ocean seems to bring her a sense of peace, and she hasn't been so restless since she started waitressing —"

"Waitressing?" he interrupted. "Are you kidding?"

Damn! She'd played right into his hands. "I'll have her call you," she said.

"I think Joanna may end up disappointing you after all, Mrs. Finelli," he said.

Or you, she thought to herself after they hung up. Obviously things were not going well for him. He reminded her of Frankie, her older son, middle-aged men of an in-between era. The sons of World War II and Korean War veterans who were brought up to be strong physically and emotionally, yet rarely showed their feelings. Life for them was about hard work, responsibility. Sean, just ten years younger, was born on the cusp of a new breed of man, more expressive, more self-indulgent.

It was nearly eleven when Joanna came home from work, later than Grace had expected. She was smiling and seemed relaxed. Grace assumed she was becoming friendly with the other waitresses. She hoped so. Joanna was not very talkative and guarded her feelings carefully. Some might consider her standoffish. Grace often wondered if it was her nature or if something in life had caused her to hold back, as if afraid of sharing some vital part of herself.

"Your husband called," Grace said, as Joanna took the pad from the counter to make a grocery list for the morning. Grace saw the smile disappear and her face close up.

"Oh, I'll call him back tomorrow."

"I think you'd better call tonight, Joanna. He seemed upset."

Joanna looked at her and flushed. "I'm sorry you had to —"

Grace put up a hand to stop her apology. "The only thing I'd like, Joanna, is to know I won't have to be second-guessing your decision every other day."

"I *told* you . . ." Joanna stopped, then added more softly, "I gave you my word, Grace. I'll be with you for the full six months."

And then Joanna went upstairs, the grocery list forgotten on the counter.

10

Paul picked up the box with his personal belongings and walked out the door of his office. He passed by Diane, his secretary, who looked up at him with red-rimmed eyes.

"Good luck," she mouthed, her lips twisting in sorrow.

He kept going, head high, briskly making his way past the pool of secretaries, all focused on keyboards and files to avoid the embarrassment of meeting his gaze. Blessedly, the elevator doors slid apart as soon as he pressed the button. When they opened again, he stepped out and walked across the impressive atrium of V.I.C., where less than two months ago he'd been lauded for his achievements.

"And although he's heading toward the half-century mark," he could still hear Ted joking over the microphone, "Paul is the youngest vice-president in our company's history."

And now he was out of a job.

It was warm outside, the mountains already dotted with the pink and white brushstrokes of flowering dogwood. Tossing the box in the trunk of his BMW, Paul sneezed violently. As he pulled out of the lot, he reached for his sunglasses to dull the brightness of the glorious spring day.

When he got home, he took an antihistamine and lay on the couch, a fist of pressure behind his eyes. He stared at the ceiling for a long time, too drained even to think, until, like someone hypnotized, he could keep his eyes open no longer. He was startled when he woke up and saw that it was nearly noon.

An odd feeling enveloped him. The house felt eerily quiet and empty despite the bright midday sunshine streaming in the large windows. It reminded him of the first time he stayed home from school sick, after his mother died. His father was at work and the house felt quiet and lonely. The lighting, too, was different, sad somehow, and unsettling, as he wasn't used to being home at that time of day.

He lay on the couch now wondering what to do next. The house was spotless, the cleaning lady having been there just a few days before. His lawn and shrubs were meticulously maintained by a landscaping company. The garage freezer was still stocked, as always, by his wife, who took care of everything else for him. Or had.

He realized as he looked up at the soaring cathedral ceiling in his family room that there was very little he did for himself in his own life. He was a privileged individual, his work so consuming that every detail of his personal life was efficiently handled by someone else. Even his occasional car appointments were effortless, his BMW picked up at work and a loaner left there for him. Diane, his secretary, had taken care of those personal things he couldn't leave to Joanna: gifts for her, theater tickets, dinner reservations.

Besides work, there were only two things he did: run and occasionally play golf with a client. He hated the game, never was good at it, despite taking lessons every once in a while. But his good-natured attitude and his ability to court his clients on some of the country's best courses made up for his lousy scores. It also gave him a human side, something his clients liked.

He thought about running now. His insides were restless and jumpy, and he realized he hadn't run in days. Maybe a good long run would calm him down. Forcing himself off the couch, he got up and went to change into his sneakers and shorts.

He ran out of his neighborhood onto the winding county road that took him west, into the hills, past fields and farms that gave this part of New Jersey a New England feel. He felt good at first, his tight muscles stretching with each step, the power of his legs propelling him. The sun was warm, bathing the countryside with a golden light, and he broke a sweat before his first mile was through. Up Snyder Road he ran, the toughest part of this route he knew like the back of his hand, a steep, winding road that was thankfully at the beginning of his five-mile loop. Halfway up, he faltered as a wave of fatigue washed over him and his legs began to tremble. His head was too congested, he realized, and he slowed his stride. A chill ran through him as his sweating skin turned to ice. He slowed to a walk. And then his heart slammed in his chest like a heavy door closing.

He stumbled into the woods, leaned his back against a tree trunk, and slid down until he was sitting on a musty pile of decaying ferns and rotted leaves. Slowly, deeply, he sucked air. He thought suddenly he might be having a heart attack, but there was no pain. Life just seemed to be leaving his body. Closing his eyes, he leaned his head back on the tree as tears slipped down his face.

He could hear his father's voice. College, he'd warned, as Paul worked landscaping jobs through high school to save for tuition, would not guarantee a successful future. Edward Harrison was an ex-marine and World War II vet who'd left high school at seventeen, had gone from the football field to the battlefield with a forged birth certificate to defend his country. Hard work was the only way to achieve security, he'd told Paul. Learn a trade. Colleges were the ruination of the country, he was also fond of saying, especially as the turbulent sixties stretched into the seventies and drugs and demonstrations captivated campuses nationwide. Four years of avoiding the real world, he'd called it — partying, sleeping, and squeezing classes in when necessary.

Four years of good grades, degree in hand, weren't enough to deflect his father's unvoiced disappointment when Joanna got pregnant and law school was abandoned. A liberal arts degree in the seventies was a guaranteed ticket to a sales job, about as low as his father thought you could go. Awards, promotions, bigger houses — none of it ever seemed to make much impression on the man who lived out his life in the same house he'd bought at twenty years old when he married Paul's mother. He was programmed to save, not spend, and could never understand Paul's thirst for a better lifestyle, a nicer house, a newer car.

It seemed to him now, sitting alone in the woods, that he'd spent most of his life worrying about money. Taking loans and working nights and weekends to get through college, too proud to ask his father for help. Then marriage and babies and the terror of so much responsibility and so little money. Living paycheck to paycheck. And then the big gamble, taking a sales position within his company, relying on commissions to make ends meet. He'd found his niche, though. After that, things got better and better, with quarterly bonus checks on top of building residuals. The economy exploded in the eighties, as his sales career took off. Things he never thought they could afford were suddenly in reach. Then Jo began pushing for him to work less, saying they could live with less. She didn't understand, he'd realized, what it took for him to get to that point. And you didn't turn down transfers and promotions because your wife didn't want you to work as much. In the back of his mind he was always thinking ahead, always worrying about the next deal. That was the nature of sales. Promotion to management ten years ago took some of the worry away, but he was only as secure as the sales team he headed. When he made vice president a month ago, he thought he'd finally bought the ticket to real security, a golden future.

As he sat there, his breathing finally slowed. The cold slick of sweat dried to a salty grit on his skin. He opened his eyes. Sunlight splashed the shaded forest floor. Too drained to move, he sat there, content to listen to the whispered breathing of the trees. Beside him a line of ants marched by his leg, a cargo of debris on their backs. A purpose to their existence. What would his purpose be now? he wondered, closing his eyes again.

When he got home, he showered and dressed, and prowled the empty rooms of his house, searching for something to do. Later he called his son, Tim, in Montana and was disappointed to find he was away on a field trip. Then he called his daughter, Sarah. She was curt, and it didn't take longer than a few minutes of forced pleas-antries for her to begin criticizing him.

She'd been waiting, it seemed, for this confrontation.

"I can't believe you're surprised Mom left," she said in that tone she'd begun using on him somewhere in her teens. "Dad, you're never there. She has no life. With us gone, what's the reason for her to stay?"

"Sarah, I'm not in the mood. I've given your mom more than a month now to indulge her need for some time. I've worked damned hard for all of you. I didn't see you complaining about my job when I was making those hefty tuition payments for you."

"Oh, come on, Dad, you and I both know my grades were good enough for a scholarship. We just didn't qualify financially. And I've always been grateful to you for my education. I've got a fabulous job, and I might even be moving to Paris."

"Paris? When did that come about?"

"Martin has a fellowship at the Sorbonne, and I've applied for a position at a really cool gallery right in Paris. My boss sent a glowing recommendation and says it looks good. We might even pick up a sublet from one of his friends."

"You and Martin are moving in together?"

"Oh, come on, Dad. I'm nearly twenty-five. And I love Martin."

"Funny, I've never even heard his name

before. Does your mother know all this?"

"Christ, Dad, don't you think Mom has enough on her mind? Have you ever given a second's thought to how she feels?"

Two minutes later he hung up, wondering why in ten years he hadn't been able to have a simple conversation with his daughter that didn't end up this way. He hadn't even told her about losing his job.

And then he called his wife.

Still damp from her shower, Joanna tossed her towel on a chair and stood naked in front of the dresser mirror, far enough back to assess her body with a stranger's eyes, when she heard the phone ring. Grace would get it, she thought, examining her limbs, long and lean, brown from the sun. Her breasts and backside were the blue white marble of unexposed flesh. Twisting around to catch the full view of her rear end, she caught a few dimples of cellulite beginning to spread and ignored the ringing of the phone. All in all, not a bad body for a middle-aged woman, she thought.

She was getting ready to have dinner at Hank Bishop's, a few jetties up the beach. It was nothing romantic, strictly casual. Yet she began wondering how she looked to other men. Her thoughts were interrupted by the familiar knocking on the wall, Grace signaling that the call was for her. She picked up the extension.

"It's me," Paul barked.

As she reached for her towel, she wondered if he was angry she hadn't returned his call the other night. "How are you?" she asked cautiously, pulling the towel around her.

"I'm great," he said, his voice dripping with sarcasm.

"Paul, please . . ."

"I hope you're making lots of money waitressing, because I'm officially out of a job."

"What are you . . ."

"Terminated, Joanna. We were bought out and all the top guys axed. Ted bought a sailboat, says he always wanted to see the world."

"Paul, there's got to be —"

"Nothing. There's nothing for me there. I very pleasantly vacated my office."

"But there's got to be some kind of severance, a buyout?"

"Joanna," he said slowly, as if speaking to a child, "I'm out of a job. We have a huge mortgage, car payments, tuition for Timmy, insurance. The buyout will keep us for six months."

"But you'll find another job."

She heard him take a deep breath. "I'm middle-aged, high-priced, and easily expendable. That's what I learned today. Twenty-five years of experience buys nothing these days, it seems."

She could picture him pacing as he talked. She'd seen him do it in airports, rest stops, pulling at his tie. "Something will come up," she said more softly.

"We should sell the house," he said. "It just doesn't make sense —"

"Wait," she stopped him.

"Joanna, you're not here. Tim and Sarah don't live here anymore. What's the point?"

"It's still our home. Their home." Pulling the towel tighter, she sat on the floor in front of the open sliders, her breath coming in spurts.

"Was, Jo," Paul said. "It *was* our home."

There was a long silence.

"It's half mine, and I don't want to rush into anything," she managed to say.

"By the way, you'd better call your daughter," he said, before hanging up. "Seems she's running off to Paris with some artist."

She set the phone on the floor beside her and pushed the door open wider. It was late afternoon, and the beach stretched before her quiet and golden as the sun dropped behind the houses. A few minutes ago, she was thinking about other men, wondering if there wasn't something else out there for her. Now, within minutes of hearing Paul's voice, she thought of one thing. Home. Her children's bedrooms, still ready for any visit. Her gardens, the columbine that had taken two summers to coax into bloom.

She sat there on the floor, counting slowly, in and out, as she tried to slow her breathing. She watched the ocean wash across the sand, then draw back into itself, a rhythmic cleansing as certain as the beating of her heart. But there were no more certainties, she realized, not since she walked out on their life and put this whole thing into motion. It was as if the whole of her past life lay in scattered pieces like the tiny grains of sand that were, at that moment, being pulled into the sea.

11

Joanna looked in on Grace before heading up the beach for dinner at Hank Bishop's. There was stuff everywhere and the remains of the old woman's dinner were scattered across the counter. Grace sat before the slider, head buried in a crossword, a glass of wine on her table, humming. She seemed oblivious to Joanna, or the chaos of the room. Joanna was tempted to ask why she'd told Paul about her job. Just then Grace looked up.

"You look all settled for the night," she said. And before the old woman could reply, she called out, "I'm off now," and crossed the room to go out the deck door.

It was just after seven and the sky was already darkening, blending with the deep purple of the sea. Joanna was grateful for the change of time recently and the longer days. To her left, in the breaks between houses, she caught the blood-streaked sky over the marsh and thought once again how lonely this time of day always seemed.

Walking up the beach, she wondered if the turtle project wasn't a line Hank Bishop used on new women. He'd been in for dinner again and persuaded her to learn more about the loggerheads, which she did find fascinating. She fingered the wedding ring on her left hand and figured that would put an end to any misinterpretation on his part.

Hank lived in the historic section. Three jetties up the beach she saw a tattered flag with a yellow pineapple, a symbol of welcome in the South. She walked up plank steps that climbed through a tangle of trees and scrub to Hank's house. Lights blazed cheerfully inside, and through a window she saw him at the sink, his back to her. And for a moment she wondered if she hadn't lost her mind, going to a strange man's house. But Goody was adamant; Hank was a nice man who'd been devoted to the turtle project for years. Joanna thought it might be a good diversion. She couldn't remember the last time she'd gotten involved in anything.

Grace was glad to be left alone. This wasn't a good night. The dull pain that gnawed at her stomach all day had finally subsided, leaving her spent and rattled. She wondered if it was the cancer already. It was hard to differentiate between the normal pain of aging, the body wearing down, and new pain that came on slowly but would soon, she knew, overtake her. At her age, eating and going to the bathroom were sometimes major accomplishments, as with new infants. Routine and regularity. Happiness was getting a meal down without event, or to relieve herself. One day soon, if not this day, the real pain would arrive and she dreaded it. Fuzzy-edged days. Long, endless nights, an ordeal to get through.

The nights were the worst for her with Frank. Even when he could fall asleep, he would thrash in their big bed like a wild animal subdued, so that she couldn't sleep beside him anymore. But she'd lie there, refusing to give in to one more separation between them, the final one coming soon enough. She would watch him, his face sinking each day, his skin stretched tight over his bones. He hadn't been that thin since she first met him on a dance floor at the end of World War II, and for a while, after the heaviness of age melted away, he'd been thin and handsome again, his features suddenly sharper, younger. But the flesh kept disappearing until his face took on a mask-like quality. *He's slipping away,* she remembered thinking one night, as he lay on the couch looking at the television but not really watching it. He'd entered a different dimension, a world controlled by pain and drugs. A world she'd soon know firsthand. But only to a point, she told herself now. She'd do for herself what she couldn't, in the end, do for Frank.

She put down her letters, unable to concentrate any longer. In her heart she still felt eighteen. In her soul still beat the eager, wide-eyed girl he'd walked across a church hall and asked to dance. So tall and handsome in his uniform. It was just before the war had ended, and as she watched him coming their way, it appeared he was heading for her cousin Rose, who was sitting beside her. At the last moment he turned to her, shyly asked for a dance. That quiet, handsome soldier was everything she'd waited for during those dreary war years.

In one of Joanna's rare, unguarded moments a few nights earlier, when she'd sat on the deck with Grace, unable to sleep, Joanna had confessed that she'd totally misjudged Paul when they'd met. It was his eyes that drew her to him in the darkness of a crowded bar, deep green eyes that convinced her of sensitivity and a similar need for affection and belonging. It wasn't until after they were married that she realized his quiet ways reflected a man who simply didn't feel comfortable sharing much about himself. They'd already had a child.

"Do you think you're the first woman in the world to fall in love with your illusion of the man you're with?" Grace had asked her. "Misjudging a man is a sin committed by women over and over again. We're romantics; we see what we want to see. Later, when reality hits, you have to hope there's enough goodness there, and mutual respect, to keep it together."

"What about you?" Joanna had challenged her. "Was your handsome soldier everything you thought he was?"

She'd thought about her dead husband and smiled. Fifty years had gone by like the flash of a shooting star, the good moments still shimmering while the rest were lost somewhere in the darkness of the years.

"He was a good man," Grace had told her. "And some dancer."

Grace sighed and went back to her letters — long, fictitious missives to her children, full of card games, walks on the beach, the choir they thought she'd joined, the Rosary Society. A full life, not a marking of time.

She still longed to dance. To feel Frank's

arm around her, his warm hand holding hers, gliding across the floor in a smooth fox-trot. Even now she sometimes forgot and reached for him in bed, or expected him to come walking into a room. Her dances were over, though, and she realized again that Joanna was her only real human link with the world now.

Soft jazz filled the room along with the clink of china. Halfway through a glass of white wine, Joanna began to feel comfortable in the old, sea-battered cottage, which had been sitting on the island for decades before other houses. As he prepared dinner and she sat at a counter stool, Hank explained the loggerhead turtle project. But her thoughts kept drifting to Paul's phone call, Sarah's answering machine.

"Only one in ten thousand turtles makes it to maturity," Hank said as he finished cleaning the last shrimp and tossed it in the strainer. "So you can see how important this project is."

"It seems so sad," she said, sipping her chardonnay, watching him at the sink as if she were giving him her full attention.

Hank layered the shrimp, caught fresh that morning from a boat he once owned, in a baking dish and began squeezing garlic through a stainless-steel press.

"We know the turtles navigate with the stars or the sun, probably follow smells and even tastes in the water, currents and waves," he went on, slicing chunks of butter and arranging them in the baking dish. "More than likely they've also got a kind of internal compass. You know, to pick up magnetic signals from the earth. Homing pigeons operate that way."

"So they always know where to go back to," she thought out loud, the few sips of wine humming lightly through her already. She decided to put her husband and daughter out of her mind until later.

"It's better than that," Hank said, turning on the broiler and sliding the baking dish into the oven. "What's really amazing is that scientists believe when a female loggerhead is old enough to mate and lay eggs, she'll find her way back from hundreds, probably even thousands of miles away to the same beach that she was hatched on."

This was astonishing; Joanna felt a catch in her throat. "So she goes home, like her mother before her."

"That's right, darlin'. It's called the 'natal beach,' " he went on, pulling dishes out of the cabinet and setting the small table.

Outside, a full moon began to inch over

the black ocean like a huge, glowing pearl, casting a bar of light across the water that seemed to carry to Hank's door. She could feel its pull, the tug of primitive forces inside, and wondered if a shift in hormones accounted for the tears that suddenly filled her eyes at that moment. She got up and walked to the window. The room was spare, filled with a few worn pieces of furniture that beckoned comfortably. A few seascapes hung on the wall, one a painting of Hank's old shrimp boat by a local artist. On a table near the stairs, next to a piece of driftwood, Joanna picked up a framed photo of a woman sitting on the sand beside a little girl. They were both blond, smiling into the camera, as the little girl scooped sand into her pail.

"My wife and my daughter," Hank said, beside her suddenly, smelling like garlic, shrimp, and lemons. "They were killed in a car accident."

"Oh. I'm so sorry." He hadn't mentioned a family. For that matter, neither had she. For a moment she pictured her own children, wondered if it was ever possible to get to a point where you could talk about something like that without falling apart.

"It was a long time ago," he said, taking the picture, looking at the faces caught in a moment of pure joy. "Sometimes it's like they were never really here at all."

He put the frame back and went into the kitchen to check the scampi. She couldn't take her eyes off the picture.

"Dinner's ready," he called, a moment later.

After coffee, Hank explained what would be expected of her as a volunteer in the turtle project. In May and June the mother loggerheads would begin to come ashore at night. Their heavy bodies, weighing as much as five hundred pounds, would leave a trail across the sand to the place they'd lay their eggs, usually high up near the dunes where the tide couldn't wash them away. During that time, Joanna would be assigned a stretch of beach to patrol a few mornings each week, to look for evidence that a nest might have been laid. Any nest would be staked with sticks and rope and then monitored until late summer or fall. Then they'd begin sitting watch each night, waiting for the eggs to hatch. As Hank talked, she could hear the wind rattling outside. Yet his gentle voice and soothing drawl were like a comforting blanket, drawing her into a snug place.

"You don't seem like the waitress type,"

he said suddenly, getting up to refill the coffee cups, bringing her back to the conversation.

"Well." She smiled, embarrassed. "I don't really know what to say to that."

"You're a bit too refined," he said, drawing out the "i" in refined with his lovely drawl. "And somehow I don't really see you as live-in help either."

Now she laughed. "You're right. I've been a corporate wife for more than twenty-five years." She paused a moment, unsure how much to reveal. "Anyway, a few months ago I decided I'd had enough and here I am," she added with an air of finality she hoped invited no more questions. She was surprised she'd told him as much, having never said a word to the people at The Chowder House.

He insisted on walking her back to Grace's. The beach was still windy and she pulled her hooded jacket around her. The moon was higher now and the sea seemed to tremble in the white light. Hank told her he'd been a shrimper for more than thirty years, that he'd lived his entire life on Pawleys Island. Was he really that rarity, she wondered, a simple man? Then he mentioned a meeting with the rest of the volunteers the next week at his house, and he asked if she was in.

"I'm in," she said, as they stopped in front of Grace's house.

He took her hand in both of his and clasped it warmly. For a moment she thought he was going to lift it to his lips. When he was gone, she sat on the deck steps for a while, watching the moon cross high above and begin its journey to the other side of the world. She was amazed at what she had done tonight, gone to a man's house, made another commitment. And finally spent nearly an hour or so not even thinking of her other life.

12

The second Monday of April dawned clear and crisp. A light frost glistened in the early sunlight as Paul shuffled barefooted down the driveway to get the paper. He read it at the kitchen table, sipping a cup of instant coffee, black because he was out of milk. He turned the front page, uninterested. He scanned the gossip columns, the comics, unable to connect with anything the world had to offer today.

In the back section, the classifieds stared at him like a guilty reminder. His insides hummed with Monday morning anticipation, his body programmed for commuting, traffic, early meetings. He should have contacted a headhunter or two by now. The long columns of tiny newsprint, for auto mechanics, sales clerks, telemarketers, teachers, editors, and truck drivers, blurred in the dim light of the kitchen at that hour, depressing him with their possibilities. He closed and stacked the paper in the recycling bin. The day loomed ahead long and empty.

He'd had his share of condolence calls over the weekend. Everyone, it seemed, had a bit of advice. Ted, who'd already listed his house and bought the sailboat he'd always dreamed of, told him to take some time and have fun. Diane, his secretary, gave him a pep talk that could have coaxed a suicide off a bridge, certain someone would snatch him up in a few weeks. Then a surprise, Karen from legal had called, her clipped, breathy words transporting him back years.

It had happened at a symposium, just after he'd moved his family back east from Naperville, a Chicago suburb. Joanna had been unhappy and unsupportive, as usual. Sarah had been sullen and nasty about walking into a new school as a freshman, not knowing a soul. Tim had been uncomplaining, as always.

The day after the moving van left, while his family settled into the new house and Joanna began scouting the schools and doctors, he flew to a conference at a Hilton in Boca Raton. At four o'clock everyone headed for happy hour, where ties were loosened, high heels kicked under tables, and an attractive attorney who'd been hired a few months before cornered him after his third Heineken. Their conversation quickly turned to a flirtatious banter. He knew, as the afternoon wore on and the room emptied, that he should leave. But he dreaded the long night ahead in his hotel room and continued to drink, flattered by the attention. Afterward he lay in Karen's bed, sobering quickly, numb with the realization he'd committed adultery. Wondering if anyone had seen them leave together.

He'd slipped out of bed, hoping to escape in the early hours, but found Karen quietly crying when he turned around from gathering his clothes. Tears slipped down her cheeks as she looked up at the ceiling with a small smile. She was forty, she then told him, older than him by five years. At her age, she'd explained, the chances of landing a husband were tougher than winning the lottery. But that didn't take away the ache to be touched and held, the need to make love. She knew he would be safe.

She was passionate and needy, far different from the cool persona she presented in the office each day. He got back into her bed, pulled her to him as she nuzzled the hollow of his neck, and Paul felt his own empty places fill up for a while. Her fingers lightly stroked the hairs across his chest, grazing his nipples reverently, as if he were a long-awaited prize. The next day he'd watched her head a legal debate on cable rights, prim and efficient again. He stared at the buttons of her silk blouse, the sheen of her stockings running up her long legs, hardly able to believe what they'd done.

When he returned home, Jo was still cold and begged him to look for another job that would demand less travel. He'd known there were some who could easily justify a double life. And with all his time away, it wouldn't be that difficult. But he couldn't. Always, it was as if his father's disapproving eyes were watching, so that in spite of his need, his loneliness, he couldn't continue. He'd been with Karen just twice that week, but the guilt still haunted him.

Karen had called Sunday afternoon to say she was worried about him. She offered no glib advice, urged him to try echinacea and quercetin from the health food store after he exploded in a sneezing fit. She never asked about Joanna or his family.

By Tuesday afternoon, Paul was heading west, driving a sleek blue conversion van, fitted with two fold-out beds and a tiny kitchenette. The BMW was gone, a trade-in, a rich relic of another life that had abruptly, he realized, come to an end. Having cruised along Route 80 since morning, he was already in Ohio and hoped to stop at a KOA in Illinois later that night. He couldn't stand another motel room, each one a carbon copy of the next, the inevitable remote and ice bucket sorry companions. With the van he'd be in control, able to keep to himself, and from the moment he sat behind the wheel in the soft leather captain's chair, a sense of adventure he hadn't felt in years had surged through him. Maybe Ted had the right idea.

He knew he was behaving impulsively, but he wanted to see his son. His wife and daughter seemed to want nothing to do with him, and loneliness propelled him west now in the hope that when he got to Montana, somehow he could reconnect with Timmy. He hadn't seen his son since he'd been home for a brief visit last summer. Paul drove on, fat tires whining along the asphalt while the sun slipped lower in front of him. For the first time since he'd walked out of V.I.C., the visceral tremors eased, as his mind, programmed for the minute-by-minute gear-switching of his job, was free and began to wander. He stared ahead, white lines racing by, arm cast lazily out the open window, his thoughts floating through the past.

He pictured Joanna kneeling in the garden in the early morning light, plying bulbs apart with a tenderness she hadn't shown him in years. Then scooping up last year's mulch from the flower beds, her face intent and serene. Each spring she started anew. Her simple gardens grew bigger with each house, as she distanced herself from him, he now saw. The complaints eventually stopped, her caring and attention turned to bulbs and seeds. Roots he couldn't give her.

By late afternoon, the highway slowly clogged with shift and corporate workers, truckers and the occasional late school bus as he approached Cleveland. Paul pulled into the left lane, the heavy van smooth at his touch.

A memory of himself as a teenager, standing outside the garage, drifted into his mind. He was watching his father lift a new sheet of wood onto his workbench. Before he cut it, his father's hand slid up and down the smooth plank, the movement almost a caress. Paul had watched transfixed as he put his nose to the hard surface and slowly breathed in the wood's pungent scent. Paul had never seen that look before. Certainly not when his father left for the plant each afternoon as Paul was coming in the door from school. There were few words between them. *Get your homework and chores done,* he would say as the door opened. *Then see if your mom has anything for you to do.*

Then his mother had died. Her loving touch, her gentle affection suddenly gone. His father switched to a day shift, and his silent presence filled Paul with more loneliness than an empty house ever could. He wondered now if his life would have been different had his mother lived. If he would have been more like her, able to pull the best out of those around him instead of indifference and resentment.

At seven o'clock it was nearly dark, and he pulled into the gravel drive of the KOA campground just past Toledo. Small trailers and long motor homes, some permanently staked, lined the tree-shaded dirt lanes that wound back to the office. Inside, a small gift shop shared the space and offered travelers authentic Indian jewelry, mugs imprinted with clever slogans and "World's Best Pop-Pop," T-shirts and sweatshirts emblazoned with grizzly bears, the Great Lakes, and "Campers Make Better Lovers." In the back there were shelves filled with canned soups, soda and chips, hot dogs and marshmallows and tiny boxes of detergent. A large sign over the front desk warned, *No Noise After Ten P.M.* Paul chose a site near the restrooms and paid fifteen dollars for his slot.

"Do you have a KOA card, sir?" the woman behind the counter asked. She was about sixty, in a housedress, a flowered cotton shift like his mother used to wear. Her hair was coiled into a gray nest that rested on the back of her neck, and her eyes smiled kindly through her wire-framed glasses.

"No, actually, I don't," he said.

"Well, if you're plannin' to do some more campin' in the near future, you may want to consider it. You'll save five dollars on each stay."

He signed for the card and then she slid a receipt along with the rules of the campground across the counter at him.

"You have a nice night now," she said, and smiled. "We close up the store at ten, but if there's anythin' you need or any trouble at all, Chet and I live in the cabin just up from the playground. You just let us know."

He walked back to his van, wondering at her cheerful disposition. She probably only ever dreamed of the things he owned in his life, Paul thought, as he folded back his bed and pulled a pair of sweatpants from his suitcase. Yet she seemed so content with her existence. How many could say that?

■ ■ ■ ■

As Joanna drove her to the doctor, Grace realized it had been nearly a week since she'd left the island. She'd been feeling worn and depressed, but today, suddenly, she felt alive again, energetic with the possibilities of whatever life still lay ahead of her. Attitude, she told herself, was everything. And there was still time.

She smiled as they rode past the marsh, swollen with the high tide, puddles of saltwater shining in the late morning light. A motorboat purred through channels that glistened like silver slashes cutting through swaths of green velvet, and she hummed with the fleeting joy of a beautiful morning.

They crossed the causeway and turned north on Route 17, heading toward Myrtle Beach. Joanna drove silently. Looking out the window, Grace noticed the flurry of development all along the highway. There was little traffic at this time of day, and the medians were blooming with spring pansies and clusters of tall snapdragons amid the palm trees.

"I'd really like to go there sometime," Grace said when they drove past Brookgreen Gardens.

Joanna turned, looking at the entryway and the tall majestic sculpture.

"That would be nice," she said.

After another silence Grace said, "How about we go out to lunch after my doctor's appointment? My treat."

"Sure," Joanna answered, and turned to her with a brief smile.

Murrels Inlet was a small fishing village about a half hour south of Myrtle Beach, worlds away from the honky-tonk atmosphere of that resort city. As Grace lunched with Joanna on fresh crab cakes and hush puppies in a lovely harbor-front restaurant, they watched shrimp boats returning from a night on the water. The dull aching in Grace's back was gone today and the doctor had told her there'd been no change in the last month.

"Let's splurge and get some wine," she suggested.

"It's awfully early," Joanna said, glancing at her watch.

It was in fact just noon, but Grace called the waitress and ordered a bottle of pinot grigio.

"To a long, warm spring," she said, touching her glass to Joanna's. "And an endless summer."

"Cheers," Joanna replied, and took a tiny sip.

"Tell me about your son out in Montana," Grace asked, hoping to prod some conversation. "What on earth made him decide on a school out there?"

"Well, my son's had a love affair with dinosaurs since he was a little boy," Joanna explained, smiling. "Here in the States the best dinosaur finds have been in Wyoming and Montana. But since he's been out there, his interest has swayed more toward anthropology. You know, lost tribes and civilizations. He's actually spent some time in Indonesia, living with a primitive tribe of people, studying their ways."

"He must be quite ambitious."

"He's not, that's the funny thing," she said, taking another sip of wine. "He's nothing like Paul. It's more a passion for him than a career. And Paul isn't crazy about his plans. He feels Timmy's just clinging to some childhood dreams, not really facing the real world. How many jobs do you ever see in the paper for anthropologists?"

"You must miss him."

"I do," Joanna said, and Grace saw sadness in her eyes. "I think about Timmy and Sarah all the time, and I do miss them terribly. But I know this is their time to find their own paths in life." She sighed. "I just wish they weren't so far away."

As they pushed their plates aside, Grace topped off their glasses with more wine.

"You're a good mother to give them that. Not all mothers are so unselfish."

"Was yours?"

Grace tried to focus the distant memory of her mother into her image just before she died in her late twenties, when Grace was just a little girl.

"She never had the chance to let me know. After she died, my father left town to find work. This was during the depression, you see, and I ended up living with my cousin Rose's family."

"I'm sorry," Joanna said.

"Frank's mother was definitely the type who wanted to keep her family close by," she said and then found herself telling Joanna more than she'd intended.

Twelve weeks after she and Frank had their first dance in that parish hall, they were married in the church next door. They left her hometown in Pennsylvania and took a bus to Atlantic City, where they spent their wedding night. The next day they took another bus to Brooklyn to meet his family, and that's where they spent the rest of their honeymoon. A week later, his leave was over and he was gone from her life. Grace had planned to return home, but Angela, his mother, begged her to stay so that they could get to know each other better. "You're family now," she'd insisted. Grace had no idea that she wouldn't leave that house for almost ten years.

While Frank was overseas, she discovered she was pregnant, and Mama and Papa, as she came to call his parents, couldn't do enough for her. But she soon saw that Mama was a strong, domineering woman who ruled her family with a fist full of guilt and innuendo. Grace would often escape to the yard and sit with Papa, a gentle man who smoked his cigar as he tended his fig trees or grafted roses. It was as if she was living someone else's life then, like in a novel, and Frank was a vague memory that was beginning to fade already. In her third month she came across a picture in a drawer, a handsome man with full hair she thought must be a cousin she hadn't yet met. But it was Frank, younger, heavier, looking little like the man she married. It was then she realized her husband was a stranger to her.

"We stayed on with Frank's family long after the war was over. Papa had had a heart attack and Angela leaned so much on Frank."

"Why didn't you just move out and live nearby?" Joanna asked her.

"This was the forties and the fifties," Grace explained. "Times were still hard. After Papa died, though, Angela finally went with Annette, who was her only daughter, after all, and expecting her own first child."

"My God, you must have felt so free."

"You would think so," Grace said, and felt her heart twist at the irony of Joanna's words. She felt a quiver of sadness in her throat, thinking of all of them, gone now. And the scared, lonely girl she was back then. She swallowed the last sip of wine and picked up the check. "But that's another story, for another time."

Grace's legs felt weak from the wine as they left the restaurant, and the sudden glare of sunlight hurt her eyes. Giggling, she realized she was a bit tipsy. She took hold of Joanna's arm as they walked down the ramp to the parking lot.

"My mother would be shocked at me," she laughed, "tipsy so early in the day. I've been told she only ever had an Irish cream on holidays."

"My mother was usually bombed by lunch. By the time I got home from school,

133

she was either downright nasty or passed out," Joanna said, and Grace looked up as Joanna's hand flew to her mouth and she began shaking her head. "I can't believe I said that."

Grace pulled Joanna's arm until she stopped and turned to her. Joanna, too, was a bit drunk, she saw. And her mouth was twisted with emotion.

"I don't think we should drive home yet, dear," she told her. "Why don't we sit and watch the boats for a while."

Joanna didn't want to sit. She was mortified at her outburst. She stood staring over the water as the boats docked in the little inlet bobbed and swayed in the afternoon breeze. Without turning, she asked Grace, who sat on a bench, "Did you ever dream about what your life would be like? When you were a young girl, that is?"

"Oh, I think we all have grand plans when the world lies before us as a big possibility," Grace answered.

Joanna turned to her then. "No, I'm talking about real dreams. What was it you wanted more than anything?"

Grace smiled. "To be an artist," she said, and then gave a little laugh. "Yes, to capture the beauty of the ocean, the sunset, the stars in the night sky. To move people with my vision."

"You, an artist? I'd never have guessed," Joanna thought and then realized she'd said the words out loud.

Grace gave her a quick look, obviously insulted by her emphatic reaction. She turned away, watching the boats again. She shouldn't have had the wine.

The weather was picking up. Tiny white clouds raced across the vast blue of the sky, and before them a cormorant dove below the water's surface in search of fish. The sun slipped quickly behind one of the small clouds and a moment later emerged again, hot and bright.

"I was about to go to school for art when I met Frank," Grace went on behind her. "I wasn't sure I had any real talent, but I knew how I felt when I had a brush in my hand. I didn't really care what anyone else thought, painting simply made me happy."

"Did you paint after you married?" Joanna asked.

From the corner of her eye, she watched Grace's gaze shift as her mind drifted across the years.

"A little at first. But in the day-to-day reality of babies — remember washing machines and dryers didn't exist yet for most people, and ironing was a major chore each day — there just wasn't time. Oh, occasionally I joined Papa in the garden and sketched a little while the children were napping, but at some point, I can't remember exactly, I just stopped."

Joanna turned and Grace looked up at her. "But why didn't you go back to it, later on?"

"Oh, I thought I would," Grace said, giving her a sheepish smile. "I'd planned to, of course, one day, when the children grew up. When free hours existed again." Grace shrugged. "But it never happened. By the time there was opportunity, the desire had simply slipped away."

Joanna turned and looked at the boats again, swaying in the stiffening breeze. She'd never wanted anything grand. Just a home. A family.

"I went to college for a few semesters," she told Grace, "but nothing really interested me that much. I thought of maybe going into nursing."

"There's nothing wrong with wanting to be a wife and mother," she heard Grace say. "It's the most noble, giving vocation a woman can pursue. I have no real regrets."

"Really?" Joanna said. "But here you are all alone. Your children call, but never come.

What good did all that self-sacrifice get you?"

"Joanna, I'm alone by choice," Grace said, a slight tremble in her voice.

"I'm sorry," she said, embarrassed. "That was rude. Maybe we should go now."

She held out her arm and Grace took it, slowly getting up. Walking to the car, she watched the beautiful afternoon disintegrate as clouds thickened and the breeze grew cold. It was ironic, she thought. All she'd ever wanted was a family.

Yet here she was, all alone, just like Grace.

13

Joanna opened the cardboard box she'd hidden in the back of the closet. Sitting on the floor, she began to pull out papers, old photographs, and the journals she'd kept all her life, pausing to look at none of it. And then she reached the pink diary with the tiny gold lock, designed to keep her thoughts secret from the world. Pressing the clasp, she pulled the pink cover open. There on the first page was her mother's neat script, which she'd always righteously referred to as her Catholic-school handwriting.

Happy 13th Birthday to Joanna.

She turned the page to the first entry, March 30, 1966, and there was her own slanted scrawl. As she sat on the hard wooden floor of Grace's little apartment, she remembered writing alone in her room late that night so many years ago. After her father had quietly told her girlfriends, who were supposed to stay for a sleepover, that

138

they had to go home. Her mother wasn't feeling well. She'd heard them whispering as they left, and she could still feel the shame creeping up her neck, flushing her cheeks like a stain of sin. *I hate my mother,* she'd written, *I wish she'd die.*

She got up and opened the sliders. A rush of ocean air blew through the room, tossing papers off the table and napkins onto the floor. She didn't care. She took deep breaths, watching the heavy afternoon clouds race across the sky. She hated Grace, too, at that moment, for insisting on drinking earlier.

She grew up in a quiet house, in a neighborhood of narrow homes on narrow lots where you could stand on the front porch and reach far enough to touch the house next door. Their neighbors were postmen and mechanics, worked in the local grocery or the foundry on the edge of town. Her father was a brakeman on the railroad and gone for days at a time. When he came home, he went right to sleep. More often than not, the phone would ring before he'd wake, giving him his two hours' notice to be on the next run.

Her mother had all the windows covered with heavy curtains, and the rooms were dark and hushed, like walking into an empty church. Joanna could remember coming home from school, passing some of the other mothers sitting on their porches or even standing on the corner waiting for their kids to appear after the long day's separation. Her mother was always inside, watching a game show or a soap opera. *Supper's at five,* she would call out as Joanna tossed her books on the table. When her father was home, they rarely talked, and she couldn't recall a sign of affection between them ever.

It wasn't until she was in fifth grade that she learned about her brother. It was Alice Lilly's mother who'd slipped one afternoon when she was over at Alice's having a Creamsicle after they'd come back from the library. Sally Pearson, another neighbor, who'd been expecting, had just arrived home from the hospital. Alice and Joanna stood on the sidewalk waiting to see the baby as Mrs. Pearson emerged from the car. But they could tell by the look her husband flashed them as he came around and opened her door that something was wrong. They went in the house slowly. There was no baby.

Mrs. Lilly explained that the Pearsons' baby had been stillborn, and said sometimes that was easier than when you had a baby for a year or two, like Joanna's mother had. And then Mrs. Lilly got all nervous and tried to change the subject. Alice was having none of that, and Joanna began to cry. She begged Mrs. Lilly to tell her more.

It was before Joanna was born, and her mother, well, her mother was different then, Mrs. Lilly said, tugging at her apron. Her mother would sit on the porch knitting little baby things while her father was at work. When the baby was born, it was her father who held him proudly for the neighbors to see. When he was two, Jonathan, a name she'd never heard, woke up with a fever one morning. By the next morning he was gone. Septicemia, they'd called, it, a violent blood infection. Mrs. Lilly was crying by this time, too, as she told her that her mother's screams could be heard up and down the block. At one point she ran out of the house, just running and running until her father caught her and brought her back home.

Joanna was born six months later. Everyone assumed her mother would snap out of it, Alice told her days later, thriving on the high drama and her importance in learning the rest after her mother abruptly ended the story. But Joanna's mother was never the same. For weeks Alice dragged Joanna around, watching Mrs. Pearson across the street with new vigor to see what would unfold there. But all they saw was her husband taking her for walks, holding her hand or curling his arm around her protectively. She looked at him with such love. And by next summer's end there was a new baby sleeping in a handsome carriage while Mrs. Pearson sat on the porch staring happily about her.

Joanna looked out the glass doors at the darkening ocean, a dull gray now, and her mind flashed forward from then, to her own porch, when she was a young mother. One of those ordinary moments that seize you with emotion, and you know you'll always remember it as other, larger moments disappear in the vast days and years of your life. It had been raining. They didn't even have porch chairs yet. Sarah and Timmy were toddlers and they sat on the porch floor, their backs to the brick wall of the little house, reading a stack of picture books from the library. Sarah, who was four, could practically memorize a book after just a few readings, and loved to pretend she could actually read. She insisted she wanted to read to Timmy. Free for a moment, Joanna opened the front door and ran in the hall to grab sweaters, as the summer storm was pushing in a cold front. When she came back out a few seconds later, she found Sarah, picture book in her lap, "reading" earnestly, turning pages slowly and pointing to each picture for emphasis with her chubby little fingers. Timmy, she obviously hadn't noticed, had fallen asleep. Not quite two, his head rested on his sister's shoulder, his chubby baby cheek pushed up, his mouth open, drool dripping down his chin. A gush of love overtook Joanna, squeezing her heart until it hurt. Oh, how she longed to keep them that way, innocent and tender forever. If she could just protect them always. And it occurred to her in that moment that her mother had never felt that way about her.

She threw the pink diary back in the box and tossed everything else on top of it. She was tempted to carry it out to the beach and set it all on fire, but thought she'd provided Grace with enough drama for one afternoon. So she shoved it far back in the closet and closed the door. Then she climbed on the futon and pulled the blanket over her, the room spinning as soon as she closed her eyes.

Joanna was glad for work that evening. She took a long shower, slipped on her black pants and white shirt, grabbed her apron, and remembered, when she headed out the door, that it was Wednesday. Hank would be there for his weekly dinner.

Wednesdays were always jammed — crab legs, all you could eat for $14.95. She was barely able to keep up with the tables, but at one point, taking an order for a party of six, something she could do with her eyes closed now, it occurred to her as she jotted down their dinners in her little pad that simply smiling, making polite chatter, and helping people could do wonders for a mood. She talked, served, demonstrated the best way to crack a crab claw, and for a few moments was part of their lives. And they were part of hers. It was a good way to get outside herself and ease the loneliness.

Hank called a greeting across the bar as she waited for a drink order. Joanna caught him watching her a few times as she raced around the restaurant with dinners and drinks, handing out checks, collecting tips. Goody was right, she thought; he was a nice man. But there was an intensity about him that made her heart beat a little faster when she found his eyes on her.

That night she joined the other waitresses for an after-work drink at the Mermaid, a local bar that closed at two in the morning. She just didn't want to go home yet, and she drank a Virgin Mary, much to their jeers. Carol, who'd been married twice and was living with a guy with her two kids, said she was thinking of moving on, but didn't know how she'd afford it without his income since her husband rarely sent his child support. Jolene, the only black waitress at The Chowder House, who was civil to Joanna but not much more, complained about the rising taxes in the area, which were pushing out the locals. Dee, who looked close to sixty and had been waitressing all her life, was talking about Goody and Les, the cook, having a nasty fight in the kitchen that night. Joanna didn't feel right gossiping about Goody, so she gave Carol her full attention.

They were nice people and she was glad for the company, but somehow she still felt like an outsider. She left after one drink. When she got home, she couldn't sleep and sat on her small deck wrapped in a blanket, watching the waning moon begin to appear in the breaks between the clouds.

The next morning Grace woke up worried about Joanna. She hadn't seen her since their lunch the day before. Several times that afternoon she'd put down the book she was reading and nearly gone upstairs to talk to her. It was obvious she had unresolved issues over her mother. But in the end,

Grace decided it was probably best not to push it. As she fixed her coffee now there was a quick knock at the door. It was a Fed-Ex man, who handed her a slim cardboard package.

Grace couldn't imagine what it could be, and tore the strip across the top and reached inside to pull out an envelope. In it was a round-trip plane ticket to Japan, tucked inside a birthday card. *I know this is early, but we'd love you to spend your birthday here with us. Love, Marie.* Her knees turned to jelly and she sank quickly onto the couch staring at the ticket, dated May 15 out of Charleston airport. Just a few weeks away. Her birthday was May 21. Closing her eyes, she imagined spending this birthday she'd been dreading, surely her last, with Marie and Jerry and her two sweet granddaughters.

She got up and began pacing the room, her mind racing with the possibilities. She felt fine. Perhaps it was possible. In just weeks she could see Marie's face. She hadn't in nearly a year. She'd thought she never would again.

She had to decide carefully. Anticipation filled her with renewed energy, and she stepped out onto the deck. The weather had turned warm again, as it often did in April.

She imagined a golden spring morning burning off the nighttime frost at home in New Jersey. Here, the beach stretched out before her like a dream. In her restlessness, she decided to go for a walk. She hadn't walked alone since Joanna came to stay with her, but she felt strong and confident. Barefoot, she slipped on a loose shift and pulled on a straw hat to block the brightness that caused her to squint. Slowly she descended the deck steps, feeling now as if she could make it to the end of the island.

The sand was soft and her feet sank. Each step was heavy and slow. She headed for the water's edge, where the waves broke and spilled and the sand was hard-packed. There she began to walk more easily. The sea slid toward her, washed over her feet, and she smiled. The water was warm and silky. She turned and headed south, the bright sun behind her. Her goal was the rock jetty about fifteen houses down the beach. Muscles she hadn't used in weeks squeaked back to life as she passed the jetty, deciding to try for the next one. It was too early yet for the summer visitors. Full-time island dwellers were at work or busy with life's chores, so the beach was deserted. Alone at the edge of the ocean, Grace felt exhilarated.

She imagined Marie and her family meeting her at the airport. She could picture them all driving through the crowded streets of Tokyo, her tucked in the backseat between her granddaughters, heading to the apartment she'd never been to. With two whole weeks they might even go to the country, stay in a villa high in the mountains, play rummy and Scrabble. One last chance, she thought. If she was well enough, they'd have no idea when she left that they wouldn't see her again.

She walked on past a few more jetties, but the tide was coming in and soon she was forced to move up to the softer sand as the waves rushed higher onto the beach, soaking her legs and the hem of her shift. Her feet sank with each step and the walking grew tedious. She turned and headed back, looking for her house, but it was gone, evaporated somewhere in the long line of houses that stretched to infinity, it seemed. Slowly her legs worked as the soft sand held her feet and her breath quickened with each step. The morning sun was in front of her again, blinding her as she headed back. Beads of perspiration began trickling down her face. She stopped, searching for her house again, her legs aching with the effort of walking. A sudden panic began to grip her in its clutches. What if she couldn't make it back?

She turned her face, directing her eyes over the water and out of the direct glare of the sun. *Hail Mary, full of grace.* Her lips moved silently. *The Lord is with thee; blessed art thou among women.* The slow rhythm of the words began to quiet her hammering heart. *And blessed is the fruit of thy womb, Jesus.* She passed the first jetty back, saw the next one ahead. *Holy Mary Mother of God.* She'd made a mistake, misjudged her strength. Plodding slowly along, she knew this was most likely the last long walk she'd take. *Pray for us sinners.* And that Japan was a gift she'd never see. *Now and at the hour of our death, amen.*

When Grace made it up the deck steps and entered the house, she saw that she'd been gone only an hour. It seemed as if she'd been walking forever. Her legs trembled and even her hands, she saw as she poured a glass of water, shook. Too weak to stand and drink, she sat at the counter and her eyes rested on the FedEx envelope sitting there. With no warning, a wail of grief escaped her. She would not see Marie again. Or her granddaughters. She dropped her head on the counter and began to sob. It almost seemed possible. The absence of pain, the brief strength of her body, the promise of a summerlike day, had filled her with false hope. But that was gone now. When there was nothing left but tiny whimpers of sorrow, she stumbled into the bedroom to lie down.

While Grace was out walking, Joanna was just waking up. She heard knocking at her door and glanced at the clock, shocked she'd slept until almost ten. She assumed it was Grace and didn't bother grabbing her robe. A moment later she faced Hank Bishop in nothing but a nightgown.

"Hank." She reached for the robe on her bed and threw it on.

"I'm sorry to barge in, Joanna, but Grace wasn't in so I came right up," he said, coming in and closing the door. "I've got some bad news. The Chowder House burned to the ground last night."

"What?" She couldn't believe it; she'd left the place just hours ago.

"Les has been badly burned. He's in intensive care and they're not sure he's going to make it."

She sat on the rocker, stunned, and he began to fix her coffee pot.

"The reason I thought you should know is the police are sure to be here soon. Seems they've already started questioning people."

"About what?"

He hesitated a moment. "Arson," he said. "They've got Goody in for questioning right now. Seems he drove Les to the hospital and has got some burns on his hands. Doesn't look good, if you know what I mean."

"But that doesn't make sense, the place is a gold mine."

She got up and pulled cups out of the cabinet and took the milk out of the refrigerator, moving as if in a daze. Then she remembered the comment at the Mermaid about Goody and Les fighting in the kitchen. "You don't think Goody had anything to do with this, do you, Hank?"

"No, darlin', I truly don't. But Les, well, I'm not so sure."

He was standing at her glass doors and pulled them open, letting in the morning air. They drank coffee and talked for a while about what had happened, and then he was gone. She was out of a job, she realized, and would have to find another restaurant. She liked the informal intimacy of The Chowder House and knew it was going to be tough to replace. Most of the newer places were more upscale and structured.

151

And the country clubs were out — too snooty.

She lay on the futon, staring at the ceiling, feeling as if she were back to square one. But she felt stronger than when she'd first come. She'd find something. She showered and dressed finally. Then she made her bed, had some cereal, and washed the dishes and cups. Longing to hear a familiar voice, she dialed Sarah.

"Good morning, Grayson Gallery, this is Mindy."

"Hi, Mindy, this is Joanna Harrison. I was wondering if I could talk to Sarah if she's not busy."

"Sure, I'll go get her."

She pictured her daughter, lovely, polished, self-assured, so different from her at that age. Or even now.

"Mom, hi." She heard the breathless rush over the line. "You'll never guess. Daddy just walked in five minutes ago."

Her mouth opened but no words came out.

"Dad, it's Mom," she heard Sarah say. "Do you want to talk to her?"

"How are you, Jo?" Paul asked a moment later.

"What on earth are you doing there?"

"I'm visiting my daughter . . ."

"I thought you were looking for another job . . ."

"No, I decided to take Ted's advice and enjoy a few weeks off first," he said dryly. "So, I traded in the BMW for a camper and drove cross-country."

"I don't understand . . . What are you doing?"

"It's simple. I miss my kids. It's been a long time since I've really been with them."

"Your timing is just odd, Paul."

"No time like the present," he joked lightly, and she knew from his tone that Sarah was probably still standing there. "I'll put Sarah back on."

A surge of jealousy rushed through her like an electric current. She'd dreamed of a trip like this for years, the two of them driving cross-country, sightseeing like other people. Spending precious days with their children. Only now Paul alone would be spending those days with them. She was committed to Grace.

"Can you believe it?" Sarah whispered when she came back on the line. "Oh, and you should see his beard. He looks awesome."

Paul's actions lately were completely out of character, she thought as they hung up. Instead of meeting with headhunters and going on job interviews, he was driving a camper across country, growing a beard, and visiting his daughter whom he didn't get along with, who seemed almost delighted with the surprise. He didn't ask when Joanna was coming home this time. Or if she was coming home.

Her family's lives, she realized, were going on without her.

14

Within minutes of hanging up, Paul watched Sarah's initial excitement at his arrival seem to evaporate. In those first moments of surprise, he realized, she'd let her guard down, forgotten the baggage of so many years. Become the loving daughter he'd once known.

When he'd walked in a short while ago and seen her across the gallery talking to someone, unaware of him, he'd thought to himself: she looks so much like Joanna. She'd turned then, looked at him, and it was a moment before he saw recognition and then surprise register on her face.

"Dad?" she'd said. "Oh my God, are you really here?"

In his mind, watching her come to him, fifteen years had vanished and he was walking in the door from a business trip to her squeal, "Daddy's home!" Tears had filled his eyes as Sarah came to him, slow and tentative. He hadn't seen her in nearly a year.

"Dad, you look . . . so different," she'd whispered, fingering his beard and then putting her arms around him.

She was almost as tall as him in her black boots with the high platforms. Her dark curls had been cropped to her ears, where they framed her face in an eye-catching wedge. He'd buried his face in her shoulder, breathing in her citrusy fragrance.

"And you look beautiful," he'd told her. "Just like your mother."

And then a girl had called out that Joanna was on the phone.

Now he watched as confusion clouded her eyes and the low-voiced questions began. "How could V.I.C. just let you go after all these years?" and "Why didn't you tell Mom you were coming to see me? She sounded upset."

Until Martin walked in.

If Paul had been able to hand-pick a mate for his daughter, it wouldn't have been Martin. He was a study in raw umber, Paul thought, and almost laughed out loud, the Crayola color popping into his brain from somewhere back in childhood as he shook the young man's hand. He was handsome, with coffee-colored, almond-shaped eyes, and long brown hair pulled back with a piece of tan leather, his skin the reddish-bronze of one of the islands in the Caribbean. A tiny gold ring pierced one eyebrow and seemed to wink at Paul, capturing the glare of the gallery lights.

"A pleasure to meet you, Mr. Harrison," he said quite formally. He was from New York, had gone to private boarding schools. His manners were impeccable.

Within moments Paul was pulled along on a tour of Martin's work, which would be opening that weekend at the gallery. Exhausted from days of driving, still operating on East Coast time, he floated past sculptures and collages of metal and stone, gorgeous pieces that impressed even his untrained eye.

"Curves," he heard Martin explain. "With the human form, everything is about the speed of curves."

Then the gallery's owner walked in and Martin excused himself. Paul watched as an intense conversation erupted concerning the display for Martin's showing.

"Listen, honey, I can see you're busy here, so I'll get out of the way," he said to his daughter. "How about we meet for dinner after work?"

"Sure," she said slowly, as if unsure. Then, "Wait."

She left and then came back and handed him keys and a little map she'd drawn.

"Why don't you go settle in at my apartment, take a nap and relax. I'll try to get home early. Then we can decide on dinner."

As he pulled open the gallery door to leave, he could hear the murmur of her voice and then Martin's, louder and more distinct.

"He doesn't seem anything like you described him."

Sarah lived in the historic district of Denver. Tiny white lights twinkled in the trees lining the streets as Paul walked. A few patrons took advantage of the mild spring day, sipping hot drinks at sidewalk cafes, steam rising in the cooler air. If not for the antiques shop windows filled with Western memorabilia, Paul thought he could have been in any city. Office buildings and high-rises encircled the old homes and stores, blocking out the white-peaked Rockies in the distance.

The apartment, just four rooms on the second floor of a brownstone, was spare and sleek, like his daughter. High ceilings, curved arches, wood floors polished to a gleam, and little furniture, testament more to her budget than her taste, he thought with a smile. A Van Gogh print above a decorative fireplace. Sunflowers, always her favorite, he remembered. A hint of the little girl lingered, he realized, in the sophisticated setting. Next to the bedroom, with a double bed that Paul didn't want to dwell on, there was a small study with a twin bed pushed against the wall, pillows arranged artfully to look like a couch. He dropped his bag in there and then went to shower.

In the bathroom he found an old claw-foot tub and decided to indulge, turned on the taps. When he stepped in about ten minutes later and slowly sank into the hot water, laid his head back on the sloped surface, he let out a moan of pleasure. He couldn't remember the last time he'd taken a bath. He and Joanna never really used the Jacuzzi tubs in their master baths. Over-sized, they took forever to fill and then cooled off quickly. Here in the old claw-foot he fit perfectly, his body cradled and warm.

His original intent yesterday, as he drove west through Nebraska, had been to go to Tim in Montana. Afterward, he'd planned to head south to Colorado and see Sarah. But as he approached Big Springs on the western edge of Nebraska, something pulled him south and he took the exit for Route 76 that would take him to Denver. He'd arrived late, and had taken a cheap motel on the outskirts of the city, needing a break from the van. This morning, he stood across the street from the gallery, unsure how his daughter would react at seeing him. He turned the hot water on again and closed his eyes, glad he had come.

He slept afterward on the twin bed and woke to early afternoon sunlight streaming through the front windows. He dressed and went out to get a sandwich. Paul found himself surrounded by tables of laughing, relaxed people, and wondered why he couldn't be like them and enjoy this time off. The guilt of too many days out of work surged through him now like a flood. Too many years worrying ahead about the next sale, paying the bills, living with the weight of family and responsibilities forever eating into his free moments. *The more you make, the more you spend,* he could hear his father say. He'd known for a long time his father was right. They could have lived with less. Smaller houses, simpler cars. Local colleges. But it was easy to indulge in the luxuries that lay before you like a hard-earned reward in the face of sacrifice. The big house, the prestigious car, private schools.

Why shouldn't you feel rewarded for all you give up? he thought.

His father had never gone for the extras, had clung to his simple existence until the end. He died in the garage of a heart attack after washing his car. Sitting on the concrete floor, slumped against the wall, his teeth, most likely taken out at the first pain, resting in his hand. When he got there, Paul had pounded the car with his fists, tears streaming down his face, whispering overand over, "Why couldn't you just go to the damn car wash like everyone else?" Paul had always thought that someday he and his father would finally open up to each other. That someday was gone, he'd realized, as he'd beat the shiny white Ford Galaxy with frustration. Now he hoped it wasn't too late for him with his own kids.

He left half the sandwich uneaten, got up, and walked through the neighborhood, restless. He even found himself wandering into several shops, searching aimlessly, for what he didn't know. Then in a gourmet deli he bought some things for dinner and headed back to the apartment, his arms full of bags, glad to have something to do.

Grace opened her eyes, stared at the ceiling, and didn't want to move. She was so tired. *Why don't I just die now?* she thought. And then she heard loud knocking and realized someone was at the door, and that's what had woken her. Slowly she got up, then trudged to the door as if she was dragging a weight behind her.

"Grace, are you all right?" she heard Joanna calling. "Grace, answer the door."

She opened the door and saw the relief on Joanna's face. Joanna came inside and as they walked into the kitchen, Grace noticed she was carrying a large present, with pretty paper and a fancy pink bow.

"Are you feeling okay, Grace? You don't look well. Should I call the doctor?"

Grace waved her hand in dismissal. "No, I just walked too far this morning. A stupid thing, really," she said. "Just an old woman feeling a bit young for a few moments."

Joanna looked at her with concern and then, as if remembering, held out the box.

"What's this?"

"I wanted to do something to make up for yesterday," Joanna said, her face turning pink. "I think I ruined your lunch out."

"Joanna, there's no apology necessary," she told her. "We're getting to know each other well enough to realize there'll be times we each . . . well, give in to our emotions. Don't you agree?"

"Lately I just seem to be blurting things out, without even thinking."

"Maybe you've held things in too long," Grace suggested. "Look, I know there have been moments I've tested your patience. Let's just assume it'll all even out in the wash."

But it wouldn't, Grace knew. One day she would be pushing Joanna's patience to the limit. And she hadn't been fair. She really must tell her soon. Should have told her from the beginning, but she could not bring herself to utter the words. *I'm dying.* She commanded them to come now, but her lips didn't move.

Joanna held out the pretty box eagerly. "Open it, please."

Grace pulled off the bow, tore the paper, and slipped the top off, certain to find a sweater or nightgown. Watercolors, brushes, charcoals, and sketching paper filled the box. The odor of the paints, brief and bitter, stung her nose with a smell that took her back almost fifty years.

"What on earth . . ." She looked up at Joanna, who was smiling, pleased with her surprise.

"You can't say you don't have the time now, Grace."

The irony of her words filled Grace with

fresh grief.

In the middle of the night, Grace sat in the dark in front of the glass doors overlooking the ocean, sipping tea. There was no moon, and the sky was now a soft black canvas, dotted by thousands of stars. It was a rare night anymore that she slept through until first light. Rather than let thoughts and fears that kept her sleepless swallow her like a slow quicksand, she would get up. A book, a cup of tea, thoughts of something else other than the coming pain, the letting go of her life, were her remedy.

It was Joanna's gift that took up most of her thoughts now. Just when she had the free time to paint again, her time was running out, each day a tiny piece of her eaten away, until one day soon she would disappear. She looked at the stars, knowing some had already ceased to exist. Yet the remembrance of them lived on, if only for a while, in the light that flickered above in the night. What was she leaving behind? Her children, her grandchildren. Her blood beating in them as surely as that flickering starlight.

She grew cold and pulled a blanket off the couch, wrapping it tightly around her. The chill of these darkest hours had its hold on her, and soon she began to shiver. Then she switched on the lights she'd extinguished earlier so as not to interfere with the night sky, and turned on the heat. She wasn't at all tired, and wondered if she was becoming like an infant that has its days and nights confused. She winced at the analogy, knowing that later, as the disease progressed, she would revert back to the complete helplessness at which she began her life on this earth. But she had time yet. She was lucky, really. With pancreatic cancer, some lived a nearly normal life until the very end.

She went over to the table, sat, and opened the white box that still lay there. The paints, the brushes, the blank sheets of paper lay before her like a challenge. How easy it would be to put the top back on the box, place it in a closet, and close the door. She could die without ever doing this, she told herself. At this stage of life, what would be the point?

There were a few times over the years when she had toyed with the idea of painting again. Each time it was so easy to put off, as she'd told Joanna at lunch, blaming the busyness of the moment. As she removed the lid from a tin of paint now and pulled it to her face, she inhaled. She knew that it was not really a lack of time that kept her away. It was fear.

A tear slid down her chin, splashed into the well of green paint. She dipped her finger, swirled the wetness until the color bloomed brightly. She wiped her finger across the inside of the box, a streak of green that ran vivid and then dulled, like a firework across the night sky, as the color faded from lack of moisture. Why was it scarier to try again after all these years, than to put it away? Putting it away should have been more frightening, the final letting go of one's dreams. But she knew, had known all along, and fooled no one but herself. It was fear of failure. And of erasing a part of her identity that had traveled along the years with her, unfulfilled as it was. She gave up her passion, her art, for her family.

She got up, filled the teakettle, and turned it on. She stood in front of the glass doors, and across the black expanse of ocean, she saw the nearly imperceptible brightening of the horizon. Morning was not far off. In Japan it was a different day entirely, and she wondered what Marie would do with hers once the girls left for school. How lovely it would have been to spend the day with her, to see her smile. In New Jersey, Frankie would be busy with his son's baseball games by now, squeezing a personal life into the too few hours left each day from his accounting business. Sean could be anywhere. The last they'd spoken, he'd taken the New York–to–Canada route and might be spending his layovers cruising the museums in the city, or perhaps he'd bumped up to a West Coast run by now.

The shrill whistle of the kettle broke her thoughts. She noticed a faint band of pink light now over the ocean, slowly pushing away the darkness, as she turned to the kitchen. She put the tea things away, suddenly too tired. Then she lay down on the couch and pulled the blanket on top of her. As she reached to turn off the lamp, she noticed in its halo of light the dried smudge of green paint on her finger, bright as a beacon, before the room went dark. Closing her eyes, she imagined getting up at daybreak, sketching the rose-colored dawn over the ocean from her deck. Her throat tightened at the momentary flutter of joy that ran through her.

Who says my last days have to be a marking of time? she told herself.

It was late when Sarah finally came home from work that night.

"Mmm. What's that smell?" Paul heard as

the door closed.

Then Sarah was in the kitchen, nearly taking his breath away, she was so lovely.

"You're cooking?" she asked with incredulity.

"Let's just say I'm putting things together, helping them along," he laughed, the counter full of bowls and pots as he read the directions on packaged pesto sauce and turned on a pot of water to boil tortellini. "One thing I will take credit for. I make some mean garlic bread, broiled not baked, with a drizzle of parmesan."

"You're joking!"

"No, no, I actually cooked a bit after my mother died," he said, slicing the long loaf of Italian bread. "Had to. My father could barely make toast without burning it."

"You've never really talked about that," Sarah said, her tone now serious.

He looked at her across the kitchen. "Sometimes it's just easier not to."

"Dad, I'm really sorry about your job," she said, putting her purse and bag down.

"I know. Something will come along," he said and quickly changed the subject. "Is Martin coming?"

"Uhm, probably later. He's not happy with the display for this weekend so he's still there rearranging things," she said, taking a bite of a radish.

They ate dinner by candlelight on a small table in the corner of the living room that served as a dining area. Light jazz played softly as they talked, catching up on the months that had passed, and Sarah told him about life in Denver, how she'd met Martin last year at an art museum and that her dream was to one day have a gallery of her own.

Martin showed up after eight, just as Sarah was pouring coffee, not as polished as when Paul had met him that morning.

"I've been up and down that scaffolding all day," he said, sitting at the table. "I don't know, Sarah, no matter how I adjust things, it just doesn't look right to me."

"Umm, I know. It really sounded like a great idea, so sleek and modern. But I think all those lines and angles from the scaffolding are too distracting," Sarah said. "They pull the focus away from the pieces themselves."

She explained to Paul then how they'd been trying for weeks to find an effective way to display Martin's work, how the idea of using scaffolding to showcase the pieces had seemed so brilliant. But it wasn't working, and now they were out of time.

"Grayson thinks it's fine," Martin said.

"Of course he does," Sarah said dryly. "We're out of time."

"Why don't you use wood?" Paul asked.

They both looked at him blankly.

"Well, you're working in natural materials and wood is a natural material. You could use it as a backdrop to frame your work," he said. "Use different shapes and stains, depending on your piece."

Martin's raised eyebrows nearly touched his hairline.

"It's just a suggestion," Paul said, embarrassed by his sudden inspiration and Martin's obvious dismissal.

"No, no, go on. You just surprised me."

Paul's thoughts took off. He could envision a simple board, perhaps stained mahogany, sitting behind the silver dancer to highlight its color and curves. And then he nearly laughed as he caught himself using Martin's lingo. Or a whitewashed, empty frame of wood, surrounding the granite piece, lending focus to it.

"I'm intrigued," Martin said, a smile growing. "But we've only got three days and we've exhausted the gallery's budget for my show."

"I could do it," Paul said.

This time Sarah's jaw dropped.

"Daddy, how could you possibly?"

"My father worked with wood all his life," he said. "I know a few things about woodworking."

Martin left at eleven. Sarah grew quiet, retreating into herself again, Paul thought, as they cleaned up. When it was time to say good night, he walked across the kitchen and kissed her on the cheek.

"I like Martin," he said, and he could see her surprise. "I didn't expect to. I don't know what kind of future he can give you and I'm not sure he's husband material, but he's a nice guy."

"Dad, I don't think I know you at all anymore," Sarah said.

15

Joanna spent the weekend scanning the local papers for jobs of any kind. On Monday morning, in a skirt and heels, she drove over to an upscale strip mall out on Route 17 where Langston Realty was located. They weren't the biggest office in the area, but they were locally owned and, she hoped, willing to train.

She was quite pleased with herself when she convinced Mr. Hubbard, the broker, that her corporate lifestyle would give her a definite advantage as a realtor. Then, when he handed her pamphlets and schedules for real estate courses in the area, her momentary joy was deflated.

"Eighty hours? I didn't realize it took so long to get licensed."

"Well, you can get licensed in as little as three weeks if you go full-time," he offered, smiling.

She couldn't. She had her commitment to

Grace. But she thought of Paul with no job, bills piling up, and the money she'd brought dwindling away.

"Well, Mrs. Harrison, you can't sell real estate unless you're licensed," he said, and then paused a moment as something occurred to him. "Perhaps, though, there might be a way to make a little money while going to school part-time."

He flipped open a book on his desk then. "One of our top agents, Shelby Reynolds, is busier than she can possibly handle right now. I've often told her she should get an assistant. Someone to help with signs and lockboxes, open houses, photos and such. But so far she hasn't gotten around to it. If she's agreeable, it won't be a lot of money, but it would be good on-the-job experience. By the time you get your license you'll already be trained to sell."

It sounded plausible. In fact, it seemed like a good way to get her feet wet. Mr. Hubbard called Shelby Reynolds on her cell phone and arranged for Joanna to meet her in a little while at a new development she was handling.

The long drive into Rice Fields Plantation reminded Joanna of Tara in *Gone With the Wind.* Huge old live oaks draped with Spanish moss stretched like a canopy to the original plantation-style mansion that was apparently being converted into a country club. From there future streets, just dirt roads now, curved to the left and right, and she followed the one that pointed to the open house, her hopes fueled by the historic beauty and the gorgeous sunny day. She passed staked lots, marked with the names of future homeowners, then passed an area of open marshy fields where slaves once toiled in the heat and battled malaria-infested mosquitoes to harvest rice. In one of Grace's books about the area, she'd read that the rich plantation families spent their summers on Pawleys and other nearby islands, where ocean breezes kept the mosquitoes and disease at bay.

The model, a Charleston-style colonial with a side porch and tall windows, was unlocked, so she went in. Sunlight streamed in, flashing off strategically placed mirrors and polished tabletops. Joanna paused a moment.

"Hello?" she called.

There was no other car in the driveway and Shelby Reynolds was obviously late.

The beautifully furnished rooms held an eerie quiet. She walked through to the back of the house, stood in the breakfast nook, and watched the Waccamaw River winding through tall grass in the distance, past the old rice fields it once fed. And it was as if she was reliving every time she'd done this: trying to picture herself in this particular house, that neighborhood. Pulled along by one realtor after another as she slowly let go of another home, another town. Another life.

And then Shelby Reynolds rushed in with a swish of silk. She floated through the kitchen on a cloud of sweet perfume.

"Welcome to Rice Fields. I'm runnin' just a little late and I do apologize," she gushed in the deepest accent Joanna had heard so far. A stack of brochures dangled precariously from her outstretched arms. "I've just been so busy. Things are booming these days, you'll find our prices are incredible for what we're offerin'."

She realized then that Shelby must have seen the Jersey plates and thought she was a buyer. She said nothing to clear up the confusion.

A half hour later Joanna sped up Route 17, certain that no one left the model without putting a binder down. She'd left with just a brochure, and the same depressed mood that each relocation had once dumped on her. By the time she crossed the small causeway over the salt marsh, the island stretched before her like a living thing in the spring sunshine, simple, unpretentious, breathing new life into her with every salt breath.

Moments later, she was pulling into the driveway beside Grace's beach house, the weathered gray clapboard and sparse tufts of grass suddenly looking shabby, but welcome. When she was halfway out the car door, she heard Grace's voice and looked up to see her at the open door.

"Your husband's on the phone," Grace called down. "I think he may be having some sort of trouble."

Her first thought was the kids. Something terrible had happened. She flew up the steps, her heart pounding, and ran to the phone.

"Paul? What's wrong?"

"Nothing's wrong really, I just need your help," he said. "I'm on the road somewhere in northern Colorado and my van is giving me trouble. I tried calling Timmy, but it seems they've cut my calling card off already, so I tried yours but it's not working either. And there's no cell service here."

A sudden flood of relief was quickly replaced by anger at him for frightening her. She sank down on one of the counter stools, trying to catch her breath.

"I haven't used my calling card since I moved in with Grace," she said, watching Grace go into her room to allow her some privacy. "Isn't that a new van you bought?"

"Did you pay the bill for the calling card?"

"Of course I did. I paid up every bill before I left. I'm certain that was in the stack." Joanna remembered that morning clearly, sitting at her desk as the sun was coming up, trying to put her affairs in order. "Anyway, can't you just get one of those prepaid phone cards from a Seven-Eleven or something?"

"Joanna, I don't think you realize where I am," he said, and she could hear the sarcasm. "There is no Seven-Eleven here."

"Well it's not my fault you decided to buy some luxury van and take off cross-country," she shot back with equal sarcasm.

She could hear his annoyed sigh.

She didn't want to fight. And she was relieved there was nothing wrong with the kids. "What is it you'd like me to do, Paul?"

"First, I'd like you to call Tim for me. You'll get his machine, but just let him know I'll be there in a day or two. Then I think you'd better look through the checkbook and figure out if everything is paid up. I'd hate to get home to find the water turned off and the grass a foot high."

"Haven't you paid any bills since I left?"

"There's a pile of mail sitting on your desk. I saw the mortgage and car payment and took care of those, but I haven't gotten through the rest of it yet. God, there must be a hundred catalogues and twice as many offers for platinum credit cards."

"Are you joking?" She couldn't believe this. He was like a child. "Some of those are probably the credit card bills. Do you think those bills get paid by themselves?"

"No, but I was always busting my ass making the money to pay for everything so I didn't have time to notice. I thought that was your job."

"Not anymore." She slammed down the phone.

Joanna's hand was still on the receiver when she realized she hadn't gotten his number. She sat on the stool, staring across the room to the ocean outside, deepening to a cold, steel gray as the sky clouded over. The fear and then anger that had shaken her insides just a moment ago were gone, burned up in the orgasmic release of silencing him. She felt calm and spent. Her breathing was even normal. Slowly, a tiny smile curled one corner of her mouth as she watched the blue gaps of sky close over while the heavy gray clouds connected like the pieces of one of Grace's jigsaw puzzles. A moment later the phone rang.

"Make sure you pay Grace for these collect calls," her husband ordered. "Here's the number before you hang up again."

Calmly she jotted down the number and hung up. And then she noticed the paint supplies she'd given Grace, all laid out but unopened on the counter.

It seemed as soon as the road began to climb and Paul entered Wyoming, the world became a different place. Towns became fewer and the land opened up on all sides. The trembling anger that had seized him when he called Joanna an hour ago began to quiet, finally. The anger was with himself mostly, for losing his temper. As soon as he'd heard that cold tone of hers, it was as if they'd fallen into the same old patterns. She'd throw up the wall of resentment and he'd try to tear it down in frustration.

And yet he'd done so well with Sarah. The gallery opening of Martin's work had been a success, and Sarah was glowing that morning when Paul left Denver, feeling satisfied. Each day she had warmed up to him a little more. When they said goodbye, her reticence was gone and she began telling him all about their plans for Paris. They would be leaving at the end of the summer.

At the opening Martin had cornered him and thanked him again for his help.

"I've gathered you don't approve of Sarah and me moving to Paris together," he said.

"I know it's considered an archaic attitude, but I believe if you're ready to live with someone, you should be ready to commit for good." His father's voice had come out of his own mouth.

"I am," Martin had assured him. "It's Sarah who says she isn't ready for that step yet."

That had surprised him. Why wouldn't she feel ready if she loved Martin? He'd realized in that moment he still had a long way to go in understanding his daughter.

As he approached Laramie now, Paul wondered if any of that had to do with him and Joanna and the struggles of their own marriage. Who knew? As he drove, he found his nerves settling, soothed by the open land and vast sky. Soon after Laramie, the high desert plains stretched to the horizon wherever he looked, rolling like a dirty green carpet to the foothills. Sagebrush dotted the plains and prairie dog and antelope were the only signs of life. Occasionally a dirt drive broke the curving thread of road that took him northwest, toward Montana. What kind of people, he wondered, chose to live here?

After a while, he saw swinging metal gates on the side of the road that were used to close the road when the snows came. When he realized he'd seen no signs of a human, not a car or a house, in nearly an hour, he pulled over and got out of the car to stretch his map out on the hood. Medicine Bow was another thirty miles. He'd pick up some things there; get more gas, even though he had nearly half a tank. He looked all around him, nothing and no one in sight. The wind blew steady, its rippling rush of air in his ears the only sound. He hadn't used his voice since he'd stopped to put oil in the van hours ago and he'd chosen to leave the radio off. The late morning sun was bright, warming the plains and the road so that heat shimmers danced ahead just above the blacktop. He stood there a long time in the absence of sound and people, realizing that in the unceasing noise of his everyday existence, it was difficult to think. It was so peaceful that he got up on the car, lay across the hood, and watched clouds skitter across the cobalt sky, reminded of summer afternoons at the beach, gifted with the long, carefree hours of youth that were spent lost in simple thought. In the endless quiet that now surrounded him, he experienced a pure serenity.

He thought of the two days he'd spent in the gallery's basement, shaving planks of wood, his hand gently stroking the boards' edges to gauge his finish. Mitering corners precisely so that the angled ends of wood came together, met perfectly, and formed a frame. The clean, sharp scent of lingering sap and then the pungent odor of stain as he brushed it on. There were moments he was back in the garage with his father, listening to his curt directions in between whining blasts of the electric saw. While his hands moved, his mind settled into a comfortable rhythm of thoughts, and a peacefulness he hadn't known in years descended on him. He wondered now, sitting up, looking out over the plains, the sagebrush rippling with the wind, if that was what his father found in woodworking, a simple release from life's pressures and tensions. He slid off the hood and stood next to the car, no other life in sight, and felt alone in the world. Not the lonely tugging that had pulled him to connect with his family, but the primal connection of man with his universe. And he understood, finally, the simple pleasure and satisfaction of using one's own hands to provide. He realized how difficult it was to be a man today, so far removed from the physical responsibilities once necessary for survival. Even in his father's day, just a generation ago, expectations had been much clearer.

He got back into the car and drove, his windows down, the rush of the wind filling the car. A half hour later he pulled into Medicine Bow, population sixty-four. A rundown gas station and grocery store were the heart of the town that consisted of just a few blocks of small old houses and trailers. He thought of all the places he'd lived in the past twenty-five years and wondered at what point in life some people decide this is the best they can do and settle.

Continuing north toward Casper, midway up Wyoming, surrounded by desolate prairie, Paul let his thoughts drift back again on the last few days. Sarah had changed so much. Gone were the frantic emotions of her teen years and the know-it-all attitude of young adulthood. Caught up in his job as he'd been during those years, he never gave more than a few minutes a day, if he was around. His daughter had grown up without him, he now realized, become a woman while he was away on trips, and those moments in Denver just weren't enough to catch up. After their few days together, he felt he had a foothold on a new relationship, a possibility of continued closeness. But he would have to keep at it, he saw now. Without attention, people grew away from you, like a plant seeking a new sun. Like his wife.

He drove on, winding through the sagebrush-covered plains, the sky blue and wide, the earth a physical presence in the absence of people, buildings, cars. He saw a historical marker and pulled onto the side of the road. HERE CROSSED THE OREGON TRAIL. Outside the car he wandered, searching for signs of the wagon train. And then he saw it, alongside the road, the precursor for the blacktop that now stretched before him into the horizon. Two long ruts worn into the earth, winding through the sagebrush and into the distance.

The wind blew like a warm breath across the plains, the movement of air the only sound that broke the quiet. His eyes followed the wagon-wheel ruts that stretched in front of him, gouged in the thick limestone earth, and he tried to imagine what it must have been like. He remembered the snow gates to close the roads and imagined the wind, stronger, colder, as it had been just a month or so ago, roaring across the plain like a giant monster. How did these people survive? What caused them to endure such hardship, to place themselves, their wives and children, in such peril? Man, he thought, always driven to search for a better life. Was he any different, really? He probably would have been on that trail, carving his groove into the earth like those before him and those after him, taking his family along for the ride. With no guarantees of the life that lay at the other end like a long-awaited prize. Or that you'd even make it. It's what he'd done, he realized now. Taken them with him on his corporate journey, looking for that better life. Certain the risks along the way were worth it.

Now, alone in Wyoming's quiet desolation, he could see that he'd lost them somewhere on that trail. And the only thing he was certain of was that he wanted them back. His family.

That evening Joanna went to Hank's for the first meeting of the turtle group. It was a nasty night for the end of April, cold and windy with bouts of hard rain, so she drove over. When she pulled into his driveway and saw all the cars, she was tempted to back out and leave. She was never good in crowds, especially when she didn't really know anyone. All the years she'd gone to corporate functions and dinners with Paul, she never strayed far from his side, adding her cursory comments here or there. Ted's wife, Jean, was the only one she really felt comfortable with, but they'd divorced long ago.

A petite blonde greeted her at the door, very pretty in a classic Southern way, perfectly outfitted in a black turtleneck dress with pearl earrings, her hair sleek and bobbed. She looked like she'd spent her life at the beach, her skin tanned and dewy, her tiny feet perched in wedged sandals.

"Well, you must be the mystery woman from up north," she said in greeting to Joanna.

Heads turned and she wished she'd followed her instincts outside and gone home. Apparently, she was the only non-local there. Smiling, she stretched out her hand, wondering for the hundredth time why Southern women always seemed so self-assured, as if they were privy to some secret she would never in her lifetime know.

"I'm Joanna Harrison."

"Lovely to meet you." Her voice was light and hushed, her Southern accent like music. "I'm Rhetta Stretton, Hank's sister-in-law."

"Oh, I didn't know Hank had a brother."

"No, honey. I'm Hank's wife's sister," she

said, closing the door. Then she flashed a quick smile. "Or ex-wife I should say."

She remembered the photo of the pretty blond woman and the little girl who died. Had she and Hank divorced before the accident?

"Joanna!"

She turned, grateful to find Hank beside her.

"Before we start the meeting, I'd like to introduce you to everyone."

Everyone knew everyone else, it seemed, and had been doing the turtle watch for years. They were nice people and tried to make her feel welcome, but it was a tight group. Once again, she was the new person in the neighborhood, as she had been so many times before.

First Hank assigned a stretch of beach for each person to begin combing the next week. They were to get out early in the morning and look for fresh tracks leading to a possible nest site, where eggs would have been deposited by the mother loggerhead. Once a nesting site was determined, it would be staked off with rope and poles and then watched, especially in the event of high tides and storms, to make sure the water didn't wash away the eggs. They would wait, then, until late August or September, when the all-night vigils would begin, to make sure the hatchlings made it safely into the water.

"I don't have to tell y'all how much harder this is getting, with more building, more people, more lights," Hank went on. "Even lights as far away as Litchfield Beach are enough to confuse the little creatures."

She watched Rhetta looking at Hank as he talked and wondered if something was going on there. There was something possessive about her. Afterward Rhetta played hostess as Hank poured coffee, slicing a homemade blueberry buckle that seemed to be a crowd favorite. Then Joanna saw Hank waving her over.

"Joanna, this is Harley Henson, he was a little late arriving," Hank said, introducing her to an older man beside him as he handed her a cup of coffee. "Harley runs the local paper."

She shook his hand, the skin cool and papery, and looked up at brown eyes that appeared huge behind thick glasses. He smiled.

"Hank tells me you're between jobs," he said in a slow, deep voice that seemed to tremble with age. "I'm lookin' for someone at the paper. Entry level, but could lead to things."

"Oh, I don't know . . ." She hesitated and gave Hank a look.

"It could be fun. Small articles, wedding and funeral announcements, a picture now and then of a store opening."

"I haven't written anything really since college . . ."

"We'd start you off slow," he assured her. "A small piece here and there."

"It's not really what I was looking for."

"Darlin', no offense, but you're way too intelligent for waitressing," Hank said, resting a hand on her shoulder.

"Why don't you just stop in tomorrow and I'll tell you a bit more about it," Harley Henson said, and then moved on to another group of people before she could reply.

"Don't be mad," Hank said. "Somehow, Joanna, I get the feeling you were just hiding from the world at The Chowder House."

She was annoyed, but just smiled, and decided it was a good time to leave. She was the first to go, and as she began saying good-bye, Rhetta sashayed over.

"Listen, honey. I know you may be needin' a good lawyer one of these days. You just let me know. My divorce lawyer is the best around." And then she gave her that warm smile again. "Besides, he's real cute, too."

■ ■ ■ ■

Joanna lay in bed that night, unable to sleep. Silly as it seemed, a lawyer had never entered her mind. When she'd put her plan in motion, she hadn't looked that far ahead. She was just trying to get by, day by day. She'd left her husband, her life, and that had been enough to deal with. She never really thought of divorce.

Now tears filled her eyes as she stared at the ceiling. Divorce would mean the end of her family. Her children would have to choose who to spend holidays with, who to visit on vacations. Slowly, like lost rafts, they would drift away from each other. And nothing would ever be the same again. Like it or not, this was where she was headed.

16

Three quarters of the way through Shoshone National Forest, on a road Charles Kurault had labeled the most beautiful highway in America, Paul's van began acting up again. As he ascended the mountains, driving switchbacks that curved past pine forests and then rose above the tree line, a red light flashed on the dashboard: *check engine.* He pulled over, opened the hood, poured some water into the radiator, and checked the oil once more. He couldn't find anything wrong. A Winnebago crawled by, cresting the summit and then gliding down the other side of the mountain, where he soon followed, the acrid smell of burning brakes filling the air.

By the next mountain, he could see the Bear Tooth Pass in the distance, almost into Montana, a jagged piece of rock wedged between two peaks, like a giant incisor pointing to the sky. He drove down and up again, the highway pulling him along like the tracks of a roller-coaster ride. When he was driving up the final peak, the jagged bear's tooth lost somewhere straight above, the van began to buck like a horse too weary, or too stubborn, to go on. But with nowhere to pull over, he had to keep going, slowing the van down to nearly a crawl. At the top he veered into a pull-off and turned off the engine, smoke or steam seeping from under the hood, evaporating into the high mountain air.

He stood there a long time, letting the van rest, looking out at the earth, stretched below him like a gift from God. Patches of snow dotted the scene and lakes glistened in the afternoon sunshine like the miniature mirrors in Joanna's Christmas village. He waited a half hour and said a prayer of thanks when the engine turned over on the first try. He descended the last mountain in low gear, arriving finally on a flat stretch of highway in a gorge between two mountains where a road sign greeted him: *Welcome to Montana, Speed Limit Prudent and Reasonable.* He'd heard there was no speed limit in Montana, but always assumed it was an exaggeration. Fifteen minutes later, he rolled into Red Lodge, a tiny town with a two-block Main Street that was quaint enough to have been erected as a movie set. He noticed a small garage on a side street and turned in. The engine died as soon as he stopped.

Inside a two-bay cinderblock building, a skinny kid who looked no more than thirteen slid out from under a Bronco, white teeth flashing a smile in his grease-blackened face.

"Hey," he greeted Paul, wiping his hands on his pants. "What can I do for ya?"

"I was hoping you could take a look at my van right away. I'm heading to Bozeman and it started acting up on the Bear Tooth Pass."

The kid shook his head with a laugh, walked out to the van, and lifted the hood. "That's no road for these things," he said, chastising Paul as he fiddled with plugs and wires. "The worst's those damn RVs haulin' ass up those peaks and then burnin' brakes on the way down. Half of 'em don't make it past Yellowstone after that."

"Well, I just bought it and it has a ninety-day warranty, but I'm a little far from home right now," Paul explained.

"I'll say," the kid said, looking at the New Jersey plates. "I'll tell ya what, you're gonna have to leave it here awhile. Harve's out sick. This is his place. I'm just the help, and I'm backed up days here. But I'll try to get under the hood before the afternoon's out."

What could he do? "Anyplace to stay in town?"

"There's a bed-and-breakfast on the outskirts of town, views and all. But without wheels you might want to stay at the Super 8. You can just walk to it on the other side of Main Street."

Paul got out and took his small suitcase, leaving the rest of his things in the van. He began walking back toward Main Street. He hadn't really eaten since breakfast in Cody, Wyoming, and it was nearly dinnertime when he passed the Red Lodge Cafe, a rustic-looking bar where the smell of steaks grilling floated out to greet him. The sun was gone behind one of the high peaks and as early darkness began to settle in the valley, a cold wind blew off the mountain, rushing down Main Street. Fooled by the afternoon mildness, he now regretted leaving his heavy coat in the car. A few doors past the cafe, he turned around, cold, hungry, the thought of a good steak and a beer pulling him like a magnet. The Super 8 wasn't going anywhere.

The sounds of friendly voices, country music, the hiss of steaks on an open grill, and the comforting clink of dishes lifted

Paul's spirits. Silence, he realized, had become a big part of his life. He enjoyed it for the most part, but he saw now that too much of it could be a lonely thing.

Forty minutes later, a charcoal-grilled rib-eye settling in his stomach, his second beer nearly gone, Paul felt warm and content. Around him friendly chatter flew between the patrons and the bartender and waitresses. Red Lodge was the kind of place where everyone seemed to know each other. Harve, owner of the only garage in town, where Paul's van now sat, had been out with pneumonia for a week, he learned, too stubborn to take care of the bronchitis he'd started out with.

"Would you like another beer?"

He looked at his nearly empty glass and thought of the night ahead, alone at the Super 8. "Sure, one more, thanks."

The waitress, a small redhead with silver studs that curled around her ear from lobe to top like a question mark, set the glass before him with a smile.

"Where ya from?" she asked, directing a look at the suitcase sitting beside him.

"Back east," he said. "My van broke down, so I guess I'll be at the Super 8 for tonight."

"Hopefully just one," she laughed and

then seeing his face, added, "Nah, Brent's my boyfriend and he's a whiz with cars. If anyone'll get it fixed, it's him."

Later that night, snow began to fall, fat white flakes that covered the ground in moments. He opened the curtains in his room and got into bed, watching the snow pile up on the small patio outside. How many nights had he spent in motel rooms in strange cities where he didn't know a soul and didn't care? But tonight, somehow, surrounded by friendly people who seemed to know each other's lives intimately, who watched out for each other, he felt like such an outsider. There was a camaraderie that pulled these people together in the middle of nowhere. Something that had been missing from his life for too many years. At that moment he longed to be one of them, included, cared about, even talked about. Part of something, even though few of them would ever have traveled in his circle of life back home.

He turned over on his side and pulled the other pillow to him, folding himself around it the way he wrapped himself around his wife, chest to back, like spoons. He thought about calling her again, but quickly decided against it. When he'd called about his phone problems, he'd expected a kind word, an offer of sympathy. Her anger had stunned him. In his frustration he'd lashed back and he now regretted that, wishing his arms were wrapped around her instead of the pillow.

She was right, though. He should have been more careful about details before leaving. He worried now about what exactly lay in those unopened envelopes on her desk. After a few days with Timmy, he decided, it was time to get home and put his life back in order.

17

Paul stood at the edge of the soccer field and watched his son run by. Back and forth he went in a seemingly thankless effort to retrieve the ball from the other team and dribble it back to his own side, making his way to the goal. And then it was stolen away, again. Paul had never enjoyed watching soccer. He just didn't see the same excitement, the play-by-play action of the football he'd loved.

Timmy reminded him of himself at that age, tall, thin, long in the arms and legs. But he ran with a grace Paul had never felt. As he rushed by, there was a touching beauty to his motion, cheeks flushed, eyes bright, intensity burning within him at that moment. Paul's eyes filled with tears. Again and again Timmy ran by without even noticing him standing alone on the sidelines.

When he'd driven into Bozeman a few hours ago, he got lost looking for Timmy's apartment. His roommate told Paul that Tim was at a game and wouldn't be home for a few hours. So Paul had driven to the campus and walked across the fields behind the buildings, the spring sun warming the valley, all traces of the previous snow melted and gone. Stretching around him on all sides were the mountains, gorgeous white peaks encircling him like a string of jagged pearls.

He watched now as a flag went up, signaling a penalty. His son bent over with his hands on his hips, catching his breath. Paul thought Tim had even glanced over at him, but a moment later the ball was back in play and his son was gone like a comet.

He tried to remember the last time he'd seen Timmy play. In high school, he'd made a few games, but toward Tim's senior year those had dwindled. Paul missed the play-offs and barely made the last period of the state championship, where they lost in a shoot-out. Joanna had been more upset that Paul had missed most of the game than she was about the loss.

The final whistle blew now, and as the players began to leave the field, Paul walked over to Tim. His son looked over and his face lit up with surprise.

"Dad!"

Tim stood there a moment and Paul could see he felt awkward. Tim's hand came forward, as if to shake Paul's, but then Paul stepped closer and pulled his son into a hug. Neither said a word then, and they began walking toward the parking lot.

"I didn't recognize you with the beard," Tim said. His cheeks were flushed and a sheen of sweat covered his face.

"Well, I finally got a lucky break. Brent, the kid who fixed the van, found a used transmission. Anyway, it turned out not so bad after all. Red Lodge is a nice little place."

Tim gave him a look. "I figured you'd be losing your mind after two nights there."

Paul smiled. "How are things going? Are your tests done yet?"

"One more tomorrow. And one more game the day after that."

"And then what?"

"Back to Siberut for a month, to finish the project we began last summer."

"That's the island off of Indonesia? Where you lived with some tribe?"

"The Mentawai, Dad. Not just some tribe."

They reached the parking lot and Paul was glad to shift the conversation. He could hear the defensive edge beginning to creep into

Tim's voice.

"How about some dinner?" he asked his son.

"Sure. Why don't you follow me back and let me shower first."

They went to the Spanish Peaks, a restaurant and microbrewery on the other side of town. It was odd ordering a beer for his son, who'd been twenty-one since February, but Tim seemed to know half the people in there.

"Lots of college kids work here," he explained. "The tips are good. So is the food."

"Well, I'd like to think you do more with your free time than chugging beers," Paul said.

"Come on, Dad, I've been on the dean's list ever since I've been here."

"I was teasing you," Paul said, regretting the comment. "I know you're no slouch."

They sipped their beers in silence and then the waiter took their order.

"So what's with you and Mom?" Tim asked.

Paul wondered if this wasn't tit for tat over his crack about the beer.

"I wish I could tell you," he said. "Your mom seems to be going through a strange time right now. Maybe it's the changes,

201

although I think she's a little young."

Timmy didn't reply.

"Are you upset about it?"

"Sure, I'm upset," his son said. "I talk to her every week. But one minute she seems fine and the next time she sounds like she's trying not to cry."

"She misses you. And Sarah. It was hard for her when you two went so far away."

"I know she's lonely, Dad. But maybe she's missed you, too," Tim went on. "Kids are supposed to leave, but husbands are usually around."

The waiter brought their salads and Paul was grateful for the interruption.

"Look, I know I've spent a lot of time on the road and wrapped up in work," he tried to explain. "But I had a family to support. Still do."

"I get that, Dad, but Mom's really lonely. She has been for a long time."

"What would you have had me do, quit my job, stay home, and hold her hand?"

"Come on, Dad. That's not what I meant and you know it."

The waiter was back again, and they hadn't yet touched their salads. He pushed those plates to the side and set their entrees down. Again, Paul was glad for the break in tension. This wasn't how he wanted things to go.

"Look, things are different for a man," he said to Timmy when the waiter was gone. "We don't always get to do what we want to do. There were times I would have liked to be home more, maybe moved less. But I did what I thought I had to do. I never shirked my responsibilities, no matter how difficult they were."

"Let's just eat, Dad," Tim said, picking up his fork. "I'm starving."

Afterward, they said good night in the parking lot. Paul was going to the KOA nearby, where he'd reserved a small log cabin. Timmy was driving back to his apartment on the other side of Bozeman.

"I'll be here tomorrow," he said. "I'd like it if we could get together after your final."

"Sure, Dad," Tim said, getting in his car. "How about a hike?"

"Sounds good."

Paul waited while Timmy's car took three tries to start.

"You'd better get that battery checked out," he said as his son began pulling away.

"Yeah, Montana winters are tough on a car," Timmy called out the window and then drove off.

Paul's cabin had a real bed, a desk, an

electric heater, and a porch, and although he still had to use the communal bathroom, he preferred it over the motel in Red Lodge. He enjoyed walking the wooded paths, and the waves and smiles from other campers.

By midnight, he was still awake, staring at the black ceiling. He remembered when he was Timmy's age thinking that his father was an unfeeling hardass, that all he thought about was work and responsibility, although his opinion had softened over time. Thinking about their conversation over dinner, he got the feeling Timmy thought of him that same way. Sure he was the breadwinner, but somehow that wasn't enough anymore.

The wind howled from the north as Grace sat on the beach in front of her house, bits of sand flying in her face and down the neck of her sweater. The crease of her book filled with gritty particles that she constantly brushed away. The ocean rolled at her from all directions, white and frothy, a churning brew that foretold a storm somewhere. But the storm, she realized, was inside of her. She was frustrated. And she longed to go home.

Grace missed the familiar things of her everyday life; her own stores, her church, her friends and neighbors. Today she felt she couldn't go on with the charade. It began when she hung up with Marie that morning, thanking her for the gift and explaining that she just wasn't ready for such a trip. She wanted to hurl her lies through her beautiful windows. She was not ready to let go of her children and grand-children. Above all, she was not ready to die.

Rain began pelting her, large, cold drops, soaking her sweater before she could stand. She plodded toward the house in the down-pour. She couldn't bear being alone there today, but now had no choice. By the time she was inside, her dress was soaked. She took off all her clothes and pulled on a warm terry robe. Then she put the kettle on for tea. There on the counter, the painting things Joanna had given her stared her down like a challenge. She'd tried to paint that morning. Standing before the glass doors, she'd watched sea and sky come alive with the changing weather. It was all there, colors shifting, darkening clouds, the churning sea, everything an artist could ask for. But it was all elusive to her. She simply didn't know where to start.

That morning, she'd gone so far as to wet down a sheet of paper. Anxiously she smeared watercolors across the sheet, only to watch them run in rivulets off the edges just seconds later. Again she'd started on a clean sheet, stroking a blue background across the sky, blending red and black in an attempt to create the dimpled mosaic of gray clouds. It had looked like a child's drawing, and she tried to will joy at that little bit of progress, to enthuse herself and keep going. But she'd only felt defeat. It was too late, she'd told herself, packing her things back in the box on the counter.

She poured her tea now and sat again at the counter. She looked at the paints and brushes, knowing in her heart that this, really, was all that was left for her. If not this, what? An endless stream of puzzles and books until the end? In her heart, she wanted more than that. Needed more than that. The challenge of this possibility filled her with a certain hope that had been dead for months. Hope for what, she wasn't sure. But it was the only word she could think of to describe the feeling that perhaps some-where deep inside her, a glimmer of the girl she once was still existed.

Grace picked up a blank sheet of paper then, but instead of prepping it for watercol-ors, she pulled a charcoal pencil out of the box. She began to sketch, long, smooth strokes. Her hand flew, and as daylight faded, the strokes shortened, her hand busy with shading, her mind lost in the vision of her creation. It came unbidden, from some hidden part of her, as involuntary an instinct as breathing. Finally, she put the pencil down, held the paper before her, and laughed aloud. It was Frank as he looked when she'd first met him, thin with a nearly shaved head, his Marine cap at an angle. And then the laugh caught in her throat and a moment later she was sobbing.

How was it all gone so quickly?

Joanna came home late in the afternoon with groceries, books from the library, and a bag of Chinese food. The wind still roared across the beach, and although sunset was hours away, the sky was nearly dark. Grace was glad she was home.

Over supper, Joanna began to tell her about a job she was considering at the local newspaper, writing wedding and birth announcements, obituaries and store openings.

"Except for my journals years ago, I've never done much writing," she told Grace.

"Well, how do you really feel about it? Do you want to try it?"

"Yes, part of me does. It's scary, but also exciting to think about doing something totally different."

"It's natural to feel nervous," Grace said, thinking about her own nervousness at painting. "But imagine how good you'll feel if you try it and find you like it."

"What if I'm not good, though?"

Grace nearly smiled, wondering if God was constructing this dialogue to get through to her after her frustrating day. "Well, you'll never know unless you try."

Joanna nodded. "I guess you're right. It's just that every job I've ever had in recent years was not really a commitment, if you know what I mean. I punched numbers in a computer. There was no 'me' involved."

"Maybe it's time you started making a real commitment to your future."

Joanna got up and began clearing the plates. "I know you're probably right."

This would be the perfect time to tell her, Grace thought. It was the most open Joanna had been. But she hesitated. Joanna hadn't even started the job yet. If Grace pulled the rug out from under her now, she might even run again. She should wait a little longer, maybe a week or two, just long enough for Joanna to settle into the job a bit and feel anchored to something.

Later, after Joanna went upstairs, Grace sat with the pile of books from the library.

Flickers of lightning danced over the black ocean in the distance. She glanced through the titles and stopped at a large hardcover, *Introduction to Watercolors.* How thoughtful of Joanna. The beautiful pictures illustrating colorful techniques immediately absorbed her. Color had always been her love; she would brush it on unhesitatingly, feeling her emotions shine through in the vivid splashes of reds, yellows, greens. The rumble of thunder moved closer and she put the book down, finally, her eyes closing.

The nagging thoughts that had troubled her earlier drifted back. She was never good at lying, and in truth she was uncomfortable with it now. Yet what was the alternative? To begin telling her children that she was dying, and then they would tell the grandchildren? To spark an ember of fear, a counting down of days, that would soon flame into gut-wrenching grief for all of them? She couldn't bear that.

And for once in her life, she was putting herself first.

The drive up to Hyalite Canyon was breathtaking. Within a mile of Timmy's apartment they were riding past horse farms and rustic-looking chalets and cedar homes. The road began to climb and snow dotted some of the higher elevation, covering the sides of the road, the fields, and then the floor of the woods. Soon they were winding beside a tumbling stream, frost-edged from the night's cold, while the surrounding trees and grasses were slowly greening back to life.

They parked beside a reservoir encircled by mountains, reflecting blue sky and puffy white clouds. Timmy led him to a trailhead that would take them up a mountain to a waterfall. As they hiked through open meadow, the midday sun warmed the air and Paul pulled off his sweatshirt. Soon they were in woods, the trail narrowing and beginning to rise sharply. Timmy had been keeping a brisk pace in front of him, and Paul now felt the first beads of sweat begin to roll down his back.

His last thought before sleep finally took him the night before was that he needed to get a job as soon as he returned home. Bills were no doubt piling up and money was disappearing fast. The transmission job was over a thousand dollars. Now as he followed his son up the mountain trail, the wind and the birds, the thunking of their boots on packed snow the only sounds to break the quiet, he felt his tension slide away.

"There's an overlook just up ahead," Tim

called back. "We'll rest there."

It wasn't much more than a rock ledge, but it was sunny, with no snow. They sat, legs dangling, the reservoir a mere puddle below flashing in the sunshine.

"It's beautiful," Paul said.

They hadn't spoken much. Paul had tried several times to initiate a conversation, and then finally given up to the rhythm of walking.

"Yeah, it's one of my favorite places," Tim said, gazing into the distance. "It's a good place to clear your head."

Paul could hear snow melting, dripping all around them and running down the mountain, a peaceful gurgling sound.

"Are you having problems?" he asked. "Anything you want to talk about?"

Tim shook his head. "No, it's nothing like that. Sometimes, I just need to get away from the world for a while. It's hard to explain."

They sat in silence, a light wind rustling the trees around them.

"Did you ever think, Dad, that we're really here by an accident of birth?" Tim said. "The rest is by choice. I mean, we live in this great country, a place people from other countries risk their lives to get into. Yet I see other places, simpler, more primitive places, where I think they've got it all over us."

"Are you talking about Siberut?" Paul asked.

"Well, for one," Tim said, and picked up a twig and began snapping it as he talked. "We think everyone lives the way we do. Or should. But all over the world, people live differently. And sometimes they seem a lot happier."

Paul felt they were on delicate ground and wasn't sure what to say. "I guess it's all a matter of what you're used to," he tried.

"Exactly," Timmy said, approving of his response. "When I stayed with the Mentawai last summer, for the first few days, all I could think was, these people are lazy. They don't do anything. They hung out with their families and their friends; when they needed food, they'd get it. There wasn't a lot of thinking ahead. Nobody worked hard. Or worked much. They got by with just what they needed. But they were so happy." He laughed out loud and turned to Paul, as if he'd just told a good joke. "Do you get it? They had nothing, but every day they woke up with joy at their existence."

Paul didn't know what to say.

"Look, Dad, I know this isn't realistic in our society. I know that, so don't flip out. But we're so far removed from who we are, physically and emotionally. Look around us here," he said, waving an arm at the mountains. "When was the last time you did something like this?"

He shrugged. "I tried to make time for running, or golf —"

"No, Dad, that's different. You ran to stay in shape and you golfed to court clients. Anyway, I know you never really liked golf. I'm talking about taking time during the day to just be, to lose yourself in your thoughts."

"So are you saying that's how you want to live? No responsibility, survive for the moment —"

"No, no, Dad, listen." He shook his head in frustration. "Why do we have to have so much? We're so caught up in *stuff*. The more people have, the more they want . . ."

It was his father he was hearing, his father's words coming out of his son's mouth. *The more you make, the more you spend.* He turned to Tim, who was still speaking.

"I just wanted you to know some of the things I see, Dad, that's all," Tim said, tears in his eyes. "I know you're disappointed in my major and there's not a lot of money in academics, but —"

"Stop. That's not true. I've never been

anything but proud of you. I've tried . . ." He paused, his throat tight with emotion. "I've tried to be a better father than mine was to me, but he *was* a good man. He taught me responsibility —"

"I am responsible, Dad," Tim said, his hand suddenly on Paul's arm, as if to make him understand. "I just want different things than you do."

Without thinking, he reached over and pulled his son into his arms. He held him for a long time with his eyes closed, the warm wind brushing his face.

Paul left Bozeman the next day on an evening flight after his son's last game. He left the van for Timmy, knowing his Toyota wouldn't make it through another Montana winter. He figured he'd already gotten his money's worth with what he'd saved on camping and driving. Tim sat with him in the small airport while he waited to board, telling him more stories about his time in Siberut and how they feared it was a way of life that was going to disappear soon, as the modern world encroached. When the final call to board was announced, they stood and he pulled his son into a hug.

"You're a good kid, Tim. I love you." He couldn't remember the last time he'd uttered those words. Words his father had never spoken to him.

"I love you, too, Dad."

There was no pressure in his ears, no pain after takeoff, and he realized then that his sinuses had been clear for days. He looked at the earth stretched out below, the jagged peaks of the Rockies giving way to the wide checkerboard fields of Midwest farms. Below him, people were living their lives, going about their daily business. Soon he would be landing at Newark Airport, and he'd have to take a limo or taxi back home. He had no choice; there was no one waiting for him.

His life, though, *was* waiting for him. It was time to contact headhunters, get the house back in order, pay the bills. And to bring Joanna home.

18

By the third week of May, Joanna had fallen into a daily routine that gave her, finally, some sense of peace. Three days a week, she went into the newspaper, and there waiting on her desk were stacks of birth and death announcements, weddings, press releases for store openings and local business affairs. They were formula pieces, and soon she learned how to take the information at hand and convert it into a sensible, succinct piece of writing. She'd even gone out once to take a picture when the regular photographer was busy elsewhere. Nervously, she grouped the mayor and some local businessmen in front of a new strip mall that was opening. Her hands were shaking as she clicked the pictures, and she prayed they wouldn't blur. She'd been given little instruction, just handed the camera, shown where to press, and then used gut instinct to group the men. She was pleased with herself when, looking through the view-finder, she noticed that the store's sign appeared to be growing from the mayor's bald head, and moved the group over a few feet. The picture was only slightly blurred.

Now as Joanna walked the beach on her morning turtle watch, she thought about the things she'd written in the last week. Harley had asked her to proofread a few news pieces and try to get a feel for the format of them: a lead that hooked the reader in, and then all the basic questions answered — who, what, when, where, why, how. She'd never really paid attention before, but news stories, she now saw, did follow a basic formula, and she began reading the papers with a new eye.

Joanna loved the early morning beach walks. The weather since the nasty lightning storm a few weeks ago had turned summery, and she stepped out onto the warming sand each morning with a sense of anticipation. Perhaps today she'd find something, see something, to lead her to a turtle nest. Occasionally she'd meet others at the end of her own stretch of territory, and they would wave or shout a greeting. As she walked that morning, her thoughts turned to Paul, who'd called her when he returned home from his trip.

"The kids are well, I thought you'd want to know that," he'd said, a bit awkwardly at first.

"They look well? And Timmy's taking care of himself?" She worried about him in particular since a nasty bout with mono the previous year.

"Yes, they look great, healthy, happy." She heard him give a little laugh. "They're damn good kids."

She smiled wistfully. "Yes, they are."

And then there'd been a silence. Joanna sensed he wanted to say something.

"Anyway," Paul went on then, "I left Tim the van. Turns out the odometer had been turned back, but it's all fixed up now. His little Toyota was shot."

"That's great," she'd said, surprised and relieved her son would have a bit more metal around him driving through the snowy Montana roads.

"Well, the bills are all paid," Paul said. "Nothing was turned off when I got back."

That was his way of apologizing, she'd realized when they hung up.

Now, scanning the beach for signs of turtle tracks, Joanna pushed thoughts of lawyers and divorce into the background again. She'd spoken to Hank only a few times since that first meeting, and found that her

218

annoyance with him — at nudging her about the newspaper job, at obviously telling Rhetta details of her life — had already evaporated. She was a married woman, after all, here without her husband. Hank may have told Rhetta nothing more than that. And she was beginning to like the job, although there were still moments when she doubted herself.

Up ahead there appeared to be something in the sand, and she picked up her pace. The tide had come in just before dawn, and now wet sand stretched across half the beach, leaving a clear line of sea debris, shells, and strawlike matter where the tide had stopped. Just at that edge, a trail left the wet sand and traveled across the dry toward the dunes. It looked to her as if huge tires had rolled up the beach from the water. With a little intake of breath, she turned to see if there was anyone else around. Could this be the evidence of a mother loggerhead laying her eggs?

She turned and glanced at the ocean. The sea was sliding back into itself, and low tide was not for a while yet. The nest, if there was one, was more than safe. Turning again, she began to run up the beach toward Hank's, just a few jetties away. She was nearly breathless from sprinting when she saw the tattered pineapple flag and veered left, up the path that wound through high dunes and finally up the wooden steps that led to his house. She knocked and then remembered how early it was and began to feel a little uncomfortable. Perhaps he was still sleeping. Or wasn't alone.

He answered the door with a towel tied around his waist, beads of water glistening in the salt-and-pepper hair that matted his wide chest. Her throat went dry.

"Joanna!" he said, obviously surprised.

"Oh, God, Hank, I'm so sorry," she stammered. "I found some tracks, at least I think they might be tracks and I wasn't sure . . ."

"Hold on," he said and turned and walked across the room, calling over his shoulder, "I'll be back in a minute, darlin'."

She waited on the porch, listening to the morning waves lapping quietly as the tide went out, picturing how he'd answered the door. He was lean and strong, and there'd been an instant physical pull when she saw him. She was not prepared for that.

She sat on the steps in a puddle of sunshine that began to peek through the heavy layer of crape myrtles and other shrubs that nearly hid his house from the beach. A tiny lizard that reminded her of a salamander Timmy once had raced by on a low limb, stopped, puffed out its neck like a red ball, and then skittered away. An image of Hank and her, naked, embracing in bed, flashed across her brain like a bottle rocket and was gone. She stood up again, uncomfortable with where her mind was going; and then she heard the door slam and Hank was coming down the steps behind her. She got up and walked ahead of him so he couldn't see embarrassment flushing her cheeks.

She led him to the spot and he stood for a moment, looking down at the tracks. Then he walked around farther up toward the dunes, looking carefully down at the sand. Finally he bent down, spread his hand, and slowly seemed to caress the sand with an intent look on his face. He stood a moment later, shaking his head.

"I think it's a false crawl," he said, walking over to her. "There's no nest."

"What do you mean?" She was terribly disappointed.

"If the mother turtle is disturbed, or can't find a good nest site, she'll simply go back into the ocean," he explained.

"But this looks like a good spot, nice dunes, not a lot of houses."

"Who knows? Maybe sometimes it just doesn't feel right to her," he said, and then smiled. "We've all got our instincts."

"Well, won't she come back tonight? If she's ready?"

"Sure, but you don't know where exactly on this beach she'll come back up, or when." He lifted her chin and smiled again. "Hey, don't be so disappointed. You did fine, Joanna."

"The tracks look exactly as you described, like those from a tractor tire."

"When she lays her clutch, you'll see those tracks go up much closer to the edge of the beach," he said, pointing farther up toward the dunes. "There the mother will use her rear flippers and dig an egg chamber cavity, oh about eight inches wide and about eighteen to twenty inches deep. After she digs, she'll rest awhile, and then she'll fill the hole with a hundred or more eggs, about the size of golf balls. When she's finished, she'll gently cover the eggs and spread sand all over the area with her front flippers to obscure the exact location of the chamber. When she's all done, she'll crawl back into the water."

"That's why you seemed to be stroking the sand?"

"Yes. Sometimes, if you've done this enough, you can feel the little differences in sand that's been disturbed. Those mammas are darn good at hidin' their babies."

"Yet they don't stay and protect the nest or nurture the babies, like birds or other animals."

"That's true. The female sea turtles never see the nest site again. And it's a good thing, really. People can be cruel and stupid. We've even had them hangin' out on the beach, drinkin', and then trying to get up and ride them," he said. "Shall I walk you back?"

"Sure," she said. "Thanks."

They walked a few minutes in silence. The sun was well above the ocean now, warming the air quickly. She unzipped her sweatshirt and tied it around her waist.

"Listen, I think I owe you a bit of an apology," Hank said, a moment later. "The night of the meetin' I sort of pushed Harley on you."

"No, it's okay," she interrupted. "I was annoyed with you, but as it turns out, Harley's a sweetheart. And I'm starting to like the job."

"Really?" He turned to her, eyebrows raised in mock surprise. "I thought you might."

"What did you tell Rhetta about me?" She plunged ahead, since they were on the subject of that night.

"Uh-oh. Did Miss Sweet and Sour Tongue give you a hard time?"

"Well, she did offer to give me her divorce attorney's number . . ."

"Oh, I am sorry, Jo. When she asked if you were married, I simply said I thought you were in the process of ending it."

"I see."

"Look, Rhetta's a nice lady but she sometimes gets a bit too involved in her friends' affairs."

"She implied you were more than friends," she said, looking at him. "She told me she's your sister-in-law."

He didn't say anything for a moment.

"She was my sister-in-law. Before Lacey and I divorced. We've stayed friends, but I think she gets a bit too protective of me, to tell you the truth."

Sure, she thought, or she wants you, which Joanna thought was more likely.

"I'm sorry, she just confused me. I knew your wife had died . . ."

"Yes, but we were divorced several years at that point," he said, then sighed. "It's a long story, Joanna. One I don't really want to get into right now, if you don't mind."

She put her hand up. "Please, I didn't mean to pry."

"No, darlin', I know you weren't pryin', but I should have explained about Rhetta before."

"Okay, let's just forget it," she suggested. They were nearly at Grace's. "I'd ask you in for coffee, but I have to get ready for work. Harley's expecting me at nine."

"I was wrong, Joanna. To assume things about your marriage. And to discuss them with Rhetta."

"No, it's okay. It's bound to come up, and I can't just keep dancing around it. It's just so hard to deal with." She paused a moment. "It feels like a death."

"I remember well," Hank said softly. "In some ways it's even worse."

She popped in on Grace before leaving for the newspaper, to see if they needed anything she could pick up on the way home. Grace had been quiet lately and she found her staring out the glass doors, the paint supplies scattered across the table. Joanna saw the sketch pad, a vibrant splash of color she couldn't make out. A moment later, Grace quickly turned it over. Grace seemed lonely, and Joanna wondered again why none of her family came for a visit.

Grace turned then, smiled at her, and asked if she'd pick up some flounder. She was going to cook for them that evening. Of course, Joanna said, glad for the offer. It was supposed to be her night to cook.

■ ■ ■ ■

Joanna was always quick on a keyboard, and that afternoon, when Harley saw the pile on her desk melting away, he pulled up a chair and sat down.

"I'd like you to go talk to a Bosnian refugee I've been hearin' about," he drawled in that low, trembly voice she loved. It was the voice of another time and place.

"I don't understand," she said. "Talk to her about what?"

"Well, try to find out what she ran away from, why she chose to come here. How she's gettin' on, things like that," he went on.

"You mean interview her?" she asked. "Harley, I'm not trained for that kind of thing."

"Now, hold on, Joanna," he said, seeing her reluctance. "I've been puttin' this off 'cause the rest of the writers have been busy with other things. And this is just a matter of sittin' down really and lettin' this woman talk."

"But, Harley, proofreading's one thing. I'm not one of your reporters," she protested, wondering what she could possibly say to this woman.

He smiled.

Ten minutes later she was riding down Route 17 with a brand-new legal pad on the seat next to her, a few cursory questions jotted on it. She was annoyed with Harley, but she was always one to cave when it came to confrontation.

Joanna knocked on the door of the motel room. A moment later, it was opened by a woman who she guessed was in her mid-thirties. She was tall and solid looking, wearing cutoff jeans and an old T-shirt. Spikes of blond hair escaped the scarf that was tied around her head.

"Hello," the woman said slowly. "You are from newspaper?"

Joanna nodded and smiled. "Yes, I'm Joanna Harrison. You are Tenevya?"

"Yes. Please to come in," she said, holding the door wide.

The room was sparse and clean, with a bed, dresser, microwave, and an ironing board set up. Beside it sat five laundry baskets, brimming with clothes. She caught Joanna's glance and flushed.

"I do the laundry as side job, besides cleaning here, so sometimes my room get messy."

"Oh no, it's very nice. I didn't realize you

live here, too." Joanna thought she just worked at the motel.

She nodded. "Yes, I live here. For now."

Joanna sat in the only chair and Tenevya sat on the edge of the bed. There was an awkward moment of silence. She took a pen from her purse and picked up the legal pad with her questions. "I'm sorry, I've never actually interviewed anyone before, so please bear with me."

Tenevya laughed, nodding. "Me, too! I never work cleaning before. In my country, I be lawyer."

"A lawyer? Well . . . then why on earth are you cleaning here?"

Tenevya gave her a sad smile. "Not so easy to do, really. You all be free, yes, but the laws . . ." She shook her head. "Everything different."

Her education, she explained slowly, carefully choosing words, meant nothing here. A legal degree in Bosnia was useless in America. Here, she would have to start all over. With nothing. No money. No family. Everyone dead except a sister she was still trying to locate.

"Weren't you afraid?" Joanna asked. "Of leaving your home, your career, everything that was familiar?"

Tenevya stared at the gold carpet for a

long moment. Then she looked at Joanna, nodding her head. "I be scared, of course. To stay would be easy, yes? Even when there is pain, it is . . . how do you say that? Familiar?"

"Yes, familiar is what we know. What we're used to."

"Yes, it be more easy to stay. Familiar not so scary. But . . . I know here," and she put her fist to her heart, "there be nothing more for me there. I must be strong. I must leave, start new life."

"You're very brave," Joanna said.

Tenevya smiled and shrugged. "People be nice here. It so pretty and warm. The ocean so beautiful. A good place to start new, yes?"

"Yes," Joanna said. "It is a good place to start over."

It was nearly quitting time when she returned with fifteen pages of scribbling.

"Here are your notes, Harley. I tried to write as neatly as I could. I probably should have had a tape recorder," she chided him. In truth, it was hard to keep writing when she was so caught up in Tenevya's story.

"Those are your notes, Joanna," he said with a slow smile. "Let's see what you can do with them."

"What? You can't expect me to know how

to take all this and make it into something. I wouldn't know where to start."

"Well," Harley began slowly, "how about with your own feelin's. How'd she make you feel?"

"I don't understand. What's that got to do with *her* story?"

She couldn't do this; it was unfair. Talking to the woman was one thing. Taking two hours' worth of conversation that bounced all over the place and turning it into a coherent article was another. It was worse than writing a college term paper. She had a mass of jumbled information and no clear idea of how to put it into any kind of order.

"I'll tell ya what, Joanna. Why don't you just think about it until you come in again day after tomorrow? That's all, just kind of write down how you felt about this woman and her story."

She had to leave, go to the store, get the flounder home to Grace.

"Fine," she said, not bothering to hide her frustration.

19

It was quiet the following morning, the only sounds the waking birds. In the pale early light, Paul scooped a shovel full of mulch from the brimming wheelbarrow and tossed it in the flower bed, the rich fragrance of cedar mingling with the musky, flat scent of newly turned soil. Again and again he shoveled and pitched the shredded bark, making his way across the flower beds that lined the front of his house, until the wheelbarrow was empty. With the hem of his old T-shirt he wiped the beads of sweat that were beginning to roll down his face, thinking to himself that May had to be the most beautiful month in New Jersey. All around him, the world was bursting with new life.

Mulching was a job done each year by the landscapers, along with aerating and fertilizing the lawn, trimming the hedges, pruning the trees. This year, he was doing it all himself. He'd been working twelve-hour days since he got back from his trip out west, clearing up the bills, organizing the things that were beyond the cleaning lady's domain. He'd even had a moment when he'd thought of canceling her, too, but wondered if that wasn't going too far. Last week he'd cleaned out the basement, organizing boxes that hadn't been opened in too many moves and throwing out a fair amount of useless junk.

Contentment filled him as he pulled at a mound of mulch with his rake. The dark mulch set off the tiny shoots and tender leaves of Joanna's perennials, which were already marking their territory in the earth. As he worked across the bed, he noticed coreopsis and coneflower, veronica and yarrow. Mounds of forget-me-nots, pale blue blossoms on dainty foliage, were peaking right now. Each year Jo swore they were her favorites, snipping clumps for miniature bouquets. The daffodils and tulips had long since faded, withering already around the edges, and as Paul made his way across the bed he stopped intermittently, folding them neatly in half, binding them with a rubber band. They wouldn't look as unsightly as they went through the necessary decay that would send nutrients to the bulbs to ensure next year's flowering. It had been years since he'd done yard work, and it amazed him how much came back to him from his landscaping days in high school.

By late morning, the sun beat on his back like a heat lamp, and he could feel wetness tugging at his old T-shirt as he moved. He was tempted to pull it off and get a little color, but thought better of it as he glanced around at the quiet, well-kept homes that surrounded him. He was beginning to look at his home and his neighborhood differently. Clotheslines were prohibited in the deed restrictions. So were above-ground pools and certain shades of house paint. Everything had to present a picture of prosperity. He thought about the campgrounds where he'd stayed, with tents and pop-up campers, lines strung to hang shabby towels and wet bathing suits, plastic lawn chairs and picnic tables for dining. Where unpretentious people enjoyed their free time and the outdoors. How different it was here.

Halfway across the left flower bed, he'd fashioned a small rock retaining wall yesterday, where they'd been having some drainage problems on this lower side of the house, causing dampness in a corner of the basement. Then he'd filled up the area with topsoil, creating a raised bed. Now as he mulched it, he wondered what he should plant there. If Joanna were here, she'd be full of ideas, planning carefully and sketching it out to make sure no one plant hid another. He thought of calling her now, asking her advice or preference in what to use, perennials or flowering shrubs, or simply an annual bed. But he decided not to. It was time he faced facts. It didn't look as if Joanna was coming back to him.

When he'd called her after returning from Montana, she'd been polite. He thought talking about the kids would bring her around, but she still seemed distant, and the words he'd planned to say, *I love you, I want you to come home,* had stuck in his throat. It was too late.

Shoveling another pile of mulch, he thought about his appointment with the headhunter tomorrow. He had mixed feelings. The guilt he felt every day as he went to the mailbox and brought in a fresh stack of bills told him it was time to get back into the real world. But since he'd begun working around the house, his days busy and productive, another part of him warred to hold on to this hard-won freedom to be his own man. And there was even a piece of him that wondered if there couldn't possibly be a way of doing both, somehow.

He heard the cordless phone ring, where he'd left it sitting beside the wheelbarrow. He pulled off his work gloves, resting the shovel against a tree.

"Hello?"

"Paul, it's Jean."

Jean? Then he recognized the voice, Ted's ex-wife, whom he hadn't spoken to since their divorce four or five years ago. She sounded exhausted or ill. And then it hit him: her voice was full of pain.

His stomach clenched. "What's wrong, Jean?"

"Oh, Paul. It's . . ." She stopped, unable to get the words out, and he knew. "Ted's gone. He's dead."

Paul sank onto the front steps. In some part of his mind, he noted that the brick felt cool and soothing on his heated body.

"He died on that damned boat he always dreamed about. Someone found him drifting near Tortola. They think it was a heart attack. Oh, Paul," she moaned, and he could hear the sobs.

His head dropped and he closed his eyes, picturing Ted alive and smiling on the deck of his boat. Thinking he had all the time in the world now to finally enjoy his dream.

He sat on the deck, drinking a cold beer

although it was just past noon. A trembling, unreal feeling vibrated inside him. The sun was still shining, bright and hot. The birds still flitted and chirped, searching for food, twigs, mates. The world was still turning, although it seemed it should stop. More than sadness, more than grief, shock had shut him down when he'd hung up with Jean. Ted, gone. It couldn't be, he kept thinking. Ted was one of those larger-than-life people you couldn't picture the world going on without.

He picked up the cordless phone.

"Jo, it's me," he said, when she picked up. "I thought you'd want to know, Ted died of a heart attack a day or two ago."

He could hear the sharp intake of breath.

"Oh, Paul. Oh, God . . ."

"Jean called me. They think he had a heart attack on his sailboat. He must have been alone. Another boat saw his drifting and then Maydayed the coast guard, but it was way too late."

"Oh, how sad. He was such a great guy. God, he was the life of every party." He heard her sniffle. "Who didn't love Ted?"

"You know, he took the buyout so well," Paul said. "The sailboat was his dream for years and he said to me, 'Well, Paul, I thought about waiting another five or ten years for this chance and thought, nah, life's short.' " He felt his throat tighten. "What if he hadn't? He'd have died and never have . . ."

He couldn't talk. Silent tears filled his eyes. He wiped at them with the hem of his T-shirt, clamped his mouth, and cleared his throat in an effort to get control of his emotions.

"I guess we have to be thankful he had that little bit of joy," Joanna said softly.

"The funeral is on Friday."

"Oh, Paul, I don't think —"

"No, it's fine, I didn't expect you to."

"It's not that. Please understand," she explained. "Grace has been acting a little odd lately."

He didn't know what to say.

"I'll call Jean. And I'll send a card from all of us," Joanna continued. "Maybe you can get a nice arrangement of flowers? He was a good friend, Paul. I know that, I'm so sorry."

"He was my only friend, really."

Grace had been strangely quiet at dinner the night before. Several times, Joanna caught the old woman watching her, as if about to say something, and then going back to whatever it was she'd been doing.

Now, as she hung up with Paul and glanced across Grace's great room to where she sat out on the deck reading, Joanna wondered if she should try to go to Ted's funeral. He'd been a part of her life for so many years. And Paul seemed devastated.

She went back to cleaning out the refrigerator and made a list of things they needed to stock up on, and was surprised to look up after a while and find Grace sitting at the counter, as if she'd been waiting for Joanna to finish.

"Oh, I didn't hear you come in," she said, closing the refrigerator.

"We need to talk," Grace said, her hands folded in front of her.

Her mind had been drifting between Paul's phone call and the fifteen pages of notes from her interview with the Bosnian woman, sitting on her desk upstairs.

"I'm dying, Joanna."

She looked at Grace. "What?"

"I know I should have told you from the beginning, but I was afraid you wouldn't stay."

"But . . . but you seem fine. How could you . . ."

She stood there stunned, and she began remembering little things. The walk that did Grace in a few weeks ago. Quiet days when she seemed to retreat into herself, pale and distant. The trips to Dr. Jacobs. Obviously not for B-12 shots.

"I have pancreatic cancer," Grace went on without emotion. "I have some time yet, probably until the fall."

Panic ripped through Joanna. "Grace, what are you saying?"

"Just this, Joanna . . ." And then Grace paused.

Joanna saw that she was struggling for control.

"We'll go on as we have been," Grace continued, "you helping me, shopping, cleaning. But soon, I'll be doing less. And then less. I'll get a home health aide at that point. It's not like some cancers. We could go on quite normally until the very end. And then, well . . . it won't be long really. Six months at the most."

"But your family . . . ," she began and then realized. "They don't know, do they?"

Grace didn't say anything.

"Oh, Grace, they have a right to know. They should be with you. How could you do this to them?"

"Do what? Can't I, for once in my life, do what I want?"

Joanna watched her stand and walk slowly to the window. "This is the way I want it," she said coolly, and then turned and went into her room.

That night, Joanna couldn't sleep. She opened the sliders, needing air, feeling again as if she couldn't breathe. She stared at the lined yellow pages of her interview, blue ink scrawled from top to bottom. How could she make sense of all this material? She couldn't even concentrate. Yesterday her life seemed so much easier; things were falling into place. Now it seemed as if everything was starting to crumble around her. Grace was dying. Timmy was leaving for Indonesia in a few weeks for the summer. Sarah would be next, going to Paris with Martin at the end of the summer. She was probably facing divorce.

She thought of Tenevya, or Tanya as she now called herself, the Bosnian refugee. A quiet woman. A hero, really, with problems and losses that made her own seem trivial. Going on each day, surviving, working to bring her sister, her only living relative, to this country. Although Joanna grieved knowing she wouldn't see her children for a long time, Tanya would never see hers. They were dead. Yet a quiet hope burned in her eyes and she spoke with strength, a certainty that one day she would be with her children again, in a better place.

Joanna prayed she could be that strong.

20

Ted's funeral was a testament to a life well lived. His ex-wife, Jean, who'd remarried a few years ago, cried as if she still loved him. His three sons gave loving eulogies of a father who seemed to be everything to them. There was a photo display, and at the center was a snapshot of Ted on his new sailboat. Paul could read the block letters across the bow: *Yet To Be.* An odd name for a boat, and then he remembered Ted's favorite expression: *The best is yet to be, Paulie my boy. Let's go for it.*

He recognized a lot of faces. He saw Diane, his former secretary, and gave her a hug and a kiss. A few of his old sales team were there. And then he saw Karen, in a sleek black suit and spike heels, blonder, tanner than he'd remembered her.

"Hello, Paul," she said, and brushed a light kiss on his cheek.

"Karen, how are you? You're looking well."

"And you, too, I must say," she said and smiled. "Listen, I really was sorry about you . . ."

He put up a hand. "It's old news. I'm over it," he said and then glanced over at the casket. "I'm just glad Ted was smart enough to enjoy a little of it."

"And what about you? Are you doing okay?"

"Sure. I took a little vacation, went out west to see my kids."

"Good for you," she said. She put a hand on his arm and then seemed to hesitate. "I heard you were separated . . . I'm sorry. What horrible timing."

He gave a short laugh. "Well, I guess a lot of things are up in the air with my life."

"Paul, if you'd ever like someone to talk to or just go to a movie or take a walk," she said, her sympathy beginning to feel cloying, "I hope you'll call me."

He thanked her, then moved on quickly to another familiar face.

After the burial and luncheon, he went home and sat on his deck for a long time, drinking a beer. There was no one to call. No place he wanted to go. The grass was cut, the flower beds mulched. There was nothing, really, for him to do. He thought of going for a run, but felt too drained. He sat staring at the woods behind his house. After finishing his second beer, he changed into his work clothes and walked down to the end of the driveway. Surrounding the mailbox was an old bed of Black-eyed Susans, which had choked out anything else his wife had planted there. He bent over and began to pull out handfuls of the deep green leaves, ripping out the roots, as well. Joanna had always talked about planting a clematis there, to climb the mailbox and cover it with blooms.

"Excuse me."

Paul turned to see a silver Lexus SUV pulled up beside him.

"Are you lost?" he asked.

It happened all the time. People pulled into the development and then became entangled in the maze of streets that wound through the neighborhood, ensuring the builder as many lots as possible.

"No. I was wondering if you were interested in more work?"

She looked about thirty, thin and fragile in appearance, with a shock of brown frizz she had pushed back with a headband. Large pearls hung from her ears like iridescent moons.

"You see, we moved in a few months ago and our place was a little neglected by the former owners, so I have lots of outside work you could do."

"I don't —" he began, but she quickly cut him off.

"I'm just a few blocks over. I've been watching you as I ride by each day; you do beautiful work. In fact, I'd love you to do a rock wall like that one for me."

Again he tried. "I'm sorry —"

"Don't say no. I know you guys are so busy you just don't have time for new customers, but I'll pay you cash and I'll pay you well."

Paul smiled. He couldn't believe this.

Her name was Buffy, and she didn't care that he lived in the neighborhood. Or that he was out of work. None of it fazed her. She had jobs to be done. Her husband, Erik, taught and did research at the local university, and she would be teaching a course or two next semester, as well. Right now, she was trying to get them settled and get her five-year-old daughter, Emily, adjusted.

Paul went to work. Whoever had done the original landscaping on her house had not planned ahead for the growth of shrubs and trees that were simply too close to the foundation. One by one Paul pulled, twisted, and ripped them out, using a chain saw he'd rented. It was exhausting work, and his shoulders and arms burned as muscles he hadn't challenged in years slowly came back to life. At night he was too tired to do much more than watch a little television after his hot shower, and often found himself falling asleep on the couch. Now he sat watching the ten o'clock news, his mind drifting over the two interviews he'd been on so far. One was with a burgeoning regional cable company looking for an aggressive sales manager as they planned to expand their market area. It was the kind of job that would consume him. Taking on the competition and trying to grow from a basic toddler position and become one of the big boys would be no easy feat. It was for someone younger, fresher than him, he thought, who hadn't already paid those kinds of dues. The other position had been with a rival of V.I.C.'s, but the position was two steps below the one he'd left and he didn't think he was desperate enough for that yet. One thing was certain — money was flowing out of his bank account like water. He'd never realized how expensive his lifestyle was. The mortgage, car payments, taxes, the car insurance, tuition, and credit card payments. He'd always heard people talk about going someplace cheaper to live. Now he understood a little better.

He turned off the TV and began hitting the lights as he made his way upstairs. Maybe it was time to start thinking about downsizing. The house and grounds were in good shape. It wouldn't take him long to do a little touch-up painting or replace some of the cracked tiles in the laundry room. Without the mortgage and taxes, he could free up more than three thousand dollars a month. Thirty-six thousand a year. There were people who lived on that much.

But the house was half Joanna's. She would have to agree.

The morning sun sent shafts of yellow light through the long side windows of the church as Joanna knelt beside Grace, who was intent on saying her rosary. Grace's lips moved silently as her fingers traveled along the crystal beads, from one decade to the next. At that moment, Joanna recalled seeing her puttering around the house or painting, her lips moving without sound, and realized that Grace was now praying much of the time.

Her thoughts drifted to her article about the woman who'd fled Bosnia. It was finally finished. After Harley spent an hour grilling her about her impressions of Tanya and her situation, he had asked her to take those notes and write them into complete thoughts and ideas. Gradually, he had her add the story. Then he showed her how to cut and paste the pages, the old-fashioned way, he called it, so she could play with rearranging some of the sequencing. By simply moving paragraphs or sentences, she was able to improve the flow of the piece. Then he showed her how to compose a simple transition sentence to connect each part of the article to the next idea or point, and like the pieces in Grace's jigsaw puzzles, it all suddenly began to fall into place. Each time Joanna thought she was finished, Harley had her write the article again and again. Finally, at the end of nearly two weeks, she laid it on his desk with a sigh of relief. And satisfaction. She felt like she was back in school, with Harley a slow, methodical teacher. But unlike when she was in school, she was enjoying learning. And as the article began to come together, one page at a time, excitement took root within her. She could do this. For the first time in a long time, she was challenging her mind. She wasn't sure why, but when she typed the final draft on the computer, she suddenly clicked the cursor between Joanna and Harrison and typed in her maiden name, Billows. Joanna Billows Harrison.

She sat back from the kneeler and let Grace slip by on her way to communion. Joanna didn't go up to communion. She hadn't been to confession since she was a girl, although she always went up to communion when she'd taken the kids each week. Paul had only come with them on Christmas and Easter. She thought of him now with a stab of pity. Out of a job. His only real friend had died. And she had left him. He was totally alone. She wondered if that was why he was calling her now sometimes late at night, just to talk to someone. She was stunned at first when he told her he was doing yard work in the neighborhood. He'd quickly explained he was going on interviews, as well, but nothing good had turned up yet. Paul seemed different, somehow. As if his hard edges were beginning to soften. He described the work he was doing, even asked her advice on flowers. Surprisingly, she began to enjoy these conversations.

She sat back on the pew again, letting Grace through, and the old woman knelt heavily beside her with a sigh. Her own knees were beginning to ache. Joanna looked up at the large crucifix above the altar, wondering if Grace was in pain yet. Guilt washed over her like a cold, uncomfortable rain. She'd been so angry with Grace after she told her the truth. She withdrew, acted cold and distant, and realized now that this was the same treatment she'd used for years on Paul when she was angry or resentful. Grace was trying to make amends. In the car that morning on the way to church, she'd suddenly broken the silence.

"I know you're upset with me for not being honest with you, Joanna, and for that I am sorry," Grace had said, staring ahead as she spoke. "But I need you. I know I should be saying that to one of my own children, but I don't want them suffering through this, too. And I don't want them remembering me that way, the way they'll always remember their father." She gave a big sigh.

Before she could respond, Grace went on in a firmer voice.

"Besides, I want to be here. At the ocean. I want this time for myself. I know that's selfish . . . but it's what I want."

What could she say?

"It's all right, Grace. I understand."

The woman was dying. Joanna had to let go of her resentment. But more than feeling resentment, Joanna was afraid. She wasn't sure what was in store for Grace. Or herself. As they bowed their heads for the final blessing, she prayed that Grace's end would

250

be as quick and painless as possible. She had a moment's vision of Ted, collapsing suddenly on his boat. Maybe he was lucky, after all.

21

Grace saw the world changing, as it did each spring. May wasn't yet over, but it was as if summer had already begun. Houses up and down the beach that had been dark and quiet were suddenly alive on the weekends with vacationers and owners who'd returned. During the days she heard laughter, mothers calling their children, and in the evening kites puffed up in the sky as walkers strolled by searching for precious shells. By New Jersey standards, things were still quiet and unhurried, but on Pawleys Island, it meant the vacation season had begun.

Her senses seemed to sharpen with all of this coming to life. She stepped out onto her deck and the smell of blooming jasmine climbing up decks and porches drifted over like an exotic perfume. Japanese mock orange blossomed everywhere, massive shrubs that stretched like fortresses around many of the homes beside hers, filling the air with the sweet smell of orange blossoms. Even the air, hot and bright with sunshine, seemed softer on her skin, like a whisper of summer.

Grace wondered if it was her attempts at painting that accounted for this sudden clarity, making the world seem so much more real, as if she were seeing it through one of those 3-D View-Masters the kids had years ago. The light, the colors, the smells, the beauty — she wanted to capture it all, somehow, hold it in her hands like a fragile butterfly for just a moment before letting it go.

Yesterday, finally, it left her. Her fear of failure. She'd taken her paints and paper out on the deck, the warm morning beckoning her, and begun a quick sketch of the beach, ocean on one side, the wide strip of sand, and then a line of four or five houses at the opposite side of the paper. And it just happened. There, suddenly, was dimension. The flatness, the lack of relief that had marred each effort so far had disappeared, and each house stood a little smaller than the one before as the beach narrowed in proportion, all of it projecting distance. It was the little bit of progress she needed to go on, and the fear of not being good enough evaporated suddenly on one of the soft breezes. Good enough for who? she'd thought, finally brushing a color. She'd decided that pleasing herself was enough.

When she woke today, it was with a different feeling than all of the other days since she'd been here. There was a little buzz of anticipation when she lay in bed drifting to wakefulness. She would try that beach scene again, this time with more nuance. She would add shrubs and flowers, darting birds. She would detail more precisely the line of dark, jagged jetties that began in the foreground and then softened into the distance. She would capture the quiet beauty of the beach that stretched north of her house.

In the distance, Grace saw a tiny figure coming up the beach. It was still early, and a moment later she realized that it was Joanna out on her morning turtle watch.

"Good morning," Joanna called as she approached.

Grace lifted a hand and waved.

Then Joanna was climbing the deck steps and Grace had no time to hide her painting.

"Can I take a look?" Joanna asked.

Grace hesitated. "Oh, why not?"

Joanna stood before her painting and Grace felt nerves thrum through her, her heart quickening. The colors were a bit bright, she knew, and she'd exaggerated some things, those things she loved, like each tender, swaying leaf of dune grass in the forefront and the pelicans skimming over the waves.

"It's lovely!" Joanna exclaimed, surprising Grace with her enthusiasm.

"You really like it?"

"Oh, yes. It's . . . it's this," she said, waving her arms at the beach before them.

Grace was pleased at Joanna's reaction, and also that her anger seemed to be gone. She smiled as joy and satisfaction bubbled inside her. And then anticipation.

What would she paint next?

Paul walked through the house slowly, surveying each room carefully before the realtor arrived. In each of his kids' rooms he stopped, sat down on the beds, and looked at the last traces of Sarah and Timmy this house would see. Most of their belongings were with them, but there were still things that branded each room as theirs. Sarah's tie-dyed bedspread and lavender walls, clusters of colorful candles on the dresser, a poster of the Eiffel Tower, ironically. Tim's room was more spartan. On his walls hung framed pictures of the various teams he'd played on, a few pennants, and some National Geographic maps tacked above his desk like a collage. An old soccer ball lay in the corner.

It would be different this time, Paul thought. When this house sold, they wouldn't all be moving on to another one together. He picked up the soccer ball, rolled it around in his hands as he paced the room, the leather smooth and worn. They would all be going their separate ways. That was the way it should be, he told himself. Sarah and Tim were carving their own paths in life, and he had no problem with that. But there was the certainty in the back of his children's minds, he was sure, that home would always be there. That he and Joanna would be waiting for them with open arms on their vacation or holiday visits. Joanna. There were still times he came in the door and expected to find her in the kitchen or kneeling in the yard working on her flowers. She'd been part of his life, a constant in it for so long, it was hard to imagine she could soon be gone forever. He'd called her a few times at night, when he couldn't bear the silence of the house anymore. When he just needed to hear another voice. At first, she was cool and untalkative, but gradually he began making inroads. What could he plant for a shade garden at Buffy's? What did she do all day? How was Grace to live with? She'd gotten a job on a newspaper, she'd explained, and he could hear a tinge of excitement in her voice as she told him about her article on a Bosnian woman. Things with Grace were far more complicated than she'd imagined, she said, but didn't elaborate. And she'd seen turtle tracks on the beach, but Hank from the turtle project had called it a "false crawl." Little by little he felt her disappearing from their life and becoming rooted to Pawleys Island.

He turned out the lights and went into his own bedroom, checking that he hadn't left dirty clothes lying around or drawers half-open. He remembered the routine from all the houses they'd sold. Uncluttered and neutral. Clean as a whistle. Joanna had been a fanatic. Until each house was under contract, there was little trace of anyone living there. No newspapers piled up in the laundry room or shoes lined up by the back door. And there was never a dirty cup or dish in the sink. It was tough, and they were constantly annoyed with her, but each house had sold quickly.

He looked at the white iron bed they had shared, where he now slept alone. On her nightstand was the twenty-fifth anniversary picture the kids had framed as a gift and given them last year. He thought about the diamond band he'd given her on their twentieth, her surprise when she opened it. He wondered if she was still wearing it. Sitting on the bed he looked at his own plain gold band, twisted it around his finger, and saw the circle of white flesh beneath it, where the sun didn't reach. He couldn't remember the last time he'd been so darkly tanned. And he couldn't recall the last time they'd made love on this bed that wasn't quick or routine. One more thing to be squeezed into a busy life. He smoothed his hand over the cream-colored quilt, knowing that if she were here at that moment, there would be nothing rushed or mechanical about their touching. The doorbell rang, and he straightened the pillows before getting up off the bed.

They sat at the kitchen table after Sandy, the realtor he'd called who had also sold them this house, finished walking through from top to bottom. When she gave him the price, he was surprised. He could make a 25 percent profit over what he'd paid. That would be a big help since there would be no relocation package paying for the movers and all his closing costs. This time he was on his own. If the house sold before he got another job, he decided he'd just go into a month-to-month rental at a local garden apartment complex until he had a better grasp on his future. In addition to cutting expenses drastically, having the house out of the way would free him to take a job anywhere, without having to worry about coordinating it all. Unlike transferring within the same company, new positions didn't typically pay your house sale expenses.

"Would you like to get started tonight?" Sandy asked him, pulling out the listing papers.

He needed a few weeks, he told her, but promised the listing was hers when the time came. She suggested he paint the lavender walls in the upstairs bedroom if he had the time. It was after six when she left, and he picked up the cordless phone and called Joanna. Now that he had all the facts, it was time he told her. But she wasn't home. He told Grace it was nothing pressing; she could call him when she had a chance.

He wondered again how she would react. When he'd threatened to sell the house after she'd first left, he'd heard her gasp of alarm. He hadn't been serious then, just looking to scare her. But things had changed. Months were passing, and it seemed ridiculous to hold on to something that was draining them financially.

Unless there was a chance she would come back.

That same afternoon, Hank called Joanna

"What are your plans today?" he asked.

She recited a litany of chores, cleaning her apartment, doing her laundry. Now that she was working two jobs, the newspaper and taking care of Grace, she found herself letting her own life go a little. But she didn't mind, really. Joanna liked being busy again. And she looked forward to going to the newspaper.

"And what is it that you do for fun once in a while?" he went on.

"Fun?" She thought about it a moment. "I don't know. Walk on the beach?"

He gave a short laugh. "Darlin', that's become just another job now with the turtle watch."

"But I enjoy it," she protested.

"I know you do, but I have something a little more entertaining in mind," he said. "Meet me at my dock about six o'clock. And wear old shoes."

She hung up with a smile.

■ ■ ■ ■

It was much more elaborate than just a dock. Across the narrow island road from Hank's garage, a long boardwalk stretched into the marsh. As Joanna carefully followed him across the narrow walkway, they made their way over what appeared to be fields of glistening green. The sun was still high, but beginning to drop on the other side of the wetlands. She was suddenly aware of the quiet, broken only by the occasional trill of a bird, the lapping of the water, and the rhythm of their footfalls on the planks. A deep, earthy smell, strong and pleasant, surrounded them. The smell of the marsh, she realized, and felt as if she was entering an exotic world. Hank's footsteps stopped and she looked up at the large, weathered gazebo. Several steps led down into the water, where two kayaks were tethered to the railing. Hank saw her alarm and smiled.

"But I've never done this, I don't know how —"

"Don't worry, you'll be a pro before the evening's over."

The tide was coming in, but she could still see shells and fish and even a crab in the shallow water. She stretched one foot into a kayak, wobbled for a moment, and before Hank could grab her arm, felt the old sneaker on her other foot plunge through a foot or so of cool water before hitting soft bottom. Gradually she balanced herself in the kayak and sat watching as Hank untied them both and gracefully hopped into his, then handed her a paddle. He gave her a quick lesson in paddling, and although she felt stiff and awkward as she dipped hers into the water, one side and then the other, trying to establish an even rhythm, in just minutes they were gliding as smoothly and quietly as fish through the marsh.

Joanna could see water glistening between the reeds in the early evening sun, and realized that what looked like little grassy islands were simply wetlands in the ebb and flow of the tides. Every so often, she would lose the rhythm of paddling and veer crookedly toward a bank. She paddled furiously to one side, then, until she straightened out. Hank was just ahead, turning every so often to check on her progress. Smoothly they slid through the narrow channels that wound through the marsh, passing the occasional fisherman or families on other docks, waiting for the sunset.

As they headed deeper into the marsh, surrounded by tall, green reeds, they didn't speak and the only sounds were the gentle gurgling of the tide pushing through the mudflats and a soft popping noise that she thought must be crabs. Rounding a bend, she caught a flash of white just ahead and stopped paddling, following Hank's lead. A snowy white egret perched majestically just a few yards away, still as a statue. As they watched, its fluid neck stretched gracefully and then it dropped its long beak, poking through the reeds, rooting in the rich mud for food. When the kayaks began to drift, she dipped a paddle into the water and the egret looked up at her for a moment before opening its great white wings and lifting into the sky. They paddled on.

As the sun dropped, sky and marsh took on a golden hue. A little later Hank turned and pointed and there, gazing at them with regal grace from a slight opening in the reeds, was a great blue heron. With its neck stretched, it must have been six feet tall. They stopped paddling, but as they drifted closer with the incoming tide, it spread its giant wings and ascended slowly, like a prehistoric creature swooping above them toward the beach. As they paddled back through the meandering waterways, dusk began to settle where they sat low on the water. In that soft gray light, Joanna felt the calm and quiet of utter peace. And then a pang of something else. Regret, perhaps, as it occurred to her how much she'd missed in her life, eyes always facing forward.

They glided back to the dock just as the sun was dipping below the horizon. Hank tied up the kayaks as she climbed up the gazebo steps, her arms trembling slightly from the exertion of paddling. Then they sat on the steps watching the last inches of the sun bleed red across the sky. When it was gone, the clouds lit up like golden streaks of fire and then faded slowly as the sky melted into a soft muddle of rose and orange.

"That was wonderful!" she told Hank. "Thank you so much for taking me."

"My pleasure." He smiled warmly and then looked at her with that intense gaze of his. "Somebody's got to make sure you have a little fun in your life, girl."

She felt herself coloring.

He went back to the house and returned a few minutes later with frozen piña coladas. They were sweet and slushy, and she felt the drink slide down smooth and fast. They talked about the turtle watch and the lack of real activity yet. Hank was disappointed and afraid that perhaps Pawleys was just becoming too busy for the turtles. Each year there seemed to be fewer nests. And vacationers were famous for leaving their outside lights on, confusing the poor creatures.

As darkness quickly settled around them, tiny bugs began to attack, nibbling viciously at any patch of exposed skin. So they took the empty glasses back up to Hank's house. Joanna was tired and feeling a bit dreamy from the exercise and the strong drink. But as she turned to say good night, she saw Hank popping a CD into the stereo.

"Do you like beach music?"

He was still on his knees, fiddling with the buttons.

"What do you mean by beach music?" She'd heard the term down South, but was never really sure what it referred to.

"Oh, you know, good old dancin' music. Oldies." He got up and turned to her and music began to fill the room. It was the Beach Boys. He held his arms out. "Do you know how to shag?"

Her heart began to beat faster. She'd never been much of a dancer. Hank wrapped an arm around her waist, pulling her closer, and then he set her left hand on his shoulder, folded her right hand in his. He looked down as he began to move and she did the same, following his steps with her eyes and then, a beat later, with her own feet. Slowly, out of time with the music, they began to sway and move around the floor. She stepped all over his feet, and her embarrassed giggles soon turned to laughter, but Hank just kept moving with the music, laughing, too, as he watched her. By the end of the first song, she was almost over her clumsiness, and by the second song, she was getting used to him touching her. Then a faster number came on, something by the Everly Brothers, and he picked up the pace and she lost the rhythm, giggling and apologizing, embarrassed at her lack of coordination. And scared and thrilled to be so close to him. Finally, he lifted her in the air and placed her feet on top of his and she danced like a little girl, her feet going wherever his led.

Afterward, he made a fresh pitcher of piña coladas.

"Just one more," she said, trying to catch her breath. "Then coffee."

She lost track of the songs. And the night. Just a few dim lamps were lit, and as darkness blackened the outside, inside they were in a magical world of music, golden light and laughter. She was having so much fun. She couldn't remember the last time she'd laughed so much. And Hank, usually so reserved, was so relaxed and easy to be with.

A slow song came on, then, "Unchained Melody," by the Righteous Brothers, always one of her favorites, and Hank pulled her closer. Her breath caught, and as she felt the length of him against her, a tightening spread like warm honey, sweet and delicious, deep inside of her. She didn't know if he moved first or she did, but they looked at each other a long moment, the laughter gone. And then they were kissing. Soft, so soft, his lips barely grazed hers, back and forth, a whisper of a touch that seemed to melt her insides until her knees grew weak and trembly. He ran his mouth across her cheek and then buried it in her neck with a little moan. They danced like that for a while, just swaying to the music, their feet not moving at all. And then they were kissing again, wild and deep. Lust burned through Joanna and she thought her skin must be on fire as he pulled her even closer, his hand on her ass now, pressing into her.

Together they sank to the floor as the music shifted to something fast that only fueled their frantic kisses. He was on top of her then, and she spread her legs as he pressed into her jeans. They kissed and ground into each other until neither could bear it and they tore their clothes off. He was inside of her in an instant, his smooth hardness piercing her with excruciating reality. She stopped moving. Oh, God, what was she doing? In twenty-five years she hadn't been with anyone but Paul.

Hank began moving, slow and deep. Filling her and then releasing her, his low moans growing with each stroke. Lust overtook reason, and her body, too far into it to turn back, moved without will. She lifted her hips, meeting his thrusts, longing for the sweet release she couldn't seem to stop. They moved and moaned in a glorious rhythm until she cried out loud, her voice echoing in the quiet room. The music had stopped. Sudden tears sprang to her closed eyes, slipping down the sides of her face as she came.

She slipped out later, like a thief in the night. Hank was asleep on the floor beside her. Her jeans were still wrapped around one ankle and slowly she pulled them on, not zipping them for fear of waking him. She pulled her shirt and sweatshirt on and then picked up her old shoes, the one still wet, and tiptoed to the screen door on the beach side of the house. The night air hit her like a cold slap. She raced down the steps through the thicket of shrubs and trees and came out on the beach, all lit up with white moonlight.

She pulled up the zipper of her jeans and ran barefoot in the cool sand toward Grace's house, thinking over and over: *I must have lost my mind. Oh, God, how will I ever look at Hank again? Why did I drink so much?* She should have known better.

She took a long, hot shower. Afterward she lay in bed, the evening running through her mind like one of those sexy music videos — Hank's lips brushing hers, the two of them melting to the floor. His smooth hardness filling her. And all the while guilt and desire warred within her until she finally turned over, her insides aching.

22

The next afternoon as Joanna drove her to Dr. Jacobs, Grace noticed she was subdued again. She'd gone out last night and wasn't home yet when Grace went to bed, although it was quite late. Joanna had the car's air-conditioning blasting and the windows open halfway, and Grace thought that was a fair description of the younger woman's demeanor toward her these days: hot and cold. Could she really blame her?

This was a regular visit to the doctor. They'd been going every few weeks now, and Grace wondered if perhaps she should tell Joanna more about her illness. Obviously she now knew they weren't going for B-12 shots. She looked over at Joanna's troubled face and then decided not to.

Grace loved Dr. Jacobs. She'd deliberately sought out a general practitioner when she first arrived months ago.

"There's no need for an oncologist," she'd

told him when he began arguing with her that first visit. "I don't plan to have any kind of treatment."

Dr. Jacobs had shaken his head and grimaced.

"What would you do if you were in my shoes?" She'd challenged him then.

That was the end of the argument.

He was an old-fashioned doctor. In a few years he'd probably be retiring. Grace guessed him to be her age or even older. But his office was always full.

"You should have a CAT scan," he told her now, after listening for a long time to her breathing with his stethoscope.

"You know the answer to that," she told him.

He sighed. "There may be lung involvement starting."

What he meant, she knew, was that it might be spreading already. And once the lungs were involved, things could escalate quickly.

"At least an X-ray, then. I can't tell for certain without some tests."

"How long?" she asked him.

He paused before speaking. "Well, it's hard to say for certain. For some people, a few months. Others have actually gone a year or more," he said. "I just had a man

271

who had no real pain until the very end. It was remarkable."

So the doctor in New Jersey may have been wrong after all. He'd given her nine months back in January. When she'd gotten to Pawleys Island, she figured she had six or seven left. She'd taken a year's lease on the house, just in case.

"There are no guarantees, Grace."

The ride home was almost unbearable. Joanna became talkative and now tried to cheer Grace with conversation. But Grace just stared out the window.

"Perhaps we should go there next week," Joanna said, when they passed the giant sculpture in front of Brookgreen Gardens. "Maybe you could bring your paints."

Grace didn't respond.

"We could go early in the morning when it's not too hot," Joanna suggested.

But Grace continued to stare out the window.

Paul had been working at Buffy's off and on for nearly two weeks. He'd finished ripping out all the overgrown shrubs, replacing them with smaller plants that would grow more manageably. And he was nearly done with the flat rock wall that now curved around the front of her house, giving it an elegant, yet rustic look. Bill, a retired pilot who lived across the street, had come by yesterday and asked if Paul might be interested in power washing his massive deck, then staining and sealing it. Paul wasn't sure how long it would take, so he gave him an inflated hourly rate that would afford his either buying or renting a power washer. Bill said fine. Delighted, Paul promised he'd be there first thing Monday morning. Then he remembered his interview and changed it to late morning.

They were in the middle of a June heat wave. As he worked, the damp, heavy air slowed his efforts as he laid the last of the flat rocks around Buffy's front entryway. The front door opened and Buffy came out, set a huge, ice-filled glass of tea on the brick step, and smiled. She'd had him hopping these past two weeks, determined to get every minute of work out of him that she could. The first day, when she invited him in to have lunch, he looked down at his sweaty, dirty clothes and laughed. So she brought a tray of sandwiches outside and ate with him on the deck while her daughter watched television. She was lonely, Paul realized. Her husband, Erik, was heavily involved in a new research project at the university, she explained, and was also doing the circuit presenting papers at various conferences over the summer. He was rarely home. By the fall, she hoped things would ease up and she could teach a course or two when Emily started kindergarten. But she was already worried, she confessed, as Emily had never stayed at any of the preschools she'd been in unless Buffy sat in the back of the room. He felt weird at first, as Buffy let out her life story in a frantic stream, in between deep breaths. It was like talking to a smoker who shot off a machine gun full of words in between drags; only there was no cigarette. Eventually, he found himself spilling out the details of his own life, finally explaining how she came to find him working outside his house that day.

"She'll be back, mark my words," Buffy rattled. "She'd be a fool not to, my God, you're handy, good-looking, you've got a brain. And you talk, unlike a lot of men."

"Well, you didn't see me before," he said with an uneasy laugh. "I wasn't much different than your own husband, running here, there, and everywhere. I think she was unhappy for a long time, I just didn't pay attention."

"I'm not unhappy, necessarily. I just like everything done like right now. And Erik doesn't have the patience for that," she went on. "In fact, if you're done eating, can you come inside? I have an idea."

He pulled off his work boots and brushed off his clothes. She led him to the brick fireplace in the family room.

"There, on either side, I would love bookshelves. I think it would make the room. Besides, we have so many books, between all my math books, Erik's biology books, and then we have a collection of old books, as well. What do you think?"

He could envision what she had in mind. On either side of the fireplace was a blank wall about five feet wide, from floor to ceiling. It was dead space, and he could imagine shelves rising to the ceiling on either side, framing the fireplace. But he hadn't done anything like that since he'd helped his father years ago. He thought about the simple wooden pieces he'd made in Colorado. Tinkertoys really.

"I don't know," he began.

"Oh, don't say no right away," she pleaded. "At least think about it."

Technically, it was just a series of straight boards. The back could be lined in panels of matching wood to give it the effect of a piece of furniture. Not really that difficult, either. Straight cuts, some mitering. He thought about the tools he would need. He didn't have any. And then he remembered the corner of his basement, the dark area near the crawl space where his father's saws and tools were shoved in a corner, covered with old bedsheets. Why had he saved them? If he'd been paying for the moves, he knew he would never have dragged them from house to house. But after the first move, he'd never had to think of them again. They were just part of the household being packed up and taken away by the movers. He'd never had to lift a finger.

He wondered if they even still worked. The blades could be rusty by now. He thought of that day long ago, watching his father in the garage as he worked, sawdust filtering to the ground like fine snow as he caressed a plank of wood he'd just shaved, like some men caress a woman's skin.

"I can probably do it," he said slowly and turned to see her smiling triumphantly. "Let me just check my tools."

"What about doors?" she asked, as he was on his way back outside. "Do you think we could put on some doors, too, to dress it up, maybe with little glass panes?"

She didn't see him rolling his eyes.

Later he saw her husband pull in and rush into the house with his briefcase. He heard loud arguing, then bursts of angry voices, but was thankful he couldn't make out the words. A few minutes later, Erik left through the garage and Paul saw Buffy throw him a kiss and a wave.

Maybe he and Joanna hadn't fought enough, Paul thought, as he dumped the last of the mulch on top of the beds he had created with the rock wall. They didn't have screaming matches. Long ago, he could remember her yelling more, but he was usually on his way out the door. By the time he'd come back, she would greet him with a cool distance. After a while he stopped expecting anything else. Maybe if he'd stayed, taken the time, they could have aired their problems and put them to bed. But he never really thought he had the time.

That night he went to a movie alone. He ate a large bucket of popcorn for his supper, too tired to think about cooking. When he got home around ten, he dialed Joanna's. She still hadn't phoned him back since his call after the realtor had left. She was out again, Grace told him. Nothing important, he said, hanging up the phone a little too hard.

23

I slept with Hank Bishop.

It was Joanna's first thought when she woke the next morning. And every morning after that. She had altered her life in one brief moment. And it was absolutely foreign to her that she could have done such a thing. She had never had casual sex in her life. There was only one boy before Paul, and with both of them, there was the rationale that she was in love. As days went by, she felt more confused. She didn't really know what to think about what had happened that night with Hank.

She skipped the next turtle meeting and avoided answering the phone. Hank called several times, Grace told her. So did Paul. She called neither one back. Even Grace seemed to look at her differently. Could she possibly know?

The Pawleys Island Gazette came out just once each week. On Wednesday, late in the day, Harley tossed a copy of that week's edition fresh from the press onto Joanna's desk as he walked back to his office. There on page one of section two was her article, "A Lesson in Quiet Greatness," by Joanna Billows Harrison. She wasn't sure about the title. It was a quote, lifted from one of her personal impressions, but Harley had felt that was the real focus of the story. "In this era of instant fame, when even criminals have graced the cover of *People* magazine," her article began, "there are those who walk quietly among us living lives of quiet greatness. Tenevya Zajac is just one of those heroes."

She read it through again, pleased. It flowed from point to point with smooth transitions. The story was interspersed with poignant quotes from Tanya. Joanna had managed not only to tell her story, but also to weave in and out of it her own feelings about it all. She was just finishing the final paragraph when the phone on her desk rang.

"Yes?" she answered, still skimming the last lines.

"You've been avoidin' me, Joanna."

She closed her eyes, unable to speak.

"Look, darlin', I really want to see you. I think we need to talk."

"I'm sorry, Hank —"

"Wait," he quickly interrupted. "Before you say no, just listen. I'd like you to just stop by after work for ten minutes. That's all I ask."

She imagined facing him finally. She could feel her face flame.

"Please, Joanna," he said. "We need to straighten this out."

Never good at standoffs, she agreed.

She thought about Grace and stopped home first, not sure if she needed anything for dinner. Grace was already eating a sandwich and her painting things were out on the deck, scattered across the table. Joanna had picked up an easel for her a few days ago, and now she saw a canvas propped on it, colorful but indistinct from where she stood.

"I have to go out for a little while," Joanna told her. "I'll be back early. Maybe we could play cards or something?"

But Grace seemed to be off in some distant place right now, caught up in her painting, she assumed.

She changed into a sundress. The newspaper office was freezing, or she still wasn't used to the Southern custom of keeping the air-conditioning on frigid, so she always wore stockings or pants and long sleeves. But it was past the middle of June and the summer sun blazed fiercely outside. Even here in the house, where Grace preferred the windows and doors open, the ocean breeze blowing through was warm. She stood in front of the mirror, surveying herself, then scooped up her hair. It was getting long and frizzing with the humidity, so she fastened it up off her neck with a gold clip.

She drove over, and as soon as she walked in Hank's front door, he took her hand and pulled her back out the screen door toward the beach. They walked down the wooden steps through the jungle of growth that now nearly hid his house on the beach side.

"Come on, I want to show you something."

Ruby red honeysuckle was blooming in a tangle through the trees like some kind of exotic vine. She saw the tiny lizard scamper under the steps as they walked by, a flash of green. At the bottom of the steps, she pulled off her sandals before stepping on the sand.

"Over here," Hank called over his shoulder.

She followed him and a few doors down from his house saw a square of sticks and string no bigger than a beach blanket far back in the sand, almost into the dunes.

"First nest of the season," he said, when

they both stopped beside it. He opened a small blanket she didn't realize he'd been carrying and they sat beside the nest, nearly touching.

"Now what happens?" she asked.

"We wait," he said, looking at her with a smile. "Incubation usually takes about fifty to fifty-five days. Hopefully, if we're careful, we'll be able to be here when they hatch and make sure as many make it into the water as possible."

The sun was dropping behind them, and the oppressive heat of the afternoon was being swept away by the ocean breeze. Along with it went her discomfort at being with Hank. He was such a nice man.

"So they all hatch at once?"

"They sure do. Could be a hundred of them at the same time, pushing through the sand and clambering for the water," he explained and then laughed. "It can be a pretty crazy couple of minutes, what with turtles racing in all directions. Especially if there's lights distractin' them."

"I hope I get to see it."

"I hope you do, too," he said, and then hesitated before continuing. "About the other night, I hope you don't think I was trying to take advantage . . ."

"No, please, it was as much my fault. I

shouldn't have had so much to drink."

"You only had two drinks."

"I know, but somehow things just got out of hand. Sex is . . . It's not something casual to me," she stammered

"I hope you don't think that what happened was casual for me, either," he said, and reached over, tracing the curve of her cheek with his finger. "You're so lovely, Joanna. And so serious all the time. It was nice to see you happy for a little while."

He reached behind her neck and pulled out the clip. Her hair fell, settling softly on her bare shoulders, and then the wind lifted it gently, grazing her skin like a caress. He just stared at her, those light blue eyes melting into her. And then he leaned toward her, lowering his lips until they barely touched her own. Kissing was okay, she told herself, lifting her lips toward him. Just kissing.

Later that week, she had that feeling again. As if she was somewhere above the room watching herself below, in Hank's old bed, the sheets twisted around them. She could see the length of him, lean and tan on top of her, until she nudged him over. As she rolled on top of him, the sheet went with her, binding them together like a wide ribbon. Placing her hands on either side of his neck, she lifted herself above him, her breasts dangling in his face with each thrust. He lifted his head and wrapped his lips around a nipple, sending a dagger of heat between her legs. She heard herself moaning now, as she lifted herself and slid down him again and again while he nibbled on her breasts. Candles surrounded them, on the nightstand and the dresser, bathing the room in a soft, golden light. The windows were open and she could hear the ocean thundering out on the beach as the tide came in. From her place on the ceiling it looked so beautiful and romantic. Hank ran his tongue along the tan line under her breast where brown skin and white breast met, whispering that it was the sexiest place he could imagine. She watched as she moved faster, this Joanna who was living a life she couldn't really imagine. She exploded into a million delicious spasms and then collapsed on his chest, laughing softly. She watched, transfixed, as their breathing slowed and they seemed to doze.

"You know, I don't really know a whole lot about you, Mr. Bishop. Aside from the fact that you sold your shrimp boat to your cousin, retired, and work on it occasionally," she mumbled in his ear, still on top of him. "Oh, and that you have this passion for turtles."

"And you, darlin'," he laughed, squeezing her ass.

"No, seriously," she said, and propped herself on an elbow to look at him.

"Well, what would you like to know?"

"What were you like as a teenager, for instance? Were you quiet or wild, did you break all the girls' hearts?" she said to tease him.

"I was fairly quiet. And I didn't go out much. I was one of those guys who had a high school sweetheart I thought was the one. I got a scholarship to play football at UNC in Chapel Hill, but to tell you the truth, I hated it. I stuck it out, though, so we could have some kind of future. But after graduation I spent that last summer on my dad's shrimp boat and I realized I didn't want to go anywhere else. Didn't want to be a businessman and make lots of money. I was happy right here, workin' the boat. I remember one night out on the boat under the stars, my dad, he knew how torn I was. 'She wants some kind of fancy life,' he told me. 'You're a simple man. Nothin' wrong with that.' "

He sighed then, as if he could see it — the confused young man he was, listening to his father's advice on that shrimp boat as they sailed into night.

"So I stayed here. Eventually took over the boat. Then got married anyway, which was a big mistake."

She pictured the photograph of Lacey, young and blond, with their daughter.

"We were only married five years. She went to California, married again, and a few months later the three of them were killed in a pileup on the freeway. Bad fog."

"Oh, Hank. I'm so sorry."

"It's my fault. If things had been different, they'd still be here."

"No, you can't say that," she said, holding his face, forcing him to look at her. "You can't still feel that way after all these years."

He grunted bitterly. "Funny thing about guilt. You can get away from it for a while, but eventually it rears its big ugly head . . ."

"Enough!" she nearly shouted. "I'm sorry I started this."

She covered his face in kisses. He began kissing her back, and slowly she could feel the heat building between them. She glanced over at the bedside clock.

"Oh, God, it's after eleven, I have to go."

"For God's sake, you're not some teenager on a curfew," Hank whispered in her ear.

"But I need to get back to Grace."

"I don't understand your obligation to

her, but I respect it," he said, and then kissed her neck. "But I sure wish you'd stay the night just for once."

From high above the room, she saw this other Joanna get up and walk across the room, naked in the candlelight, and begin to pull on her clothes. Heard her laugh and say:

"I wish I could, too, so we could do it again."

She did feel like a teenager, sneaking up the stairs, trying not to waken Grace. Her lights were all out. When the phone rang, just as she slipped through her door, she grabbed it on the first ring.

"Joanna, it's Paul."

It was nearly midnight. Her heart squeezed in fear. "What's wrong?"

"Nothing, everything's fine. I just need to talk to you, and whenever I call, you're not there. I figured you had to be home by now."

She knew he'd called a few times. She sat, her heart steadying, listening to her husband's voice nearly a thousand miles away. And she could smell her lover all over herself.

"I've been doing a lot of thinking. About finances, the future," he said quietly. And then she heard him sigh. "About the house."

"What about the house?"

"I had a realtor in and got a price," he said. "We're losing three thousand a month hanging on to it."

"You want to sell the house now?"

"Unless things change, Jo, it might be the smartest move financially."

Which meant, really, unless she was coming back.

"I don't know what to say. Is this really what you want?"

"I don't think what I want has had much to do with anything in my life lately," he said with a little laugh that held no humor.

What could she say? *I just came in from my lover's, you caught me off guard, and truthfully, I find it impossible to look ahead more than a month or two?* She was being unfair to him.

"Can you give me a day to think about it, please?" she asked.

"Sure."

She couldn't sleep. After a while, she pulled her rocker out onto the deck and sat there in just her nightgown under the star-filled sky. It was still warm, but the breeze off the water was soft and cool. Her skin felt as if it was still burning from Hank, while her heart felt heavy for Paul.

In the morning, she called him.

"Sell the house if you think that's best," she said.

■ ■ ■ ■

II
MIGRATING SOULS

■ ■ ■ ■

24

By the first of July, it had been raining for more than a week, and Paul felt as if he was climbing the walls. He'd been spending most of his days down in the basement, where he'd uncovered his father's saws and woodworking equipment. He was working on Buffy's shelves.

After a few days surrounded by the dark cinder-block walls, he realized why his father had taken over the garage with his equipment. With the door open, it had been as if he were outside. Paul toyed with the idea. It would be a monumental task moving everything up a flight of stairs and out into the garage. He would need help; he couldn't do it alone. So he kept working, listening to the unceasing rain pelting softly against the grass just outside the tiny, high basement windows he kept open.

He hadn't listed the house yet. He was ready, though, everything touched up and neutralized as Sandy had suggested. She had called him a few days ago, and once again he told her another week or two. He knew it was time, but somehow he couldn't seem to take that last step and sign. After that, he knew it would all be out of his hands.

He'd been offered a job in Atlanta, but he turned it down. He didn't really know why. The money was good, he even liked Atlanta, having traveled there often on business. But it just didn't feel right. He'd turned down a few interviews, too. Trapped in the basement, he wondered if he could ever spend fifty to sixty hours a week indoors or behind a desk again. That now seemed like a sentence to him.

His mind wandered while he worked, music playing on a small stereo he'd moved into the basement. He wondered how Tim was doing in Indonesia. Paul worried about the travel over there, small charter flights and the infamous ferries across the Indian Ocean to the island jungles. He'd spoken to Sarah a few nights ago and mentioned he'd painted her room. When he told her why, she became silent.

"Sarah, I'm not making this decision lightly. But this is a big house for just one person," he'd explained. "And you'll be off to Paris soon." He hoped talking of Paris would lift her spirits.

"I know, Daddy. It's just that . . ." She stopped. "What if Mom came back?"

"I already talked to her. I don't think that's going to happen."

"Oh."

"Listen, I haven't put it on the market yet. We'll see."

He worked late that night. The frame for the bookshelves was already cut, stained, and nailed to the walls beside Buffy's fireplace. Now he was working on each shelf, cutting, sanding the edges, and then staining. Last would be the doors. Yes, Buffy would get her doors.

He settled on the couch at nine and ate a take-out pizza while he flipped channels. By eleven he was in bed.

The phone woke him in the dark and he glanced at the bedside clock as he picked it up. Two-forty-three in the morning.

"Hello?"

"Paul?" He heard a whisper. "It's Buffy."

"What's wrong?"

"My alarm system went off. I'm sorry to call in the middle of the night, but . . . could you come over, please? I turned it off fast, so it wouldn't wake Emily. But now I'm freaked. I know it's probably nothing, but

Erik's away, I don't know anyone else, really. Please?"

He sat up and ran a hand across his eyes, trying to rub them awake.

"I'll be right over."

He pulled on sweatpants and a T-shirt, and when he was backing his car out of the garage, he threw it in park, hopped out, and grabbed a baseball bat and then a can of toxic weed spray. The house was dark when he got there, but when he knocked, he saw lights go on one by one as Buffy made her way down the stairs.

"Emily was sleeping with me. I let her when Erik's away. And when that fucking bell went off, I just leaped out of bed and hit the off button next to my bedroom door."

He'd never heard her curse before. She was wearing one of those sumptuous white terry-cloth robes that made her look tiny and fragile. He could see she was rattled.

"Anyway, then I got to thinking, what if it's the real thing this time, you know? But I don't want to call the cops, because what if it isn't? And Emily is still sleeping."

"It's okay. Where's the master panel?"

It was right there in the hall. The alarm, it appeared, had been triggered in the basement.

"Oh, God," Buffy whispered. "Maybe we should call the cops after all."

Paul shook his head. "Why don't I just go down and check. It probably is nothing."

"I'll be up here with the phone ready," she said, pulling the cordless phone out of her robe pocket. "Just yell if there's anything wrong. I've got 911 on speed dial."

Luckily they had lots of lights in the basement, and they all went on together with a flip of the switch at the top of the steps. Boxes were still lined up along one wall, and there was a small bike and skates where Emily apparently rode in circles around the support columns. He didn't see anything and there didn't seem to be any place to hide. He picked up a flashlight on a shelf near the furnace and checked the alarm sensors. Then he caught a movement in his peripheral vision. Leisurely crawling across the basement floor was the biggest spider he'd ever seen.

"Oh, God." Buffy shuddered when he brought her down. "It's got legs like pipe cleaners! Do you really think that did it?"

He nodded and smiled.

"It's even creepier than a burglar," she said, making him laugh.

She made coffee and they sat at her kitchen table, listening to what they both hoped was really the last of the rain.

"Listen," she said, sipping her coffee, her knees drawn up on the chair like a little girl at a sleepover. "What are you doing tomorrow? I'm taking Emily to see *The Lion King* on Broadway and I have an extra ticket. Erik screwed up the dates, but he says I screwed them up. Anyway, why don't you come?"

He laughed, embarrassed.

"Oh, come on. It'll be great. When was the last time you had a day off? I promised Em we'd take the ferry over, and it's supposed to be nice and sunny. It'll be fun," she pleaded.

What could he say?

They sat in the top balcony. "Nosebleed seats," Buffy hissed angrily when they got off the elevator. "I've got vertigo," she whispered to Paul, a bright smile plastered across her face for Emily's benefit. "I hate heights."

Emily was rapt with excitement as an array of animals sang and danced across the stage in a breathtaking spectacle of color and clever costumes in the opening act. Paul's mind immediately began to drift. It had occurred to him on the ferry from Weehawken that he hadn't left Sparta in weeks. As they crossed the Hudson into Manhattan, sunlight glinting off the skyscrapers, a warm river breeze buffeting them, a feeling of freedom came over him. He watched Buffy point out the Empire State Building and other landmarks to Emily.

Once off the boat, they'd hopped a shuttle bus that dropped them at Times Square.

"Now that we live so close, I'd love to come and see the ball drop on New Year's," Buffy had remarked as they passed the infamous spot. "Could you imagine?"

He couldn't, he realized, watching as the boy lion returned to the stage, not dead after all, but full grown. New Year's Eve was still nearly six months away and he had no idea where his life would be at that point.

It was a long play, and toward the end, as he listened to the high wailing of the young lioness, he wondered if life was passing him by. His stomach did a little flip as an instant of panic gripped him. Perhaps he should have taken the job in Atlanta. What if there were no other offers? He'd been floating, waiting for something to happen, he wasn't even sure what. For his wife to come back, or something to fall at his feet, maybe. He'd turned himself into some kind of neighborhood handyman, but could that really be a future? He had skills and talent and education. He had the ability to make lots of money. Those weren't things you just let go.

It was nearly midnight when Buffy dropped him in front of his house.

"Thanks for coming, Paul. And thanks for carrying Emily to the ferry, she's really dead weight when she's asleep."

"Sure," he smiled, opening the car door. "It was fun."

"You know, you're a lot different than most other men I've known. Do you think Erik would have changed his plans or even pretended to be upset he couldn't go today? Oh no, what he's doing is always the priority. I know making a living is tough and all that. But Christ, stop once in a while and have a conversation. Learn to look around at what's going on in your life."

"I think maybe that's difficult for most men to do. Unless your life is pulled out from under you."

"Your wife's a fool," she said, and gave him a quick kiss on the cheek.

He went right to bed, tired from the long day. The next morning at nine sharp he called Sandy and told her to bring over the listing contract for him to sign. Then he would send it to Joanna for her signature.

25

Grace didn't want to come to Hank's Fourth of July party. After the third time Joanna had begged her, she finally agreed. She didn't leave the house much now, caught up in her world of light and color and imagination. And years ago, when she'd been just a girl, it had been the same when she'd been lost in the act of creating. It was a good thing now, she told herself, as it was consuming her time and attention. She was sleeping a little better at night, too.

But part of her was afraid. Slowly, little by little, she was cutting herself off from the world. As she had after she was married and had her babies, trapped in a dizzying orbit of fears she could not understand. Or push away. She'd spent a lifetime making sure she never descended to that dark place again. Fear of it propelled her to Hank's Fourth of July party.

Grace sat in a rocker in a corner of the

porch that faced the beach. She felt as if she was in a tree house, high up in a tangle of shrubs, trees, and vines. Her chair was sideways, so she could look through the windows into the house or, if she tilted her head in the other direction, catch a glimpse of dunes barely visible through the oaks and crape myrtles. Her eyes were fixed in the house now as she watched Joanna, who was standing across the room from Hank while he talked to someone else. Joanna's eyes followed him as he greeted people, fixed drinks, ran outside to fire up the grills. Her eyes were filled with wanting.

And for Grace, the pieces slowly fell into place as she watched. Joanna, she realized, was having an affair.

It was probably inevitable that Joanna would find someone, she told herself, sipping an iced tea garnished with a sprig of mint. It was placed in her hands just moments after she walked in, by a polished blonde who introduced herself in a breathy drawl as Rhetta. A woman who seemed as comfortable in this house as Hank, as she pulled baskets out of cupboards and filled them with chips and pretzels.

Joanna had been consumed with loneliness, and it shouldn't be surprising that she needed to fill the emptiness in her life. But

Grace was disappointed. Joanna was, after all, still a married woman. It was none of her business, she told herself now, watching Joanna and Rhetta talking. Rhetta was all friendly smiles and fluttering hands, but Joanna appeared stiff and guarded in her presence. Hank was back in the house then, grabbing lighter fluid and matches. Joanna's eyes followed him, not knowing it was all over her face. Then she went into the kitchen where Grace could no longer see her.

Her mind drifted to her painting. She'd been working inside on a still life, a vase of mixed summer flowers on her table, since it was too hot to work outside, which she preferred. After copying each petal and leaf of the cosmos, daisies, snapdragons, and nicotiana, she stood back, less than impressed with the result. It was too precise and boring. She'd started again, dabbing the colors on more boldly, the orange, gold, rose, the different greens of stem and foliage, and then sponging them away while still wet. The effect was much more subtle yet dramatic, the colors blending into a fusion of shades and light. The simple, old-fashioned bouquet had come alive on the paper.

"Is this seat taken?"

Grace turned to find an older man at her side. He stretched a hand toward her.

"How do you do, ma'am. I'm Harley Henson. I work with Joanna at the newspaper. You must be Grace."

She smiled at him politely, taking his hand and shaking it. "Yes, I am Grace."

He lowered himself slowly into the rocker beside hers. "And how are you enjoyin' life here in the low country?" Harley asked Grace in his deep drawl, his words pouring forth like slow, thick molasses.

She didn't want to talk to him. Didn't want to like him. But when was the last time she'd had a conversation with anyone other than Joanna? And when had she last spoken to someone her own age, who understood that each day was a gift, that aches and pains were now part of the process? Within minutes she learned that Harley lost his wife five years ago. That there had been a few years before that when his Mary didn't even know him, when he'd finally had to feed her. He said the word Alzheimer's the way she remembered others once utter Auschwitz, a world of agony for which there were no other words. Finally, he'd put his wife in a nursing home, and Grace knew how he felt. The guilt of betrayal that never left you. Could you have done more? He himself now suffered from arthritis, he told her, and was even driven to acupuncture to keep his fingers moving on the old Smith Corona typewriter he refused to trade in.

She found herself telling this stranger about Frank's death as he nodded and smiled, eyes soft with sympathy. He reminded her of a big old basset hound, long ears and drooping brown eyes full of kindness. And sadness. As the words spilled, something else flowed with them. Relief. Here was someone who understood. Who'd been there, as well.

After a while he brought her a glass of white wine. "What is it you miss the most?" he asked.

She knew what he was speaking of, didn't need him to explain. She closed her eyes a moment. "Dancing," she said softly.

He smiled. "I miss a good late night card game."

She was glad she had come.

I'm like a junkie, Joanna thought. *And Hank Bishop is my fix.*

She watched him rushing across the room, taking care of a dozen little things as people arrived and the room filled with voices and laughter, the clinking of ice in glasses. It was a scorching, airless day, and although this was an outside party, everyone was waiting for shade to hit the beach. Hank was wearing shorts and a T-shirt that now clung to him with sweat as he rushed in and out of the house. She wanted to rip it off him and dry him with her own skin.

But she continued talking to Lois, one of the librarians who was also on the turtle watch. Lois heard that she'd found a nest near Grace's house and assumed it was on one of her morning patrols. Joanna didn't tell her that she stumbled on it late one night, racing home from Hank's bed. The moon had been little more than a curved sliver, throwing just enough white light so that she could see the sand and avoid any stray shells or debris to protect her bare feet. Glancing ahead, she'd seen a huge dark object that appeared to be moving. As she slowly made her way closer, her hand flew to her mouth to stifle a shout of joy. A mother loggerhead was laboriously digging her nest. In the little bit of moonlight, she could see her flippers methodically scooping sand. She stopped, ducked behind the nearest jetty, and waited, her heart pounding with excitement. After a while, the turtle stopped digging and then rested, as if catching her breath. Then she sat in the big depression for a long time. Joanna was so tired, but she slowly moved to the inner edge of the jetty and sat on the sand, leaning her arm against the hard rock and resting her head against it. She was hit with the strong smell of fish and salt. She didn't know how long she sat there, but she must have fallen asleep after a while. When she opened her eyes with a start, the mother turtle was gone. Slowly, she'd scanned the beach with sleepy eyes, but there was no trace of the loggerhead. She wasn't sure exactly where the nest was. She hadn't picked a landmark for a target because the turtle had been there; she was her landmark. Walking cautiously across the beach, her eyes glued to the sand, Joanna had searched carefully. And there it was in front of her, the tracks left by dragging flippers leading back into the ocean. She followed the tracks up toward the dune and there, where they began, the sand was smooth and flat. She took off her sweatshirt and laid it out on top of the nest to mark it.

"You're so lucky." Lois sighed. "I've been doing this for nearly twenty years and have never had the good fortune to find a nest."

"Yes, I am lucky." Joanna smiled, and felt her face grow warm as Hank gave her a look across the room.

She turned to check on Grace and saw

her out on the back porch, sitting by herself. A needle of annoyance jabbed at her. At first Grace didn't want to come. Then, after much cajoling, she agreed. Only now she was deliberately keeping herself apart from everyone.

"Hello, Joanna."

And there was Rhetta, all smiles in a short white skirt and blue halter top that made her look tanner and blonder. A string of freshwater pearls encircled her long neck.

"I'm supposed to be nice to you," she drawled sweetly. "I apologize if I came on a bit strong last time."

They both knew who'd chastised her.

"Forget it," she said. She didn't want to get into it. As far as anyone in the room knew, she and Hank were just friends.

"Why don't you and I do lunch one of these days, get to know each other a little better?" Rhetta asked with a lift of her eyebrows.

"I'm literally working two jobs," Joanna told her, and flashed a phony smile of regret. "I just don't have that kind of time." Then she excused herself and went to get another iced tea.

Hank was in the kitchen, filling the ice bucket, and they exchanged hungry smiles.

"Havin' a good time?" he whispered

"This is really hard," she said softly and then giggled.

"Rhetta behavin' with you?"

She rolled her eyes. "Yes."

He began dumping bags of ice into a large cooler. "She's not a bad person. She just can't stand not bein' the most beautiful woman in the room."

The funny thing was, he made her feel like it was true. Then he lifted the cooler with a grunt, his brown arms corded with muscles as he carried it past. "Later, okay?"

She watched him walk across the living room and out the back door. And then saw Rhetta watching her.

She sauntered back into the living room and drifted into a conversation about hurricanes.

"Could be the worst season in years, I heard them saying on the Weather Channel the other day." This was from Gus, who ran the gas station just off the island.

"I'm just sick of all this el niño, la niña bullshit," said Hank's cousin, Sam, the one who'd taken over his shrimp boat. He sounded angry, and she wondered if he'd had too much to drink. "If you ask me, these guys are just making stories to justify their airtime."

Nearby she could hear another conversation going on about the fire at The Chowder House. Goody's name was being thrown around, and she thought she heard someone say the cook had just gotten out of the hospital from his burns.

She glanced over at the back porch and was surprised to see Harley sitting next to Grace. She was amazed, too, that Grace didn't get up and walk away; she was so determined to be alone. Grace's face lit up with a smile then, something she couldn't recall seeing in a long time, and that same needle jabbed her now with guilt. What must it be like to know you're going to die? To have a timetable where you count out the days, like they used to do with the kids at Christmas. She thought about Grace never seeing her children again. The courage it would take to endure that alone, far from home, to spare them. How could she question Grace's motives, or the right or wrong of what she was doing? It was her life. And her death. Joanna made a promise to try harder with Grace.

"They should never have let them rebuild these beachfront houses after the last bad hurricane," she heard as her mind came back to the party. "Thinking you can keep a house there for any length of time without some kind of catastrophe is pure folly."

"I'll tell you what's pure folly, the buildin' goin' on in those old rice fields. When's it goin' to end? When there's no land left?"

"All those Northerners lookin' for better weather and lower taxes . . ."

She slipped away, feeling once again like an outsider. No matter how entrenched she was becoming in life on Pawleys Island, she would always be different. She even spoke differently. Quicker, sharper, than their soft, slow drawls. She passed Hank carrying another tray across the room and he nodded for her to follow.

Slowly the house emptied as the partyers made their way down to the beach, cooler now as the sun began to set. The smoky aroma of grilled chicken, hamburgers, and hot dogs floated in on an ocean breeze. Hungry now, Grace and Harley made their way slowly down the wooden steps, kicking off their shoes when they reached the sand. It was cool and soft on Grace's feet, and a sudden longing filled her to take off all her clothes and lie in it, let it caress her whole body. She felt more alive than she had in years, despite a sleepless night spent worrying about an ache in her back. Turning over to ease the pain, fear had hit her in the middle like a fist. Once it hit the spine, she knew, things deteriorated quickly. But by this morning, when the rosy dawn spread across the ocean, she'd convinced herself it was simply stiffness from too many hours painting. Years ago, after painting, she would stretch to ease the aches and kinks and bring life back to her limbs. She would start stretching again.

Harley offered her a hand as they trudged toward the beach where the party was in full swing. The music, the smells, the colors, the shifting light were suddenly in sharp focus, and she had an urge to capture this moment in vivid watercolors.

She ate more than she had in a long time, savoring the taste of charcoal on her hot dog, slathering her corn with butter and lots of salt. Harley brought more wine. She was aware of the constant wash of low tide. Later, when sea and sky melted into a dark canvas, the fireworks began. With a whoosh, each shot into the sky, exploding in sparkling reds, greens, and golds. For those few seconds the whole beach lit up, and Grace saw all the faces look up, as if in collective rapture. Then each firework faded, fluttering to earth like glittering fairy dust as another flew up through the settling smoke. A surge of joy rushed through her. She wished the night would never end.

■ ■ ■ ■

Joanna, too, could not remember feeling so happy in years. Hank had lit tiny citronella candles and scattered them throughout the sand to keep the bugs away. It was like a dream, she thought, the flickering candles casting puddles of golden light, the soft laughter, the gentle backwash of the waves as the tide went out. And the soft breeze caressing her flesh as those blue eyes watched her with burning anticipation across the crowd. She wished the night would never end.

When the first firework rocketed into the sky and exploded above, streaks of red glitter shooting across the night, she thought: this has nothing to do with my life before. Paul, Sarah, and Timmy were like people from another existence. A different Joanna. She watched the colors light up the sky, falling like shards of colored glass over the black water, and felt herself melting into it all. This, she realized, was her life now.

26

The following week, Harley asked Joanna to take pictures of a demonstration at a new development on the Waccamaw River. The Barony was just the latest in the upscale building frenzy catering to wealthy locals and transplants from other states looking for better prices and taxes, Harley explained. Northerners, he meant, but she knew he was too polite to say it.

She sat at her desk with the camera, a roll of film ready to be loaded, and Harley's scrawled directions. But she couldn't move. Also on her desk was the mail she'd scooped up on her way to the office, and in the pile was a thick envelope from Paul. The contract to list the house for sale. Seeing it in writing was different than talking about it on the telephone. 848 Butterfield Drive. Their home.

Lately she'd been so happy she stopped thinking about everything that had to do with her former life. She wasn't ready to deal with it, but soon would be. Remembering how fragile she'd felt when she first got there, she just wanted to concentrate on building her new life. And enjoying the little bit of happiness that finally seemed to have come her way. Now she was looking at a blatant reminder of all she was choosing to ignore.

Just sign it, she kept telling herself. But every time she picked up the pen, she wound up twirling it, chewing it, putting it down again.

"I just heard on the scanner that the police may be headin' over to that demonstration," Harley said as he passed her desk. He must have been wondering what was holding her up. So she loaded the film into the camera, grabbed her purse and the directions, and headed out the door.

Getting into the car was like getting into a preheated oven. The blast of hot air that blew out at her after opening the door had her sweating instantly. Quickly she turned on the ignition, flipped the air-conditioning on high, and slammed the door, waiting beside the car. She knew people who went from one air-conditioned environment to another, barely spending more than a few minutes in the sweltering summer heat. The

Weather Channel said the Northeast was suffering an endless spell of cool, rainy weather. Right now she would have welcomed some gray skies and rain.

She opened the car door and it was as cool as her office. Driving across Route 17 southward to a dirt road just past a local diner, she turned right toward the river. The woods grew heavier on either side and the trees canopied the road, blocking out the sun. Where the road ended just before the river, a new road was cut through the thick trees to the right. *The Barony,* a regal sign proclaimed, *Estate Homes & River Lots Available.* And there walking up and down the road was a group of everyday people, mostly black, just pacing back and forth and carrying signs that read, *Development is Pushing Out Locals, Development = Higher Taxes, Save the Land from Greedy Builders.*

It didn't look like much of a story. Joanna sat for a moment, unsure of what to do. She could see the dirt paths of new streets, branching off the main road of the development, and the framework of what was probably the model home. Tractors and backhoes pushed dirt like Timmy's old Fisher-Price toys. In the distance she caught a gleam of white, the old plantation house, being renovated as a country club. There wasn't much to photograph besides the people marching past the sign for the development. If she shot at the right angle, she might be able to get it all in.

Getting out of the car, Joanna crossed over to the throng of people. They kept marching. She pulled the camera to her eyes and took a look through the viewfinder. Through the tiny square of magnified glass, she saw eyes turning toward her. She lowered the camera.

"I'm from the *Gazette*," she announced loudly, to no one in particular. "I'm just going to take a picture."

She felt like an idiot as she snapped a dozen shots, moving a few steps here and there to shoot different views, hoping to get their signs at the right angle so that the readers could make them out. Beads of sweat rolled down her chest, into her bra, and she could feel a band of wetness grow on her upper lip. She couldn't wait to get out of there. She snapped the last picture, heard the automatic rewind begin to whine, and turned to leave. Then she caught a familiar pair of eyes on her. Jolene, from The Chowder House.

She hesitated. She wanted to leave, but thought that would be rude. Jolene, however, had never said more than a few words to her, and Joanna wondered at times if she didn't actually dislike her, although she couldn't imagine why. They barely knew each other. Now Jolene stared her down across the dirt road, a sign high above her reading, *3 Generations Forced Out.* Joanna walked over to her.

"Hi, Jolene. I got a job on the newspaper," she said stupidly.

"I can see that." Her voice was very soft, her drawl slow and deep.

She didn't say anything else and Joanna stood there a moment awkwardly, wishing she'd just left. Jolene's dark skin glistened, as if she'd just run through a hose, but Joanna knew it was perspiration.

"Have you found another job?" she asked politely.

"Yeah, waitressin' at another restaurant."

Another pause.

"Well, it was nice seeing you," she said, and started to leave. "Good luck."

"What you think about all this?" she heard her say. She turned back. "What you gonna write about?"

"Oh, I'm just taking a picture, I'm not doing a story," Joanna explained with a nervous laugh.

"That's all we get, huh? Just a picture?" Jolene turned then and began walking with the others. "Figures."

She didn't bother to cool the car this time, just got in and drove off, sweat trickling down her face, her back plastered to the seat. She handed Harley the film and the camera when she returned to the office.

"I hope these turn out okay," she told him. "The cops must have come and gone because it was pretty peaceful."

"Mmm," he said, absorbed in something on his desk. She turned to go.

"Here, this is for you."

He handed her an envelope addressed to Joanna Billows Harrison at *The Pawleys Island Gazette.* She couldn't imagine what it was. She went back to her desk, sat down, and opened it.

Dear Ms. Harrison,
I was deeply touched by your article on the Bosnian woman who is trying to bring the rest of her family to America. It was nice to read about someone good when all we ever seem to hear about are the bad. I've enclosed a small check that I hope you will forward to Tanya. I hope it helps her to achieve her dream.

Isabel Delaney

She was giddy with pleasure and ran right

back to Harley's office, waving the letter and the check, one in each hand.

"Why are you so surprised?" he laughed. "That was a wonderful piece."

"I don't know, I guess I just thought of it as a job. Once it was printed, it was done. Now this."

"That's the thing about writin'," Harley said, leaning back in his chair. "It's never just a job. You make people think, you sway their feelin's. It's a gift. And a power."

She thought about Jolene for a second, her disappointment that she wasn't writing about her plight. "You're right," she said. "But who would have ever thought I . . . I could do this."

Harley smiled.

"I know you offered this to me because of Hank."

"Now, hold on," he said, straightening in his chair. "Hank Bishop had nothing to do with this."

"But when you asked me about the job that night at his house . . ."

"I remember. At the turtle meetin'. I didn't even know who you were at that point. I watched you that night, though, how you looked around the room, observin' everyone. Taking it all in. Quietly assessing us. And I knew you had it in you. The best writers are people who simply observe the world around them. The harder part is digestin' it and gettin' it back out again in your own way. And you seem to be able to do that just fine."

She stood there, amazed.

"I guess I had a feelin' about you." He smiled. "Besides, years ago someone gave me the same opportunity, and I saw a chance to somehow repay the favor."

It was the first time she really thought of writing as more than a job. It wasn't an innate talent, she knew that now. It was hard, hard work. But she could do this, she realized, excited suddenly by the possibilities. Moving people, as she had done with the woman who wrote the letter, was a power. There was a check in her hand for Tanya that was a direct result of her written words. That felt incredibly good.

"Thanks, Harley, for giving me the chance."

"You're very welcome, my dear."

She turned to leave and then hesitated.

"You know, Harley, that demonstration I just photographed? Maybe you should think about doing an article about it. I mean, the picture shows the demonstration, but you've got to wonder what it is that drives each of those people to stand there in the sweltering heat."

He nodded. "I'll give it some thought," he said. "By the way, Joanna. Do you think it might be all right if I called on Grace sometime?"

She wasn't about to say anything to open this can of worms.

"I think you'll have to ask Grace that, Harley."

27

The early July rains had finally given way to a stretch of blistering, humid days, what most people thought of as a real Jersey summer, and Paul's life began to take on a comfortable rhythm. He rose early and began his outside jobs before the sun was above the mountains, so that by late morning, when an oppressive haze brewed by the intense heat and humidity seemed to suffocate him, he was ready to move indoors.

He enjoyed the quiet of early morning. While his neighbors were still sleeping, he listened to the first chirps and whistles of the birds waking, watched as the jays and finches began darting over him in search of food. Occasionally, deer would stray into a yard from the surrounding woods, oblivious to him as he worked. Then one would look up and spot him and somehow, a moment later, they would all stand frozen, their huge brown eyes staring at him with innocence and fear. A lot of the neighbors complained of the deer, which had a fondness for tulips and lots of other shrubs and plants. Paul began leaving apples on the edge of the woods for them.

He felt his body getting leaner, stronger, and his skin browned a little more each day in spite of the sunscreen he occasionally slathered on. A few times when the heat was unbearable, he turned the hose on himself, and thought there was nothing so glorious as a blast of icy water on a steaming scalp. Those were moments he felt almost happy.

But by the afternoons, when the heat became so intense he could feel his skin shrinking, he switched over to whatever indoor work he was doing and the old uneasy feeling drifted back. He should be working at a real job. He should be making real money. Not that he wasn't surprised and pleased at what he was bringing in with the landscaping and odd jobs. But after twenty-seven years of being accountable to someone else, of looking beyond the last sale to the next one, he found he was having a hard time letting go. He didn't really know if he could.

He couldn't have asked for a better pitchman than Buffy.

"This is more than just shelves, this is

furniture," she gushed happily, dragging in every neighbor she could. The result: he was now building a cedar closet in her neighbor Elyse's basement and an identical set of shelves for the Skinners, who had the same model as Buffy a block over. So he was busy; he had plenty of work, and was exhausted by the evenings. But a restless feeling still nagged him.

One afternoon, after he showered and threw a frozen dinner in the microwave, he scooped up the pile of mail by the front door and began to leaf through it. There was a note from the postman about a delivery, and he opened the front door to find a package wrapped in brown paper sitting on the steps. He didn't recognize the return address. He took the pile into the kitchen, opened a cold beer, and sat at the table, ripping it open. A moment from his past stared up at him and he felt his body go still. It was he and Joanna, Ted and Jean, about ten or twelve years ago, smiling with joy at him. He remembered when the picture had been taken, on the fourteenth hole at Spyglass, overlooking the Pacific Ocean. They had their arms around each other and behind them the Pacific shimmered in the late morning sunshine. Joanna still had long bangs and that straight, prim pageboy. She looked so young. They all did. Just before the stranger they'd asked to shoot the picture had clicked it, Ted turned to him and said quickly, "Does it get any better than this?" Ted had just made vice president and Paul had broken every sales record that year. They were riding high on success.

Five years later, Ted was divorced. Now he was dead. And Paul was alone and out of a job. How could they know, with those bright smiles, their eyes on the future, what that future held? It was a certainty that things would always be the same. Or, if you worked hard enough, better. But here he was, living proof that didn't always hold true. He opened the note that was taped to the back of the picture.

Dear Paul, the boys found this picture in Ted's locker at the country club when they were cleaning it out. I thought you'd like to have a copy. Although we were no longer married, I miss him and can't believe he's really gone. But I guess in life there are no guarantees and we should make the most of each day. I like to believe that Ted did. Thanks again for being such a good friend to him.

Love, Jean

He sat staring out the window for a long time. He didn't want to die alone, the way Ted did. He didn't want to spend the rest of his life alone. He wondered if his wife ever missed him. He didn't think so. For a while there, he'd hoped he might be able to bridge the distance between them, when they began talking frequently on the phone late at night. There was a softening then, in the way she began speaking to him, as opposed to when she'd first left and everything was laced with her cold determination. Now it seemed she was never there, and after a while he felt foolish and called less and less.

He began sorting through the rest of the mail — bills, credit card offers, and a thick envelope postmarked Pawleys Island, S.C. He swallowed the last of his beer and opened it, knowing what it was. On the bottom of the first page of the listing contract was Joanna's signature, dated July 20. She hadn't sent it right away, and he'd begun to hope it meant she was having second thoughts about selling. About leaving him. But apparently he was wrong. Perhaps she'd just been too busy to get to it.

He got up and turned the microwave on to reheat the frozen dinner that had now cooled. He called Sandy, his realtor, to tell her the papers were ready. She'd be over to pick them up in a few hours, she told him enthusiastically. When the microwave rang, he opened it, pulled out the dinner, and threw it in the garbage. Then he pulled on his shorts and sneakers and went out for a long run.

On Friday evening, Paul went to dinner at Buffy's. Her way of saying thank you, she kept insisting, when he kept saying no. She was lonely, he knew, but she'd slowly been making more acquaintances in the neighborhood. Now as he stood at her front door with a bottle of wine in hand, he felt awkward. They'd developed an easy intimacy he'd never shared with another woman before. There was none of the push and pull of a romantic relationship, which he'd always found to be the case in the past. Not that he had any romantic feelings toward Buffy. He found her attractive in a quirky way and wondered for a moment if he could feel more if she were unattached.

Erik opened the door. "Welcome," he said, stretching a hand and shaking Paul's with vigor.

Paul hadn't expected him. In all the times he'd been at Buffy's over the past weeks, Erik had only been there once, the time they'd fought and Erik quickly left. Traveling, lecturing, working late, Buffy always explained. And when she'd mentioned dinner, she hadn't said he'd be home.

"Please, come in," Erik said, pulling the door wide open.

"Thanks," Paul said, handing him the bottle.

Buffy was in the kitchen arranging a platter of shrimp cocktail. Her halo of frizz was swept back in an elegant chignon and silver studs gleamed in her ears. She wore a gauzy Indian print sundress and looked about eighteen.

"Hi, Paul." She smiled across the room. "Aren't we lucky? Erik's home early from Indiana."

She hadn't known her husband would be there, he realized. She'd dressed like that for him. He suddenly felt uncomfortable.

"I'll uncork the wine," Erik said, holding up the bottle.

"And I'm going to scoop up Emily and take her up to bed."

Paul could see the little girl stretched out on the couch in the adjoining family room, the TV still playing.

"So, you've been a great help to my wife," Erik said, pouring the wine. Then he handed Paul a glass and raised his own. "I appreciate it."

Paul sipped his wine.

"Why don't we go sit out on the deck," Erik suggested. "It seems to be cooling off a bit out there."

Dusk was settling and Paul could see the first fireflies, pinpoints of yellow light, beginning to lift from the grass and dart through the yard like glowing embers.

"Buffy tells me you're between jobs right now, that all this handyman stuff is temporary," Erik said between sips.

Paul laughed. There was an edge to Erik. He wasn't sure if he was innately formal or if he was trying to needle Paul.

"That's right."

"What is it you do?" Erik asked. "Normally, that is."

"I was a vice president with V.I.C. before the merger. Normally I'm in sales."

Erik looked at him and then smiled. "I apologize. I believe I've offended you."

"Not necessary," Paul said, taking another sip of his wine.

Erik stood up, took a long-nosed lighter from next to the grill, and began lighting citronella candles around the deck.

"The bugs can be ferocious sometimes. My wife's latest idea is a screened porch so we could sit out here in peace."

Paul had an idea where this might be going. "I think all the rain this summer has made it worse," he said. "You might want to get a citronella plant, they work pretty well."

"I've never heard of it," he said, putting down the lighter, turning to Paul with a smile. "You really are an amazing wealth of information."

"I also have a background in landscaping."

"Well, you'll have to tell my wife about this citronella plant. I'm afraid a screened porch is not in the budget right now."

They both turned as the French doors opened.

"Who's hungry?" Buffy asked, the platter of shrimp in her hands.

By the third bottle of wine, Paul felt almost drunk. Erik had loosened up and was regaling them with one hilarious story after another of lecture hall gaffes from when he first began teaching college. Buffy's cheeks were flaming, from the heat and the wine, he assumed, and she began fanning herself with a placemat. Little wisps of hair curled around her face, and in the firelight Paul thought she looked beautiful. Erik had begun touching her every chance he could, and now held her hand across the patio table.

"Oh, God, I almost forgot," Buffy said, jumping up. "I made a strawberry short-cake."

When she'd gone into the house, Erik smiled at Paul across the table. He, too, was flushed and perspiring and his eyes seemed to hold some deep secret. Paul remembered the day they'd screamed at each other and how Buffy had thrown him kisses later when he left the house.

"It's nice to be home," Erik sighed. "I get tired of rubber chicken dinners and sometimes my cheeks hurt from those endless polite smiles. But Buffy understands. She likes nice things and on a regular professor's salary, well . . . we wouldn't be living here."

"I understand," Paul said to commiserate, feeling more amiable toward the man. "If I had it to do over again, I think I might have put my family first a little more often."

"Some of us don't have that luxury."

It had come out wrong. It seemed Erik was insulted.

"I'm just saying there were times when I could have done things differently that I didn't. You know what they say about hind-sight."

"Ah, yes, the sensitive man. Women love that, don't they?"

He was needling him again.

"How about some port?" Erik asked then, gathering the nearly empty wineglasses.

He went in to get the bottle as Buffy was coming back out. She set the cake on the table.

"I don't think your husband likes me very much," Paul said in a low voice.

"Erik?" she said, surprised. "Oh, he's probably a little jealous at all the time we spend together." And then she giggled. "It'll do him good."

He left right after dessert, anxious to get away from Erik's condescension, and walked home in the moonlight. It bothered him that Erik's condescending attitude had provoked him. The neighborhood handyman, he'd called him. For as long as he could remember, he'd defined who he was as a man by his job. The more he sold, the more he made. And the better he felt about himself. Now he made just a fraction of that. The funny thing was, he liked woodworking, enjoyed landscaping, and was beginning to get used to the freedom of being his own boss. Why couldn't that be enough?

He saw the *For Sale* sign on his front lawn as he neared the house and then the lockbox dangling from the front doorknob. The list price he'd insisted on was too high, his realtor had cautioned, but she took the listing anyway. He was out of work. She knew he'd have to drop it eventually.

He went up to bed, closed his eyes, and moaned with weariness. Maybe it was time to just let it go. Joanna, the house, the past. It was eating away at him. On his own he could live simply, maybe even buy a small place for cash. Then he could pick and choose what he wanted to do about a job. Where to live.

He could live anywhere, really.

28

One morning on her way to the office, Joanna realized with all the fanfare of an epiphany that she had indeed carved a new life for herself. She had settled into a comfortable niche on Pawleys Island with a job she loved. In fact, two jobs, if she counted Grace. And a boyfriend. No, she thought with a smile, that sounded too juvenile. A lover, yes, that was better, whom she spent every free moment with. In a few weeks she would begin to sit night vigils at her turtle nest. She had full days, a busy life. She realized that in a few days, July would be gone. A shiver ran through her and she turned the air down in her car. Once again, as in her teens, she was spending a summer with an older guy. Love? She wasn't going there just yet. She was simply following her feelings. And the feelings she had for Hank were raw, intense, and almost painfully exquisite. Like that summer at the

Sand Bar when she was crazy about the lifeguard who was a few years older, she'd sometimes lose her breath at the sight of him.

Things with Grace were back on an uneven footing, as in the beginning. It seemed to begin again right after Hank's party a few weeks ago. Perhaps it was just Harley. Grace did nothing to encourage the attention Harley was beginning to pay her until one day, probably deciding he wasn't going to get anywhere on the phone, he just showed up at the house. Joanna was glad. Harley was kind and genuine, and she thought he could be good for Grace, so she found herself encouraging him when he was about to give up. Why shouldn't Grace have a little companionship, even though she thought it unwise at this point? Perhaps Grace was annoyed with her for encouraging the man.

She pulled into the parking lot of *The Pawleys Island Gazette,* her mind still on Grace. She seemed to be resting more between her painting sessions. And her face looked thinner, as if she'd suddenly lost a lot of weight. When Joanna asked how she felt, the answer was always the same, "Fine." Yesterday, however, Joanna had been stunned when she drove Grace to Georgetown and they parked in front of a small brick building on a side street, the Natural Healing Center of Georgetown.

"I might be a little while," Grace had said, getting out of the car. "Why don't you go for a ride or something."

Joanna had driven to the docks, wondering if Hank's old boat was in. A few nights each week he would go out shrimping with his cousin, Sam, and Joanna would lie in bed, eyes open, looking for their lights in the black ocean just beyond the glass doors. She enjoyed missing him. And she always got a bag of shrimp the next day, horrified at first to see them in their true raw state with the heads still on. Hank would laugh. The boat hadn't been in yet, so Joanna walked up and down the River Walk killing time.

When she'd gotten back to the Natural Healing Center, Grace was waiting for her on a bench outside. Her eyes were closed and she seemed to be asleep. But as soon as Joanna pulled up, she smiled and got in the car. Grace didn't say a word, and had seemed almost peaceful on the ride home.

The newsroom was busy as she walked through and settled in at her desk. It was just eight-thirty. She turned on her computer and checked her e-mails first. Harley, with an idea for an article on local reaction to The Chowder House fire. It had indeed been arson and Les was now in jail. Goody, it seemed, had gone back to the restaurant and caught him in the act.

Her last e-mail was from Sarah, whom she'd been e-mailing regularly since she got the job and had access to a computer. It felt like she was part of her life again.

Dear Mom,
I have a perfect, perfect idea. At least it will be if you say yes. Everyone else has agreed. What would you say to a small family reunion at the house, one last time before it's sold? I e-mailed Tim and he's actually coming into JFK airport from Indonesia the end of this week, switching flights to go back to Montana. Only he's coming home instead and pushing that flight back. Daddy, of course, will be there. And I've gotten a few free days and will be flying into Newark on Saturday.

She looked up from the monitor and rubbed her eyes. Sarah had not taken the house going on the market well. Although they'd been through this routine so many times before, this was different, as Sarah kept pointing out. This was the last house they'd all lived in as a family. Joanna knew it, but forced herself not to dwell on it. Sarah's words struck her first with guilt, then annoyance. She was acting like a petulant child.

It all hinges on you, Mom. Please let me know by Wednesday.

That was today. Her daughter had sent the e-mail late Monday evening, knowing she wouldn't get it until this morning. Sarah could be charming and manipulative when she wanted something badly. She stared now at her daughter's words on the screen. How could she just leave? And what about Grace? And then she imagined them together, her son and daughter. A chance to see them both. Hold them in her arms. How could she not go?

She hit the REPLY icon. *Of course I'll be there,* she typed. *I can't wait to see you. I love you dearly, Mom.*

She felt a tremble of excitement as she clicked SEND. My God, she was really going to see them in just a few days. When she'd first come to Pawleys Island, when the days were long and empty and unendingly lonely, it was what she'd dreamed of more than anything.

That evening Joanna had supper with Grace, a wonderful cold gazpacho she'd made with salad and rolls. Grace told her she had a doctor's appointment the next day and would need to be driven in the late afternoon.

"I hope I won't be interfering with any plans of yours," Grace said pointedly.

Once again, she seemed to be dancing around something she wanted to say.

"Actually, I have dinner plans, but it's not a problem. I'll change them."

"With Hank Bishop?" It sounded like an accusation.

"What are you getting at, Grace?"

"It just seems you've been spending a lot of time with the man," she said. "And I've seen the way you look at him. A person would have to be blind not to know what's going on there."

"And what is it you think is going on, Grace?" She was embarrassed. And annoyed. She was a grown woman and her employee. This was none of her business.

"You're having an affair," Grace said, looking up from her soup.

"An affair?"

It was a dirty word from another era. Did

people really have "affairs" now? She hadn't thought about what she and Hank were doing as something illicit. They were two consenting adults.

"Joanna," Grace said gently, as if trying to explain something difficult to a child. "You and your husband may be separated by distance, but legally you're still married."

"Not really," she protested. After all, she'd left her husband months ago. The legal thing was something else. It was like an unpleasant detail she wished she could just eliminate.

"Look, I apologize. It really is none of my business," Grace said, gathering her dirty dishes. "It's just that we live together and I can't help being drawn into your life. I don't want to see you make a big mistake. Years ago I kept my mouth shut when I shouldn't have, with Sean and his wife. I swore I wouldn't make that mistake again."

Joanna took Grace's dishes, stacked her own on top, and got up to put them in the dishwasher.

"Just don't confuse loneliness with love, Joanna," Grace said behind her. "It can easily happen."

She cleaned up the dishes in silence. Grace stepped out onto the deck and Joanna was glad to be left alone. This wouldn't be a good time to tell her about the trip home. Tomorrow she would tell her.

It was nearly dawn and Grace stood at the countertop, where she was cutting a pill in half, glancing up for a moment to see the first bloody tip of the sun poking above the horizon. She took the half pill and cut it in half again. Just one quarter of the pain pill was all she'd allow herself. It was the first one from the bottle she'd gotten at Dr. Jacobs' a few weeks ago. Swallowing it, she saw that the sun was already half up, igniting the ocean in shades of crimson and gold.

The backache was still with her as she walked across the great room and opened the sliding doors. Sitting on the deck, she watched the world slowly come back to life. The beach was quiet, the hushed lapping of the waves the only sound. She heard the door above slide open and remembered: Joanna was leaving this morning. She told Grace she would be gone just for the weekend, but Grace felt lonely already. If it weren't for her affair with Hank Bishop, she would have worried Joanna might not return. She wondered now what it would be like for her, going home to her family after sleeping with another man. In her fifty years of marriage, Grace had never even touched another man. In truth, she'd never been tempted. But things were different today.

She could see Frank's face, alive and smiling, just before he'd gotten sick. That was how she liked to remember him. Before. Before she'd lost him, because he'd left her long before he died. She remembered the chemo sessions, hours in the hospital, a tube pumping toxic chemicals into his arm. He would throw up for days, bent over and retching his insides until there was nothing left to come up but his soul. And it did, a little at a time, until one day he was a gaunt and ravaged shell of the man she loved.

The ache in her spine was easing, and she knew this was how it started. You gave in, a little at a time, to drugs that dulled your mind and eventually silenced your spirit. Pain would wear you down until you just let go. When Joanna had taken her to the Natural Healing Center, she'd thought, why not? It helped Harley with his arthritis. She'd lain on a soft table and closed her eyes, soothed by the gentle music and the gurgle of water from a nearby fountain. She felt little as needles were pressed into her from head to toe. There was a dense thicket of them over her abdomen where the cancer was, and when she opened her eyes she saw they were aflame, like tiny torches igniting her body. Strengthening her chi, the therapist had said. She'd fallen asleep and awoke feeling peaceful and refreshed. And the pain had been absent for days, returning just the night before.

She wasn't looking for a miracle. Grace was too old to believe in such things. But if she could get through her last days without descending into a drugged fog, well, that would be enough. She had work to do. Ideas that burned within her that she needed to put on canvas. Just a few more, at least. Last night, near midnight, as she sat in this same chair and watched the stars glitter in the black sky, she thought of Van Gogh's *Starry Night*. The stars like swirling pinwheels against a backdrop soft as black gauze. She couldn't remember ever doing a night scene. It would be different, a new kind of challenge, and a definite change in colors.

Tonight, she decided, she would begin.

29

Joanna looked down on the smooth, rolling hills of northern New Jersey, lush and green from the midsummer rains. This was where she had worked and shopped and cooked and cleaned, driven the curving roads that wound through those hills like ribbons of blacktop. She'd had a life down there, an existence that now seemed foreign to her from thousands of feet above, looking out the window of the plane. A kind of life, anyway. She'd left all those months ago, after all, because it had been so empty. And it still amazed her that she had done it — just walked away. Now with the clear vision of time and distance, she could see what a different person she'd been then. Fragile and numb. Lonely. Scared most of all because she wasn't really certain she could survive on her own. But here she was, having crossed the threshold of a new life that made coming back to her old one a little unnerving, despite the fact she couldn't wait to see her children.

She pictured Hank when she'd kissed him goodbye last night. He left then for the shrimp boat, where he would be working all night. So she drove herself to the airport just after watching the sun come up over the ocean. It was better that way. She wasn't sure why, but Joanna was uncomfortable with her past and present coming so close together. As the plane began its descent, she realized Hank was probably just getting home to bed after docking in Georgetown and off-loading their catch. She grew so lost in her thoughts of him that she didn't even realize the plane had stopped until the passenger beside her got up and began pulling his bag out of the overhead.

She hadn't told her family what time she'd be in, preferring to take a cab from the airport. Leaning her head back on the black leather seat, she closed her eyes, tired, excited, her breath suddenly coming in short and slippery spurts. She wondered if she was walking into an ambush of sorts. With all of them together, did her children — Sarah, especially — hope she would have some miraculous change of heart and come home for good? She needed to brace herself for the arguments and persuasions that were bound to be leveled at her. But at the moment she could think of only one thing — seeing them.

Before she knew it, the cab was driving through Sparta, already clogged with Saturday morning traffic as shoppers began their weekend errands. Pots of flowers sat in front of the antiques shops, coffee houses, and boutiques lining Main Street, and gas lanterns graced each corner. Then they were on the winding county road that would take them out of town to Greenwich Hills.

Everything looked different, as it does when you've been gone a long time. And she'd been gone nearly half a year. In spite of the fact that as they got closer her nerves seemed to hum with the familiar anxious feeling of getting home and seeing her family, that strange surreal feeling overtook her once again. She wasn't really in this cab, but somewhere up above, watching this all happen to someone else. Then the driver pulled onto Manor Drive, into her neighborhood, riding past stately brick and Tudor homes, all meticulously landscaped. As they turned into her driveway, Joanna felt a sudden surge of tears clog her throat. The house looked so different. A beautiful stone wall curved around one side of it. Flowers bloomed everywhere, and she saw purple

clematis clinging to the mailbox, a gardening project she'd long talked about but
never gotten to.

She hesitated when the car pulled away,
wondering if she should ring the bell. She
was a visitor in her own home. She pulled
out her keys and went in the back mudroom
door. Morning light flooded the kitchen as
she walked in. "Hello, anybody home?" She
saw the note on the center island, where
they always left such notes for each other.
Gone to the store. Tim went to pick up Sarah.
Be back soon. Paul.

She walked through the house one room
at a time like a stranger seeing things for
the first time. Seeing the ghosts of them in
each room, as they had been. Little things
had changed, she assumed because of selling the house. The stenciling it had taken
her weeks to paint over the kitchen cabinets
was gone, covered with good old antique
white paint, the harbinger of a transferee
sale. Sarah's room had lost its lavender
glow, also the victim of neutralizing. The
whole house was immaculate, uncluttered,
homey, and inviting. Paul had done well
keeping things up, inside and out.

The biggest surprise was when she went
into the garage, intending to get some
gardening books she'd left behind. They

weren't near the back wall anymore, but stacked neatly next to her gardening tools on a lovely new potting table, something she'd wanted for years. Her spades and trowels, the big potting tray where she mixed soil, all of it beautifully laid out on the stained shelves, looking like a picture from a gardening magazine. And then she saw the saws and workbench in the empty bay her Jeep used to occupy. She couldn't believe it. Paul's father's things that they had carted from house to house for years, that were still sitting in the basement when she'd left last March. A sudden, loud buzzing made her jump and she turned to see the other garage door slowly open as a small green Honda pulled in. It wasn't until he got out of the car that Paul looked up and noticed her standing there.

"Joanna!"

He was surprised to find her there, she could see. And for a moment she just stood there, frozen, her heart firing like a trip-hammer.

"Hi, Paul . . . ," she said, as he said, "I picked up some groceries for the week-end . . ."

They both laughed.

Should she kiss him on the cheek? Offer a friendly hug? Before she could decide, he went around and opened the trunk.

"I'll help you bring them in," she said, filling her arms with bags instead.

Like the house, he looked different. As if he was the one who was spending the summer at the beach. He was tanned to a deep brown and his green eyes were striking under those heavy, straight brows now flecked with gold. Even his sandy hair was bleached yellow on the ends. He looked younger and handsomer, reminding her of when she first saw him across that bar nearly thirty years ago.

"Timmy's here already?" she asked, putting the bags on the counter and going back for more.

Paul followed. "He got in last night. He looks good. Lost a little weight on that jungle diet, but he's got some amazing stories."

"I've missed him so much. Not that I haven't missed Sarah, but she's so much easier on the phone. Tim talks two minutes, then he's antsy to get off."

"I know what you mean."

It seemed like an endless supply of bags piling up on the counter. "What did you do, buy the store out?"

"I haven't really kept much in the house. I do a lot of takeout or microwave stuff, so I needed to stock up. But I did get something for everyone," he laughed, pulling a box of Lucky Charms out of a bag.

She laughed, too. "I think Sarah has outgrown those. I'm sure she's into something healthy for breakfast like fruit and yogurt."

"Wrong," Paul interrupted. "I saw a box in her kitchen out in Colorado."

"Really?" She was more amazed that Paul had noticed than that her thoroughly modern daughter still had the taste buds of a child.

They put the food away like any normal married couple doing their Saturday morning chores. Paul didn't just look different, he seemed different to her. She couldn't quite put her finger on it. The restless energy that always made her feel as if he had something more important to do was gone. He seemed genuinely happy in the moment. Yet she caught him looking at her a few times, as if she were a stranger he was uncertain about. And in a way, she realized, she was.

"I think I'll put my things upstairs and freshen up. Can you manage the rest?"

He smiled and nodded and she caught the irony of her question. He'd been managing the house without her now for months.

She took her small suitcase up the stairs and paused in the hallway, about to turn to their bedroom. Then she realized: it's Paul's bedroom now. She took her things to the spare room down the hall, filled with mismatched antiques and an old sleigh bed, a cheerful yellow room she'd decorated with the same care as all the other rooms in the house. Never imagining she'd be coming back one day almost a stranger and sleeping in it. It was odd, too, being in her house and not having a dozen things to occupy her time. In the past, she'd always done two things at once — balancing the checkbook in between loads of wash, paying bills while returning phone calls. Now she stood in the spare bedroom wondering what she and Paul would do while they waited for their children.

"I thought we'd have a barbecue tonight," he said, when she came back down to the kitchen. He was pouring marinade into a plastic bag filled with chicken pieces.

"I think I'll go cut some flowers for the table," she said, opening the drawer where she kept her shears.

"They're out in the garage."

"Oh, yes. I saw the potting table."

Without turning, he said, "I was trying to organize the garage and I remembered you saying that would be the perfect thing for storing all your gardening tools."

She didn't know what to say. "It's lovely," she managed, and then slipped out to the refuge of the garage.

Her gardens, where she'd spent so many hours trying to bring her visions to life over the last few years, were at their peak. Tall seas of Shasta daisies, deep pink coneflowers. The mounds of monarda she'd put in just last fall were covered with humming bees, feasting on their sweet fragrance. As she began snipping blooms, she thought: this was where I spent so many hours, from the first mild days in April until the first killing frost in fall. She loved to garden, to create beauty where there had been nothing but barren ground. But it had also filled the many hours she'd spent alone.

The beds were free of weeds, the leaves all healthy and intact. Whatever Paul was doing to combat the ever-present slugs, which often left her foliage looking like tattered rags, it was working. She held an armful of flowers and was just rounding the house when a car pulled in the driveway. She watched as her son and daughter sat for a moment, then got out and stood beside the car, laughing at some shared joke, unaware of her. They looked older, taller. Then she saw Sarah's face grow serious and Tim walked around the car and put his arms around her. Joanna stepped back quickly so they wouldn't spot her. She'd waited for this moment for so long, had thought she would run at first sight of them. But now she couldn't move. She bit her lip to keep the sudden tears back. Then she turned and walked around the house and through the back kitchen door. She was standing there with Paul when they came in through the garage a few minutes later.

"Oh, my God, Mom, you're here," Sarah screamed, dropping her bags and running to her, pulling her into a tight hug. Behind Sarah she could see Tim, smiling almost shyly, waiting his turn.

"Look at your hair!" her daughter gushed, pulling away. "You look fantastic. Hey, Dad, what happened to your beard?"

"Too hot," she heard him mutter.

Tim walked over then. "Do you mind?" he asked, pushing his sister aside.

His arms went around her like bands of steel, holding her so tight she nearly lost her breath. She inhaled the musky scent that had always been him, and felt the first tears slip down her face. "Oh, Timmy, how I've missed you."

"Me, too, Mom," he whispered.

They separated then and the four of them stood there for a moment in silence.

"Who's hungry?" Paul called, opening the refrigerator.

She watched him across the room, pulling out cold cuts and rolls, and she thought, that's my part. That's what I do. But the three of them began making sandwiches and Tim went searching in the depths of the fridge for his infamous honey mustard, while she just stood there, watching them.

They had sandwiches on the deck, an early lunch since everyone was starving. Except Paul, who said he'd probably go for a run soon. They could have been any normal family, the conversation and laughter flowing nonstop. First Tim, grossing them out with his jungle menu of grubs, larvae, and dog. And Sarah, so thrilled over Paris she reminded Joanna of when she was a child, working herself into a fever of excitement on Christmas. Paul laughed and joined in, but a few times she found him staring across the yard.

From that moment, it seemed to her as if the weekend revolved around food, none of which she made. Her family treated her like a guest in her own house, eager to feed and please her, but try as she did, she couldn't seem to slip into a comfortable place.

■ ■ ■ ■

Joanna lay in bed that night, exhausted but unable to sleep. It was ironic that something she had thought would make her so happy had thrown her into an abyss of guilt and uncertainty. Too little, too late, she thought. It was the kind of time she used to dream about when they lived as a family. All of them together. The emotions that had choked her all day came flooding now in a rush of silent sobs as she lay in the dark, listening to the low bass beat of Pink Floyd playing in Timmy's room.

There was a short knock and her bedroom door opened. She could see Sarah standing there in the hall light.

"Are you sleeping?" Sarah whispered.

Quickly she wiped her face with the sheet. "No, come in. Just turn on that small light over there; the one overhead is too bright."

Sarah came in and sat beside her on the bed. Her daughter's hair was pulled back in a ponytail and she wore a pair of chic blue striped pajamas.

"Are you crying, Mom?"

Wiping the tears, she stupidly shook her head no.

"What is it?" Sarah asked nervously.

Joanna was always the one who wiped away the tears, comforted hurts and sorrow. Convinced her children that everything would be all right. Now her daughter tried to soothe her with soft whispers.

"It's just very emotional," she said softly. "Seeing you all."

"I know, it is for me, too."

They were quiet for a few moments and then Sarah pulled the ribbon out of her hair and began playing with it as she talked.

"You know, Mom, I told Tim I was afraid you might think this was some kind of setup. Daddy's changing and all, but I know how lonely and unhappy you've been for a long time. Tim does, too." She hesitated a moment. "I'm adult enough to know that what I want can't always be. You've always given us everything. Daddy, too. You have a right to choose your own life now." As she said it, Sarah's own eyes filled with tears.

What Sarah wanted and didn't say, Joanna knew, was for them to stay a family. She'd never had that herself, a close, loving family, and had wanted it in the worst way for her children. That no matter how old you were, there would always be that one constant in your life: home.

"So tell me about your job." Sarah smiled, changing the subject. "Writing for a newspaper sounds exciting."

"Well, I'm starting at the bottom, taking real baby steps. But I'm learning. Sometimes I think it may be a future for me."

"Wow. My mother the writer."

"Oh, I wouldn't go that far yet."

"Martin asked me to marry him again," she said suddenly, as if Joanna had known about the other times.

"Well," Joanna said, taken aback. "You've obviously said no before, then."

"I haven't said yes yet, let's put it that way."

Sarah stretched out beside her on her back, looking up at the ceiling. She watched her daughter, those incredibly long lashes that had amazed her when she was a baby. The tiny scar on her forehead where Tim had accidentally hit her with a golf club at a driving range when they were little. But a woman's face now.

"I don't know. I love him, I'm sure of that. And the thought of us going to Paris together is so incredible it almost seems unreal. Like a dream you always have that you think can't possibly ever come true. It's hard to explain," she said and then turned to look at her. "It's like it's so good it's scary."

Joanna thought of those first years she was

married and the fierce, protective love she had for her two babies. The joy she felt being with her husband, sharing that intense love for them. And the realization that her dream of love and a family had come true. She remembered, too, the fear that went along with it. Could something so precious really last?

"How long have you known Martin?"

"Over a year. The thing is, we were friends first. I had no idea we'd end up falling in love. He's so kind, he's got the best heart of anyone I've ever known."

"That sounds like one of the best qualities you could hope for in a guy. So what is it that's holding you back?"

She didn't answer at first, and then gave a little shrug. "I don't know. I can't really put my finger on it."

Joanna had always thought of marriage for life. And had not taken her own vows lightly. The last thing she ever wanted to endure, or watch one of her children endure, was a divorce. Hank was right, the agony of those first months after she'd left was worse than a death. It had nearly paralyzed her with anguish. She was stronger now, yes, but it wasn't over.

"Why don't you quit beating yourself up and just give it more time? It doesn't sound like Martin's going anywhere without you."

"I know," she said, a tear slipping out of the corner of her eye. Joanna brushed it away with a finger and then Sarah turned and came to her and they held each other for a long moment.

"Oh, honey, how I love you."

"Me, too, Mom." She kissed Joanna's cheek. "Good night."

Joanna lay again in the dark for a long time, thinking about how hard life was. Did you ever really know what the right thing was? she wondered. People followed their hearts like some sort of divining rod, hoping it would lead them to happiness. She thought of herself when she'd first met Paul. It wasn't what Sarah described. There was instant attraction followed by a longing to always be together that they both assumed was love. And maybe it did grow into that after marriage and children. But Joanna had gotten pregnant and the choice, really, had been taken away. She knew in her heart, though, that she had no regrets. Whatever went wrong, there were good times in the last twenty-six years. And two precious gifts, her children.

Grace didn't get to begin her painting of the night sky that evening, after all. After napping in the afternoon to make up for the lost hours of sleep the night before, she fixed a light supper. It was quiet without Joanna popping in, or just hearing her footsteps overhead. But the houses around her were busy with the usual commotion as the Saturday rentals changed hands. Families left and, a few hours later, new families moved in for their week or two of vacation. Occasionally they would wave or chat about the weather, but no one was ever there long enough to do more.

As the afternoon light began to fade, the beach was alive with after-dinner activity. Grace took her canvas and supplies outside. Kites were flying in the early evening breeze; walkers strolled by followed by dogs leaping in the surf. And then she saw a familiar head coming up her deck steps. Harley.

"I knocked on your front door a few times and then thought, if I were living on the beach, where would I spend such a beautiful evenin'? And here you are."

He smiled, and reached for her hand formally, as he did every time he saw her. Not shaking it, just a polite squeeze of affection.

"Actually I was just getting ready to work."

He flushed with embarrassment. "I do apologize," he said, backing away. "It was presumptuous of me to just drop in."

How could she be so rude? Her mother would have put soap in her mouth.

"No, please, it's all right," she said, putting down her pencils. "At least stay for a cup of tea. Or would you prefer something stronger?"

He turned and smiled then, giving in quickly. "I do enjoy a drop of bourbon now and again," he said, almost shyly.

Before she knew it, night had settled around them and they were still on her deck, he on his second bourbon, with lots of ice, she still nursing her first. It was a gorgeous summer night again, the air soft, the stars glittering in the clear black sky with an intensity she was certain she'd never seen before. She would remember this and paint it tomorrow, each quiver of light that seemed to tell her: *There's more than you know.* She thought of Van Gogh, sipping on his absinthe, looking at such a night, and she understood his masterpiece. Such beauty was fleeting, almost painful.

They talked of books and old movies, the changes the world had undergone in their lives. And then, as if reading her mind, Harley asked her: "Are you afraid to die?"

She was taken aback, at first. But they were both, after all, near the end of the journey.

"No, not really. I've certainly seen enough of it, though, to scare me."

"I'm not, either. I believe we do go on. I don't know how really, perhaps in some other dimension. Or perhaps the Hindus are right. We just come back here all over again and get a chance to do it right."

"I am afraid of losing myself, though," she said. "I saw that with my husband."

"I saw it with my wife," he answered quietly.

"Do you have any regrets?"

He didn't answer right away. She wondered if he regretted putting his wife in a nursing home, as she did with Frank. Wondered if he ever shared her unspeakable thoughts of rescuing him from his hell on earth.

"Oh, I guess just the usual," he said then with a sigh. "Work less, worry less. Be with my family more."

She smiled, understanding.

"What do you say to a game of cards?" she asked, ready to change the subject.

They played for several hours. They talked easily and he made her laugh with some of his newspaper stories. It was late when he finally rose to leave. She'd given him two cups of coffee, while realizing she hadn't thought of her illness all night. At the door he took her hand again, this time raised it to his lips.

"I can't, Harley," she said suddenly. "You can't expect . . ."

He interrupted. "Friendship. That's all. I'm just looking for a friend."

She said nothing and closed the door, wondering if that wasn't too much to ask.

30

Joanna opened her eyes, and through the lace curtains she could see the sky was a soft gray. It was early, the sun not even up yet. But she was wide awake, and decided to go for a walk. She dressed quietly, tiptoed downstairs, and found her son lying on the family room couch, flipping channels.

"What are you doing up so early?" she asked him.

He clicked the TV off and turned to her. "I'm all screwed up. Still on Indonesian time, I guess."

"Sarah was up late, still on mountain time. I guess we're all a little out of sync."

"Going walking?"

"Uh-huh. Want to come?"

He hesitated. Normally, it would be a quick no thanks.

"Okay. Just let me get my sneakers."

They followed the serpentine streets that wound through the neighborhood like a maze, leading to the walking trail in the woods that surrounded it. It was the route she'd walked hundreds of times, nearly every morning before work, in her other life. It was quiet now and they didn't speak for a while as birds flitted above them. The only other sound was the alternate soft thud or rustle of their sneakers as they traveled the footpath that was dirt and pine needles with an occasional stretch of dried oak leaves. Through the trees she could see the sun just beginning to peek above the horizon. She hadn't even realized it, but she missed the woods. The hushed quiet as if you could hear the trees themselves breathing, the tranquility that never failed to fill her with peace. For months now her feet had felt only sand, while her ears heard the endless washing of the ocean.

Joanna looked over at her son. "So, in a few weeks you'll be starting your last year."

"Not exactly."

"What do you mean? You're planning to finish, aren't you?"

"Oh, sure. But it won't be my last year. I'm gonna start right on my master's next summer."

"Really?"

They slowed their pace, picking their way around a puddle.

"The head of the department offered me a teaching assistant's position, which means my tuition will be free. I'll just have to get a job for living expenses."

"So besides teaching, you'll take graduate classes and work a second job?" It sounded like a heavy load. She glanced over at him again, baseball hat on his head, eyes down on the trail. "Have you talked to your father?"

"I don't expect him to help me anymore after this year. Especially with the job situation."

"And how does he feel about you continuing on?"

He turned to her with a little laugh. Their pace was brisk and they spoke in quick, almost breathless spurts.

"Actually, I think he's okay with it. When he came to see me I sort of laid the groundwork. Anyway, he knows I'm not him, never will be."

She was surprised. And pleased for Timmy. This battle had been waging since he'd first left for college and announced his plans to study anthropology.

"Besides, Dad's changed a lot. I hate to say it, but I think leaving V.I.C. has actually been good for him. Except now he might be going back."

"What?"

"Yeah, they offered him a consulting position."

"Really?" She stepped in front of him as she wound her way around a fallen tree. "When does he start?"

"He hasn't taken it yet," Tim said. "I'm hoping he doesn't."

She slowed and waited for him to make his way around the tree. "Why?"

"I don't know. I guess I shouldn't say that. But when I got here Friday, he asked me to help him bring up all Pop's tools to the garage. And then he started telling me about all the work he's been doing, the landscaping jobs and all. He made these shelves for a lady named Buffy that were really incredible."

"You saw them?"

"Yeah. She dropped off that tray of homemade cookies the other night and we got talking and ended up going over. Mom, I couldn't believe Dad could do something like that. It was really nice, kind of like our wall unit."

She thought of the potting table.

"Anyway, she got him all these other jobs and he's been building things all over the neighborhood," Tim went on. "The thing is, he seems happy and guilty at the same time.

Like if you're enjoying it, can it really be work?"

They were out of the woods again, coming into the other side of the development. The sun was on them now, and already it was heating the morning air.

"Maybe those things don't really pay enough?" she suggested.

"Nah. I don't really think that's it. Besides, if it's just him, how much does he really need? He won't have a big house to worry about."

They were both silent for the next block. She couldn't see Paul not taking the job. Not the Paul she knew, anyway. They began to slow down as they approached home, their breath evening out. Paul had considerately put the *For Sale* sign in the back of the garage for the weekend.

"So, I guess you'll be out in Montana for at least another few years, then?"

"Realistically, five. Until I finish my doctorate."

"Dr. Harrison, I presume?" she said to tease him and he laughed.

But Joanna was just trying to cover her own sorrow. He and Sarah would both be so far away and for such a long time. After being together these few days, it was harder to accept again.

"It's really not so far," Tim said, as if reading her thoughts. And then he reached and put his arm around her. "I'll come visit you, wherever you are, Mom. And I want you to promise you'll come out and spend time in Montana. You may not want to leave."

Sarah was still sleeping when they slipped back in the house, but Paul was out on the deck having coffee and reading the Sunday papers. He'd already gone out and gotten a bag of their favorite bagels. Joanna thought of this Buffy he'd mentioned a lot, whom Tim had met. Who almost seemed to be a part of his life. She wondered if there was something going on there. But, really, who was she to question? Or judge.

That Sunday morning Grace took a taxi to church. She prayed for her children, as she did every day, and said a prayer for Joanna's safe return. Then once again she asked God to give her the strength to get through her illness gracefully. She added a final prayer for Harley.

When she came out it was already hot, but family and friends were congregating in front of the church, and it struck her what a lonely life she'd pushed herself into. She smiled at the faces she saw each week, got into the air-conditioned cab, and remem-

370

bered all the Sundays her family gathered around her table for dinner. She sighed. At least her children were all alive and well.

She stopped at the bakery on the way home, and while the cab waited, she picked up a pecan coffee cake. Her clothes were getting loose, although she still ate. But she joked to herself that she might as well take advantage of the situation. Pulling into her driveway, she noticed a strange car parked beside her house and thought it must be one of the vacation renters at the wrong address. She climbed out slowly, holding the white bakery box tied with string.

"Hey, lady. You need help with that cake?"

She looked up. Her son was sitting on the steps beside her front door.

"Sean," she whispered, her heart squeezing with joy. She hadn't seen him in nearly eight months.

In a moment he was crushing her in his arms and she began to cry. Sobs threatened to overtake her and she pushed him away.

"Let me look at you," she said, wiping her eyes. "You look wonderful."

He laughed. "Sure, only a mother doesn't notice the thinning hair and the tire around the middle."

"Now, Sean. You look the same."

"Well, forty does things to a man."

"You're hardly middle-aged," she said and then laughed. "But you're getting close."

"And you look like you've lost weight," Sean said.

"Oh, you know what they say," she quickly replied. "You lose your taste for things as you age, and it's quite true. Plus I've been walking more."

They went into the house, and while he put his things in the spare bedroom, she gathered her art supplies and tucked them in the hall closet. Sean would only be with her a few days, she told herself. Her projects could wait.

She made coffee and they had cake while he told her of his life in the last months. Lately he'd been working the Silver Meteor, Amtrak's New York–to–Miami run. He had five days off and decided to deadhead back to Charleston and rent a car to come and visit her.

"Are you seeing anyone?" she asked.

He smiled. "You never change," he said and she detected a note of chastising. "Yes, I'm seeing a nice lady from Tampa. But it's nothing serious."

He got up and took their plates.

"I thought I'd go out exploring a bit this afternoon and then I'll take you out for dinner. Pick the nicest restaurant around."

Before she knew it, she was alone again. She stretched out on the couch, glad for the time to catch up with her thoughts. And she needed the rest. Naps had never been part of her daily routine, and she didn't want to worry her son. And then she remembered her appointment the next day, another acupuncture session. She reached for the phone and left a message, canceling.

Her son charmed her again over dinner. As he charmed everyone. He was full of stories of his travels, and Grace wondered, not for the first time, if it was this ability to draw people to him that kept him from committing to a more traditional life. This need for attention. His travels gave him an endless supply of adventures to share.

Already he was talking enthusiastically of the Santee River Delta, just south of Georgetown, where he'd gone that afternoon. The only delta on the East Coast, he told her. From the foot trails he'd seen some rare birds and thought a boat would give him an even better look at the wildlife.

It was dark when they returned from dinner, and they sat on her deck for a while, enjoying the cool night breeze.

"You don't get lonely here, all by yourself?" he suddenly asked.

She was surprised by the question. Sean rarely got this personal.

"I've got some friends. I keep busy. And it's so beautiful here," she answered vaguely. "It's a good place for me to be right now."

"Marie's worried about you."

"Did she send you to check up on me?"

He turned and looked at her, reached over and took her hand. "No, that was my idea. I think about Dad and know I should have been around a little more," he said.

Guilt flooded her. If he knew, what would he think of her? Did she really have the right to lie to her own child? As she struggled with what to say, he suddenly stood.

"It's a beautiful night. I think I'll go for a walk on the beach and work off some of that dinner. You don't mind, do you?"

"No, of course not." She was relieved, in fact. This dance was difficult, like an extended game of charades.

He went down the deck steps, and in the moonlight she could see him walking up the beach, just like any vacationer passing by. But it was her son. He was really here. Tears filled her eyes at this unexpected gift. Sean. From the time he was born, he was different from her other children. Blond, while they were dark, wild and high-spirited where they were responsible. She'd named him Sean after her father, because from the beginning he seemed to be sprung from her Irish roots. Everyone, including his older brother and sister, spoiled him. Everyone except his father. They'd clashed right from the beginning. Sean had a mind of his own and could never follow Frank's old-fashioned ways. Sometimes she thought she'd spoiled him most of all to make up for the fights and silences with his father.

She leaned her head back and closed her eyes, exhausted from the long day and the tumbling emotions her son had brought. Then she sat up, remembering. Joanna would be home tomorrow. And Sean would still be there.

Could she trust Joanna to keep her secret?

31

Joanna was glad Paul stayed behind when she went with the kids to the local flea market that was held every Sunday in the summer. He'd never been one for shopping. Now she walked with Sarah and Tim up and down the long stretches of stalls and tables filled with antiques, clothes, collectibles, and anything else imaginable. A high pressure system had rolled in from Canada and the sky was a clear and vivid blue, the air warm yet crisp with no humidity. It reminded her of a New England summer day.

As she bought Tim a handmade sweater and Sarah silver jewelry, she was reminded of the end of summer back-to-school shopping she'd always loved. It seemed like old times. Joanna found a light blue shirt the color of Hank's eyes and held it up, picturing it on him.

"That would look great on Dad with his tan," Sarah said, coming up behind her. It was spontaneous, innocent, so she just smiled. "It would. Let's get it for him." In the past, they'd always brought him something.

At a kiosk loaded with books, magazines, and school supplies, she picked up a leather-bound journal and flipped through the blank pages. How many years had it been since she'd written in a journal? Twenty? Twenty-five? She paid for it and for a book of poetry for Hank, and held the bag as if it were some tangible link to the new Joanna, who seemed to be quickly evaporating as she felt herself slipping back into her old life.

It was late afternoon when they returned home. Paul was outside with the hose, watering the flowers. Her old job.

"Hey, Dad, you hungry?" Tim called as they got out of the car. "Let's order some pizza."

"I can make us something," Joanna offered.

"Ooh, Nicolosi's pizza," Sarah drooled. "You don't really want to cook, Mom, do you?"

She did, but she just smiled. "Are you kidding?"

They went in while Paul continued watering. By the time the pizzas were delivered, he'd joined them out on the deck. Sarah and Joanna were each having a glass of wine, and he and Timmy each held a bottle of beer.

"I forgot, you're legal now," she said to Tim. It was just something else to get used to, another milestone, like when your child reached high school, or got a license.

"Don't worry, Mom. I don't abuse it," he said with a smile. "Besides with my schedule, I don't really have a lot of time for fooling around."

She knew that and was grateful once again for such levelheaded kids.

"Oh, Dad, we got you something at the flea market," Sarah said, and ran inside. She came back out a minute later with the bag and pulled out the light blue shirt.

"Very nice," Paul said, taking it from her.

This was part of the ritual, too. They always brought something back for him and he always complimented their selection. He held the shirt up. Sarah was right, Joanna thought, the light blue against his tan skin lit up his eyes and made his hair even blonder.

"Thanks, guys." He even smiled at her.

When they were tossing the paper plates inside the pizza boxes, Sarah asked, "You guys wouldn't mind if Tim and I went to a movie tonight, would you?"

"What's playing?" Joanna asked.

"Oh, just a screamer. Nothing you guys would be interested in," Tim said. "Some kids made a movie with their own cameras for a couple thousand bucks, and it's the biggest movie around."

"Yeah, let's see how long Tim can go without hiding behind his popcorn," Sarah said, teasing him.

And then they were gone and Joanna and Paul found themselves suddenly alone on the deck, across the table from each other. She thought back to her conversation with Sarah last night, and reminded herself this wasn't a setup.

"Timmy tells me you were offered a consulting position with V.I.C."

He nodded.

"Are you going to take it?"

"I haven't decided. I can't seem to make up my mind. Five months ago I would have grabbed it. Now," he paused, "I'm not sure I want to go back to all that."

This was amazing to her. This was the man she'd begged to turn down a transfer once and a promotion another time. A man who could never say no. "What would you do if you didn't?"

He laughed a little. "Actually, I'm not sure

about that, either. I like working outdoors, I like woodworking. And I like being my own boss."

"The potting table really is beautiful," she told him and could see his pleasure. "If I had seen that in a store, I don't think I could have resisted."

"Well, it's yours to keep," he said, giving her a long look. "At some point we're going to have to figure out what to do with everything else in the house."

"I know. Not now, though, okay?"

"Okay."

They seemed to run out of things to say then. Paul went in to watch television and she sat with a cup of tea, paging through *The New York Times* until it grew too dark on the deck. Then she went upstairs to take a bath. She was grateful for the time alone. She felt emotionally spent, and the thing she kept holding at bay, wouldn't even let herself think of, was tomorrow. When they would leave, one by one.

After her bath, she lay on top of the sleigh bed with a magazine, so sleepy it was an effort to turn the pages. But she was determined to stay awake and see the kids when they got home. Their remaining time together was too precious.

■ ■ ■ ■

She heard a noise and opened her eyes, realizing she'd fallen asleep after all. Turning over, she was startled to see Paul, sitting beside her on the bed.

"What time is it?" she asked, her voice thick with sleep.

"Near eleven."

"Are the kids back yet?"

He shook his head. "They called to say they were going to Porter's Pub to shoot some pool, so I don't imagine they'll be in for a while."

"Oh." She was still deep in the throes of sleep and fought a yawn, struggling to keep her eyes open.

He stared down at her as he lifted a hand and began stroking her face with soft fingertips, barely touching skin. Then he ran his fingers through her hair, again and again, as if combing it, a lovely whisper of a touch that sent her drifting. Her eyes closed.

"You're so beautiful," she heard Paul say, as if somewhere in a dream.

"Mmmnn . . ." She was floating back to sleep.

Then his lips touched her forehead, each cheek, her nose, like a butterfly's wings searching her face until finally alighting on her mouth. Her breath caught. And with that breath came a flood of emotions as she drank in a smell from her past, the sweet fragrance of the outdoors, sunshine and fresh air and cut grass. The way he came to her once upon a time on Saturday afternoons when the kids napped and he'd just finished yard work and they'd make love in a hurry of soft laughter, with the yellow afternoon light streaming through the window. A scent she'd all but forgotten. And now in this dream, she was back there in that time of joy and babies and youth.

He cupped her face and she opened her eyes. His eyes burned into her. Then before she could speak, he kissed her again, with urgency, as he shifted and lay beside her, pulling her to him, her body melting naturally into his as it had done for years. He pressed against her and longing flooded through her middle like a rush of hot liquid. She breathed him in and put her arms around him, pulling him to her, her lips seeking the old scar on his neck as they always had.

As he kissed her, his fingertips brushed a path up her arm, across her shoulder, and down her collarbone until they found her breast and began tracing circles around her nipple as she moaned.

"Oh, Joanna . . ."

He buried his lips in her neck as his other hand lifted her nightgown, pressing his hardness into her, and as she felt herself falling away, she suddenly saw Hank's face. Hank . . .

Her eyes flew open.

She shook her head, pushing on Paul's chest to pull away from him. She had to stop this.

"Nnno . . . ," she tried to say, but it was a mumble as her own mouth was crushed against his shoulder. She pushed harder. "No, Paul, stop."

Suddenly he was still. They lay side by side, just a few inches apart, her eyes riveted to the scar on his neck, unable to meet his face. He was breathing hard, as if he'd just stopped running. Then he pulled in a long, slow breath and let it out in obvious frustration. She looked up. He was staring at her. His eyes were full of hurt.

"I'm sorry. I can't," she said.

His face hardened and a moment later he sat up. She lay there unable to speak, a heavy chain of guilt wrapped around her heart. This man was still her husband. And she was sleeping with someone else.

A moment later he stood and walked to

the window. He stood there a long time without speaking.

Then, with his back still to her, he said. "So, there's no turning back? This is what you really want?"

She closed her eyes. How could she turn back? After everything it had taken her these past six months to find some little happiness in her life, how could he expect that? This wasn't real anymore. This was just a moment of nostalgia, and she had to be careful she didn't mistake it for something that once was, but could never be again. Still . . . she felt his pain.

She sat up, searching for the right words, and spoke to his back. "You know, for the past twenty-six years everything I've done was, I thought, in the best interest of our family. It probably seems like I'm being selfish right now. I mean, here we all are, gathered one last time because I'm breaking up this family . . ." She choked on the last words and couldn't continue as she tried to compose herself.

He turned to her then. "I could say the same thing. Everything I've ever done, even though you may not have thought so, was what I thought was in the best interest of this family. I worked hard for us."

He stared at her and she couldn't bear it,

she looked down at her hands, which were twisting the hem of her nightgown. They were silent for a while.

"I'm sorry," she said. "I know you did. But, Paul, you never even listened to me. Everything for you has always been duty, responsibility, work. I've felt like just another obligation to you . . ."

"That's unfair. I loved you."

"You had no time for me."

"Do you think I felt loved? When was the last time you showed me any affection? After the first few years, and you know we were happy then, you began putting that wall up. Sure I had to work and travel, but Christ, I had a wife and two kids to support. I was scared shitless. And it seemed like nothing I did could ever please you."

"Now *you're* being unfair. I was lonely, Paul. Lonely as hell. But you always found time to run or golf. Everything else always came first. Not me."

He looked down at the floor and she could see he was grinding his teeth. After a moment he said, "I'm sorry. Maybe I was being selfish. But I thought I was doing the right thing."

"And so do I," she said, but it came out little more than a whisper.

He heard, though, she saw it on his face.

"So that's it, it's over for good?"

If there was a way she could have wiggled out of that moment, she would have. Years of resentment suddenly slipped away as she faced this man she'd been married to for more than twenty-five years. A good man who she still had so many feelings for. A man who obviously didn't want to let her go. Her heart was now breaking for him. And as she felt her emotions begin to overwhelm her, she told herself she had to be strong. Because it was too late for them, really. No matter how she felt at this moment.

"I'm sorry," she said, through the lump in her throat.

He walked to the door and gave her a pained smile.

"I guess that's it," he said and closed the door behind him.

When she left the next morning, Joanna didn't cry. She got up early, dressed, then went downstairs while everyone else was still asleep and began fixing a big breakfast. They knew she had to catch a mid-morning flight, so before long, her son and daughter and her husband were sitting at the table while she slid strips of bacon and stacks of strawberry pancakes onto their plates. She sat with them, ate quickly, and began clearing things before they were even done.

"Mom, stop," Sarah said. "You're making me feel guilty."

"It's okay, honey," she told her from the sink, where she rinsed plates. "I like doing this."

So they let her. The truth was, she needed to keep busy, to force her mind to pay attention to the little details at hand so she wouldn't think about the dwindling minutes and how before she knew it, she would be gone. And then they would be gone. It would all be over.

How do you say goodbye to your children when you're not sure when you'll see them again? A quick embrace, an almost polite kiss on the cheek, was how she held it together. It must have seemed cold to them, but she was in the cab before she knew it, the three of them standing in the driveway. As she was pulling away, she heard Sarah call out and the driver stopped. Joanna rolled down the window.

"I just had a great idea, Mom. How about Christmas in Paris?"

Joanna looked at her, stunned. She hadn't thought that far ahead. She'd been too busy these past months, just getting herself through the moment.

"What a lovely idea," she called out.

As the limo pulled out of the driveway, she thought of Grace. Was it possible she could still be alive at Christmas? Her obligation was for six months. If things went longer, would she really be able to just leave her? And Hank, how would he feel about Christmas apart?

It wasn't until she was strapped in her seat and the plane began to taxi that Joanna started to cry. Slow, silent tears that came unbidden. Paul and Sarah would be in his car by now, taking Timmy to JFK. Then they were spending the afternoon in the city. He would have her to Newark Airport by seven and she'd be on her way back to Colorado and Martin, arriving before midnight, mountain time. And Paul would go back to the house on Butterfield Drive by himself. How ironic that they would all leave, and he'd now be the one left alone. He'd barely looked at her that morning. Did he hate her for pulling away from him last night? He'd stood in the driveway in the new blue shirt, which Sarah insisted he wear, looking so handsome. And so hurt. She pictured him in the garage working late at night, sawing, sanding, easing his loneliness by keeping busy. Whatever had come before was nothing compared to the unbearable ache of grief that now filled her heart.

After a while she went to the restroom and rinsed her face. The cloud cover that had obliterated the earth since Newark was breaking up, and through the clear patches she could see the ocean below, shimmering in the morning sun. Grace was waiting for her at home. Joanna decided to take her out for a nice dinner. Then she'd go see Hank, give him the book of poetry she'd bought, and they would check on the nests. By the end of the week they would begin sitting vigils, waiting for the tiny hatchlings to appear. And on Wednesday she'd be back at the newspaper.

Back to her life, as it was now.

32

Paul sat on his deck in the dark thinking about the last three days. One by one they'd left, first his wife, then his son, and finally, earlier that evening, his daughter. But the hardest by far was watching Joanna leave. No kiss goodbye, no sign of affection, just a wave of the hand and a glance at him as the limo pulled away. She'd changed so much since the last time he saw her, all those months ago. Standing on the blinding white beach she was still his wife, even as she was trying to pull away from him. He had felt he could still reach her somehow. Now, he realized, he'd waited too long. She'd removed herself from him emotionally. And he was stupid to try to make love to her. He'd just felt like it was his last chance, so he took it. And lost. From now on when they were together, most likely because of their kids, he would be regarded as an old friend and nothing more.

She'd been lonely, the way he was now. How had he not recognized that? Because he'd been too busy. He didn't listen to her, and he knew he was guilty of that if nothing else. After the kids left home, when he would travel for days at a time, did she sit out here by herself trying to escape the silence of the empty house, as he did now? He wondered if his mother had ever been lonely with his father gone sometimes sixteen hours a day. She'd never complained. But it was different. His father was home every night. Paul recalled months when he hadn't spent more than five nights in his own bed.

The trees began to rustle as the wind kicked up, and he wondered if it meant more rain coming. Maybe it really was time to get back to the real world. He thought about the offer to go back to V.I.C. as a consultant. He would actually be an employee of the consulting firm, not V.I.C. But he'd spend his days back on his home turf, trying to beef up their wireless communications sales, which had plummeted in the last two months. Last week he told them he'd think about it. Now he decided to call them in the morning.

He went back into the house, where a single light burned in the kitchen. He was hungry, but didn't feel like eating. It had been like that all weekend. Food, he'd realized, was an easy thing to hide behind. He'd shopped, fixed things, cleaned up, and it had given him a place to stand back and watch. Joanna, he could see, was uncomfortable with that. Stripped of her job in the kitchen, it was as if she'd stood naked before them. On the last morning, she could endure it no longer and beat them to the kitchen, cooking for them, eating away the minutes until it was time to leave. It was so apparent. She was cool and efficient as she worked her way around the kitchen, and it made him wonder how often in the past she'd hidden from him like that. And he hadn't noticed.

When he wasn't busy doing something for them, he'd made himself scarce. He didn't like taking the time to run from the too-few hours they had together, but he could only endure so much. And Joanna, he knew, expected him to say no when they left for the flea market Sunday afternoon. So he had, and simply lay on the couch thinking of them the whole time they were gone.

When he'd pulled into the garage Saturday morning and gotten out of his car to find her standing there, he'd had a moment of hope. The way she'd looked at him. He almost went and pulled her into his arms. She looked so beautiful, her skin sun-bronzed, her hair curling about her face, her wide gray eyes beating at him like a frightened deer's. But pride held him back. And then when the kids came, he felt such joy fill the house, fill her, that he felt his hope growing again. But there was always a reticence when it came to him. Her looks were never too long, her smiles a bit too formal, and the night they'd ended up alone out on the deck, he'd felt her standoffish armor go up as soon as Sarah and Timmy left. He argued with himself for over an hour before he went to her room to see if there wasn't some chance they could salvage things. Her kindness should have been easier to take than her initial anger and resentment months ago, but it wasn't. That was when he knew it was really over. That there was nothing left for her.

He closed the refrigerator, not even realizing he'd opened it. Or how long he'd stood there looking at the weekend's leftovers. He turned out the kitchen light and crossed the room in the dark to go upstairs to bed. That's when he saw the tiny red light blinking on the answering machine.

The first message was from Sandy, his realtor. The couple from Ohio who'd seen the house earlier in the week were definitely interested. But they thought the price was awfully high.

"You know how it is," he heard her voice in the dark room, "they're already in sticker shock at our prices in New Jersey compared to where they're from. And we did discuss that you're probably about thirty thousand dollars higher than you should be. Anyway, they're talking about making an offer, so I'll keep you posted."

She was trying to wear him down; he knew the drill. At the moment he wasn't much interested. The next message was Buffy, who must have called when he was sitting outside earlier, with her usual breathless, run-on sentence.

"Hi, Paul. Hope you guys enjoyed the cookies. Your son's a doll, I'm so glad I got to meet him, he's really a clone of you, you know." Not really, he thought. "I forgot to tell you I'm having a little surprise party for Erik's birthday Saturday night, hope you can come."

He didn't think so. In spite of the awkward beginning to his dinner at her house last week, he'd actually had a good time. Or maybe it was because of the three bottles of wine they'd had. But he came away with an odd feeling about Buffy and Erik. He wasn't really sure what was going on there. He did miss her company, though.

The following afternoon, Paul found himself pulling into the visitors' parking lot at V.I.C. He sat in his car a moment, the air conditioner still blasting, remembering the last time he'd been there. The mountains were turning green, the dogwood just beginning to blossom. It had been early spring. Now it was just a few weeks until Labor Day, the official end of summer. For all those months, people had come here day in and day out, sitting at their desks, making calls, going to meetings, all in an effort to make this corporation money. And more money. While he'd been home filling his hours with manual labor and finding his mind, for the first time in nearly three decades, free to roam. Did he really want to give that up? It was inevitable that as he walked through the atrium filled with trees and shrubs reaching up toward the sun, and the rushing cascade of the waterfall, he would remember that night, the party for his promotion. Joanna had been stunning in a green beaded dress that glittered as she moved around the room.

He stopped at the reception desk, something he'd never done before, and was told to wait. Within a few minutes the elevator opened and he was stunned to see Dan Rogers, who'd been a rookie on one of his sales teams a while back, come to greet him with outstretched hand. He'd expected Rich Casey, who'd been his contact so far. Dan took him to a conference room just off the main lobby, and it galled Paul that he was treated as any visitor, not allowed into the inner sanctum of the company offices. Not yet, anyway. Dan laid out charts and spreadsheets across the table and talked about the fierce competition in the wireless communications field.

"To be honest, it's a market we're slipping in, especially in the past six months," he said. "We think there might be some dead wood in the field, maybe in middle management. With your past track record, you may be just the guy to bring us up to speed."

Paul sat a moment looking at the charts and graphs, the spreadsheets. He had an urge to swipe them off the table onto the floor. He wanted to know why someone as young and inexperienced as Dan Rogers was sitting here telling him all this. He knew, though. They could get Dan at half the price of someone with Paul's seniority. But apparently, what they were finally realizing was they were also getting his inexperience.

"Where exactly would I fit in?" Paul asked.

"Well, first we'd like you to take an overall look at sales production, so you can target the trouble spots. Then we'd actually like you to meet with each regional sales team from top to bottom and troubleshoot anything you see fit."

"Wouldn't this normally be done within the company?" Paul asked. "I mean, you must have an idea from all the information you've gathered, your quarterly sales reports, who's producing and who isn't."

"Sure, we do, of course," Dan said a little too heartily, Paul thought. "But with your experience, we think you may find things we've simply just missed. You're the best, Paul."

He wanted to smack the solicitous grin off Dan Rogers's face. Dan was obviously in the hot seat and Paul was his ticket off. That's why he'd asked him to come for this meeting so quickly. Dan opened a folder.

"Here's an outline of what we're proposing, as well as compensation," he said, sliding a stapled stack of papers across the conference table.

Paul picked it up, flipped through the pages. "Obviously, I need to give this some consideration," he said, and then stood up.

"Of course," Dan said, standing a moment later when he realized Paul was bringing the meeting to an end.

"I'll be in touch," Paul said, as he opened the door.

"When," he heard Dan call out, "do you think we might hear from you?"

"Give me the weekend," he said and walked out.

He spent the rest of the week working in the garage, trying to finish the shelves he'd been making for Buffy's neighbor Elyse. His mind went back and forth. He should take it. Because they didn't have to give him benefits, the money was excellent and the smart thing was to make it while he could. How long could it last? But he knew guys who'd been consulting for years with the same companies, who might as well have been hired as regular employees. There was a certain amount of satisfaction that they needed him. But there was also the bile he'd have to swallow every time he reported to Dan Rogers, who'd always been mediocre at best. Obviously, though, Dan knew how to play the game. And the game, it seemed, was now played differently.

Paul and Ted were testament to that.

33

When she returned to Grace's from the airport earlier in the week, two surprises waited for Joanna. Grace's son Sean was there for a visit. And Hank had left a note for her. There'd been an accident on the boat. His cousin Sam got tangled in a shrimp net and hurt over the weekend, so Hank would be taking the shrimp boat out for him all week. Being in charge meant even longer hours, so he'd have to stay at Sam's house in Georgetown rather than driving back and forth to sleep. *I'll call you in a few days* was how he'd left it.

Grace was preoccupied with her son and seemed anxious when Joanna was around. Joanna was certain she knew why. But it was easy to make herself scarce since she took an instant dislike to Sean. At first she thought he was charming, his stories entertaining. But after a while they grew stale, and she resented the time he spent gallivanting around, looking for new sights and adventures, eating into the minutes she knew were precious to Grace. More than once he'd kept Grace waiting when she cooked special meals for him. Joanna wondered if she was really blind to his faults or if she'd just managed to accept him for who he was — a selfish man who would always tend to his own needs first.

She was relieved to get back to work on Wednesday. There was a stack of press releases, weddings and birth announcements, waiting on her desk, familiar tasks that had become almost rote now that she had the routine down. Before she knew it, the morning was almost gone. A little while later she looked up, surprised to see Rhetta walking into the office. She came right over with the friendliest of smiles.

"Hello, Joanna. I was hopin' we might have lunch together."

"I'm really way too busy, Rhetta. I wish you'd called first."

"Nonsense," Joanna heard and turned to see Harley walking into the room. "You take all the time you need, Joanna. You eat in every day you're here as it is."

She stood there, wishing she were the type of person who could just be rude and tell Rhetta that she didn't want to be near her.

But she wasn't. A few minutes later she found herself being driven to the Soundside, an upscale restaurant that had recently opened and was packed every time she drove by.

They made small talk about the weather and the turtle watch coming up the next week. But Joanna felt her discomfort move up a notch when they were seated and Jolene, the black waitress she'd worked with at The Chowder House, came over.

"Hi, Jolene," she said as Jolene handed them menus. "How are you?"

"Just fine, Joanna," she said without smiling. She took their drink order and left.

"So, I hear you went home for a visit," Rhetta began.

She bit her lip, wondering how she was going to get through lunch. She didn't pretend to herself this woman was looking for friendship.

"Yes, I did," Joanna said slowly. "To see my children. My daughter's moving to Paris and my son lives in Montana. We don't see each other often."

"That must have been nice." She smiled sweetly. "And difficult, having to say goodbye again."

"It was hard, yes."

Jolene was back with the drinks and they

ordered lunch. She hoped the service was quick.

"It's a shame about Sam gettin' hurt, isn't it? He's lucky to be alive."

Now Rhetta had her curiosity. She'd had no details from Hank's note. "What exactly happened?"

"Oh, you know, they get so used to working those boats that sometimes they just turn away for the wrong moment and boom, they get their feet caught in a net and the next thing they're gone, pulled overboard."

"Oh my God." She imagined getting dragged into the cold, black ocean at night, wrapped up in a net.

"Well, they got him good and quick," Rhetta went on. "But his leg got cut up pretty bad when Bobby, who'd jumped in after him, began cuttin' up that net with his knife to free Sam."

"How horrible. He's going to be okay, though, right?"

She gave Joanna a sympathetic smile. "That's right, you must be missin' Hank, off coverin' for Sam every night. Well don't worry, Sam should be fine."

Jolene set their sandwiches down, and she was glad for the interruption.

"What is it you do, Rhetta?" she asked before taking a bite. She'd never actually asked where she worked, and hoped that might eat up the rest of their lunch.

"Well, I have a little interior design business I run. With all of the buildin' goin' on, I've just been swamped. Nothin' like a new house with all those bare white walls cryin' out for some attention," she laughed.

She was always so stylish and impeccably dressed, Joanna imagined she was probably very good at it.

"I decorated the model over at that new development goin' in, Rice Fields."

For some reason that really galled her. But she listened to Rhetta rattle on about her clients and her new projects, glad to be on neutral ground as they ate.

"You and I might as well face facts," Rhetta said, after Jolene had cleared their plates. "We'll never get any further than the back of the line with Hank."

"Look, Rhetta . . ." She really didn't want to talk about Hank with her.

"Because the number one place in his heart," Rhetta went on, "will always be occupied by Lacey."

"That's ridiculous. Lacey's dead."

She laughed. "Yeah, you would think that it's ridiculous, wouldn't you? But dead means you suddenly lose those human flaws we all seem to have." She shook her head,

as if Joanna just didn't get it. "Dead sometimes elevates you to saint status."

Jolene came over with the check then, and
Joanna could have kissed her. She threw
money on the table and got up. "My treat,"
she said to Rhetta without a smile. "I really
have to get back now."

She was almost at the door when Jolene
called her name. Joanna turned and Jolene
was beside her a moment later, with a tray
of drinks in her hand.

"I was just wonderin' if you gonna be
takin' any more pictures down there at the
Barony?"

"Um, I don't know. Why?"

"Well, the builder just made a bunch of us
offers on our houses. Seems he plans to just
tear 'em down and use the land to put up
some more of them fancy, expensive ones."

"But you don't have to take the offer.
Especially if you don't think the price is
fair."

She laughed, as if Joanna were a child.
"You think we have a choice? Eventually
they'll run all of us old-timers out with the
taxes climbin'. Nothin' but rich whites'll be
left. That's what your picture don't show."

She didn't know what to say and then
Jolene turned away, carrying her drinks to a
table. Joanna walked out feeling uncomfort-

able. No, she realized, guilty was a better description. And then she had to get back in the car with Rhetta, who'd been waiting for her.

"Friend of yours?" she asked.

"I worked with her."

"Oh, right. The Chowder House."

She wasn't falling for the bait again, and remained silent until they got back to the newspaper.

"You seem like a nice person, Joanna," Rhetta said as she got out of the car. "And it seems like this might be more than just a summer romance for you. I just don't want to see you get hurt, that's all."

"Right," she muttered, closing the door.

She thought about Jolene the rest of the afternoon as she worked. Harley had left early so she didn't have a chance to remind him that she thought they should do something on the Barony situation. She tried to ignore Rhetta's annoying words that kept poking into her thoughts as well. Rhetta had really stepped over the line this time, and she wondered if it was worth mentioning to Hank. Perhaps that's exactly what Rhetta wanted her to do.

When she got home, Grace was cooking up a storm and invited her to have dinner with her and her son. He was out somewhere, and while they waited for him, Joanna set the table and made a pitcher of iced tea. Grace was making shrimp marinara with angel-hair, a dish she'd picked up years ago from her mother-in-law. She seemed so happy to Joanna, her cheeks flushed from the heat of the stove. Every so often she pulled off her glasses to wipe the steam that kept fogging them.

"Well, let's just hope the prodigal son is back before these shrimp start to get tough. He has a habit of getting caught up in his escapades and losing track of time."

It was as if she were talking about a small boy, Joanna thought.

"He always says he won't die with any regrets," Grace went on, turning to her and pulling a strainer from the cabinet. "But I have to wonder if at some point he won't regret not having a wife to grow old with. And children. I can't imagine dying without knowing you're leaving something of your-self behind."

"Oh, Grace." Joanna went to her.

"No, no." She waved her away. "I'm not feeling sorry for myself. Sometimes I just think that years ago, when Sean's wife was so unhappy, I should have done more. She was a schoolteacher and struggled to keep him home. And I would simply say to her, that's the way he is, as if he couldn't change. I'd vowed never to get involved in my children's marriages, not like my mother-in-law did. And I tried to live by it."

"Do you really think there was anything you could have done to make a difference?" Joanna asked her.

Grace lifted the lid on the saucepan and gave it a stir. "I should have tried harder. When Alaina came to Frank's funeral with her second husband and pulled out pictures of their two children, I thought — that's what Sean missed."

"Come on, Grace, quit beating yourself up. From the little I've seen of your son, I'd say his life is exactly as he wants it."

Grace sat on the stool and suddenly looked old and tired, the flush of cooking gone. Sean showed up an hour late. He'd found an eagle's nest down at the Santee River Delta, where he'd spent the afternoon. Joanna watched Grace's face light up again at his mere presence, and she thought of the weekend she'd just had with her own children, the maternal longing for them that never truly left you.

"Smells great," Sean said as Grace began ladling shrimp over the pasta. "You know you don't have to cook every meal for me."

"I like to do it," Grace said a little too quickly, and Joanna realized she was trying not to cry.

"So tell me more about the Santee Delta," she urged Sean then.

He talked throughout the meal, while she and Grace listened. She thought: what if this was me and I knew it was the last time I'd see my son? She couldn't bear it, watching Grace as Sean chattered on, oblivious to his mother's pain.

After dinner she went for a walk, glad for the time away from them. She thought about Hank, awake now, getting the boat ready to take out for the night, hauling in nets full of shrimp. She hadn't seen him in five days.

Her nest came into view then, and she walked up toward the dunes and stood before the small square staked out with sticks and string. In a few days the group would begin vigils at every nest, three-hour shifts all night long. It seemed an amazing commitment. She looked down at the square of sand, imagining the tiny eggs, the little creatures beating inside, ready at any moment to burst forth into the world. And the mother loggerhead, probably thousands of miles away by now, heedless of the perils of her offspring. She hoped she was lucky enough to see them hatch, but she'd already been warned that the odds were against it. There were people who'd sat watches year after year, only to miss the hatchlings by a shift. And some who sat at nests that mysteriously never hatched at all.

On Friday morning, as soon as Harley came in, Joanna went into his office.

"Do you remember that picture you had me take at the Barony weeks ago?"

"Now, Joanna, you're improving all the time. I don't want you to dwell on things that don't come out perfect."

"No, that's not what I was getting at. I think maybe we should do an article to follow up the picture."

"Oh, I think that situation's quieted down. There's not much goin' on there anymore."

"It may appear that way, but there's a lot going on to the people being affected by the development."

He looked up from the stack of papers on his desk. Now she had his attention.

"Harley, I think we're missing the big picture here, so to speak, with this development. You're always asking me to look for my impressions, well what about the individuals, the families? How they're being affected. Isn't that the real story?"

He sat back and gave a big sigh. "What is it you had in mind, Joanna?"

"What if we did a piece focusing on one family and how all of this development is impacting them?"

"Umm," he said, in that slow Southern way that meant he was thinking about it.

She waited.

"Tell you what. Put a few rough ideas in writing, don't get too carried away, and I'll take a look at it."

"Thanks, Harley."

She went back to her desk, satisfied but also a little miffed. Joanna thought this was a great idea and couldn't understand his hesitancy. But then she almost laughed at herself. How long had she been working there? Was she suddenly an authority on what constituted a good article or deserved space in the paper? She was still just a novice.

After lunch she began gathering ideas, and then called Jolene and made an appointment to talk to her the following week. She seemed wary at first, especially when Joanna explained that she wasn't sure if this would even see print. When she hung up the phone, she felt the little needle of guilt that had been jabbing her all week ease up some.

When Joanna got home, she was barely in

the door when Grace called out that she had a phone call.

"Hey, darlin,' " Hank said as soon as she got on. She could hear the smile in his voice.

"Hi," she said, nearly breathless, conscious of Grace just a few feet away.

"How about a date tomorrow night?" he asked, teasingly. "It is Saturday night, after all."

"You'll be home?"

"Yeah, I'll be done after tonight, so I'll head back after sleepin' a bit tomorrow," he went on. "Interested in a quiet little dinner for two?"

"Sounds perfect."

"See you tomorrow."

Sean would be taking Grace out for dinner since he was leaving on Sunday, so she didn't have to worry about any complications there. She hung up the phone and looked across the room. Grace was busy reading. Joanna hadn't told her that Sean had cornered her outside the house when she'd returned from her walk the other night.

"My sister Marie is worried about my mother," he'd said as they stood on the dark beach in front of the house. "Is everything okay?"

What could she say to that? Part of her

411

still felt Grace was being too selfless and deserved to be surrounded by her family during her last months. And wasn't she also being selfish, in a way?

"I think this is just where she wants to be right now," she said to Sean. "Tell your sister that."

34

By Saturday, when he was putting the final coat of polyurethane on Elyse's stained shelves, Paul was no closer to a decision about the consulting job. He wished again that Ted was still alive to talk it over with him. He'd thought of calling Joanna and discussing it with her, then decided against it. Buffy had called that morning to remind him about the party, but he didn't bother to tell her he wasn't coming. He knew that would spark a twenty-minute monologue to persuade him.

His realtor called late morning to say the Ohio couple had finally made an offer. She'd stop by that afternoon with the contract to go over it with him. He knew that meant it was low. Lower than what he was asking anyway. When he'd given her his list price weeks ago, her eyebrows had shot up in surprise. He knew it was too high, but the market was crazy and at the time he wasn't in a hurry. In truth, back then he was hoping listing the house would be the catalyst to finally bring his wife home. But that wasn't going to happen. If the offer was decent, he wasn't sure what he would do now.

It was nearly five when the doorbell rang and he let Sandy in.

"These are great buyers, Paul," she said as they sat at the kitchen table and she pulled a thick file out of her bag. She opened the file and pulled out a check.

"Here's their initial thousand-dollar escrow payment. And this is a letter from their mortgage company showing they're already approved for the loan. Plus, there's no house to sell on their end, the company is buying them out . . ."

He knew the drill; transferees were the best buyers around. Hadn't he been one enough times? "I understand all that, Sandy. Why don't we just get to the terms."

"They're coming in with their best offer, rather than fooling around and going back and forth." She slid a contract in front of him. They were offering him $600,000. He was listed at $639,000.

"They've looked at the comparable sales in the neighborhood, of course. You know how educated buyers are today."

"It's still well under my asking price."

"Well, Paul, you know when we put it on the market, I thought your price was about thirty thousand dollars higher than market value."

"And they're ten under that."

"I have a feeling if you go back with something reasonable they'll come up."

"I thought this was their best shot."

"Believe me, if we're close, I'm sure they'll come up some. They really need a house."

But did he really need to sell? "I'd like to think about it."

"Of course, Paul. I know you've got to touch base with your wife, too. Do you think you might be able to get me a response by this evening? They're so anxious."

"Sure, I'll call you after dinner."

After she'd gone, he sat looking at the papers. The closing date was in just thirty days. He didn't even have a place lined up yet. And there was all the furniture to be divided or put in storage. Or maybe they should sell all of it, too. If he took the job consulting for V.I.C. he could just stay, the money wouldn't matter anymore. But what was the point, really? The house was too big, so full of memories. And it just seemed to make him feel more alone. Suddenly he felt like he had to get out of there.

He left the contract sitting on the kitchen counter and went to Porter's Pub for a burger and a beer. He'd only been there once, but now on a Saturday evening it was packed and lively. He thought back to the Red Lodge Cafe, when his van had broken down in Montana. He'd had a couple of meals and begun to get friendly with the people there when he'd been snowed in. Here he was in his own town and he really couldn't name one person in the place. But he listened to the friendly banter of the regulars as he ate, talking of their kids, their softball games, vacations. After his second beer, he paid the bill and then toyed with the idea of going to a movie. He went home instead and called Joanna. It was only fair that he tell her about the offer.

When a strange man's voice answered he started to hang up. "I'm sorry, I must have the wrong number," he said.

"Who are you looking for?"

"I'm looking for Joanna?"

"Yeah, you've got the right number. I'm Grace's son, here visiting."

"Is Joanna there?"

"No, I think she went up to Hank's for dinner. Should I have her call you?"

"Uh, no. I'll call her back."

"Who's —"

But Paul hung up before Grace's son finished the sentence. Who the hell was Hank? And then he remembered her talking about the turtles, mentioning his name. And he knew. It explained her sudden absences from Grace's, the late nights she wasn't there to take his calls. She'd been seeing someone. He closed his eyes. He should have been prepared for this. In his mind he pictured her talking, laughing, with some faceless man. Kissing him. He didn't know how long he paced back and forth through the kitchen, into the dining room, the foyer, back into the kitchen, endless laps that kept bringing him back to the same place, the same thoughts. His wife with another man.

When the phone rang he grabbed it, thinking somehow it might be her.

"Paul, why aren't you here yet?" It was Buffy. "Erik will be coming soon, I don't want to ruin the surprise."

Paul went into the dining room and grabbed the bottle of Dom Perignon that Ted had given him on the night of his promotion, still sitting in the wine rack. He and Joanna had never opened it. Never celebrated. He felt like a fool.

He walked the couple of blocks to Buffy's and noticed it was already getting dark at just eight o'clock. Buffy's house appeared dark and quiet, but once inside, he saw that half the neighborhood was there, and it seemed the party was already in full swing.

"Paul, you made it," Buffy said, pecking his cheek and taking the bottle. "Ooh, Dom Perignon."

Suddenly he felt underdressed, still in the jeans and polo shirt he'd worn to the pub. Buffy was wearing a long, sleeveless black sheath with slits up both legs. Her hair was down and curly, with a flower stuck behind one ear.

"Erik's going to shit when he walks in," she went on, pulling more appetizers out of the refrigerator. "I don't think he has any idea."

He grabbed a beer and offered to help.

"No, everything's under control. Come on, I'll introduce you around. Most of Erik's department is here from school. And I think you know nearly all of the neighbors."

He was embarrassed to say he didn't, except the ones he'd met through her. When they were done making the rounds, he found a quiet corner where he watched the crowd talking, laughing, drinking. *What am I doing here?* he thought. *My wife is with another man, and here I stand in a room full of happy people.* Buffy flitted around the house like an exotic insect spreading nectar among her guests. And then there was a loud *"Shhh!"* and she somehow got them all back into the family room, where they turned the lights out.

They heard the garage door close as Erik parked his car, and a little giggle rippled through the group. They listened to his footsteps on the concrete floor and a curse as they heard the clang of his keys falling. Then the door to the family room opened.

"SURPRISE!"

Erik looked as if he'd been shot, he was so stunned. Then Buffy pushed her way through the guests and threw her arms around him.

"Happy Birthday, Erik!"

He wrapped his arms around her and lifted her off the ground, twirling her around like a little girl. Everyone laughed.

"Well," Erik said, putting her down to face the crowd. "I guess I need a drink."

"Me, too," Buffy said, wiping her brow dramatically. Again everyone laughed.

As the party drifted into other parts of the house, Paul found himself next to Elyse, who asked how her shelves were coming along. She called some of her friends over, pointed to Buffy's shelves, and Paul listened with embarrassment as they talked.

"Wow, he really made that? I thought it was a built-in wall unit."

"Are you doing cherry, too?"

"No, Paul's using a light oak stain on mine."

The women chattered about possible projects for him and said they'd call him on Monday. Eventually, he made his way back into the kitchen.

"Paul, how's the house sale going?"

It was Bill, the retired pilot.

"Well, I got an offer today, but I'm not sure I'll take it."

"I was surprised when I saw the sign in front of your house. Where you thinking of heading to?"

"I'm not really sure. I may just rent something locally until I decide."

"Lois and I have been thinking about moving. The house is really more than we need anymore, just the two of us. And now that the grandchildren are coming, she wants to be closer to them. You know women!" he laughed.

He smiled. He really didn't know women, though, he thought. He would have bet money Joanna would never have been unfaithful to him. They were, after all, still legally married. But then who was he to judge? He'd been with Karen years ago, and blamed it on loneliness.

He went out on the deck, weary of small talk, and was surprised to find a group of smokers congregated there. He saw Erik on the far side of the deck talking seriously to the blond woman he'd been introduced to as a research assistant at the university. She was young and pretty, and Paul wondered if she was just a grad student. He saw Erik lift his hand then and run his finger down the curve of her face. It was an intimate gesture and she smiled shyly at him. Paul turned quickly to the group of smokers next to him, as if he were involved in their conversation about the Yankees' current slump. When he glanced over again he saw Erik and the woman sharing a longing look and then Erik walked away, leaving her outside by herself. He could see Erik through the screen door, crossing the kitchen, going up behind his wife, and kissing her neck. She turned to him with a smile of such happiness that Paul wanted to go inside and punch him.

"Paul?"

He turned to see a short, stocky man with a beer in his hand.

"I'm Jay Garabed. We live next door to you."

"Oh, right," Paul said, extending his hand.

"The disadvantage of moving in during

the winter is you don't really meet any of your neighbors until summer."

"I know what you mean," Paul replied, remembering how tough winter moves had been. "I haven't seen you around this summer, though."

"Well, I've been traveling a lot and my wife is working and going to school."

"Sounds like a tight schedule."

"Yeah, it is. But it's nice to finally meet you," he said, and Paul thought the conversation was over. "Listen, I was wondering if I might ask you a favor. You've got some loud machines going and, you know, it being summer and the windows open and all, we were just wondering if you might be able to tone it down a little."

He knew the saw could be loud; the high-pitched whine could almost cut through you at times. But he liked working with the garage doors open. That had been the whole point of moving the tools upstairs. He was tempted to smile and say no, and see how this pompous jerk would react. And then he realized it was probably a good time for him to leave.

"I'm sure I can do something," he said and excused himself.

But Buffy cornered him as he crossed the kitchen. "Come here," she said, pulling him by the arm into the laundry room. "Open this."

She handed him the bottle of champagne he'd brought, chilled from the freezer. He twisted the top, a napkin wrapped around it, and it popped. She pulled two glasses from a cabinet above the washer and held them for him to pour.

"This stuff is too good to waste on everyone else," she giggled. "We'll just hide it in here for us."

"What about the birthday boy?" he asked. He decided he couldn't stand Erik after all.

"Actually, he never liked champagne. Gives him a headache. What a weenie."

She giggled again. Paul realized she was drunk.

"I guess we better get back to the others," he suggested.

She looked up at him then, and he could see tears welling up in her eyes.

"You're so sweet," she whispered. "Why couldn't I have met someone like you?"

She stretched up on her toes to kiss him. Her lips barely touched his and part of him wanted to pull her to him and kiss her back. But he didn't move. She stopped then and stared up at him.

"Sorry," she said, taking a sip of her champagne to cover her embarrassment.

She quickly turned and opened the laundry room door. He followed with the open bottle still in hand. When they went back into the kitchen, Erik was busy playing host.

"Oh, there she is," he called out. "And Paul, too. Well, there must have been something broken in the laundry room."

He opened his mouth, ready to let it fly, but Buffy spoke before he got the words out.

"Don't be stupid, honey," she said, holding up her glass. "You know how paranoid I am opening champagne. I asked Paul to do it in the laundry room so in case it went flying like a missile, no one would get hurt."

A few minutes later, he slipped quietly out the front door, without a good-bye to anyone. It was late and the moon had already crossed the sky. He was tired and walked slowly toward his house, realizing he hadn't called his realtor back. He looked at the oversized homes as he walked by. McMansions, he'd heard them called. Who were these people all trying to be? What kind of life did an address in Greenwich Hills guarantee you? Not one he was interested in any longer, he realized.

He'd call Sandy in the morning and counter with $620,000. Then they'd see how serious the people from Ohio were.

35

Joanna changed three times as she got ready for her dinner with Hank, settling on a simple white sundress that highlighted her tan. She thought about what Hank had said once while making love, how he loved tan lines. Her hair, which she hadn't cut since she'd come to Pawleys Island months ago, hung below her shoulders, and her bangs had grown out and fell in curls with the rest of it. She looked at herself in the mirror and remembered the baby oil and iodine summers of her youth at the Sand Bar. And here it was, all over again.

Slowly she walked up the beach, savoring the anticipation. They hadn't been together in eight days now. She thought after dinner she'd ask Hank to put on some dancing music. And maybe they'd take a blanket down to the beach later on, lie back and watch the stars. Make love.

She crossed a jetty and thought of Paul

then. She wondered what he was doing tonight. She had a vision of him standing in the driveway again, watching her leave. Ironically, she almost hoped he went back to V.I.C., just to pull him back onto familiar footing. He seemed so lost. Then she saw the tattered pineapple flag, and veered across the sand and up the familiar wooden steps through the tangle of trees and bushes. Her heart began to beat a little faster.

She could hear soft music playing and the clatter of dishes and things. She walked a few steps over to the window and peeked in. Hank was in the kitchen, as he was the first night she'd come. This gray-haired, bearded man she once thought looked like a rugged, weathered sea captain had brought out a part of her that had been asleep for years. That she had almost forgotten existed. In the beginning, she was embarrassed by her need, wanting him so much that it consumed her like a teenage girl. But the truth was, she felt more alive than she had in many years. Maybe this was the real Joanna, after all, awake again after a long sleep.

She gave a little knock and pushed the door open.

"Hey, darlin'," Hank said with that smile and she walked into his arms.

He held her so tightly, his lips brushing her neck, she felt as if she were melting into him. "I missed you," she whispered in his ear.

He loosened his hold and looked down at her. "God, you look good enough to eat."

She giggled. It all felt new and exquisite after just a week apart, and the bit of shyness she once had crept back.

"Some wine?" he asked, heading back into the kitchen.

"Sure. I'll get it."

She felt a little breathless from the excitement of being in his arms again, the strange feelings that seemed to be erupting within her. She grabbed the bottle from the refrigerator, then rooted in a drawer for the corkscrew. She poured them each a glass.

"How's Sam?"

"Oh, he's fine now. Broke the cardinal rule of all fishermen, though. Don't get complacent, 'cause the next thing you know you're hooked or netted."

"And how did you enjoy your week on the boat?"

He looked up at her and smiled. "It was lonely. I thought about you a lot. How was your trip home?"

She didn't really know how to answer that. She picked up her glass and walked over to the window. The sun was beginning to lower over the marsh and everything was bathed in a golden wash of color. "I love my kids more than anything in this world. It was wonderful to see them."

"But . . ." He raised his eyebrows. "Sounds like a 'but' coming."

"But it was kind of gut-wrenching. Sarah's going to Paris, Tim back to Montana. I'm here. Paul's the only one left in the house, and it looks like there are people interested in it." She gave a little shrug. "It's like the end of an era, you know what I mean? It's over, we'll never go back to that."

He gave her a sad smile and then she realized, of course he knew how that felt. He'd lost his family long ago. A part of his own life had ended, never to be revisited again. She walked over to the picture of his ex-wife and daughter and picked it up, looking at the smiles, captured forever, a happy moment come and gone.

"I'm sorry," she said to him. "I guess I'm so caught up in my own feelings, I forget about everyone else's."

He came over and touched her face tenderly with his fingers. "I doubt that. But it's all right, for me it was a long time ago."

She couldn't help but think of what Rhetta had said the other day.

"Maybe with time it'll get easier for me, too."

He smiled and pulled her to him. "Come on, let's go watch the sunset while we wait for supper to cook," he said.

They sat on his dock out over the marsh, watching the sun sink slowly in the sky. Joanna could see groups of people on some of the other docks, who repeated this ritual night after night, never tiring of the gorgeous sunsets. Tonight's sunset was calm, the sky a soft blend of pastels, pinks and yellows. Hank, too, was subdued. She could see that he was tired. He talked a little about his nights on the shrimp boat. But all she heard was Rhetta's voice telling her about Lacey.

"I had lunch with Rhetta the other day," she said when there was a lull in their talking. It just came out.

He gave her a sympathetic smile.

"Why does she seem to have this claim on you?"

"Sometimes I think Rhetta is my penance in life for all my past sins." A great blue heron swooped low over the water, landing in the tall grass across from them. They watched in silence for a moment.

"Is she in love with you?"

He turned to her. "Did she tell you that?"

"Of course not. I don't think a cold witch like her is capable of love. But I'm pretty sure she wants you. Or thinks she has some right to you."

He didn't talk for a few minutes, staring over the water that was rushing out with the tide. The sky softened to a deep lavender as the sun disappeared below the horizon.

"I'm sorry," he said, reaching for her hand and pulling it to his lips. "Rhetta and I have a long and sad history, what with Lacey and all. But she has no right botherin' you."

Maybe she was reading more into things than was there. Hank, after all, might be the only family left for Rhetta. Or the only link to a sister she once loved. And Joanna was an outsider.

She smiled at him and took his hand. "Let's go eat. I'm starving."

They didn't dance. After dinner, Hank fell asleep as they sat on the couch listening to music. He began to snore softly, his head thrown back at an awkward angle. She slipped a pillow underneath him and he seemed to just slide down on his side, settling into a deep sleep. She covered him with an afghan, blew out the candles, and turned off the music and all of the lights but the one over the stove. Then she leaned down to kiss him. In the dim lighting, the gray hair and beard, the deep lines of weather and exhaustion around his eyes made her pause. He suddenly looked old.

Grace lay in bed watching the morning sun dance across her walls, the shadows moving higher as the morning stretched on. She didn't want to get up, hadn't wanted to since her son left days ago. When he first arrived, she'd thought she would pick right back up with her painting once he left. That she would slip effortlessly back into the existence she'd created for herself, pull out her painting things, the canvas of her night scene that had excited her not so long ago. But the longer Sean stayed, the more she felt herself being pulled back into the Grace she used to be. And she didn't want him to leave.

She turned on her side to ease the ache in her back and heard Joanna walking about overhead. This afternoon Joanna would take her back to the Healing Center for another acupuncture session. Hopefully, it would ease her pain again. But she had to admit it wasn't the pain dulling her senses now that eroded her will to survive. It was depression. For days now, she couldn't stop the weeping. Long, silent spells where the tears ran like the lifeblood flowing from her, leaving her frayed and spent. She knew she needed something to pull her out of it, and had thought it would be her painting.

Outside, a gull cried over the rhythmic rolling of the waves. Slowly she got up, crossed the room, and threw on a loose shift, not bothering to wash or comb her hair. She didn't slip on shoes. When she opened the door to the deck and stepped out, the sun nearly blinded her. She reached inside for her straw hat and then made her way down the deck steps. At the bottom her feet immediately sank into the soft, warm sand. How many days had it been? It seemed she rarely left the house or the deck anymore.

Slowly she walked to the water's edge, where the sea washed across the sand to meet her. At first the water felt cool as it splashed across her feet. She stood there as the ocean pulled back into itself, leaving her feet wet and exposed. Then the waves built again, clear green and flecked with foam. Within minutes her feet were used to it, and the water felt warm.

The beach was quiet, and she remembered that in the South schools started in the middle of August. She was glad for the solitude. Out where the waves began, she could see fish jumping, silver flashes in the sun. Soon the dolphins would come to feed. Beside her, tiny sanderlings darted back and forth as the waves washed in, comical creatures running double time on tiny legs. The ocean shimmered like green glass and the sky was clear blue.

Turning from the water, she walked across the wet sand and the high-tide line, back to where the sand was soft. Slowly she sat, waiting for the dolphins. She'd been here before, this place of inertia where the world seemed to go on as she stood in the same spot, unable to move. Lying back, she moaned with pleasure as the hot sand beat into her spine. A vision of herself, on the stoop of the house she and Frank shared with his parents all those years ago, flashed in her mind. It was August, too, a bright hot day more than forty years ago. Frank was behind the wheel of their car, little Marie sitting beside him, her face peering up at Grace. Frank was taking her shopping for clothes to go back to school. Marie wasn't more than six or seven. She cried at first. *Why can't Mommy take me shopping?* she asked. *Why does Daddy always take me everyplace?* At that moment, Grace remembered hating herself.

How easy it was, she knew now, to give in to your fears. To let depression swallow you into a quicksand of troubling thoughts so that soon you couldn't move. She sat up, brushed the sand from her hair, and pulled her hat back on. She wouldn't give up. It wasn't time yet, despite the growing pain, the fatigue, the struggle to recapture her will. She could still move, still cook, still paint. Even if it was nothing more than another month or two, she told herself, as she saw the first black fin of a dolphin break the water's surface. She would not waste her final days.

The acupuncture did help. Carol, the practitioner, who had studied in China, added light massage now to Grace's treatment. Under her firm yet gentle strokes, she could feel the tightness leaving her, the tension slide from muscles as taut as if she'd been perched on the edge of some high place. Finally, for the first time in over a week, she relaxed. And then she slept.

That night she was on her deck with her paints and easel. It was time to begin the night scene that she'd abandoned when Sean had come. As she stood on the dark deck, Grace realized that getting the lighting right was going to be tricky. The outside lights were too bright and washed out the night and its features. She carried a few table lamps out, but they only lit what was right around them and she couldn't see the colors or even the canvas before her. Eventually she lit candles, two dozen votives, scattering them around the deck and turning out all other lights. After a few minutes her eyes adjusted and she smiled. How clever of her to figure it out.

"Oh, Grace, how lovely."

She looked up to find Joanna coming out the door, a blanket and tote bag in her arms.

"Are you going to sit your watch?"

"Yes, first one," Joanna said, smiling, her excitement apparent.

"And you'll be back at midnight?"

"Yes," she said, crossing the deck to the steps. "They're three-hour shifts. I'll be back then."

And she was gone. That meant, Grace realized, that she was not going to Hank's afterward. Although Joanna had often come home in the early morning hours, she had never spent an entire night at Hank's. She wondered now if Hank was sitting his own vigil, or if things had cooled since Joanna returned from her trip home. Grace had tried to make conversation about her trip, but Joanna's responses were short and vague, as if her mind was elsewhere, or she was just too busy.

Joanna, she realized, who once had so many hours to fill in a day, suddenly did not have enough of them. She saw the little looks of impatience or frustration now when she asked Joanna to do a little more. But things were getting harder for Grace. Her energy no longer lasted more than a few hours until she was forced to lie down. Joanna could take care of the household things; she needed to paint. Even now, after the flurry of carrying lamps and candles, she felt worn and spent. She sat on a deck chair to catch her breath.

At odd moments the guilt came back. She would be looking in the mirror, brushing her teeth, and catch a glimpse of Marie in her eyes. And each Sunday, without fail after Frankie's weekly call, she thought again of the burden she'd soon lay at his feet, executor of her estate. And there was the guilt over Joanna, who one day soon would carry out Grace's final wishes.

It was time, she realized, to begin putting things in place for her.

36

Two weeks later, Joanna was sitting vigil at her turtle nest once again. It was a hot night, even for early September, and at a little after eleven Joanna felt her eyes closing. She'd been there since nine o'clock, waiting for any sign of movement that tonight might be the night the little turtles would pop through the sand and race for the life-sustaining ocean. She took the sweatshirt she'd brought and bunched it up like a pillow, then lay back on the sand. Above her the sky was a soft black, like velvet, studded with a million glittering stars. She waited in the dark, unable to read or do anything that required light, still hoping to be one of the lucky ones and see a nest actually come to life.

The first few times she sat, Hank kept her company, but he had his own watches at another nest. He had gallantly taken the twelve-to-three shift, which was the hardest to give away. So in a little while she'd be heading back up the beach to her own bed, while he'd be settling next to his nest about a half mile up the beach. She wondered if he'd leave early and stop by for a few minutes, as he'd done a few times. Not that she'd be upset if he didn't. She found herself looking forward to these hours alone, under the night sky, the only sound the rhythmic washing of the ocean across the sand. It was a luxury, really, to have nothing to do but think. Or even not think.

Joanna closed her eyes for a moment and the noise of the water began to fade. She felt the numbing clutches of sleep begin to pull her under and sat up abruptly with a start. Falling asleep was the worst thing she could do. In an hour or two she might wake and find the turtles had hatched and gone. And have missed the whole thing. She stood up, stretching her arms overhead and yawning. Then she walked in quick little circles around the sand in her bare feet for a while. The sand was cool and soft. Across the ocean, in the blackness where sea and sky met, she saw the tip of the moon pushing over the horizon. In the sudden rush of light she turned to her nest, looking hard for any signs of movement or shifting. Any difference in the sand. Nothing. These hatchlings should have come by now, even Hank had admitted it the other night. But she wouldn't let go of the possibility that they could still come. And it wasn't hard to convince the others watching her nest to keep it up another week or so. They were all so dedicated, and each hoped they would be one of the lucky few to ever witness the miracle.

She sat back down again on the blanket and watched the waves rolling toward her. For a moment they would spill across the sand in dark pools, their foaming edges lit up like white lace in the moonlight, only to be pulled back into the ocean a moment later. Again and again she watched as the moon inched higher in the sky, until a ribbon of white light stretched across the water from the horizon to the beach in front of her, nearly taking her breath away. She thought of Grace back at the house, probably out on the deck trying to capture this on canvas. It seemed she was outside every night now in some frantic attempt to paint the night sky. Grace had changed so much in the last few weeks.

She'd been wearing loose, cool dresses all summer, so Joanna wasn't aware of the weight loss at first. It was when she watched her picking at her food one night, talking and pushing it around her plate as if Joanna wouldn't notice, that she realized Grace's appetite wasn't what she remembered. And then when she really looked at her, she could see that the bones in her face were more prominent, the skin stretched a little too thin. She was walking slower, too, stiffer, as if favoring some part of her that might be in pain. Of course when Joanna asked her, she said no, she was fine, just a little rheumatism from all her painting. A few days after that, she saw Grace lying in the sand in her clothes, with no towel or blanket, on a burning hot morning in August. She ran to the door, heart pounding, certain Grace had died right there on the beach. But the old woman got up before Joanna reached her, and then turned with a smile, pointing to the dolphins feeding offshore. At odd times Joanna would come home and hear music blaring as soon as she got out of the car. The first time it happened, she thought it must be one of the rental houses. But as she climbed the stairs and went inside, she saw Grace across the room, doors thrown open to the beach, sketching and swaying in time to the music. She would turn it down without a word when she noticed Joanna. Joanna felt as if she were watching someone cling ferociously to anything her senses could grasp — the hot sand, the pounding music, the smell and colors of her paints that now seemed to almost obsess her. She just didn't know how to approach Grace about all of it. And she was afraid of what was to come.

Tilting her watch to catch the moonlight, she saw it was nearly eleven-thirty. Just another half hour to go. In the morning, she had work, and was anxious to begin the final rewrite on the piece about the Barony and its effects on local families. The whole thing had been an eye-opening experience for her. She'd been to Jolene's house, and the houses of her family and neighbors, several times now. The first time she drove over there, she pulled up and sat in the car a few minutes, looking over the run-down homes. Some would call them shacks. And she wondered if it wouldn't be better if they were all torn down. She began having second thoughts about what she was doing. Maybe Harley was right, they'd already covered enough about the situation. Jolene came out on the porch then, and she got out of the car, walked through the old metal gate, and went up the steps to her house. From the car Joanna hadn't noticed the flowers growing in plastic milk jugs that had been cut in half, lining the porch. Confederate jasmine climbed up a broken piece of lattice leaning against the worn and faded clapboard siding. She had a quick thought that it must smell like heaven in the front yard when it was in bloom. Jolene took her inside and the house was dark after the bright sunshine. The first thing that hit her was the smell of something wonderful cooking with cinnamon. A moment later her eyes adjusted and she saw the house was drab, the furniture old and mismatched. But everything was clean and neat, and someone's handwork was everywhere, with colorful doilies and crafts.

"This is my mother, Bernice," Jolene had said, leading her to a heavy, older woman sitting on a couch. She wore a bright caftan, and her short hair was springy and littered with gray. A bag of knitting was at her feet, and her hands flew as the needles clicked and a row of stitches seemed to grow before Joanna's eyes.

"Nice to meet ya," she said in the same soft voice as her daughter. "Jolene here tells me you might be able to help us."

"Thank you for having me over," she said. "You must understand, I haven't been doing this for very long. But I'll certainly write about your situation fairly and honestly. Hopefully that will begin to influence public opinion a little bit."

As her knitting needles raced back and forth, Jolene's mother began to talk about her grandparents, the children of slaves who'd worked on the plantations that once covered the land that stretched north and south on the Waccamaw River. Her own mother remembered the stories better, and Joanna was surprised to learn she was alive and even living in this very same house, where she'd been born more than eighty years before. But she was not feeling well lately and was sleeping in one of the bedrooms upstairs. Joanna tried to imagine it, the same family on this same little piece of land for the last hundred and fifty years or so.

While they talked, Jolene's kids came in from school. They were quiet and well behaved, and watched with big eyes from the kitchen table, where they had their after-school snacks. Everyone made enough to survive, Jolene's mother explained. It might not seem like much to rich whites, but they were content. They had love and family and occasional good times. They had a lot of things those white folks in their big fancy houses would never have, she'd gone on to say.

Jolene took Joanna up and down the road

then, to meet some of the others. Her next-door neighbor had a little shed out back where he was sawing and carving, and she saw the beginnings of a little dollhouse, a business he was trying to build.

"I'm thinkin' of tryin' to build 'em identical to some of the big houses goin' up," he explained quickly in his obvious excitement. "Imagine it, buyin' your little girl a dollhouse just like the house she's livin' in. I bet they'd pay a lot for that."

"Jeremy, you're a fool," Jolene scolded and they moved on. "Some of these folks just don't get it," she said as they walked. "Already resigned themselves to take the money, maybe look for a little place in Georgetown. Not me. I'm as good as any of them folks in those big houses. I got a right to stay here."

They went in house after house that seemed to be a carbon copy of Jolene's, where grandparents, their kids, grandkids, extended families all lived together. It reminded Joanna of the story Grace had told about when she got married right after the war and lived with Frank's family for years. A way of life Joanna thought had disappeared. These were hardworking people who didn't have much. Meager houses, a few nice possessions. But she saw that afternoon that their lives weren't just about survival. They had love and friendship and the support of each other in this community. They had their songs and their ways that had been handed down and cherished. And they'd been there for generations, since slavery had been wiped out and they could get a little piece of earth for their own. In the beginning, just after the war, she learned, many of them had gone back and worked on the same plantations where they'd been slaves. But eventually that way of life simply died out. These people were the last link.

When she got back in her car and left, Jolene waved from the porch without smiling. Joanna thought she understood her a little better. Sitting on the beach now, it occurred to her that somewhere over the years, she'd become a bit of a snob. And she hadn't even realized it. The house Joanna grew up in was modest, in a blue-collar neighborhood where everyone seemed to struggle for a little bit more. But in the last twenty-five years, her houses had grown bigger and grander, insulating her from the simple way of life she once knew. And even leading her to look down on that life from her privileged existence. It made her uncomfortable now. She hoped her work on this article might be a step in redeeming herself a little bit, even if only in her own eyes. But secretly, she hoped for more of an impact than that. These humble people were looked at with a patronizing eye by those who had more. And to the developers, it was as if they didn't even count.

"Hey, Joanna."

She turned with a start to see Dennis, her replacement. He was a college student who still lived at home and commuted to Coastal Carolina University up in Myrtle Beach. He was majoring in marine sciences, and didn't mind the middle-of-the-night shift. Rarely went to sleep before three anyway, he said.

"Quiet watch?" he asked, dropping his backpack on the sand.

"Unfortunately," she said, getting up and gathering her things. "Maybe you'll be the lucky one."

He threw his small blanket on the sand and sat down, unlacing his sneakers.

"I dunno," he said, shaking his head. "Better happen soon or I guess we're done."

She walked back to Grace's, watching small clouds begin to sail across the sky from the south. The hurricane they'd been bracing for all week was now headed for the Gulf in Florida. But they were still due for a day of heavy rain tomorrow as the outer edges of it passed by. Lucky again. It seemed it had been a summer of near-misses as one hurricane after another shot across the Atlantic from the coast of Africa like jets lined up on a runway. As a result, they had a pantry full of water, batteries, candles, and canned foods to last a month. But they still had the brunt of hurricane season to get through, Hank had warned. The fall months were usually the worst.

Joanna lay in bed for a long time before falling asleep. The tiredness that had gripped her earlier seemed to have disappeared on the walk home. She thought about Sarah, leaving for Paris in a few days. She said a prayer she would get there safely. And then her thoughts shifted to Timmy, who'd begun his senior year a few weeks ago. His schedule was hectic, he was still playing sports, and she knew he wasn't eating right. Or sleeping enough. She hoped he wasn't pushing himself into a relapse of mono. And while her thoughts were locked in a middle-of-the-night worry mode, they drifted finally to Hank and herself.

She had to admit she'd been keeping herself from thinking about them, or dwelling on the nagging little thoughts that popped into her mind occasionally. But there was no denying there was some kind of shift in their relationship since she'd gone back home. A change she couldn't quite put her finger on. They couldn't seem to get back to those first trembling weeks of passion. She wasn't sure if it was him or perhaps her. Maybe it was the fact that after those days apart, she came back and looked at him with fresh eyes, hardly able to believe again what they'd done. The physical pull was still there. And the warmth and affection. But she realized she didn't know Hank Bishop as well as she should have before getting so involved. Maybe it was her, after all; maybe she did put the brakes on a little after returning, without even realizing it. But he, too, seemed a bit more reserved, although he made no secret of his longing for her. The look in his eyes across a room, when she would sometimes turn and find him watching her, was almost intoxicating. The wanting was there. It was as if he sensed her new reserve and was respecting her need to slow down.

A flash of lightning lit up her bedroom, followed a moment later by the distant rumble of thunder. Soon a drenching downpour beat against the windows, and she hoped Grace had brought all her painting things inside. It seemed she listened to the rain for hours after that.

■ ■ ■ ■

The following afternoon, Grace was riding up Route 17 again as Joanna drove her to see Dr. Jacobs. How fast time was going, Grace thought, watching the medians glide by, now filled with fall mums.

"I haven't seen Harley around much these days," Joanna said, interrupting her thoughts.

"Well, I think it's best not to encourage him," she said. "Really, where could it go?"

Joanna was silent for a moment. "Are you feeling worse?"

She'd danced around this topic as Joanna had danced around her trip home. "I have good days and bad. Nothing to concern yourself with yet."

Joanna didn't speak for a while. Grace could only imagine what she was thinking.

"And will you tell me when it's time to concern myself, Grace?" Her voice was tight and strained.

"Of course I will, Joanna."

"You see, I'm not sure exactly what it is you have in mind for me. I mean, I know at some point we'll call hospice —"

"No," Grace interrupted. "We will not call hospice."

"You can't expect me to —"

"I don't," she interrupted again. "I don't expect you to be my nurse or my bathroom attendant. I will not linger to that point."

"Oh, Grace, how can you know that?"

"Because I'm taking no treatments, no drugs, nothing to prolong this ordeal. I hope to die quickly and naturally. The acupuncture has been a great help so far."

Joanna glanced at her and Grace saw pity flash across her eyes.

"I'm sorry," Joanna said and reached over, touching her.

"Thank you."

"No, I'm sorry I've been distant lately. Since I've come back."

"I assume you have a lot on your mind," Grace said.

"I do. But I've been so caught up in my own life, I think I haven't given you enough consideration. Or been very pleasant."

She saw Joanna's eyes fill with tears.

"Sometimes it actually hurts me to see how much you love your children," Joanna said to her, looking straight ahead. "I never had that, you know. My mother never once thought of what her words or her actions did to me. It was always about her, her needs, her excuses. Sometimes I think I get angry with you for that. Or maybe it's just

450

misplaced resentment." She wiped at a tear, before it could slide down her cheek. "I'm sorry. It's just that compared to her you're . . ." Again she stopped, clearing her throat. "I'm sorry, I didn't mean to get all maudlin."

Grace felt her throat swell at Joanna's pain. Hadn't she been caught up in her own self-absorption, as well?

"My father died about five years after I moved out of my house," Joanna went on. "I'd already been married a few years by then. We weren't living near them, so I didn't really have to worry about my children around her. He was dead about two years or so when my mother called me one day out of the blue and said she'd met another man. They were going to be married. Do you want to hear the kicker?" she asked. "She met him at AA. My mother waited until after she'd ruined my life and my father's to stop drinking. She couldn't have done it for me? No, she didn't love me enough to spare me the misery and embarrassment of having an alcoholic mother when I was a girl. I think I hated her more at that moment for quitting than for being an alcoholic in the first place."

They were turning off the highway and Grace could see Dr. Jacobs' office building up ahead. Joanna's face was a mask of composure.

"I think you need to make peace with this, somehow," Grace told her softly.

"I have," Joanna replied. "She died about ten years ago, so it's really ancient history."

Joanna's anguish seemed to follow her into the waiting room, where she couldn't even pick up a mindless magazine. How we carry the weight of our past around our necks like a millstone choking us for the rest of our lives, Grace thought. Joanna had not made peace with this, Grace was certain. Grace remembered times in her own girlhood when she resented her mother for dying, for leaving her motherless. How silly it was, of course, as if her mother could help it. But the pain wasn't silly. And as much as her own mother and Joanna's were not there for them, they'd tried to make up for it with their own children. Now she had no children around to comfort her, and Joanna no mother. Perhaps for what time was left, they could be there for each other.

"Mrs. Finelli?"

She looked up to see the girl waiting for her, file in hand. Slowly she followed her to the examining room, where her heart automatically kicked into a higher gear, as it did each time.

Dr. Jacobs did not smile and joke this visit. He examined her a long time.

"Will I make Thanksgiving?" she asked as he turned to the sink and washed his hands.

He didn't answer as he finished, then dried his hands.

"Halloween?"

It struck her then how her life had been delineated by holidays, birthdays, anniversaries. She remembered the doctor telling them about Frank's mother, "She won't make Christmas."

"It's hard to say, Grace. Of course if we did some of those tests you've been avoiding, I'd have better information to work with."

She smiled at him. "Look, I know I've got your hands tied behind your back, so to speak. But give it your best guess."

He sat at his desk, opened her file, reading nothing, she thought. Just buying some time before he uttered the words. She knew what that was, that time before the words were spoken, when it was all still a maybe but not real yet. She remembered wishing they could go back to those moments before they knew with Frank. When the weight of that knowledge didn't keep them from truly enjoying another moment of life without thinking, this will be the last time we do this or see that together.

"Never mind," she said aloud. She didn't really need to know.

He looked up at her and smiled.

"You're a gutsy woman, Grace."

"Not really. I just think it's kinder not to have to count down to our final moments, like that big ball at New Year's. My husband's father died under his beloved grape arbor with probably not a minute's notice. That's the way to go, if you ask me."

"I think so, too."

"And when the time comes, I'd just like to let you know that I want no respirator, no prolonging a body that's really gone. And no autopsy. I plan to go simply and naturally. I'm leaving written instructions. I want to be cremated immediately."

He looked at her a long moment. "I understand, Grace."

Walking out to the car, she knew as clearly as if he'd spoken that she would not see Halloween. September was already a week old.

That gave her less than two months.

37

A week later, Paul called Joanna to say there was another offer on the house, a good one. The last one had come to nothing. Now he needed Joanna's okay before agreeing.

"It's a November closing, so it gives me some time to figure out where I'm going," he explained. "And to decide what to do with all of this furniture. You must want some of it."

"I do," she said. "But I'm just not sure where I'm going to be after all this, if I'll have enough room. Or if it makes sense to ship some of it down here."

"So you'll be staying there, then?"

She told him the truth about Grace finally. He was stunned at first and then sympathetic. She felt so relieved to talk about it.

"It sounds like you two have become close."

Joanna smiled at that. "I guess we have."

"She originally said six months, didn't

she?" he asked.

"Yes, but who knows? That doesn't give her much time. But to tell you the truth, I don't think she has much time."

"And where will you go, after?"

"I don't know, I guess I'll stay here." Where else would she go? "Maybe find a little condo or apartment."

It amazed her how they talked about things now. He asked again how the writing was going and she explained about the article she'd just finished on development that would appear in next week's paper.

"Send me a copy. I'd like to see it."

"Sure. And what about you? Are you glad to be back at V.I.C.?"

"I don't know. It seemed like the right thing to do, the money and everything. Anyway, how long could I play at being a handyman?"

"I didn't think you were playing at it, Paul. It seemed like you were working pretty hard. Timmy was impressed."

"Really?" He seemed pleased. "Anyway, sometimes I feel a little lost in space. I'm still not sure what I really want."

He did seem lost. His voice was quiet and she felt a flicker of tenderness, or perhaps it was sympathy, for him.

"Where will you go when the house

closes?" she asked.

"Maybe the garden apartments across town. They've got month-to-month rentals I looked into a while ago. If they have something opening up around that time, I thought I'd just go there until I figure out the big picture." He snickered again. "If I ever do."

She agreed to take the offer. Before they hung up, he said something that surprised her.

"Have you thought at all about Sarah's invitation to have Christmas in Paris?"

"Oh, just a little bit. I don't seem to be able to think ahead too much."

"Why is that?"

She was embarrassed then. "I don't know. I guess I'm not really sure what my big picture's going to be either. Why? Are you going?"

"I'd like to. But if you want to go and my being there would stop you, I'll stay here. Just let me know."

She hung up, touched by his consideration.

By Friday, the hurricane in the Gulf had worn itself out and the rains that had lashed at them for days were finally gone. It was hot and sunny, the sky a clear, vivid blue they hadn't seen in a while. It felt almost as if summer was back as Joanna drove home from the newspaper that afternoon with the windows down, feeling lighthearted and looking forward to the night ahead. Hank was taking her to the Shrimp Festival in Georgetown. He'd told her she needed some fun again. She agreed. If she'd learned one thing that summer, it was that she'd spent most of her adult life never giving herself permission to have a good time. Or when she did, feeling guilty about it. Not anymore. Pleasure, she realized, was as necessary to the human makeup as worry, which she'd always been much better at. She admitted to herself now that the reason she'd been denying herself really had to do with the complicated baggage of her past. As the hot September air rushed in the car windows, she knew that admitting that was a giant step. Tonight she would have a good time.

When she got home, Joanna found Grace dozing on the recliner she'd had delivered earlier that week. She was stretched out with the back of the chair lowered and her feet raised in the air. She had believed Grace when she told her she'd bought it because of the stiffness from so many hours of painting. But now as she watched her chest rising and falling so slightly, her face so different without her glasses, it hit her. Grace was in pain all the time now. How had she not seen that? She stood there wondering if she should cancel the evening with Hank. But Grace seemed to be sleeping peacefully, so she eventually went upstairs to change.

Twenty minutes later, when she came back down, Grace seemed to be struggling awake. The relaxed face was gone and she appeared so old, almost disoriented as she sat up in the recliner and looked at Joanna across the room.

"You're going out" were the first words out of her mouth.

"No, I think I'm going to stay here with you," Joanna told her, coming closer.

"Don't be silly, go," she ordered gruffly. "I overdid it, that's all. Tonight's your Shrimp Festival, isn't it?"

Joanna sat down on the couch across from her. "Grace, don't you think it's time we really talk about this?"

"Not now," Grace snapped, pushing a button on the side of the chair that suddenly lowered her feet to the floor. "You've got someplace to go. Have fun. I'm nearly done with this night painting, and I'll go easy tonight. I promise."

She sat there, hesitating.

"Go!" Grace ordered. "I'm going to fix a little supper now. I'll be fine."

A horn honked out in the driveway then and Joanna left, reluctantly, knowing she would worry about Grace all evening.

But she didn't. Hank was his most charming and romantic. He looked younger, handsomer tonight, with his hair cut a little shorter, his salt-and-pepper beard shining like silver against his tanned face.

"Hello, darlin'," he said, then brushed her lips as she got in his truck. "Are you ready for some fun?" His smile was sexy and suggestive. She smiled back. Yes, she was ready to have fun, after all.

The main street of Georgetown was lined with booths of food, games, and rides for the kids, and it seemed there was music on every corner. They ate fried catfish and calabash shrimp and drank fresh-squeezed lemonade as darkness began to settle and the party atmosphere kicked into high gear. Hank took her to the River Walk then, and they strolled along the water as small boats cruised by. The earthy river smell mingled with the heavy odors of fried seafood as they walked all the way down to the fishing dock and waved to his cousin Sam, just pulling out on the *Clementine,* Hank's old shrimp boat.

"What a quaint name!" she said, as they watched him sail out into the night. "How did you ever come up with that?"

"Oh, I didn't," he said with a smile, his eyes following the boat until it was lost in the blackness of the ocean at night. "It was my father's boat first. And my mother's name, believe it or not, was Clementine."

"It's lovely. Sweet and old-fashioned."

"I thought so. It was my daughter's name, too."

"Oh, Hank."

He turned to her with a sad little smile. "Come on. Let's walk back up and get back to having fun. We haven't eaten nearly enough shrimp. And you haven't danced with me yet, miss. I'll be expectin' at least one slow and sexy one, ya hear?" he said, teasing her.

It struck her as odd that she'd slept with this man and didn't know his daughter's name. He took her arm as they turned back, and she smiled up at him while thinking there was still a lot she didn't know about Hank Bishop.

They ate shrimp in every way, shape, and form until she thought she'd be sick. Then they stopped at the beer booth and she had a small cup of a local brew that quickly went to her head. She wasn't a beer drinker. And

461

then it seemed as if they danced forever. Shag after shag, mixed with the slow, sexy numbers that had them melting into each other in spite of the heat and the dampness of their clothes.

By the time they got back into his truck and headed up Route 17 toward Pawleys Island, they were both yawning and worn out. Her head felt heavy from the beer.

"Come stay the night with me," he said softly.

She looked at the clock on the dashboard. It was nearly midnight. She'd told Grace she'd be back by ten or ten-thirty.

"I'd love to, Hank. But Grace wasn't well tonight. I really need to get back."

Hank knew Grace was ill; she'd told him that much. But she'd never told him how ill. Perhaps she'd been afraid it would slip somehow when he was at the house, or that he'd be too kind or solicitous.

"I'll be missin' you all night long," he whispered with a smile.

"Me, too."

But Grace was like someone transformed when she got back. Her eyes were alert and she was animated as she admitted sheepishly she'd painted for several hours.

"We haven't seen the stars for a while. How could I pass up this beautiful night?"

she asked with a bright smile.

It occurred to Joanna then that Grace might be taking something for the pain. Or was this typical of the ups and downs of a terminal cancer patient, bad one minute, good the next? She made a mental note to do some research on the Internet when she got back to work. Something, she now chastised herself, she should have done a while back.

She said good night to Grace then went upstairs and began taking out her earrings. She thought about Hank, all alone at his house. And missing her. Standing in front of the mirror, she imagined him getting into bed. She smiled at her reflection, then put the earrings back in. She pulled a light sweater from the closet and slipped out quietly. She decided to walk up the beach instead of driving, since it was such a gorgeous night. She even stopped for a moment and talked to Lucille, who was sitting vigil at her nest. Still nothing. Joanna could tell she, too, was nearly ready to give up.

She walked in the water for a while, and it was warm as a bath as it slid softly over her feet. Holding up her skirt, she waded up to her knees, anticipating Hank's face when she walked in. Tonight when they danced had been like that first night, when they gave themselves up to the pleasure of each other without censoring their passions. Perhaps she was the one, after all, who'd brought about the quieting of their relationship. She was determined, this time, to keep thoughts of her family out of her mind.

There was the tattered pineapple flag, lifting slightly in the gentle night breeze. She walked up the wooden steps, her sandy feet barely making a sound. As she climbed higher she could hear sounds and wondered if Hank had the television on. A voice stopped her just as she reached for the screen door. She hesitated, then turned and went over to the window that looked into the living room, standing to the side so she couldn't be seen. With just a screen separating them, she could hear everything.

"What the hell are you doing with that lost little soul from the North?" she heard Rhetta hiss.

Peeking around the window frame, she saw they were facing each other in the living room, their sides to her. She inched closer for a better look.

"Only she doesn't look so lost anymore," Rhetta went on.

They had seen Rhetta at the Shrimp Festival. Joanna hadn't thought it odd; they'd seen so many people they knew.

While they were dancing she was in the crowd, watching, her sweet smile dripping venom.

"You're out of line," she heard Hank say almost wearily, and he turned away.

Rhetta grabbed his arm. "No I'm not. I'm just tryin' to save you from another disaster."

"Who the hell do you think you are, talking to me that way?" He shook his arm free and walked away from her toward the kitchen, so his back was to Joanna.

"I'm the wife you should have had all those years ago," she cried out.

To her astonishment, Rhetta began to cry, soft whimpers as she slowly sank to her knees on the floor of his living room.

He turned toward Rhetta, and Joanna quickly stepped back from the window. Standing in the dark shadows of the porch, she could hear only the sounds of Rhetta crying and the low rumbling of the waves down on the beach.

A moment later she dared to peek in again and saw Hank on his knees beside Rhetta, holding her in his arms.

38

Driving across western Pennsylvania, Paul realized he was going back to the place he'd started. Since taking the consulting position for V.I.C., he'd been working day and night, calling on the regional sales managers, examining their stats, wondering why he was killing himself for a company that cared nothing about him. Money, he admitted. It always came down to money.

Part of the reason he took the job and went back to the corporate life was, ironically, Joanna. He felt like less of a man in her eyes not working a real job. Or maybe he was just trying to punish himself in some way. And now he was forcing himself to deny what he'd known since the first day he went back to V.I.C.: This wasn't what he wanted.

What, then, was? A different kind of job, something that left a part of him alive at the end of each day. And his wife back. Still.

But Joanna, he knew, had found someone else. He also could have started seeing someone else, he told himself, as he passed Harrisburg and began to think about stopping for something to eat. Karen was available, she'd made that clear. And Buffy had been sending him signals since Erik's party when she'd kissed him. Although there were moments he longed for a physical release, he couldn't get interested in other women.

Three hours later he pulled into his driveway as darkness settled around the neighborhood. He opened a beer and went out on the deck. It was a warm night, the crickets singing, the stars covering the black sky, and it felt like the middle of summer. But the leaves were already tinged with color. And in a month the glorious golds and crimsons would fade and wither before the leaves were gone until next spring. Tomorrow he'd have to make a real effort to find a place to live when the house closed. The apartment he was counting on was no longer available.

"Paul?"

He wasn't sure where the voice was coming from and got up, then saw Buffy rounding the house.

"Paul, are you out here?"

"Up here, on the deck," he called out.

"Christ, what are you doing sitting in the dark?" she said, coming up the steps. "There's not even a light on in the house. I saw your car in the driveway and thought you might be lying in there dead or something."

He chuckled at her melodrama. Buffy always made him laugh.

"Nope, I'm fine. Just enjoying one of the last warm nights. Want a beer?"

"Sure," she said, going toward the French door. "Don't get up. I know where to find it."

Part of him knew if he walked in the house behind her and put his arms around her, he could have her in a heartbeat. He was tempted. The loneliness that had consumed him all day made him feel reckless now. Who cared about tomorrow?

"I grabbed some pretzels," she said, coming back out. "Can't drink beer without munching."

She was wearing tight jeans and a T-shirt, and her frizzed hair was pushed back with a headband. She looked like a little girl.

"Erik thinks I went to the library over at the college," she announced, sitting down and popping her can of beer.

"Isn't it a little late for that?"

"Oh no. The college library is open until

midnight. As if more than five people will be there, though, on a Friday night." She reached for a pretzel and took a loud bite. "I couldn't take it anymore, though, I just had to get the hell out of there. We've been fighting all week."

Paul wasn't sure he really wanted to hear this.

"Erik wants to have another baby," Buffy went on before he got a word out. "And I don't."

"Oh," he managed to say.

She took another long sip of beer. "He wants a son, and I can understand that, of course. You have a son, you know what it's like. I guess carrying on the name is really important for a man, and all that, but . . . I don't know, Paul. I don't really think of myself as a great mother, you know what I mean? I'm not mother material. I'm too selfish."

"You're a fine mother."

"Emily's different than other kids, even I know that. And I know it's because of me. I probably should have encouraged her more to play with other children. But with all the moves, you know it was tough just getting her adjusted, missing her old home, I didn't want to force things on her. And the next thing you know, here she is in kindergarten, she's almost antisocial. I can't get her to open up."

"Lots of kids don't want to go to school the first year. She's really close to you, it's probably a big change for her being without you."

"And what about me? I just started teaching again. Two lousy courses. I waited five years for this and I have these two courses, I feel like I'm finally using my brain, again, and he wants me to start all over." Her voice was steadily rising. "Is it wrong of me to want a career, too? Look at him, his career is everything. Why is that okay for a guy?"

"Erik, I think, is a little old-fashioned," Paul said.

"Well I'm bored. And I want to keep teaching."

"Why can't you do both?" he asked. "Women do it all the time."

She took another sip of beer, then slammed the can down on the table. "Not the mother of Erik's children. His children will never be raised by someone else."

He didn't know what to say to that.

"What about your wife? Didn't she want a career, something else just for her?"

He thought about it. "No, not really. She enjoyed being a mother and didn't even get a job until they were in high school. But we moved around a lot, too, so it was difficult for her —"

"You see," she cut in before he could finish, "I'm not like that. It's just not me. And I'm doing the best I can with my daughter."

She jumped up then. "I gotta go. I have to at least stop at the library and pick up a book so it doesn't look like I completely lied." She walked around the table and kissed his cheek. "Thanks for listening. Again."

He sat for a while after she was gone, thinking back on a time in their lives he'd completely forgotten until now. When Joanna had wanted to have another child. And he didn't. Sarah and Tim were in middle school and he thought things were finally getting easier. They'd even started saving for college. Joanna was lonely and lamenting how quickly they were growing up. He just didn't want more responsibility. If they'd had a third child, he or she would be just starting high school now, he realized. And his wife, he knew, would never have left him.

Joanna avoided Hank all the next week. The morning after she saw him with Rhetta, she called when she knew he'd be out on his morning run and left a message that Grace was still not well and she'd be tied up for days. On Tuesday night she skipped the turtle meeting, knowing Rhetta would be there.

Why didn't she just confront him? she kept asking herself as she sat at her desk, replaying the scene again in her mind. Because she felt like a fool. Something was going on between Hank and Rhetta, something that went beyond a shared grief over Lacey's death. Rhetta loved Hank, felt she had some claim on him. But what about Hank? How did he really feel about Rhetta? She thought about Rhetta's words that day at lunch. Was Joanna nothing more than a summer fling to Hank? She shook her head, clearing the images from her mind. She forced herself to get back to the article she was writing.

After work she stopped at Harris Teeter's to pick up something for dinner and ran into Lucille, her fellow nest watcher.

"We missed you at the meeting," Lucille said, pausing in the aisle with a half-filled cart. "I was sorry they abandoned our nest. But I was ready for it, too. School's open again and those late nights were getting to be too much."

"They gave up on my nest?" She thought of the litter of eggs just beneath the sand

and the bond she'd formed with them, certain they would make it.

"I'm sorry, I assumed Hank told you," Lucille said.

"No, I haven't spoken to him."

"Oh," Lucille said in that way that told Joanna she knew what was going on between them. "Well, we assume it was a false nest after all. Otherwise they should have hatched by now."

A slow tremor began to beat within her as she finished the shopping and then tossed the bags into the truck. How could he do it? How could he not tell her? Nothing in her life made sense. Her relationship with Hank was some kind of sham. Her dedication to the obviously empty nest a complete waste of time. And she was driving home to watch a woman she'd come to care for waste away before her eyes. She felt her throat clog with grief. Oh, Grace.

It wasn't until that moment that the full weight of Grace's coming death hit her. She continued down Route 17 toward the north causeway that would take her back, as it had a hundred times, to the little world that had become their own. Two women who had run away. And who'd hoped to find a way to face the future that life held for them.

When she carried the groceries in, Joanna

473

found Grace asleep on the recliner, although it was only five o'clock. She dozed soundly despite the rustling of plastic bags and the clattering of cans. Grace was nearly done with her painting, the one that had seemed to consume her for weeks now.

Earlier that day she told Joanna a few more nights would do it. Joanna glanced over at her again and saw that her once lovely face, even for an old woman, was the color of ashes. The initial bouts of stiffness she'd glibly attributed to too many hours at her easel had degenerated into a limp now, so that her step across the wooden great room floor was the distinct step-slide of a cripple.

Joanna opened a container of gourmet soup and dumped it into a pot to heat. That and chicken salad sandwiches would be supper. Light food was all Grace seemed able to handle now, and Joanna knew with certainty that after a few spoonfuls of soup, she'd more than likely push the sandwich away.

But once again, Grace surprised her. When she woke it was with a smile, now like an infant who'd been wooed to good spirits by a happy dream.

"Smells good," she called out, popping up the recliner and slowly rising. In her soft slippers she step-shuffled across the floor to the kitchen.

Determined as she was to have the conversation they'd avoided for so long, Joanna let it pass again, reluctant to dampen a pleasant moment.

"Tomorrow's the day then, isn't it?" Grace chatted amiably. "Your story will be appearing?"

"Yes, tomorrow it is."

Caught up in everything, Joanna had completely forgotten. Her article on local development showcasing the plight of Jolene's family and friends would hit the newsstands tomorrow. She'd been so excited, it was the most challenging piece she'd tackled, so far. She was actually beginning to think of herself as a writer. Last week she'd gone up to Coastal Carolina University, paid twenty-five dollars, and joined their library. She'd driven home with a stack of books on writing and journalism. She wanted to be better.

"It seems you've really found something for yourself," Grace said, interrupting her thoughts.

She looked up and Grace was smiling at her, as a proud parent might.

"I'm happy for you, Joanna," she went on. "We all need something of our own."

Joanna stood and began gathering dirty dishes, unable to deal with Grace's sudden tenderness. This wasn't going to get any easier.

On Saturday morning, Paul went to the A&P to pick up a few things and decided to grab some boxes while he was there. He had sixty days to pack up the house himself. It was a daunting task. Worse than packing, though, would be the sorting through a lifetime of memories. As he was wedging the stacks of boxes into the backseat, he heard someone calling him and turned to see his neighbor, Bill, the retired pilot.

"I see you're getting ready for the move," Bill said, a single plastic bag of groceries in his hand.

"Yeah, no company move this time," Paul said, closing the back door for the second time against the boxes.

"We're putting our house on the market this weekend," Bill said, pulling his pipe out of his pocket. "I finally gave in. My wife won't let me have any peace until she gets closer to our daughters and those grandchildren."

Paul smiled. Bill, he'd always thought, had a little too much time on his hands and could talk for hours. Paul watched now as he pulled out his pouch of tobacco and began the ritual of tamping it in the pipe's bowl.

"I'll miss it here, though," Bill went on. "I like this little corner of Jersey. Woods and farms, winding country roads and small towns like Sparta here. Especially this time of the year. I'll miss the autumn, that's for sure."

"You're right. The seasons here are beautiful —"

But Bill talked on. "Are you staying local, then?"

"I am for a while." He opened his trunk and made a show of rearranging the boxes and groceries. "I'm just looking for a short-term rental while I finish up some consulting work for V.I.C."

"Oh, yes, I heard you'd gone back." Bill nodded as he began lighting and puffing. "My wife'll miss our house, that's for sure. Of all the places we've lived, this was her favorite home. She loves the Tudor look, and they just don't build them anymore. Anyway, I was thinking of having one of those paintings done for her. You know, something she'll always have to remember this house."

"That's a great idea," Paul said, slamming the trunk and jangling his keys noisily.

"Well, I've got to get going. I've got to stop at my realtor's to pick up some rental listings. Good luck with your sale."

Bill smiled, then walked across the parking lot, a cloud of pipe smoke trailing him. Just as Paul turned to open his car door, he caught a woman looking at him from the corner of his eye. He glanced around to see Karen standing in front of the drugstore. She smiled and waved. He waved to her and she began to walk over. Trapped again.

"Hi, Paul. I see you've got a car full of boxes. Are you moving soon?"

"Middle of November."

"I see. How's the consulting thing going?"

She had on black leggings and a long sweatshirt, as if she'd just come from the gym.

"All right, I guess. Sometimes I get the feeling I'm going to end up little more than a glorified hatchet man. There's a lot of dead wood in the wireless division . . ."

"Yeah, starting with Dan Rogers. I'm sure he hasn't got the stomach for the tough stuff. I never could stand that man."

"Not my favorite, either," Paul said, surprised at her candor. But Karen always had been direct. "Anyway, let's move on to a more pleasant topic. Are you local now?"

"Uh-huh." She smiled. Her blond hair was

cut short, with a long bang hanging sexily over one eye. "I finally left the city and bought a condo here last year. I kept putting it off, thinking I'd end up getting transferred back home to California. But I'm told I'll be here indefinitely. So, I'm a happy homeowner with roots. For a while anyway," she said. "So what about you? Have you decided where you're going, yet?"

He laughed. "That seems to be the question of the day. No, actually. I thought I could get a short-term rental in one of the apartment complexes, but there's nothing coming up."

"Good. Somehow I can't picture you in a garden apartment, Paul. Can you?"

"Yeah, maybe you're right. Anyway, I've got a few more months to figure it out."

"Why don't you come for dinner tonight? I'll cook you a nice meal and show you my new place."

He was ready to say no. But what did he have to do the rest of the day but pack and ride around driving by rentals? Tonight would be lonely. And his wife would more than likely be spending Saturday night with her boyfriend. Why was he denying himself?

"Sure, what time?"

"How about seven?" she asked with a smile.

■ ■ ■ ■

At seven he was at her door and she answered barefoot, wearing a pair of jeans and a soft pink sweater. She gave him a friendly peck on the cheek.

"Great place," he said as they walked through the foyer into a sunken living room that seemed to be wrapped in glass. "And a great view."

He walked over to the triple glass door looking down from her perch on this mountain at the town of Sparta below, twinkling like fairy lights in the early evening.

"That's what sold me," she said, bringing him a beer. "The first week, I got up at the crack of dawn each day to watch the sunrise over the town. It's simply magical."

"And then?"

"Oh, it's still magical. I just don't have the energy to get up that early every day," she laughed. She looked at him then. "Sometimes I think we give up a lot of the magic with these corporate jobs."

She went to turn the television off.

"Shit," he heard her mutter, standing in front of the set.

He walked over. The Weather Channel was on and he watched the broad map of the

Atlantic, where a series of swirling blobs seemed to be coming off the coast of Africa.

"I have to fly to the Caribbean on Monday morning," Karen said, sipping her beer. "And there's another hurricane on its way. They've just been nonstop."

"Well, if it's bad, you postpone."

"Yeah, sure. You know it's not always that easy. Besides most of the time it's too close to call, so you get on that plane to show a brave face, wondering if you're being stupid and will end up dead for all your bravery."

He looked at her in surprise.

"I hate to fly," she confessed.

Karen, it seemed, was full of surprises. After a delicious pot roast dinner — his favorite, but how could she know that — he wandered through the living room, glancing at pictures and mementoes of trips gathered on the mantel over the fireplace. On the end, he picked up a picture of Karen and an older man he presumed was her father.

"That's David," she said, beside him again with a mug of coffee. "He asked me to marry him about a month ago."

Paul took the cup and looked at her.

"I know, you probably thought he was my father. We've been dating over a year. He's a wonderful, kind man. And he's sixty-five. Not a terrible age difference, really," she said, putting the picture down. "Come on, I've got apple pie. From scratch with vanilla ice cream."

They went back to the table and she cut the pie, placing generous scoops of ice cream on each piece.

"I love to cook," she said. "But I rarely bother just for myself. This was a pleasure."

"You're a great cook," Paul said. "I mean that. I haven't had a good home-cooked meal in months."

She gave him a warm smile.

Afterward, they watched the Yankee game, Karen beside him on the couch curled up with a small blanket. She couldn't commit to David, she'd told him, there was simply something missing there. It would be so easy to stretch his arm behind her and pull her to him. But in spite of her good looks, and his physical need, he no longer felt that way with Karen.

A bright orange harvest moon hung just above the mountains as he drove home. A light frost was forecast for the morning. When he pulled into his neighborhood, he noticed the *For Sale* sign shining brightly in the middle of Bill's front lawn. In the soft moonlight, the large Tudor home looked like a medieval castle or an English country estate. It was quite beautiful, he thought.

And then he remembered Joanna telling him about someone she'd interviewed who was making replicas of people's homes.

And an idea came to him.

39

Once again the comfort of routine beckoned Joanna. At a little before nine on Sunday night, she went to sit vigil at her nest one last time. The others may have given up, but she needed closure before letting go of her nest. She'd done it for too long to end it so abruptly. Besides, with Grace and Hank slipping away, her family scattered, she had to focus on something.

It was a warm September night, the kind that made you believe summer could last forever. The air was soft, with a breeze that felt more like a whisper. And the water, she found when she slipped off her sneakers, slid across her feet with silky warmth. Despite no moon, the sky was soft with the glow of thousands of stars that were beginning to pierce the deep gray of early night. It wasn't long before Joanna found her nest.

Already it had that leftover look. The sticks had shifted and now pulled at the string outlining the square until it resembled more of a crazy trapezoid. She dropped her blanket and beach bag and immediately pushed the sticks deeper into the sand until they straightened and the string fell back into its perfect imitation of a square. Then she sat beside it and waited. And let her mind drift, as it always did during these hours.

Sarah was happily settled in Paris. She was e-mailing Joanna every other day, gushing about their apartment over a little cafe, the gallery that was all she had hoped for, and Martin's first days in his fellowship program at the Sorbonne. Life was filled to the bursting point with possibilities for her, and as much as Joanna missed her, she was filled with joy and a certain sense of satisfaction that her daughter was a strong enough woman to go after what she really wanted. And had the good sense to know so young what that was.

Tim's e-mails were shorter. He was looking forward to graduation next spring so he could get on with the projects that excited him. Suddenly there was an opportunity for a six-month stay in Antarctica that he was pursuing, which meant he might put off grad school a semester. They'd had their first snow already, as they often did in

Montana while it's still officially the last days of summer, and he'd been snowboarding. She wondered if there was a girlfriend anywhere in the picture he just didn't mention.

All in all, her children were doing well. She thought about Paul then, as she seemed to always do when thinking about her family. And she assumed that was only natural. They seemed to be in a similar place, both of them about to be on the move soon. In truth, she'd been avoiding thinking about what she would do once Grace was gone. Not too long ago she'd envisioned staying here, continuing with Hank, and just seeing how far it could go. Now she wasn't sure. She was at home here, finally, even entrenched a bit in the life of the community. It was the first time she could say that about any place she'd lived in years. Roots, she realized with a smile in the darkness. She finally had them.

"I thought you might be here."

Hank. She was so lost in thought she hadn't heard him coming up the beach. She felt a little tripping in her heart.

"You've been avoidin' me." His light tone didn't match the look in his eyes.

He sat down on the blanket and faced her.

Then he took her hand and brought it to his lips.

"I'm sorry, Joanna."

He knew. But how could he? He and Rhetta had never once glanced at the window where she watched.

"I've missed you," he went on. "When you weren't at the meetin' I should have come to you, but I didn't want to intrude with you and Grace." He paused a moment. "I knew it would hurt you, givin' up on this nest. But it was the right thing to do. The others were tired and disappointed and ready to let it go."

It was a moment before she realized what he meant. "You think I've been mad at you because you ended the vigil on my nest?"

He looked at her, puzzled. Then she pulled her hand from his and stood up.

"That's not why I've stayed away." She began shaking her head. "I came to your house last Saturday night, after you dropped me off from the Shrimp Festival. Grace was doing better, so I walked down the beach to surprise you and spend the night. Only the big surprise was on me."

"Jesus," he whispered, realizing what she'd seen. He closed his eyes then.

"I didn't stay long. My last picture was the two of you on your knees holding each other. Whatever came after that, I missed it."

He stood up suddenly. "Nothing came after that," he said. "Nothing. I haven't touched Rhetta in years. You're the one I want, Joanna." He reached for her hand.

She pushed him away. "I think it's time you tell me exactly what's going on between you and Rhetta."

He turned and looked out over the water, his jaw clenched. "I've spent my whole life payin' for the mistakes of the past," he said without looking at her. "Denyin' myself any kind of happiness because I just didn't feel I deserved it. Finally, with you," he turned and faced her then, his eyes shining, "with you it seemed possible I could let go of it all. Have a chance."

"This has to do with Lacey?"

He nodded and she was stunned to see his eyes fill with tears.

"I'm a simple man, Joanna, I think you know that. Always have been. I've never had grandiose ambitions and I don't need a lot of fancy things to make me happy. In high school, I was a good athlete, got the attention of people. You can imagine what that was like in a small town like this. Rhetta . . . she was my high school sweetheart."

"Rhetta? I thought Lacey . . ."

But he was shaking his head. "No, Rhetta. She was bright and ambitious, and when the offers for scholarships started comin' in, she helped me map out a future we thought would bring us a good life. I went to UNC in Chapel Hill and she was gonna follow me the next year. Only by the end of that first year I'd had enough. I missed the beach. I was miserable and lonely, and I can honestly tell you being homesick is a real illness. I didn't go back."

He paused for a deep breath. "I'm happy here, Joanna. This is my home. And it's hard for me to understand when people seem to search all over the world for what's often right in their own backyard. But Rhetta . . . she was havin' none of that. Her goal after we were married — you see, we were engaged at that point — was for us to move to Charleston or Savannah. I was majorin' in marine sciences and she was certain I'd get snatched up by some big company, or maybe start a consultin' firm. Anyway, I finished up at Coastal Carolina, commutin' from here. She wound up at the College of Charleston. It wasn't so far, and she could come home weekends and we could be together."

A bitter laugh escaped him then. "I was young and stupid and so in love. I couldn't believe it, you see, that a girl like Rhetta, so bright and so beautiful, would want me. Our dreams were different, but I convinced myself it could somehow work. Anyway, to make a long story short, I wound up going to work with my dad on the shrimp boat. He wasn't doin' well, I'd always loved the work, and it just seemed like the right thing to do. Rhetta made it clear she wasn't livin' as a shrimper's wife and she went out to California and finished school there. She wanted so much more. And I . . . I was happy with this." He held his arms out and then looked up, as if encompassing all of the island, the stars, his boat, the sea. "I couldn't imagine doin' anything else. So, I let her go."

He seemed to struggle then with words. She realized he was trying to compose himself as he ran a hand through his hair.

"Lacey was the total opposite of her sister. Sweet and pretty and happy with whatever came her way. She didn't ask much of life, kinda like me. She was two years younger than Rhetta. She stayed local and was happy cuttin' hair, workin' at a salon up in Myrtle Beach. I know I shouldn't have married her, but it all seemed to fall into place and she was . . . she was a good woman. My dad was retirin' then and we got married and got a little place over on the Waccamaw. I took over the shrimp boat, she worked at the salon, and it seemed like it would all work. But I never really loved Lacey, not enough. I realized that as soon as I saw Rhetta again. With Lacey it was comfortable, practical. With Rhetta there was a passion we couldn't seem to kill, no matter how long we were apart. She came in and out of our lives those first few years like a carrot dangled in front of me. And just beneath the surface of her hatred for me, I could see the wanting still burning like a fever."

Again, he was silent. She folded her arms and waited. She glanced up at the sky, noticing a patchwork of gray clouds that had blown in.

"I knew then I should have ended it with Lacey, but then she told me she was pregnant. How could I leave her? I felt like I'd gotten a death sentence. But then the baby was born and I was certain I could make it work. I loved that little girl like nothin' in my life before; she was so beautiful, so innocent. But after a while I slipped up, made a big mistake, and afterward nothin' in life was the same. I slept with Rhetta." Another deep, slow breath. "I know, you're thinkin' she seduced me, it was all her fault, but it wasn't. I take full blame. The grief of our

491

situation was eatin' away at her heart like a cancer. I was tryin' to console her and it got out of hand. Well, eventually Lacey found out. We hung on a few more years but she knew, I guess, Rhetta would always be between us. Eventually she left, took Clementine and wound up marryin' a lawyer, moved out west. How could I stop her, even though I felt my heart was bein' ripped out when she took my daughter away. She was tryin' to start over, and I couldn't blame her. Then there was the accident and they were gone."

He didn't speak for a while and neither did Joanna. Whatever she'd thought had been between him and Rhetta, it was nothing compared to this.

"If I'd been a better man, they'd be alive today. If I'd had more self-control, I might have seen my daughter grow up, get married. Maybe I'd even have grandchildren right now."

She watched him sit in the sand, suddenly seeming so worn and aged. It was as if she were looking at a stranger. This man she'd opened her heart and body to — she really didn't know him at all. She sat across from him, far enough away so he couldn't touch her, and waited.

"Rhetta left, couldn't deal with the guilt.

Years went by, there were some women, but never anyone serious. Then about five years ago, Rhetta came back. She'd been married and divorced and opened her design business here, and I guess thought enough time had gone by that we could pick up again. But I couldn't look at her without seein' Lacey's face and the guilt starin' right back at me. It wasn't until you came into my life that I think she realized she might lose her chance for good. But Joanna," he looked up at her, managed to take her hands, pleading, "you have to know I was hopin' there might be a future for us."

"And Rhetta, where does she fit into that future?"

He didn't answer.

"Do you still love her?"

He shook his head. "I don't know that love is the right word. She's been like a splinter buried deep under my skin all these years, painful but a part of me."

She didn't know what to say. She was reeling from his story.

"I'm a sorry man, Joanna. I've taken my comfort where I could over the years . . ."

She waited for the words that should have come next: I love you. Because foolish her, she'd had moments when she thought she might be falling in love with him. *Don't confuse lust and love.* Who had said those words? Then she felt his fingers on her neck, pulling her toward him.

"Give me a chance, Joanna. We have something special, don't you think?"

"I don't really know what to think, Hank." She took his hand from her neck. "Except that I need some time to sort this all out."

After a moment he said softly, "I understand."

She stood up, as if dismissing him.

"I understand," he repeated, and stood up as well.

She thought he was going to kiss her, but then he simply turned and began heading home. She sat back down, watching him walk up the beach with his head down. She pictured those blue eyes she loved, that could seduce her with a look. What a fool she'd been.

She lay back on the blanket, worn out. Looking up then, she saw clouds like thin gray veils still drifting across the sky. After a while the moon rose and she watched the clouds play with the moon, like a game of hide-and-seek, until her mind quieted down. There was really nothing to think about, she told herself as she let her eyes close. It was over with Hank. It had to be. It was just a summer romance. And she was a grown-up now, not some silly teenager unwilling to let go of what never could have lasted anyway.

But she could feel the tears sliding down her face into her hair. She still felt like a fool.

Something woke her in the fuzzy moments before opening her eyes. She thought she was in bed, until a sudden thundering crash sent her heart racing and her eyes opened. She stared into blackness. Sitting up, she looked at the waves crashing fiercely just yards away and realized it was high tide. She had slept half the night away on the beach.

Groggy and bleary-eyed, she sat there a moment, rubbing her face awake as the ambient light lit the breakers and she could see the foam rushing, swirling, then sliding back into the sea. She looked up and there wasn't a star in sight, the earlier clouds having knitted themselves together into a heavy blanket of deep gray. Again the waves crashed with a thundering explosion, and she wondered if there wasn't another hurricane out at sea somewhere roiling up the waters even this far. There'd been so many storms, she couldn't keep up with them. Or perhaps it was just the lateness, the quiet of the hour just before dawn, that made the ocean seem so loud.

She began gathering up her things. It was chilly now, the sand cool on her bare feet. She pulled on her socks and sneakers, then stood and slipped on the sweatshirt that had served as her pillow. Picking up the blanket, she gave it a shake and began to walk. Something made her turn around. A motion in her peripheral vision. And in the gray darkness, she saw something scamper across the sand, like a ghost crab. Then she saw another. And another. Dozens of tiny creatures scrambling about the beach.

"The hatchlings!" she cried out loud, dropping the bundle and hurrying over to the nest.

Like a pot boiling over, tiny dark creatures were overflowing from the nest, scattering and bumping into one another in a frenzy. As if their little lives depended on it. And they did. "Oh, God," she breathed. "They've got to get into the ocean."

She was babbling out loud in her excitement, realizing that in the darkness of the moonless beach, any light might draw them off course. Blessedly, the breakers crashed loudly and she wondered if sound didn't lure them as well, because the majority of them scrambled in the right direction, as if in a giant race. But not all of them. As her eyes adjusted to the darkness, she could see errant turtles like black shadows in the gray light pushing across the sand toward the lights of Murrels Inlet, little more than glittering pinpricks in the northern distance, but enough to lure them in the wrong direction.

Running closer, she saw they were tiny, no bigger than her hand, with limbs that sprang like wings from the bumpy round shells of their backs as they flailed furiously in the soft sand. She ran around them, scooping up sand to create a barricade and then pushing them around toward the water. Their furious limbs didn't stop, and within moments they were at the water's edge. She watched the first few hatchlings catch a wave, tumble and then suddenly disappear in the next pull of the sea. Gone.

Ahead of her she saw the others, the dozens that had run in the right direction, lined up as if in squadrons. She was laughing like a lunatic then, running, talking to the hatchlings, urging on one creature after another, their little heads bobbing intently in the direction of the ocean. And Life. Suddenly, white light flooded the beach and she looked up to see a piece of the moon, exposed in the thready break of clouds.

Then she looked back around to be certain those hatchlings left were heading the right way. Behind her a handful had turned around somehow and were heading toward the dunes. Why weren't they following the moon now? She raced in front of them, scooped them up one by one, slimy and sand-covered. Holding them tenderly against her sweatshirt, she carried them down to the water, placing them on the wet sand where the next wave caught them. One by one they were carried out to the sea.

Then they were all gone as suddenly as they'd come, and the sea before her gave no hint that a hundred tiny creatures had just been enfolded in its arms. In a matter of a few frantic minutes, it was all over. She sat on the cold, wet sand at the water's edge, already soaked, unable to believe what she'd just witnessed. She laughed out loud with joy at the wonder of it.

They were off, into the cold black water to make their own way, to grow and live, perhaps as long as fifty years. One day they would return to this very beach, where their mother had carefully nestled them in the soft sand, as her own mother had left her. And the cycle would repeat, again and again. The laughter caught in her throat as a sob began and tears slipped down her face. She remembered the mother, lumbering across the sand, her heavy body weighted even further by hundreds of eggs that she carried, fulfilling a primal legacy. Hatching her litter, never to see them again.

Born, reproduce, die. It's what we all do, she thought. And in the end, we all want to go back to the place that is home.

40

Grace pulled the calendar off the wall and stared at the page for September, a grid of thirty little boxes, each one signifying a day in her life that had come and gone. She turned the page to October and looked at the photograph of a mountain stream cascading over rocks in a gush of white foam. Imprinted on the bottom was a scripture: *"Whoever believes in me, as the scripture has said, streams of living water will flow from within him." John 7:38.* She'd gotten this calendar from the little church on the other side of Route 17 the first Sunday she'd moved down. And she'd hung it up when she got home, knowing that this calendar, unlike all of the others whose pages she turned every month of her life, would not see her turn the final page.

Today was October 1. Grace tacked the calendar back on the kitchen wall as her eyes moved to the last square on the page.

October 31, Halloween. The page blurred before her. *Stop it,* she ordered. She leaned against the wall to steady herself as numbness traveled from her foot up her right leg, as it did now when she stood too long.

Then she let go and shuffled over to her recliner, afraid if she braced herself against the wall much longer, Joanna would return to find her in a heap on the floor. Or worse still, crawling across it like a baby. Each footstep was a little victory as she stepped and then pulled with her hip on the deadened limb, dragging it across the wooden floor. When she reached the chair she fell into it, exhausted, a moan of relief escaping her as she lay back, pulling the afghan over her. It was in her back, and her bones, she was certain. Little by little, her body was shutting down.

She heard the car then and pulled a tissue from the box beside her, wiping her face and blowing her nose. Then the door opened.

"Did you remember to stop at the drugstore?" she called out.

"Yes, of course," Joanna answered, suddenly beside her.

She handed Grace the small package, flashed her a worried look, and then took a bag of groceries over to the kitchen.

"Damn it," she cried, tossing the bag on the table.

"What? What is it?" Joanna cried, running over to her.

"These are suppositories! I don't want these." Frustration fueled more tears. She swallowed hard to control the trembling in her voice. "I specifically told Dr. Jacobs' nurse."

"I'll call and get you something else."

She shook her head, reaching for Joanna's hand. "I'm sorry. It's not your fault. I'm sure I'm driving you crazy lately."

"Oh, Grace. I just feel so helpless sometimes. I'm not a nurse, I don't know what to do to make you more comfortable. I wish you'd let me call hospice. We could get a nurse in a few days a week."

Grace shook her head emphatically. They'd had this conversation before and she knew she'd been nasty about it. Once again, Joanna let it drop.

"I haven't had a bowel movement in a week," she told Joanna. "Please, run over to the health food store later and get me some flaxseed oil. That may help."

"Why didn't you say something?"

If she did, it would never end. The litany of complaints could go on every waking hour. Not to mention the humiliation of talking about one's most intimate matters. And then there was the problem of trying to sleep at night. How could she burden this poor woman with that, on top of everything else?

"I'll go now," Joanna said. "I'm sure they're still open."

As she picked up her purse and sweater, she turned to Grace again.

"Harley is upset you canceled cards again. That's three weeks in a row. Maybe it would do you good if you feel up to it?"

"Tell Harley I'll think about cards again when your article appears," she said with more venom than she felt.

"Don't take it out on Harley," Joanna said. "It's a long piece, with photos, as well. And there just wasn't room in the last two issues. But he assured me it will be in this week."

And then she was gone and Grace was alone again in the silent house. She closed her eyes and thought about Joanna's offer last week. To take her home. It seemed her husband, Paul, wanted her to help him divide the furniture and things in their house. If she went, she could take Grace home to her family. Grace wanted to shout, *Don't! Don't do this to me!* It wasn't until she saw Joanna's horrified face that she realized the words that were screaming in her mind had passed her lips.

"I'm sorry," she'd said then, "I just can't. It's not possible." But the possibility had dangled cruelly before her, much as Marie's plane ticket had months before. She was becoming quite a handful for Joanna, she realized. She had to try harder for what little time was left.

She opened the little bottle of pills on the table beside her and poured one into her hand. It was half a pill only. She'd scored them all, rationing them carefully so that when she was ready there would be enough. Half a pill did not kill the pain, but lessened it enough to make it bearable. And half a pill wasn't enough to blanket the world in a fog. Exhausted, she closed her eyes, wondering how it was her body went on. Her painting of the night scene flashed across her closed lids. It was finished. Focusing on the scene, she visualized each detail — the swirling stars, the trembling white light on the dark ocean, the high dunes, smooth and cool in the night. And something else. Something mystical, a presence she liked to think of as God.

She woke, wondering how long she'd slept. Opening her eyes, she noticed the sky, amber-streaked clouds stretching above the ocean with the first light of new dawn. Morning already? She smiled, knowing she would see one more day. Then her smile faded. She was confused. It was evening, the clouds capturing the colors of the sunset above the marsh. Oh dear, it happened often now, waking and not knowing at first where she was. Or even when it was. At times it was as if she were floating in another dimension, and she wondered if this was what it felt like to die, your soul gradually carried off to some other place.

"I've got it," she heard Joanna say. She wondered what she meant.

Joanna handed her a bag and she opened it. She looked at the bottle — flaxseed oil. And then remembered.

"Thank you," she muttered.

Joanna looked at her article, stunned. It was buried on page seventeen, past the local sports and business promos. It was chopped to just half a column. The title was vague and disappointing: "Locals Protest." What would Jolene and her family and friends think when they saw this? They were mentioned only once, briefly in the third paragraph. Conspicuously absent were the photographs of their homes and the new luxury homes being offered by the builder, an effective contrast that told an entire story in itself.

She looked into Harley's empty office. He was gone for the day. He would have a logical explanation; he always did. But nothing could appease the feeling that she'd somehow let Jolene and her family down. It was only three o'clock but she gathered her purse and sweater, not caring who saw her walk out. She drove down Route 17 to the dirt road that stretched back to the Waccamaw River. She was shaking inside.

It was fall now and the October sun, low-angled in the sky, sent brilliant shafts of light through the canopy of trees. She flipped the visor down and put her sunglasses on. At home, she thought, the leaves would be starting to soften, the brilliant greens slipping briefly into paler versions of themselves before exploding into russets and crimsons and golds, one final burst of life before the long winter's sleep. Here there was barely a reminder of the change of seasons, the days still stretching warm and soft into mild evenings. The only hint that something was about to happen was the sudden activity with the birds and the sea life on the beach in the last few days. Everything, it seemed, was on the move as the migration season began.

She slowed the car as she came abreast a throng of schoolchildren walking home on the side of the road. There was laughing and shouting, that after-school sense of freedom, and she saw Jolene's own two kids in the pack, their colorful knapsacks flopping on their backs. How much longer would they be making this walk?

As she pulled up to Jolene's, she saw with dread that they were all out on the porch, enjoying the beautiful day, most likely waiting for the kids to get home. Jolene's mother was seated on a graying wicker chair beside her handiwork, her hands flying with a will of their own. Jolene sat on the top step of the porch. Behind her, Joanna could see a very old woman, rocking slowly back and forth. Her grandmother, she presumed, whom she'd never met. She opened the gate and walked up to the porch steps, the paper clutched in her damp hand.

"We seen it already," Jolene said in her soft voice, nodding at the paper.

"I'm so sorry," she managed to say. "I can't believe they cut it to —"

"Well, believe it," Jolene spat out. "You think you got more power than that big developer?" She laughed at the stupidity of it.

"Jolene! That's no way to speak to someone who's been trying to help us."

Joanna turned to the voice. It was the grandmother, hidden in the shadows of the porch. "Come up here, girl, where I can see you."

She walked up the three steps into the shade of the porch, ready to stretch out her hand, and then stopped. The grandmother was like a shrunken doll, her dark skin withered and folded in on itself like a raisin, her hair a white tuft of cotton. Her hands gripped the arms of the rocker as she eased herself back and forth.

"I'm Joanna Harrison," she said, mustering a smile.

"I'm Evelyn Johnson and I'm mighty grateful for what you tried to do for us."

"This is not what I wrote," she said, holding the paper up and waving it. "It's been chopped and hacked apart and even the pictures I took —"

"Joanna," Jolene interrupted again, reaching for the newspaper. "Let me show you somethin', girl." Jolene opened the newspaper, turning pages furiously until she reached her target and then folded it in half and pushed it back at Joanna.

"There," she said, pointing to a large ad in the back of the paper. "In case you don't get it yet, that's why your article was chopped."

Joanna stared at a full-page ad for Coastal Carolina Developers, showcasing their four new housing subdivisions in the area. Rice Fields and the Barony were highlighted.

"I can't believe Harley would cave to this . . ."

"Believe it, girl."

"Jolene!" the grandmother chastised her again.

No one spoke for a few moments. She could hear the clicking of Jolene's mother's knitting needles and the laughter and voices of the approaching schoolchildren.

"We know you sure tried," Jolene's grandmother said. "Amen. That's all one can do in this world is try." She began rocking again, humming a soft tune.

"I'm sorry," she said, turning to leave. And then she stopped and looked at Jolene. "I will do something about this."

"Yeah, sure. Good luck."

She drove home feeling sick. And when she got into the house and saw Grace, she felt even worse. Grace was asleep on her recliner and didn't hear her come in. When she walked over to check on her, Joanna could see a flush of fever in her hollow cheeks. A sheen of perspiration covered her forehead. Did she still dream? she wondered. Was each day, each moment filled with the dread of knowing it could be her last? Poor Grace. She placed a hand on her forehead to gauge her temperature, as she'd done with her children. Tears filled her eyes at the damp, icy touch of Grace's skin.

"Mama?" Grace whispered suddenly, her eyes fluttering.

Then her eyes closed and Joanna realized she was dreaming. She stood there stroking Grace's forehead, while the tears streamed down her cheeks.

Grace tried so hard to wake up. She could feel her mother's soothing hand and knew somehow that she had been sick for a long time. The hand was so warm, her mother's fingers gentle as they brushed across her forehead and stroked her hair.

Opening her eyes, she nearly cried out at the strange woman standing above her. It took a moment, her startled heart tripping in her chest, for her to make her way back across the years to the present.

"Joanna."

"Oh, Grace. Shall I call Dr. Jacobs?"

"No, that's not necessary."

She watched as Joanna sank on the couch, a frown of worry knitting her brows.

"It won't be long," she told her and she

saw the sudden flood of tears in Joanna's eyes.

"But shouldn't we . . ."

Grace shook her head before Joanna finished the sentence. "I told you in the beginning I would need you for six months or so, and it seems I've taken you a little past our initial bargain," she said, attempting a lighthearted tone. But her voice broke and she struggled a moment for control. "I just want you to know how much I appreciate how you've cared for me. I know I haven't always been the easiest person to work for."

"Oh, Grace, this isn't a job anymore. It hasn't been for a long time."

Joanna reached over and took her hand, holding it for a moment in both of hers.

"Just one more thing," Grace said. "I've left letters for each of my children. When the time comes, will you see . . ."

"Of course. Anything."

"All right," Grace said, pulling her hand back, pressing the button on her recliner. "Enough of this maudlin talk. Would you please fix me a cup of tea?"

Later, after supper, there was a knock on the door. When Joanna opened it, Grace heard Harley's deep, rumbling voice, although she could not make out their words. Slowly she made her way out to the deck, where dusk was settling over the beach, leaving them to talk in private. She felt so much better, supper or the painkillers, or maybe both, reviving her suddenly. The breeze off the ocean was like a whisper of silk across her skin, rippling her hair, and she smiled, closing her eyes for a while. Each blessed moment now was a gift. Opening her eyes in the fading light, she looked up to see the first tiny pinpricks of light as Venus and Jupiter bloomed in the sky.

"Hello, Grace."

She turned to see Harley at the top of the deck steps.

"Joanna sent me away but as I was gettin' into my car I decided I want to see you badly enough to risk bein' rude." He stopped a moment, as if catching his breath after the long flight of steps. "May I sit with you a moment on this beautiful evenin'?"

In spite of herself, she smiled at him. "Of course."

"I know you've been feelin' a bit poorly, so I won't stay long," he said, pulling up a chair. And then he reached for her hand, touched it softly with his lips, and she didn't stop him. "I've missed you, Grace. And I know you're upset with me, as well, over

Joanna's article, but she and I have just set that all straight."

"Are you sure about that?" she asked, knowing how disappointed Joanna had been.

"You have my word."

She nodded, pleased, and then couldn't help herself. "I've finished my painting," she told him, needing to tell someone.

"Well, Grace, that's wonderful. I can't wait to see it."

"Not yet," she said, a bit coyly. "Next time. I'm not ready for anyone to see it just now. How's your arthritis been?"

"Not too bad, but with the colder weather comin', it's just a matter of time."

"You should try a winter in New Jersey, if you want to give your bones a run for their money!" she teased.

As they talked, stars slowly filled in the vast blackness overhead. It was nice, even for just a short time, to forget about everything, she thought, comforted by Harley's deep voice and the ocean sounds below. She was aware of the radio she'd left on just inside the door, an old-time station that played songs from her generation, so normal and comforting. Too soon, it seemed, he got up to leave. Afraid of wearing out his welcome, she guessed.

"Harley, I've played many hands of cards with you these past months," she said softly. "And I still haven't been given a dance. How about just one before you leave? If you wouldn't mind turning up the radio a bit?"

He turned to her with a look of stunned delight. "Why certainly, Grace."

He went inside and a moment later she heard the soft instrumentals of "The Way You Look Tonight," always one of her favorites. And then Harley was before her. Holding out her hands, she laughed and said, "I'm a little stiff from sitting." Gently he pulled her up, folding her fingers in his huge hand that reminded her of a bear paw. He wrapped his other arm firmly across her back, so that there was no chance she could fall. They began to move, their feet shuffling across the deck planks in a rough fox-trot. Within moments they were gliding smoothly, although they barely covered any ground at all.

The song segued into another, "I'll Be Seeing You," but her leg was already beginning to prickle and numb. She leaned into him and they swayed with the music, her head against his chest, listening to the slow beating of his heart, wetting his shirt with the tears she could no longer hold back.

41

The next morning Joanna was up early, too excited to sleep. At a little after eight she left for the newspaper up in Myrtle Beach where Harley's friend, Daniel Burrows, was the editor. Burrows was more than happy to run her article, uncut, pictures and all, he told her a little while later, as she sat in his office. He explained that losing the advertising of one big developer would cause little impact to his paper. Not like Harley, for whom losing one big account might shut the paper down. And then he went on for a while, telling Joanna how Harley had managed to keep *The Gazette* afloat all these years despite escalating production costs and decreasing advertising dollars. Little by little each year, more and more weeklies were shutting down, he explained, and the little pep talk worked, because when she left, a lot of her anger at Harley had already melted away.

Driving back to Pawleys Island, she decided to say nothing to Jolene or her family. She would take them a copy when the article was printed in the upcoming Sunday edition. Her insides hummed with excitement. Perhaps this was for the best. She'd be reaching a much larger readership now and would have more impact. And in truth, she did want her efforts recognized. She'd put so much into the piece, and couldn't remember the last time she'd felt so proud of something she'd accomplished.

So for just a little while that morning, her sadness over Grace seemed to disappear. It was with her always now, and the little reprieve was like a piece of candy during Lent — a fleeting pleasure followed by an aftertaste of guilt. When she'd told Harley last night that she'd be leaving the paper indefinitely, he thought at first it was because she was angry. And perhaps for a moment it was. But Joanna knew she needed to be with Grace full-time now, for whatever time was left. Last night she'd been surprised to see them out on the deck, and was secretly pleased that Grace allowed herself the company.

When she checked on Grace early that morning before leaving, she seemed so much better, alert and a bit energetic, and

Joanna was briefly relieved. But then she remembered the small rallies that were often a part of terminal illness, that seduced you with hope, only to shatter you soon afterward. It had happened with her mother. She knew it was coming soon.

It was when she stopped at the grocery store, packed with people, the shelves running low on stock, that Joanna heard about the hurricane. There had been so many in the news the past few months, and so many close calls that hadn't panned out. With all that had gone on in the last day or so, she hadn't paid much attention.

"Took a sudden turn northward," she heard a girl at the checkout counter tell the customer ahead of her. "Supposed to hit somewhere near Myrtle Beach tonight."

And sure enough, as she packed the bundles in her trunk, she looked up at the sky. It had been blue and balmy when she'd gone inside, now it was light gray and dulling every moment. Apparently, voluntary evacuation was encouraged, but no one she'd passed in the aisles had been about to leave their homes. What would she and Grace do? And where could she even take Grace? She couldn't imagine them holed up in some hotel; Grace was too ill for that.

A hospital? She'd be afraid to even mention it.

When she got back home, Joanna found that Hank had been there and gone. He'd fastened the storm shutters across the windows and moved all the deck furniture into the storage shed below the house before moving on to help others. She was glad she'd been out. She missed him. Still found herself longing for him at times. They hadn't talked since that night, although he'd called a few times.

"He says the locals never evacuate," Grace told her, sitting on a kitchen chair on the deck and watching the weather roll in.

She surveyed the beach, which had been sunny and tranquil when she left that morning. The ocean had hardened to a steely gray, the swells spitting peaks of white foam. The sky was a similar shade of gray now so that the entire landscape was flat and ominous.

"I don't think we really qualify as locals," she said, turning to Grace. "We could find a nice hotel inland or —"

"Yes," Grace interrupted, surprising her. "I think that's a good idea. I don't want to be responsible if anything happens here. You have a family. Why don't you start packing."

"All right. I'll get your suitcases out first

and then —"

"I'm not leaving," Grace said, as if it was obvious.

"Grace. What do you mean?"

"Joanna, really. What's the worst that could happen to me?"

She could die. But she would anyway.

"Please, Grace, don't do this. I can't leave you here alone."

"Yes you can."

"No I won't," she nearly shouted.

A sudden wind roared up the beach, flinging sand across the deck and stinging her bare legs. Grace covered her face. Joanna felt her breath catch. This was crazy.

She turned to Grace. "We'll both stay, then. We're as good as locals anyway."

There were boxes stacked in every room. The walls were bare, most drawers empty. Paul hated living in such chaos. It was a golden October afternoon and northwest New Jersey was enjoying a long string of warm Indian summer days. As he finished taping up the last box in the bedroom, he decided to call it quits for the day. Then he showered and dressed and hopped into the car, driving west out of town, a route that had become familiar to him already.

He'd found the old farmhouse one afternoon when he'd nearly signed a lease on a rental. Desperate, he'd stopped one last time at the newspaper shop on Main Street, and there on page ten of the *Swap & Shop* was a For Sale By Owner, a handyman farmhouse on two acres with a stream and a barn. The house was a mess, but the barn called out to him: a workshop.

Now he pulled into the long gravel driveway and sat looking at the house a moment. The once-white paint was gray and peeling, the wide front porch pulling slightly away from the house, its pillars askew and needing shoring up as well. A few remaining shutters hung at crazy angles, giving the house an almost comical look. But it had a simple grace, he thought, its paned windows beautifully trimmed with now-decaying woodwork, the wide front door graced by a transom and leaded glass sidelights. He could visualize it someday with window boxes and wicker porch furniture, the wide pumpkin-pine plank floors restored to their former glory. If nothing else, it would be a good investment. With a lot of work, he could flip it someday and make a handy profit. But only if he had to. This, he decided, would be home for a while.

He got out and walked to the back of the house, where an old-fashioned back porch had been enclosed long ago to serve as a mudroom. He pictured a wall of windows and a tiny breakfast room filled with plants. It wouldn't be difficult at all. He'd be busy for months to come but that, he decided, was a blessing. Each day as he packed up the house, putting a few more pieces of their life away, he kept holding on to this house and the busy days ahead when he'd be too tired to think about his wife and children, all gone, and his future alone.

Just then he saw a movement in the woods across the stream and watched as a line of deer stepped carefully into the clearing, making their way down to the water's edge, oblivious to him. He smiled. It was a different world here.

He would be done with his consulting job for V.I.C. in another ten days. He'd worked double-time to bring it to a close, too professional to simply walk away, which was what he'd wanted to do several times. Dan Rogers could drown in the figures when Paul was through, for all he cared. He owed V.I.C. nothing. And it no longer bothered him that their standing was slipping and their stock slowly sinking. He'd already sold his and put the money into CDs. Besides, he assumed Joanna would be getting half when she filed for divorce anyway. He hadn't been to an attorney yet, although he knew he'd have to do it soon. They would divide the proceeds from the house in half, but there were other things, such as the V.I.C. stock, that weren't as simple. He had a healthy pension, and Joanna was probably entitled to a portion of that. He wondered how things were going for her now. If she had future plans with Hank. They barely talked lately.

He'd hoped she could manage a quick trip home to help him out. He knew Grace was ill, but he'd left a message at her job, asking if just one day might be possible. It would give them enough time to inventory what they had and decide what to do with it all. He needed to make some decisions very soon; the house would be closing in just three weeks. But Joanna still hadn't called him back.

On his way home, he pulled into a deli as he approached the outskirts of town and picked up a sandwich for his supper. As he passed Buffy's house, he noticed Emily on the front steps, crying with a doll clutched to her chest. Paul slowed down and then pulled in the driveway. He could hear the shouting before he even closed the door to his car. He ran to the front steps.

"Emily, are you okay?" he asked, crouching down, trying to look nonthreatening.

A little sob escaped with a hiccup. "Daddy hit Mommy."

He could still hear shouting behind the oak front door. He reached for the door handle. It was unlocked. He opened it and went inside. He stood in the middle of the sunny entry foyer, hesitating. The shouts were louder now, their words carrying through the house.

"You bitch," Erik screamed. "Why should I believe anything you say?"

"And what about you, you bastard," Buffy screamed back. "Do you think I'm stupid, do you think I don't know —"

A sudden crash ended her words and Paul ran through the foyer into the kitchen. Erik had Buffy backed into the countertop, a stack of shattered plates at their feet. They both turned to him in the same instant, a stunned look on their faces.

"Paul!" Buffy said, clearly astonished.

"What the fuck do you think you're doing?" Erik barked at him.

"Let her go," Paul said, his calm voice belying his pounding heart.

"This is my wife," Erik announced, as if explaining something to a child. "We'll deal with this ourselves. Leave."

"Buffy, are you all right?" Paul asked,

ignoring Erik.

"I'm okay, he hasn't hurt me. He's just furious because I . . ."

Her words were stopped by a vicious slap. Paul was on the man before he even had a chance to think, some innate reflex propelling him the instant he saw Erik's hand fly. He caught Erik unaware and had the advantage, although Erik was quite a bit bigger. A second later Erik was sprawled on the tile and Paul was on top of him, his knees pinning Erik's arms to the ground as his father had taught him years ago. Beneath him Erik thrashed and cursed.

"Paul, oh Paul," Buffy cried, and it was a moment before he realized she was pulling on his shoulders. "Please, get up. Let him go!"

"Why, so he can hit you again?"

"I did a terrible thing, Paul," she said, beginning to cry. "A horrible thing."

"Buffy!" Erik warned.

"No, it's my fault, Erik. I've been taking the pill and not telling him, Paul, because I didn't want to get pregnant."

Underneath him Erik roared in frustration. "Shut up, Buffy!"

But Paul held him until Erik began to quiet down.

"Please, Paul, it's okay, just let him up,"

Buffy said, crying.

"No funny stuff," he warned Erik.

"Fine," Erik muttered.

He unpinned Erik's arms and chest and stood quickly, backing away just in case.

"Your little girl is sitting out front, crying her eyes out," he said, watching as Erik slowly got to his feet. Buffy's whimpers echoed in the silent kitchen. "You might want to think about her now." He turned to go.

"I'm sorry, Paul. Please don't hate Erik," he heard Buffy call out.

As he backed out of the driveway, Buffy came outside and picked up Emily, who wrapped her legs around her mother's waist. With a stricken look Buffy watched him drive away.

At home, he dumped his sandwich on the kitchen table and saw the blinking light on the telephone before unwrapping it. He hit the play button. It was Joanna, finally.

"Paul, I am so sorry, but Grace is not well. She's really failing suddenly and there's a hurricane heading here later tonight. I can't possibly leave her. Please understand."

He watched the Weather Channel as he ate his sandwich, barely tasting it as he chewed. They charted the track of a major hurricane as it had crossed the Atlantic and seemed to curl around the tip of Florida, as if rounding toward the Gulf. But it had taken a sudden turn northward, now barreling up the seaboard like a swirling pinwheel, headed straight for the coast of South Carolina. "Jesus," he whispered, throwing the rest of his sandwich back in the bag.

They were urging all those in waterfront houses to evacuate.

42

By the middle of the afternoon, Joanna stood on the deck, watching the gray ocean churning below, as heavy, colorless clouds raced north above the foaming water. Pelicans battled the wind, flying in formation just inches above the whitecaps, hoping to make it back to their nests on the south end of the island before the hurricane hit.

She turned to look up the beach and the wind whipped her hair across her face, blinding her for a moment. As she turned around to face south again, her hair suddenly lifted like a kite. She could see shuttered houses lining the beach. There were no lights in the darkening afternoon, and a touch of panic squeezed at her stomach.

She crossed the deck and stepped inside. Grace sat at the card table working on her jigsaw puzzle, a withered version of the woman she'd first met seven months ago. Joanna watched her. Soft piano music filled the quiet now, interrupted every so often by the moan of the rising wind sneaking through invisible cracks in the house.

"It's getting wild out there," she said, and went to put the kettle on the stove.

"There's nothing like a storm at the beach to make you feel alive," Grace said. Her cheeks were flushed and her eyes bright, like a child before a party. "I've just a few last pieces here and then I'd like to go outside for a moment, if you'd help me."

Joanna said nothing at the irony of her words. She walked over to check her progress. It was a lighthouse scene in Maine, a stretch of rugged coastline and ocean filling the table with shades of blues and deep greens. Just a few patches of table showed through where pieces were still missing. Within a minute, Grace pressed the last piece into place. She pulled off her glasses then and rubbed her eyes.

"I'd like to go down on the beach now."

She wanted to say, *Shouldn't you rest first?* But what was the point? Once Grace made up her mind about something, there was no changing it.

Joanna took her time gathering her sweater and a blanket to sit on, to give Grace time to stand and get her bearings. Too much sitting seemed to sap the strength or feeling from her legs, she wasn't sure which, and it often took a few moments before Grace managed her first step. Once again, Grace was full of surprises, and when Joanna came out of her room, she was at the sliding door, waiting. The wind caught them as soon as they stepped outside, and Grace gasped a moment and then laughed. The long flight of stairs was another story, and Joanna was already thinking ahead to climbing back up. Slowly they went down, Joanna one step ahead just in case. And then they were on the sand, soft and cool through the thin blanket. The wind was warm, despite the absence of sun. High tide was over but the waves were building, sweeping toward them on an angle now, the telltale sign of treacherous waters. They broke white and foamy, frothing onto the sand and sliding toward them, a little closer each time. She turned to see Grace smiling.

"I'm a young girl," she said, "trapped in an old woman's body. I want to run on the beach, I want to walk to the end of the island and search for sand dollars." She laughed out loud and shouted into the wind, "I want to paint until my arms fall off!"

Joanna couldn't speak and reached over for her hand. It was cold.

A handful of gulls took flight before them, their wings flapping feverishly as they attempted to fly south, struggling against the wind and going nowhere. Joanna wondered if they lost their breath at such times, as she did. They pressed on and in moments were a little farther down the beach.

As if sensing her fear, Grace said, "It's not too late. You can still leave."

We could both still leave, she almost replied.

"It's not supposed to be that bad," she said instead. "It's down to a category two already and hopefully by the time it reaches us, it'll be downgraded to a tropical storm."

Large drops of rain began to pelt the sand around them, as if belying her words. By the time they were on their feet, brushing sand from their bare legs, cold rain pounded them. Hooking her arm through Grace's, she hurried her along to the stairs leading up to the deck. But they were moving too slowly, drenched already. So she pulled her near the house and under the carport, where they escaped the rain and finally went in the front door.

Inside the foyer, Joanna grabbed towels from the laundry room. Grace was shivering, so she dried her arms, then rubbed the towel up and down her legs. Once dry, they slowly made their way up the flight of steps to Grace's living room. Her face was gray now.

"I guess this is it," Grace said with a shaky sigh as she settled into her recliner and stared at the sliding glass doors. Joanna turned and looked out to see nothing but a gray blur where the beach was, as rivers of rain beat against the glass doors.

She made tomato soup and grilled cheese sandwiches, light enough, she hoped, for Grace to handle. As Joanna worked in the kitchen she tried to ignore the wind, which had escalated to a high-pitched whine, broken by occasional rumbles as a sudden gust slammed the house. They'd lost cable, but before it went out they learned that the storm had picked up a little strength as it hurtled up the coast, and was now expected to hit land just north of Myrtle Beach.

"Maybe I should pull the storm shutters across the sliders now," she suggested to Grace.

"Just a little longer," Grace said quietly, still sitting in her recliner, dozing or simply staring out at the storm, she wasn't sure which. Joanna went out on the deck and quickly practiced sliding the shutters across the wall of glass that overlooked the beach, so that there would be no problems later on. Within moments she was soaked again. She couldn't blame Grace, really. The thought of closing them, their last glimpse of the outside world, made her feel a bit claustrophobic.

While they ate, the lights flickered briefly and then went out. For a moment they sat in the dark, saying nothing. The music, too, had ended with the loss of power, and beyond the silent room they could suddenly hear the wind outside, risen to a screeching whistle. Joanna realized you could chart a storm's severity by the pitch of its breath. It was getting closer.

She lit candles everywhere. Grace went back to her recliner and she took the couch, both of them with books in their hands, although neither of them read. As the night deepened and the storm intensified, she imagined the ocean somewhere in the blackness, roaring and thrashing, a cold and frightening place. Maybe it was the hurricane or the absence of everyday things such as lights and music. Or maybe it was their individual fears. But after a while, she and Grace began to talk about things they'd both been silent about for years.

"I know you think I'm some sort of brave soul, coming down here to die alone," Grace said, breaking the quiet. "But I'm not. I know . . ."

Even talking was an effort for Grace, and Joanna waited.

"I know what it's like for fear to control you. To take over your life," Grace continued. "There was a time years ago, when my children were babies, that I couldn't even leave my house. I was so paralyzed by the world around me and all the terrors I thought it held." She paused, took a long breath, and Joanna could see this was not an easy thing for her to talk about. "Back then it was called a nervous breakdown. Today they have a fancier word for it. Agoraphobia. A kinder word, I think."

"Grace, that's so hard to imagine. You're such a strong woman."

Grace smiled at the irony of those words. "Oh, I became strong. After I realized the fear was worse than anything the outside world held for me. I was so ashamed of myself. But then, when I began to realize my children were becoming aware, I decided I had to do whatever I could. I would not pass my fears on to them. I loved them too much for that. And so, little by little, I came out of that dark place."

It was hard for Joanna to imagine Grace paralyzed by fear. Unable to leave her house. But watching her relive it now, Joanna could see the suffering she must have endured.

"Can I make you some tea?"

"Yes, I'd like that."

Luckily, they had a gas stove. Joanna struck a match and lit the pilot. While they waited for the kettle to boil, Grace kept talking.

"Life is a journey, Joanna. I know that's a cliché, but it's true," she said. "And each part of it, no matter how painful, is a revelation. My handsome soldier wasn't everything I thought he'd be. I lied to you about that. He was just a man, human and full of frailties. How could he possibly live up to the romantic image he conjured up in a young girl's heart? Frank was strong-tempered and undemonstrative, I found that out very quickly when he came back from the war. And I'm sure I must have seemed demanding and petulant. Those were difficult years. But slowly, as the years went by, we began to grow towards each other, until finally I realized what a good and loving man he was underneath his stern demeanor. But when we were dancing, it was as if this other part of him emerged, as he held me in his arms and we'd fly around a room." Her eyes were lit up as she pictured them all those years ago.

And then a gust of wind slammed into the sliding doors, with the force of a sledgehammer, sending Joanna to her feet.

"I think it's time, Grace. I don't like to feel locked in either, but I'm afraid the glass may shatter."

"Yes, you're right."

She threw on a rain slicker, took a quick breath, and opened the slider a crack. Water began to spray her face, and as she opened the door a little wider to squeeze through, a blast of wind tore through the living room, tossing papers into the air. Pushing against it, she stepped onto the deck and slid the door shut. The wind roared like a wild beast, nearly drowning out the thundering ocean. Blackness surrounded her and she waited for her eyes to adjust, as she knew they would, even in the inky dark.

Cold water poured over her as if she were standing in the shower, and the noise hammered her like blows. Her face was dripping. She stepped over to a sheltered part of the deck, where the roof hung over a few feet, so she could stop squinting and find the handle on the shutter. As her eyes grew accustomed to the night, it faded to a deep gray. In the distance she could see a swirling ribbon of white she knew must be the breakers. A sudden wind gust slammed her into the house, cracking her head. Her breath was labored, as if she'd just run for miles, and her clothes were soaked through. She felt almost dizzy, as though she were perched at the edge of the world, that indistinct line on the horizon where ocean and sky met, where ships seemed to sail off the earth.

Fear and exhilaration gripped her as she grabbed the handle of the shutter, pulled it across the glass door, then reached for the other one and pulled it so they met in the middle. She did not latch them together. She couldn't seem to seal the house that way, like a coffin. When she finished she ran down the deck steps, under the house, and back in the front door. In the laundry room she stripped her wet things off and toweled her hair, her body shaking and charged. She'd never felt so alive.

After she'd dried herself and dressed in sweats, Joanna made her way back downstairs with a candle in her hand. Through the dim lighting, she could see Grace in the kitchen.

"Here," Grace said, holding out a small glass. "I'm sure you could use this."

She took a quick sip and the brandy slid

down, warming her. Grace poured herself a drink as well, and they settled back in their chairs, candles glowing all around them.

"What are your plans?" Grace asked her. "After you leave this house?"

She looked at Grace, hating talking this way. "I don't know, really."

"You remind me so much of myself, Joanna," Grace said, surprising her. "Maybe it's because neither of us really had a mother. And we're both nurturers at heart." She took a small sip of her brandy. "The problem with nurturers, though, is that they usually take care of everyone but themselves."

Joanna sipped her own brandy, a lovely lethargy seeping through her. They sat in the candlelight, the storm muted now with the house sealed up. It was like they were in a warm, golden cocoon.

"Don't stop writing, Joanna. I think you've found something there. And I think, truthfully, you're meant to do something important with it."

"I hope so," she said, her voice barely a whisper.

Grace, it seemed, was telling her everything she wouldn't be able to say to her own children now, indulging this need to share whatever wisdom she'd earned in her lifetime.

"But you must let go of this thing with your mother," Grace said then.

"I have."

"Joanna, you haven't and you know it. How long has your mother been gone? Ten years? Yet each time we speak of her the tears are there, and the wound, obviously, is still raw."

She couldn't speak; a lump of grief swelled in her throat.

"You know, I used to blame my mother for my fears," Grace continued. "After all, she wasn't there for me when I needed her growing up. It took me a lot of years to realize how irrational that was. Of course she would have been there for me if she'd had a choice."

"My mother had a choice."

"Did she?" Grace waited but she didn't answer. "You don't really know that. Maybe she, too, was paralyzed by fear. Like I was. Maybe she chose a different way to escape hers. I didn't leave my house, that's how I coped. Maybe she needed alcohol. I'm not saying it's right, Joanna. I'm just saying we all have our demons."

She said nothing, wishing Grace would stop.

"She's been punished, Joanna. You don't have to keep punishing her. She had to die knowing she failed you, isn't that enough?"

"I wasn't there," she said, before she realized it. "When she died. I wouldn't go."

Grace's expression didn't change. "Go on."

"Before she died . . . she wrote, asking me to come and stay with her. She had liver failure from all those years of heavy drinking. We were moving again, the timing was terrible, and I wrote that perhaps in a few months . . . I really didn't know how little time was left. She wrote me again, begging my forgiveness. I . . . I just couldn't. I didn't write back. Five weeks later I got the call that she died and . . . I . . ." She shook her head, unable to finish.

She got up and walked to the shuttered sliders, feeling like she couldn't breathe suddenly.

"Joanna, it's time you forgive yourself. You're a good person. And you were hurting."

"I can't," she said, tears filling her eyes. "What I did, my God, how despicable she must have thought I was."

"Come now, you would forgive your children anything, wouldn't you? You know that, don't you? Your mother forgave you a long time ago. You just didn't know it."

"Oh, Grace, it wasn't just her. I was such a lousy daughter. I just imagine her, in this place where she's still tormented and . . ."

"No," Grace interrupted. "That's not where she is."

She looked at Grace.

"Sean told me once, a long time ago, what the Mayans believe: dying is simply waking up from this dream we call life. I like to think that's true. Your mother is in a better place now, the place she was meant to be. Her pain is over. Someday she'll tell you that herself."

Joanna stood at the closed doors, desperate for air. Pulling one aside, she reached in and separated the storm shutters. A cool night breeze came in, but no rain. She pushed hard, and the shutters opened.

"I need air," she said, and stepped out onto the deck.

It had to be almost midnight. The wind had disappeared and all she could hear was the heavy thunder of the surf, repeating rhythmically, the pause and then the crash. She leaned against the house and looked up, the sky a swirl of misty clouds. She felt the hand on her arm before she knew Grace was beside her, and then Grace was pulling her in, enfolding Joanna in her arms. As

Grace held her, Joanna thought, *How tiny she is, her back now rounded and stooped.* Grace held her for a long time, the two of them, she realized, filling in for the mother and the daughter neither one of them would ever see again.

"You're exhausted," Grace said then, pulling away. "Go to bed. The storm is over."

She was exhausted. Halfway through the door, she turned to look back at Grace.

"I'll blow out the candles," Grace said, as if reading her mind. "I'm just staying out for another minute or so and then I'll come in, too."

As she turned back inside, Joanna noticed that the beach was brighter already, and wondered if the moon wouldn't be poking through the clouds again soon.

Yes, it was over, Grace thought, after Joanna left. She shuffled slowly over to the rail, leaning against it to take pressure off her leg and ease the pain in her back. She watched the ocean sliding back and forth in the darkness, spray flying with each crash of the waves. She loved the voice of the ocean, thinking now that it sounded like the voice of God. Looking down the beach at the line of dark houses, she wondered how many hours it would be until the lights came back on.

She noticed then something bright on the southern end of the island, and she stared hard, trying to make it out. After a few moments she realized it was moving. A circle of white rushed up the beach now from the end of the island and she watched it, mesmerized, wondering if by some fantastic coincidence a UFO had chosen this moment to land. It wasn't bright enough to be called light, she thought. It was almost the absence of darkness, a halo of it that traveled across the sand and water, until it was just beyond her house.

As it raced toward her Grace's eyes followed it, drawn upward, and there above her was a clear circle of night, stars glittering across a patch of velvet sky. Her breath stopped. It must be the eye of the storm. Wild gray clouds swirled around the perimeter of the sphere of stars like steam boiling off a clam pot. A glimpse of heaven, she thought, smiling. If only there were enough time to paint this, too.

Slowly she made her way back into the house. She poured herself another brandy, blew out the candles, and went into her room, closing the door. First she opened her top dresser drawer and pulled out a small stack of envelopes, placing them on her nightstand. The one on top said, "Joanna." Her body began to shiver as she moved about the room, although she wasn't cold. And she felt off-balance, as if she might fall. The brandy, perhaps? No, that was helping to calm her. Fear? Of course. She remembered the trembling fear that was once a part of her life. Taking another big sip, she limped to her closet and pulled out one canvas at a time. She lined them up on the floor, leaning them against the walls all around the room. Then she shuffled back to her bed, fluffed two pillows against the headboard, and sat with a long, shaky sigh. Silent tears were already spilling down her cheeks.

She opened the drawer of her nightstand and took out two small bottles of pills, all that was left. Some were whole, and there were still some half pills, those she'd hoarded for this moment that was once still blessedly in the future. She poured out a handful. They were tiny, and she swallowed them all with one sip from her water glass. Pouring out another handful, willing to take no chances, she swallowed those as well. And then she took a big sip of brandy, and another, the fire momentarily burning her insides with a pain she welcomed. Within seconds, a heavy cloud seemed to descend on her, numbing her with its weight.

She wished she could have waited until dawn, to see one last sunrise. Nothing seemed quite as frightening when there was light. But that would run the risk of being found merely unconscious. To be revived, to have to face it all again. She thought of the glittering circle of night. A piece of heaven, she hoped. A promise she'd only glimpsed in her night painting. She looked at her sketches and canvases stretched around the room like a little gallery of her own, and she smiled. Not a bad effort, really. If only she hadn't waited so long. A buzz hummed through her now like a sudden charge from a faulty switch. Her head turned more slowly, scanning her works, the vivid bursts of colorful flowers, the shimmering swells under the midday sun, and finally the night, with stars exploding like fireworks above the silver ocean, alive with ambient light. God will forgive me, she told herself. He loves me as I love my children. I could forgive my children anything. He will forgive me for sparing them. They are my babies, my life. She smiled, closing her eyes, silent tears escaping down her worn face, the creases of a lifetime, of worry and laughter, as individual and perfect as the print of her finger. There was a God; she knew it now, in spite of those fingers of doubt poking at her every now and then, such perfect love seeming impossible. The love that flooded her, overflowing like the waves, for her Marie, her Frankie, her Sean, she knew now was the same love God felt for her. How else could you explain it?

Her eyes closed and her mind slowly drifted, drifted. A few moments later they opened with a start.

"Mrs. Finelli?"

She heard someone calling her name.

"Mrs. Finelli, wake up."

She was awake, she was trying to say, but her lips wouldn't move, as if she was paralyzed. She closed her eyes again.

"Mrs. Finelli?"

She was so tired. She remembered being this exhausted before, so bone-weary you couldn't imagine doing all that was asked of you. Again she tried and finally, finally, she managed to open her eyes.

"Mrs. Finelli?"

She looked over and the door was opening, a nurse with a starched dress and white cap coming in. She held out her arms to Grace with a smile on her face.

"It's a boy, Mrs. Finelli." She was holding

a baby out for Grace to take. "You have a little boy."

Grace tried to hold her arms out, to take her child. But they were so heavy, she couldn't seem to lift them. The nurse finally laid the baby in her lap. She looked down at her child, the tiny face, the eyes looking up at her with such hope. "Oh, my love," she cried, "my love." She laid her arms around him and closed her eyes.

43

The phone was ringing, and in her dream Joanna kept reaching for it. Then she realized the phone really was ringing and rolled over quickly, grabbing it.

"Joanna?"

"Paul?" It came out like a croak.

He rushed on. "I wanted to make sure you're okay. I tried all last night, but the phones were out."

She sat up with a start. The hurricane.

"Is everything all right there?"

Her room was filled with bright sunshine, the hurricane almost like a dream that didn't really happen. "Wait just a moment," she said, getting out of bed, opening the slider and stepping onto the tiny deck high above the ocean.

Below her the waves rolled on as always, but bigger, sprays of spume lifting like silver spindrift with each crash of the ocean. The beach, however, was another story. It was littered everywhere with ocean debris — shells, garbage, seaweed, and other large plants. She saw a tire, pieces of a pier that must have been stirred up from the last major storm to hit there. And there were deck furniture and umbrellas, the loss of those who'd neglected to put their things safely away. Some of the houses, she noticed, were already unshuttered, and there was a damaged deck here, a roof missing chunks of shingles there. But, all in all, they'd survived fairly well. Early walkers were already scavenging the wreckage below.

"Paul?" she said, getting back on the line. "It's okay. A lot of garbage and some minor damage around us, but I think nothing that can't be fixed."

"You're pretty brave to ride that out," Paul said then, surprising her. "And maybe a little foolish."

"Oh, I would have gone. But I couldn't leave Grace here alone. I don't think there's a lot of time left."

"I'm sorry."

"I'm sorry I can't help you with the house. Please understand. I've got to stay with Grace."

"I understand. I'll manage. I think I can figure out what you'll want to keep. I'll arrange a storage unit for you if it comes down to it, and have it all moved there."

"That's really kind of you, Paul. I appreciate it."

The great room was flooded with morning sunshine. The lights were all on and music played from the radio, which must have come back on sometime during the night or early morning, when the power was restored. Forties music that filled the room with nostalgic cheer. Joanna looked across the room, expecting to see Grace in her recliner where she slept nights now. She was surprised to see the chair empty. There were no sounds in the bathroom and her bedroom door was closed.

She knocked softly on her door.

"Grace?" she called out.

No answer. She knocked again, a little harder.

"Grace?" she called, more loudly.

A bolt of alarm shot through her. She opened the door slightly and nearly sighed with relief. Grace was asleep in her bed. Quietly, she began to close the door, but the color caught her eye. All along the bottom of the room, lining her walls, her paintings were stretched out like a gallery. As Joanna's eyes scanned them, her breath caught. She couldn't help herself, and pushed the door open wider to get a better look at her work. It was her final painting, the night scene, that pulled her into the room. At first she thought it looked like the work of a madwoman. A frenzy of swirling stars and trembling ocean, each blade of dune grass more vivid and colorful than it could ever be in real life. But she could almost feel the soft night breeze, smell the salty tang of the ocean air, and realized the deliberate exaggeration of color and light made the painting more alive than anything she'd ever seen. She glanced over at Grace again and saw her eyes were open.

"Did I wake you?" she said softly. "I'm sorry. Your painting is magical."

Grace didn't speak, her eyes remained unmoving. Joanna stared at her. "Oh, Grace," she wailed.

Her legs began to quiver violently. Walking to the side of the bed was like pushing her limbs through water. Grace's eyes were barely open. She could make out just a sliver of blue, staring blankly at some point across the room. Grace's arms were lying across her stomach, as if she were holding something, or pulling something toward her. Looking at her face, Joanna realized how much the pain had changed her over the months. But she was back now, the Grace she first knew, her mouth relaxed, her face peaceful.

"Oh, Grace." Her knees gave way and she sank to the floor beside her. Burying her head in the mattress, she sobbed like a child. And strangely, Joanna had a sudden vision of the last time she saw her mother, in a casket in the funeral home in Florida. There was no smile, like this, but her ever-present frown was gone, her face peaceful finally. What was it in those final moments that seemed to release one of all earthly worries and cares?

She didn't know how long she was on the floor. Each time she thought she was spent, a fresh wave of weeping began again. She wept for Grace, for her mother, for herself. She grieved for her children, so far away, and longing for them sent new whimpers of sadness through her. She gave in for once and let her body cleanse itself of all the pent-up grief and sadness. And finally she stood on shaky legs. She bent over and kissed Grace's cheek, already cool.

Turning from her, Joanna gasped in fright. For a moment she thought someone was there, sitting in the chair in the corner of the room. A young woman, she thought, in a blue dress, rather old-fashioned. But the chair was empty now. She stood there, wondering. Had she really seen something? Could it . . . and somehow she knew. Grace's mother had been with her. Watching over her in death as she couldn't in life.

She turned to Grace again and spotted the envelopes on the night table. She went over and picked up the top one. It was addressed to her. Then she picked up the others, one for each of Grace's children. She wasn't sure she was ready for this.

As Joanna walked, the dolphins seemed to be following her. Out beyond the waves, they traveled in schools, their sleek bodies arcing up through the water, making their way south to their winter home. Earlier that day, when she sat on the deck steps, too worn out from grief after the coroner had come and the calls had been made to Grace's son Frankie, she'd watched as a school of dolphins had circled in the water just in front of the house, blowing air through their holes, making a sort of net to trap fish. To her, though, it was a farewell to Grace, who never failed to be thrilled at the sight of them, always scanning the water for their telltale fins.

It was cooler today than yesterday, as if the hurricane had swept away the last traces of summer and fall had finally arrived. An afternoon breeze pushed at her back as she made her way to the southern tip of the island. A massive flock of gannets was moving through, black-and-white birds that never came in to land, hovering above the ocean now. As she walked, she could see them diving in the water, then bobbing on the swells as they rested.

Hank had come up a short while after she'd found Grace, to see if they were all right after the hurricane. When she opened the door and saw him, she walked right into his arms. She'd just finished reading the letter. As he held her, she told him what had happened. After a while, he sat her on the couch and brought her a small brandy. She heard him call 911 as she sat there rereading Grace's words.

My Dear Joanna,

I won't torture you with maudlin talk. I think I've managed to say everything I wanted to already. Enclosed with this note is a power of attorney for you to have my body immediately cremated. I've already made arrangements with a local funeral home. Then you must call my son Frank and let him know that my ashes will be shipped home and that you have a letter with further instructions for him. Please know that I have come to love you like a daughter and that I could never possibly repay the care that you have given me. If I were your mother, I would be so proud of you.

Love, Grace

Monarch butterflies were everywhere as she walked, and she stopped then as one fluttered on the sand, simply resting or too weak to continue its monumental journey to the mountains of Mexico. She lifted it by one fragile, golden wing and tossed it in the air, but it wavered a moment and then dropped to the beach again, swept into the sea by the next wave.

By the time Joanna reached the end of the island, where the ocean spilled into the marsh, she was feeling a little better, the heavy fog of grief and crying lifting, her head clearer again. A flock of terns, there must have been several hundred of them, stood like an army at attention, all facing south, as if waiting for some signal to take flight again and continue their journey.

She wondered at this migration, this sudden movement of all these creatures of sea and sky. How was it they knew when it was time to leave? Time to return? And why was this missing in human beings, who were supposed to be so much smarter?

Sitting on the sand, she rested. She thought of the baby loggerheads, wondering how far they'd gotten on their journey. Motherless and alone, each one making its way through the cold depths of the ocean across the world. Independent. Surviving.

She sat there for a long time. Then she got up and began walking back up the beach. She knew now what she had to do.

She found Hank pulling plywood off his windows. When he saw her, he climbed down the ladder and came to her, hope lighting his eyes. It had been there that morning, as well.

"We have to talk," she said.

She sat in his kitchen as he made them tea. He was nervous, she could see that. She thought about the Fourth of July party, when she couldn't keep her eyes, or her hands, off him. Just a little more than three months ago.

He put her cup in front of her and sat. "Joanna, I want us to start over. I never meant to hurt you."

"Wait," she said. "I've been avoiding you, Hank, because I wasn't really sure how I felt. Or maybe I just didn't want to face it. What we had . . . well, it was good. But I think we both know it's over." She saw his face drop. "We were both lonely and hurting, and we stumbled upon each other. Not such a terrible thing, really."

"I do love you, darlin'," he said softly.

How ironic. She'd waited to hear those words, and now it was too late. "I'm sorry, Hank, I just don't feel the same way. But you helped me find a part of myself that had been asleep for a long time."

He smiled. He knew what she was talking about.

"And maybe I can help you see that you need to finally resolve this thing with Rhetta once and for all."

His eyes closed at the sound of her name. When he opened them, he said, "You're right. I do."

"Now I have a surprise for you," she said, with a big smile. And she told him about the turtles hatching.

He couldn't decide what had made the nest hatch so late, after they'd given up. She told him about the unusually wild breakers, the noise, the full moon. "Maybe they're like sleepy children who need a good shake to wake up," she laughed.

"I'm so glad you got to see it," he said. "I'm glad you didn't listen and give up like the rest of us. I guess we'll learn a thing or two from this one."

She left a short while later, walking back to Grace's empty house. She couldn't stay there. She would go back now and help Paul clean out the house. It was the fair thing to do, the responsible thing. She'd find a place to live, go back to school, and pursue writing. Perhaps work for a newspaper again while taking classes. And in spite of the sadness that still engulfed her, a glimmer of excitement took root as she thought about her future. She was a different person than the woman who had come to Pawleys Island so many months ago.

She would always love this place. But it was time to move on.

44

Paul looked at Joanna across the kitchen. She was kneeling on the floor, poring through boxes that had not been opened in years, dragged along on each move for one reason or another and now being unearthed like mysterious artifacts from a lifetime ago. She'd arrived the day before, late in the afternoon, looking exhausted and worn with grief. She'd seemed startled by his beard and the length of his hair, and he'd hastily explained that he'd been too busy and simply hadn't gotten around to having it cut. After months of easy talking on the telephone, they were back to short sentences and quick glances.

He'd taken her for supper to Porter's Pub, where, ironically, he was now known by the waitresses and bartenders. After a quiet meal, she'd gone right to bed in the yellow guest room down the hall. He'd sat in the family room, pretending to watch television, unable to sleep himself. Hardly able to believe she was back in their house.

Today the reserve was still there. She was pleasant enough, but it was as if she was holding back, afraid to establish any level of intimacy at all. As if silently establishing the ground rules: they'd remain friends, that was all.

"Tired?" he asked, and she looked up at him, stray curls floating wildly about her face, where they'd escaped the clip. He loved her hair like that.

She nodded. "I feel like I should get into the moving business. After all the packing down there, driving for twelve hours yesterday. Now packing and unpacking boxes again." She laughed, finally.

But he could see the pain still lingering in her eyes. Grace's death had hit her hard.

"What do you say we take a break," he suggested, pushing his box against the wall. "Come on, I'd like to show you something."

She hesitated, looked around the room at all they still needed to accomplish, and sighed. "Okay. I guess none of this will go anywhere while we're gone."

He watched her push the front door open tentatively, as if afraid some creature or giant bug might pop out at her. Cautiously, she stepped inside and he saw it all through her eyes. Wide-planked wood floors painted blue years ago stretched before them, scuffed and peeling. The walls were enshrouded with dark paneling, the ceilings were dropped and depressing, and there was the musty odor that houses have when not lived in for a long time.

"This is a joke, right?" She turned to him with a half smile. "You're not really moving in here. It's not habitable."

He laughed. "Not yet, anyway."

He walked her through the first floor, through the living room, and then the dining room with arched doorways, pointing out woodwork that would be salvaged, windows that would be replaced. And finally, in the kitchen, with a sweep of his arm, he described the sunroom that would be a breakfast room as well, overlooking the stream and yard.

"You can do all this?" she asked again.

"Come on, let me show you something else," he said, leading her outside and across the gravel drive to the old barn. He pulled out his keys and opened the padlock on the door. It took a moment for her eyes to adjust to the cavernous darkness after the bright sun outside. There, stretched out before her, were his father's old tools, the workbenches, and some new equipment as well. He watched her taking it all in.

"With a few windows in here, I'll be able to do whatever I want," he explained.

She sat on a crate, still looking, and he waited for her reaction.

"You could really be happy here?" she asked, still incredulous, it seemed.

"I'm happy already, and I haven't even moved in," he told her, trying to make her understand. "I don't have it all figured out yet, but I know I'm done with V.I.C. and working for someone else. And I get real pleasure when I'm working with my hands. I haven't felt that in years." He saw the doubt on her face. "I'll take it one step at a time. This weekend I've got two high school kids coming to help me take down all the paneling in the house and sand the floors. They're from the vo-tech, so I get free help and they get credit for it. By the time I'm ready to move in, it won't look as scary it as does now," he laughed. "But it won't be perfect yet." *It'll never be what you and I have always had,* he almost added, and stopped.

"Wow," she said with a big smile. "It's just . . . such a surprise."

She was starting to relax, he thought. Her enthusiasm was starting to come alive in the lilt of her voice, the occasional smile.

Perhaps it was being away from the house and here on neutral territory, away from the painful reminders of all that had gone wrong for them. And then he saw her eyes travel across the room and cursed his stupidity.

"What's this?" she asked, standing and walking across the barn.

He said nothing, waiting for her reaction.

"It's our house," she said, evidently stunned.

She looked at the miniature replica of their home, 848 Butterfield Drive, sitting on a table where he'd put it days ago after finishing the final coat of paint.

"You did this?" she asked.

"Actually, I got the idea from you," he admitted, coming closer now, hoping she liked it. "You mentioned a man down on Pawleys Island who was making miniature reproductions of houses to sell."

"But they were nothing like this. This is a perfect replica of our house!"

"You like it?" he asked, finally.

"Oh, Paul," she said, looking at him then, "it's wonderful . . ."

"It's yours," he blurted out, and then regretted it as she threw him a guarded look.

"It was the first one, just practice, really. I made a few others and have sold them already. Since you gave me the idea for this little business, I thought it was only appropriate."

"Oh," she said. "Thank you."

"Come on, let me show you the property," he suggested, afraid she'd retreat back into herself. They left the barn and walked in back of the house.

"My God, that's an old money tree," she said, spotting it behind the barn. "I haven't seen one of those since I was a child."

She reached over and pulled one of the round, parchment-covered pods off the bush, rubbing it between her fingers and then pulling it to her nose.

"Wow, there's a memory," she said softly

Lilies of the valley stretched along one side of the foundation, and a towering old lilac bush nearly hid the outside cellar door. And then she turned and he saw her spot the stream.

"Oh, it's lovely," she said, making her way down the sloped lawn to the water's edge.

It was a brook really, just a few feet across, but the gentle gurgle of the water slipping over worn rocks was a sound he'd already come to love.

"You could plant iris here, along the banks. They'd take off in just a few years," she said.

He watched her turn and survey the yard again with a sweep of her eyes.

"You could do wonderful things gardening here," she said, really looking at him for the first time since she'd arrived. "It'll be a wonderful home. I'm really happy for you."

"And what about you?" he asked, almost afraid to speak the words and scare her off. "What will you do?"

"Well, as I told you last night, I want to go back to school. Continue writing, maybe find another newspaper job."

"No, I meant where will you live?"

"I don't know yet."

He hesitated a moment and then plunged ahead. "There'll be plenty of room here and . . ." He stopped. He saw the look of alarm instantly cross her eyes.

"Wait," he went on. "I'm just saying if you need a place until you figure out where you want to live, stay here. No strings, I promise."

She just smiled. "I'm sure I'll find something."

Driving back, she was quiet, and he thought about the article she'd given him just before she went to sleep the night before. She was proud of it and pleased that the family she wrote about seemed grateful for her efforts. He sensed a passion within her for writing now, and he recognized the burning need to accomplish something of her own. He wondered now if she didn't view him as some threat to her hard-won independence.

"Here's the last of them," Paul said, carrying another stack of boxes into the kitchen and unloading them on the counter.

"It's amazing how much junk we carted with us," Joanna said, heaving handfuls of stuff into a plastic garbage bag from yet another box.

"I don't know," he said, "this one has 'Do Not Throw Out' written rather nastily across the top. Your handwriting, I think."

She looked at it and laughed. "It is my handwriting. Probably another junk drawer dumped into a box and forgotten."

He watched her take a knife and slice through the tape, peeling back the lids with a smile, like a child at Christmas expecting something good. Her face immediately froze.

"Oh my God," she whispered.

She looked up at him and then slowly held up a tiny pair of black patent leather shoes. He remembered Sarah wearing those shoes when she was taking her first steps. She handed them over and dug back in, retrieving a ragged patch of cloth, gray and fraying at the edges.

"Mr. Blankey, do you remember?" she asked, and of course he did. Timmy's precious blanket, or what was left of it after one of their puppies had chewed it to bits.

He watched her pull out one thing after another that had once been a precious part of their lives, that they could not manage to part with and had somehow managed to forget over the years.

"Look at this!" she cried, lifting out a small plastic pouch, opening it and waving scissors, trimmers, and a thin-toothed comb. "The barber's kit I used to butcher your hair with."

He couldn't smile any longer, but she didn't notice.

"You didn't do such a bad job," he said.

"Are you kidding?" she laughed, still digging in the box.

"No, not at all. In fact I was just thinking you could save me a little time if you'd give me a trim."

"What?" She looked up at him with obvious surprise. "You'd trust me with the beard?"

"No, I'm keeping the beard. Just trim the hair."

Over the box she smiled at him and then

waved the scissor menacingly with a laugh.

Before she could change her mind, he grabbed a kitchen chair, pulled it across to where she stood, and then sat down, with his back to her. He heard her laughter stop and the room was suddenly silent. He was afraid to turn around and just sat there waiting.

It seemed a long time went by, but then the comb slid through his hair, smoothing it in sections all around his head. He felt her fingers lift a piece and there was a long pause. Then he heard the first snip of the scissors.

"I hope you don't regret this," she said behind him, with another laugh.

She picked up another strand of hair, her fingers brushing his neck. He turned suddenly, grabbing her hand, holding her there so that she had to look at him.

"I don't think I'll regret this," he said, pulling her fingers to his lips.

EPILOGUE

It's early morning, nearly dawn, and as Joanna walks along the Seine just blocks from Sarah's apartment, she can't help reliving last night. On the tiny balcony of Sarah's apartment they watched in awe as the Eiffel Tower, a piece of it visible in the distance, lit up from bottom to top like a match bursting into flame.

She pulls her hat closer over her ears, blocking out the cold wind blowing across the river. Somehow she didn't think winter in Paris would be as cold as at home. After they'd raised their champagne glasses and toasted the new year, she'd leaned over and kissed her daughter, and then her new son-in-law, Martin. And then, unable to help herself, she knelt down and kissed the small mound of Sarah's belly, where her grand-child is growing. She is blessed.

The tip of the sun is just peeking over the river now, sending a shower of red across the horizon, reflected in the moving water. Joanna thinks of all the sunrises she watched on Pawleys Island, and for a moment her heart squeezes with missing Grace. There was a memorial service for her a few weeks after her death, and Joanna drove to Grace's church in Glen Rock to be there. Afterward, a large crowd of family and friends walked to the adjoining cemetery where her ashes were buried with her Frank. It was incredible to meet her children, finally — Marie, who looked so much like her, but seemed to lack some of Grace's fire; and Frankie, a quiet, serious man, who couldn't stop thanking her. Sean didn't speak to her at all, his resentment all too obvious in the way he looked at her.

The city is coming slowly to life as she walks, and the new sun already warms the streets. Tomorrow she will leave Paris. Excitement hums within her as she thinks of her first courses beginning in a few weeks, when she returns to college after more than a quarter century. She's begun writing poetry, too, and finds it both comforting and thrilling to wrap her thoughts and feelings in imagery and metaphor like a hidden jewel.

Leaving the sidewalk, she crosses the street to a path that winds beside the river.

Her footsteps crunch as they hit the gravel, and beside her, Paul's steps keep perfect rhythm with her own. They were married again last night after the simple ceremony for Sarah and Martin, renewing the vows they'd first spoken twenty-six years ago. Timmy stood beside Paul, a wide grin lighting his face.

She glances over at Paul now, who smiles, still tired after just a few hours' sleep. When Joanna woke earlier, unable to fall back asleep, she quietly pulled on sweats. When she was lacing up her sneakers, he rolled over and peered at her through half-open eyes.

"Go back to sleep," she whispered.

"Wait," he said, throwing off the covers. "I'll go with you."

ACKNOWLEDGMENTS

This book would not be in your hands were it not for the following, who helped to make my dream come true. I thank you all from the bottom of my heart:

My sister, Jacky — my computer guru — and her partner, Kathy, for endless support, refuge, and beautiful places to write.

Debora Messina, soul friend, for reading endless drafts, listening to my laments, and being there always. Here's to reading pages on your deck, with a glass of wine under the moon.

Tom and Helene Timbrook, forever friends, who have been a big part of this journey.

My wonderful cousin, Janet Bejarano, who took me on The Margarita Book Tour. Thanks for the laughs and the confidence!

All the generous people who provided me with a getaway to write: Karen McFadden and Steve Maixner, Betsy McFadden and Phil Fluke, Bob and Karen Russell, and John and Linda Abromitis.

To the independent booksellers. First, a special big thanks to Harvey Finkel, Kris, Gail, Rob, and Mom, at Clinton Books, the first, and biggest, champions of this book. You are what make the independent booksellers the heart and soul of this industry. Harvey, if heaven sent me an angel, it is you!

Tom Warner of Litchfield Books. You embraced this book and made me feel like "the real deal," before I quite believed it myself. I will never forget your kindness.

And for the other independents who I owe bigtime: Carol Viall and Kristen Cernak at Sparta Books, Darryl and Ann Zinn at The Book Loft, Frazer Dobson and Frank Burleson at Park Road Books, and Jamie Fiocco at McIntyre's Fine Books. Also The Book Worm, Mendham Books, Chicklet Books, The Book Shelf, Califon Books, Harbor Walk Books, and a special thanks to Bess Long of My Sister's Books.

The many readers, book clubs, and angels

who prayed, lit candles, and went out there and fought for me and my book to get noticed, including: Lucy Heller, Alyson Reynolds, Ellie Corda, Linda Eyrich, Sr. Therese Marie, the sisters McFadden, Mary Moore, Nancy DiBlasi, Anita Minervino, Tracy Cappel, Sheila Johnson, and most especially my cousin, Liz Cornett.

Thanks to Joanne McCarthy, for allowing me to borrow from her exquisite poem, "Ripening," for my title.

Dr. John Parras and the Graduate Writing Program at William Paterson University, where it all began.

Dr. Bryon Grigsby and Centenary College. Your support has been unbelievable.

My dynamo agent, Victoria Sanders, and Benee and Glendaliz: thanks, ladies, for believing in me.

My foreign agent, Chandler Crawford. You are amazing!

And finally to my editor, Leslie Wells, and my publisher, Ellen Archer, at Hyperion. It is a thrill to be in your hands!

ABOUT THE AUTHOR

Maryann McFadden has been a successful realtor for the past twenty years, but she always wanted to be a novelist. *The Richest Season* began as her thesis project when she returned to school for a master's degree. She lives in Hackettstown, New Jersey, where she is at work on her next novel.

The employees of Thorndike Press hope you have enjoyed this Large Print book. All our Thorndike and Wheeler Large Print titles are designed for easy reading, and all our books are made to last. Other Thorndike Press Large Print books are available at your library, through selected bookstores, or directly from us.

For information about titles, please call:
(800) 223-1244

or visit our Web site at:
http://gale.cengage.com/thorndike

To share your comments, please write:
Publisher
Thorndike Press
295 Kennedy Memorial Drive
Waterville, ME 04901